About the Author

Maya Blake's writing dream started at thirteen. She eventually realised her dream when she received The Call in 2012. Maya lives in England with her husband, kids and an endless supply of books. Contact Maya: mayabauthor.blogspot.com, X @mayablake and Facebook maya.blake.94

Melanie Milburne read her first Mills & Boon book at age seventeen in between studying for her final exams. After completing a Bachelor's and then a Master's Degree in Education, she decided to write a novel, and thus her career as a romance author was born. Melanie is an ambassador for the Australian Childhood Foundation and is a devoted owner of two cheeky toy poodles who insist on taking turns sitting on her lap while she's writing.

Michelle Smart is a *Publishers Weekly* bestselling author with a slight-to-severe coffee addiction. A bookworm since birth, Michelle can usually be found hiding behind a paperback, or if it's an author she really loves, a hardback. Michelle loves hearing from readers and can be contacted directly via her website michellesmart.co.uk

Pleasure in Paradise

April 2026
Beachside Rivals

June 2026
Office Retreats

May 2026
Reunion in the Sand

July 2026
Royal Escapes

Pleasure in Paradise:
Beachside Rivals

MAYA BLAKE
MELANIE MILBURNE
MICHELLE SMART

MILLS & BOON

All rights reserved including the right of reproduction in whole or in part in any form. This edition is published by arrangement with Harlequin Enterprises ULC.

This is a work of fiction. Names, characters, places, locations and incidents are purely fictional and bear no relationship to any real life individuals, living or dead, or to any actual places, business establishments, locations, events or incidents. Any resemblance is entirely coincidental.

Without limiting the exclusive rights of any author, contributor or the publisher of this publication, any unauthorised use of this publication to train generative artificial intelligence (AI) technologies is expressly prohibited. HarperCollins also exercise their rights under Article 4(3) of the Digital Single Market Directive 2019/790 and expressly reserve this publication from the text and data mining exception.

® and ™ are trademarks owned and used by the trademark owner and/or its licensee. Trademarks marked with ® are registered with the United Kingdom Patent Office and/or the Office for Harmonisation in the Internal Market and in other countries.

First Published in Great Britain 2026
by Mills & Boon, an imprint of HarperCollins*Publishers* Ltd
1 London Bridge Street, London, SE1 9GF

www.harpercollins.co.uk

HarperCollins*Publishers*
Macken House, 39/40 Mayor Street Upper,
Dublin 1, D01 C9W8, Ireland

Pleasure in Paradise: Beachside Rivals © 2026 Harlequin Enterprises ULC.

What The Greek Wants Most © 2014 Maya Blake
Wedding Night with Her Enemy © 2017 Melanie Milburne
Bound by the Italian's 'I Do' © 2023 Michelle Smart

ISBN: 978-0-263-42162-0

Printed and Bound in the UK using 100% Renewable Electricity
at CPI Group (UK) Ltd, Croydon, CR0 4YY

WHAT THE GREEK WANTS MOST

MAYA BLAKE

To my editor, Suzanne Clarke,
for your unfailingly brilliant insight and support!

CHAPTER ONE

THEO PANTELIDES ACCELERATED his black Aston Martin up the slight incline and screeched to a halt underneath the portico of the Grand Rio Hotel.

He was fifteen minutes late for the black tie fund-raiser, thanks to another probing phone call from his brother, Ari.

He stepped out into the sultry Rio de Janeiro evening and tossed the keys to an eager valet who jumped behind the wheel of the sports car with all the enthusiasm Theo had once felt for driving. For life.

The smile that had teased his lips was slowly extinguished as he entered the plush interior of the five-star hotel. Highly polished marble gleamed beneath his feet. Artistically positioned lighting illuminated the well-heeled and threw the award-winning hotel's design into stunning relief.

The hotel was by far the best of the best, and Theo knew the venue had been chosen simply because his hosts had wanted to show off, to project a false image to fool him. He'd decided to play along for now.

The right time to end this game would present itself. Soon.

A sleek designer-clad blonde dripping in diamonds clocked him and glided forward on sky-high stilettos, her strawberry-tinted mouth widening in a smile that spelled out a very feminine welcome. And more.

'Good evening, Mr Pantelides. We are so very honoured you could make it.'

The well-practised smile he'd learnt to flash on and off since he was eighteen slid into place. It had got him out of trouble more times than he could count and also helped him hide what he did not want the world to see.

'Of course. As the guest of honour, it would've been crass not to show up, no?'

She gave a little laugh. 'No, er, I mean yes. Most of the guests are already here and taking pre-dinner drinks in the ballroom. If there's anything you need, anything at all, my name is Carolina.' She sent him a look from beneath heavily mascaraed eyelashes that hinted that she would be willing to go above and beyond her hostess duties to accommodate him.

He flashed another smile. '*Obrigado*,' he replied in perfect Portuguese. He'd spent a lot of time studying the nuances of the language.

Just as he'd spent a lot of time setting up the events set to culminate in the very near future. For what he planned, there could be no room for misunderstanding. Or failure.

About to head towards the double doors that led to the ballroom, he paused. 'You said most of the guests are here. Benedicto da Costa and his family. Are they here?' he asked sharply.

The blonde's smile slipped a little. Theo didn't need to guess why. The da Costa family had a certain reputation. Benedicto especially had one that struck fear into the hearts of common men.

It was a good thing Theo wasn't a common man.

The blonde nodded. 'Yes, the whole family arrived half an hour ago.'

He smiled at her, effectively hiding the emotions bubbling beneath his skin. 'You've been very helpful.'

Her seductive smile slid back into place. Before she could grow bolder and attempt to ingratiate herself further, he turned and walked away.

Anticipation thrummed through his veins, as it had ever

since he'd received concrete evidence that Benedicto da Costa was the man he sought. The road to discovery had been long and hard, fraught with pitfalls and the danger of letting his emotions override his clear thinking.

But Theo was nothing if not meticulous in his planning. It was the reason he was chief troubleshooter and risk-assessor for his family's global conglomerate, Pantelides Inc.

He didn't believe in fate but even he couldn't dismiss the soul-deep certainty that his chosen profession had led him to Rio, and to the man who'd shattered what had remained of his tattered childhood twelve years ago.

Every instinct in his body yearned to take this to the ultimate level. To rip away the veneer of sophistication and urbanity he'd been forced to operate behind.

To claim his revenge. Here. Now.

Soon...

He grimaced as he thought of his phone call with his brother.

Ari was beginning to suspect Theo's motives for remaining in Rio.

But, despite the pressure from his family, neither Ari nor Sakis, his older brothers, would dare to stop him. He was very much his own man, in complete control of his destiny.

But that didn't mean Ari wouldn't try to dissuade him from his objective if he'd known what was going on. His oldest brother took his role as the family patriarch extremely seriously. After all, he'd had to step up after the secure family unit he'd known for his formative years had suddenly and viciously detonated from the inside out. After his father had betrayed them in the worst possible way.

Theo only thanked God that Ari's radar had been momentarily dulled by his newfound happiness with his fiancé, Perla, and the anticipated arrival of their first child.

No, he wouldn't be able to stop him. But Ari...was Ari.

Theo shrugged off thoughts of his family as he neared

the ballroom doors. He deliberately relaxed his tense shoulders and breathed out.

She was the first thing he saw when he walked in. His lips started to curl at his clichéd thought but then he realised she'd done it deliberately.

The dress code for this event had been strictly black and white.

She wore red. And not just any red. Her gown was blood-red, provocatively cut, and it lovingly melded to her figure in a way that made red-blooded males stop and stare.

Inez da Costa.

Youngest child of Benedicto. Twenty-four, socialite... seductress.

Against his will, Theo's breath caught as his gaze followed the supple curve of a breast, a trim waist and the flare of her hips.

He knew each and every last detail of the da Costas. For his plan to succeed, he'd had to do what he did best. Dig deep and extract every last ounce of information until he could recite every line in the six-inch dossier in his sleep.

Inez da Costa was no better than her father and brother. But where they used brute force, blackmail and thuggery, she used her body.

He wasn't surprised lesser men fell for her Marilyn Monroe figure. A true hourglass shape was rare to find these days. But Inez da Costa owned her voluptuousness and confidently wielded it to her advantage. Theo's gaze lingered on her hips until she moved again, dropping into conversation with the consummate ease of a practised socialite. She had guests eating out of her hands, leaning in close to catch her words, following her avidly when she moved away.

As he advanced further into the room, she turned to speak to another male guest. The curve of her bottom swung into Theo's eye line, and he cursed under his breath as heat raced up through his groin.

Hell, no.

His fists curled, willing his body's unwanted reaction away. It had been a while since he'd indulged in a mindless, no-holds-barred liaison. But this was most definitely not the time for a physical reminder, and the instigator of that reminder was most definitely not the woman he would choose to end his short dry spell with.

He exhaled in a slow, even stream, letting the roiling in his gut abate and his equilibrium return.

As he made his way down the stairs to join the guests, the deep-seated certainty that he was meant to be here—in the right place at the right time—flared high.

If Pietro da Costa's love of excess hadn't led him down the path of biting off more than he could chew, this time in the form of commissioning a top-of-the-line Pantelides super-yacht he could ill afford, Theo wouldn't have flown down to Rio to look into the da Costas' finances three years ago.

He wouldn't have become privy to the carefully hidden financial paper trail that had led right back to Athens and to his own father's shady dealings almost a decade and a half ago.

He wouldn't have dug deeper and discovered the consequences of those dealings for his family. And for him personally.

Memory stirred the unwanted threads of anxiety until it threatened to push its way under his control like Japanese knotweed. Gritting his jaw, he smashed down on the poisonous emotion that had taken too much from him already. He was no longer that frightened boy unable to stem his fears or chase away the screaming nightmares that plagued him.

He'd learned to accept them as part of his life, had woven them into the fabric of his existence and in doing so had triumphed over them. Which wasn't to say he wasn't determined to make those who'd temporarily taken power from him pay dearly for that error. No, that mission he was very much looking forward to.

Focusing his gaze across the room to where Benedicto and his son held court among Rio's movers and shakers, he strategised how best to approach his quarry.

Despite the suave exterior he tried to portray with his tailor-made suit and carefully cropped hair, Benedicto could never mask his lizard-like character for very long. His sharp, angular face and reptilian eyes held a cruelty that was instinctively felt by those around him. And Theo knew that he honed that characteristic to superb effect when needed. He bullied when charm failed, resulting in the fact that half of the people in this room had attended the fund-raiser tonight just to stay on Benedicto's good side.

Five years ago, Benedicto had made his political aspirations very clear, and since then he'd been paving the way for his rise to power through mostly unsavoury means.

The same unsavoury means Theo's own father had used to bring shame and devastation to his family.

Grabbing a glass of champagne, Theo sipped it as he slowly worked his way deeper into the room, exchanging pleasantries with ministers and dignitaries who were eager to find favour with the Pantelides name.

He noticed the moment Benedicto and Pietro zeroed in on his presence. Bow ties were surreptitiously straightened. Smiles grew wider and spines straighter.

He suppressed a smile, deliberately turned his back on the father and son and made a beeline for where the daughter was smiling up at Alfonso Delgado, the Brazilian millionaire philanthropist, who was her latest prey.

'If you want me to host a gala for you, Alfonso, all you have to do is say the word. My mother used to be able to throw events like these together in her sleep and I've been told that I've inherited her talent. Or do you doubt my talents?' Her head tilted in a coquettish move that most definitely would've made Theo snort, had his eyes not been drawn to the sleek line of her smooth neck.

Alfonso smiled, his expression beginning to closely resemble adoration.

Forcing himself not to openly grimace, Theo took another sip of champagne and brushed off an acquaintance who tried to catch his eye.

'No one in their right mind would doubt your talent. Perhaps we can discuss it over dinner one night this week?'

The smile that started to curve her full, glossy lips forced another punch of heat through him. 'Of course, I would love to. We can also discuss that pledge you made to support my father's campaign…?'

Theo moved closer, deliberately encroaching on the space between the two people in the centre of the room.

Alfonso's attention jerked towards him and his smile changed from playboy-charming to friendly welcome.

'*Amigo*, I wasn't aware that you had returned to my beloved country. It seems we cannot keep you away.'

'For what I need to achieve in Rio, wild horses couldn't keep me away,' he replied, deliberately keeping himself from glancing at the woman who stood next to Alfonso. He breathed in and caught her scent—expensive but subtle, a seductive whisper of flowers and warm sunshine.

His friend's eyes gleamed. 'Speaking of horses—'

Theo shook his head. 'No, Alfonso, your racehorses don't interest me. Speedboat racing, on the other hand… Just say the word and I'll kick your ass from one end of the Copacabana to the other.'

Alfonso laughed. 'No can do, my friend. Everyone knows underneath that tuxedo you're part shark. I prefer to take my chances on land.'

A delicate clearing of a throat made Alfonso turn, a smile of apology appearing on his face as he slipped back into playboy mode. For the ten years that Theo had known him, Alfonso had had a weakness for curvy brunettes.

Inez da Costa had curves that required their own danger

signs. His friend risked being easy prey for whatever the da Costas had in mind for him.

'Apologies, *querida*. Please allow me to introduce you to—'

Theo stopped him with a firm hand on his shoulder. 'I'm perfectly capable of making my own introductions. Right now, I think you're needed elsewhere.'

Alfonso's eyes widened in confusion. 'Elsewhere?'

Theo leaned and whispered in his friend's ear. Shock and anger registered on Alfonso's face before his jaw clenched and he reined his emotions back in. His gaze slid to the woman next to him and returned to Theo's.

Taking in a deep breath, he held out his hand. 'I guess I owe you one, my friend.'

Theo took the proffered hand. 'You owe me several, but who's counting?'

'And I shall repay you. *Até a próxima*.'

'Until next time,' Theo repeated. He heard the disbelieving gasp from Inez da Costa as Alfonso walked away without another glance in her direction.

A thread of satisfaction oozed through him as he tracked his friend to the ballroom doors. Scanning the room, he saw Pietro da Costa's thunderous look in his sister's direction.

Theo lifted his glass to his lips and took a lazy sip then turned his attention to Inez da Costa.

Her large brown eyes were filled with anger as she glared at him.

'Who the devil are you and what did you say to Alfonso?'

CHAPTER TWO

THEO DIDN'T LIKE the idea that he'd been less than one hundred per cent thorough in covering every angle in his investigations.

His surveillance of Inez da Costa had been from afar simply because until recently he'd deemed her involvement in his investigation peripheral at best.

The extent of her role in her father's organisation had only come to light a few days ago. But even then he should've recognised her power.

Now, at the first proper sight of what was turning out to be the jewel in Benedicto da Costa's crown, the essential cog in the sinister wheel that his enemy was intent on using to his full advantage, he experienced a pulse of heat so strong, so powerful, he sucked in a quick breath.

Up close, Inez da Costa's heart-shaped face was flawless…breathtaking, her skin a silky, vibrant complexion even the best cosmetics couldn't hope to produce.

Not that she hadn't attempted to enhance her beauty even further. Her make-up was impeccable, her lids smoky in a way that drew attention to her wide, doe-like stare.

Long-lashed eyes that bored into him with unwavering demand and a healthy dose of suspicion. Her nose flared with pure Latin ire and her full lips parted as she released another agitated breath.

The pictures in his dossier did her no justice at all. Flesh and blood wrapped in red silk from cleavage to toe, she made his senses ignite in a way he hadn't felt in a long time. The earlier pull deep in his groin returned. Harder.

'I asked you a question.' Her voice held a hint of dark sultriness that reminded him of a warm Santorini evening spent drinking ouzo on a deserted beach. And the mouth that framed her words, painted a deep matt red, reminded him of what happened on the beach after the ouzo had been consumed and inhibitions were at their loosest.

She glanced over his shoulder and Theo's jaw clenched at the thought that she was more concerned with the departing Alfonso than she was with him.

'Why is one of my guests walking out the door right this moment?'

'I told him that if he didn't want a noose slipped around his neck before he was ready to be hog-tied, he needed to stay away from you.'

Her parted mouth gaped wider, showing a row of perfect white teeth. *'Excuse me—?'*

'You're excused.'

Eyes the colour of dark caramel flashed. 'How dare you refer to me as such—?'

'Careful, *anjo*, you're causing a scene. *Pai* would not be happy to see his event ruined by a tantrum now, would he?'

Her eyes didn't stray from his, her stare direct and cutting in a way that made it difficult for him to look away. Or maybe it was because, despite the boldly challenging stare, he spied a quickly hidden vulnerability that tweaked his radar?

'I don't know who you think you are but perhaps you need to be educated in the etiquette of social gatherings. You don't deliberately set out to insult your host or—'

'My intention was quite simple. I wanted to get rid of the competition.'

'The *competition?*'

The doors to the larger ballroom where the dinner fund-raiser was to be held were thrown open. Theo turned to her.

'Yes. And now Alfonso's gone, I have you all to myself. And, as to who I am, I'm Theo Pantelides, your VIP guest of honour. Maybe you should add another bullet point to your rules of etiquette. That the hostess should know who her most important guests are?'

Her mouth started to drop open but she caught her reaction and pursed her lips.

'You're Theo Pantelides?' she muttered.

'Yes, so I suggest you make nice with me to stop me from leaving. One high net worth guest departing before dinner may be excusable. Barely. Two will certainly not go down well with your crowd. Now, smile and take my arm.'

Inez reeled under the steely punch packed behind the suave, sophisticated exterior and charming smile.

Theo Pantelides.

This was the man her father and Pietro had talked about. The one who would be taking over majority shares in Da Costa Holdings until after the elections. The one her brother Pietro had referred to as an arrogant bastard.

Well, he certainly was arrogant all right. The swiftness with which he'd dispatched Alfonso and assumed he could control her confirmed that assertion. As to whether he was a true bastard...well, that was something to be determined. But so far all signs pointed in that direction.

What she hadn't been aware of was that the man spoken of with such scorn would be so...visually breathtaking.

'I thought you would be older.' The words tripped from her tongue before she could stop herself.

'As opposed to young, virile and unbelievably handsome?' he drawled.

Shock jolted though her at his unapologetic, irritatingly justified confidence. Because he undeniably was. A full head of vibrant jet-black hair was common enough among her countrymen. Even his hazel eyes, sculpted cheekbones and square jaw were conventional in the polo-loving jet set crowd her father and brother encouraged her to associate with.

On this man, though, the whole combination had been elevated several hundred notches to an entirely different level of magnetism that demanded attention and got it. There was a quality about the way he carried himself, his broad shoulders unyielding, that spelled a tough inner core anyone would be foolish to mess with.

And yet that danger Inez could feel rising off him was… compelling. Alluring.

She found her gaze drifting over his face, past the tiny dimple in his chin to the dark bronze throat as he lazily swallowed a mouthful of champagne.

She inhaled a sharp dart of air as she watched his Adam's apple move. Then jerked back when her fingers flexed suddenly with the urge to touch him there.

Santa Maria!

She fought to remember her anger at this stranger. As much as she detested her role in tonight's events—the blatant begging for campaign funds disguised as a charity event—she couldn't let opportunities slip through her fingers.

It was the deal she'd made with her father.

An education in return for serving her time. In six short weeks she would be free to pursue her dreams. Free of her father's influence, of the sleazy, horrifying rumours that had been part of her childhood and what had driven her mother to quiet despair when she thought she wasn't being observed.

She needed to focus, not moon over how coarse this arrogant stranger's faintly stubbled jaw would feel against her skin.

'*Make nice?* After you rudely interrupted my conversation and sent my guest for the evening running without so much as a goodbye?'

'Think about that for a minute. Do you really want a man who would abandon you so easily on the strength of a few whispered words?'

Genuine anger replaced the momentary sensory aberration. 'That you needed to whisper those words instead of state them in my hearing makes me wonder just how confident you are of your manhood.'

Inez was used to being the butt of male jokes. Pietro and her father had mocked and dismissed her career ambitions until the day she'd picked up her suitcase and threatened to leave home for good.

But she was still shocked when the man in front of her threw back his head and laughed. Even more so when the sight of his strong white teeth and the genuine twinkling merriment in his eyes sent her pulse racing. An alien tingling started in her belly and spread outward like fractured lightning.

'Did I say something funny?'

Light hazel eyes speared hers. 'I've been challenged on a lot of things, *querida*, but never over my manhood.'

The political career her father so desperately craved produced men who could fake confidence with the best of them. She'd seen political candidates on a clear losing streak fake bravado until they were on the verge of looking totally ridiculous.

This man oozed confidence and power so very effortlessly it was like a second skin. Couple those two elements with the dangerous magnetism she could feel and Theo Pantelides was positively lethal.

Over her thundering heartbeat, she heard the master of ceremonies announce that the fund-raiser she'd so carefully orchestrated—the platform that would see her achieve her freedom—was about to begin.

Beyond one broad shoulder of the man who seemed to have sucked the air from the large ballroom, she saw her father and Pietro heading towards her.

Her father would want to know what had happened to Alfonso. The Brazilian businessman had promised to host a polo match on his large ranch where he bred the finest thoroughbreds. Securing a time and a date and a campaign donation had been her job tonight.

A much needed win this man had cost her.

Frustrated anger flared anew.

'This can be resolved very easily, Inez,' Theo Pantelides murmured in her ear. His voice was deep. Alluring. To hear him use her given name, the version her half-American mother had so lovingly bestowed on her, made her momentarily lose her bearings. A state that worsened when his hot breath washed over her neck.

Barely managing to suppress a shiver, she snapped herself back into focus. 'Don't say my name. In fact, don't speak to me. Just…just go away!'

Inez knew she was on the verge of displaying childish behaviour but she needed to regroup quickly, find a solution to a situation that had been so cut and dried fifteen minutes ago.

She watched her father and brother approach and the dart of pain that resided beneath her breastbone twisted. For a long time she'd yearned for a connection with them, especially after *Mãe* had been so cruelly ripped from their lives following a fall from a racehorse a week before Inez's eighteenth birthday. But she'd soon realised that she was alone in the pain and loneliness brought on by the loss of the mother who'd been her everything. Pietro had been given no time to grieve before their father had stepped up his grooming campaign. As for Benedicto himself, he'd barely finished burying his wife before resuming his relentless pursuit of political power.

The only other male she'd foolishly thought was honourable had turned out to be just as ruthlessly power-hungry as the men in her family.

Constantine Blanco—one lesson well and truly learned.

'I see the rumours were false after all,' the man who loomed, large and imposing, in front of her drawled in that deep voice of his, capturing her attention so effortlessly.

She pushed down the bitterness that swirled through her at the thought of what she'd allowed to happen with Constantine. How low she'd sunk in her need for love and a desire for a connection.

'What rumours?' She infused a carelessness in her voice she was far from feeling.

'The ones that said you exhibit grace and charm with each bat of your eyelids. At the moment all I can see is a hellcat intent on scoring grooves into my skin.'

'Then I suggest you stay away from me. I wouldn't want to ruin your *unbelievably handsome* face now, would I?'

She hurried away from his magnetic presence towards where the tables had been set out with highly polished sterling silver cutlery and exquisitely cut crystal. At twenty thousand dollars a plate, the event was ostensibly to raise money for the children trapped within Rio's *favelas*, a cause dear to her heart.

Shame it had to be tainted with power-hungry sharks, mild threats to secure votes and…devastatingly handsome rogues with piercing hazel eyes who made her breath catch in a frighteningly exciting way…

The direction of her thoughts made her stumble lightly. Catching herself, she smiled at a guest who slid her a concerned glance.

Each table was set for eight. Her father had insisted their table was placed in the centre, where all eyes would be on them.

With Alfonso's unexpected departure, the empty seat would stick out like the proverbial sore thumb once the Secretary of State and his wife and the other power couple had taken their places.

She had no choice but to bump someone to the high table. All she needed to figure out was who—

'Staring at the empty seat will not make your departed guest suddenly reappear, *senhorita*,' the deep voice uttered from behind her.

That hot shiver swept up her spine again.

Before she could summon an appropriately scathing retort, her chair and the one bearing Alfonso's name were pulled back.

'What are you doing?' she demanded heatedly under her breath. She continued to stare down at the place setting, unwilling to look up into those hazel eyes. Something in their light depths made her hyperaware of her body, of her increased heartbeat. As if she was prey and he was the merciless predator.

It was preposterous. She didn't like it. But it was undeniable.

'Saving your skin. Now, smile and play along.'

'I'm not a puppet. I don't smile on command.'

'Try. Unless you want to spend the rest of the evening sitting next to the equivalent of an elephant in the ballroom?'

Something in his voice made her forget her vow not to look into his eyes. Something...peculiar. Her head snapped up before she could stop herself.

Their eyes clashed. And she found herself in that hyperaware state again. She forced herself to breathe through it. 'You created the very situation you now seem intent on fixing. Why don't you save us both time and state what your agenda is?'

A look passed over his face. Too quickly for her to decipher but whatever it was made her breath catch in a totally different way from before. Warning spiked the hairs on her nape.

'I merely want to redress the situation a little. And, as talented as you seem to think you are at hiding it, I can see my actions caused you distress. Let me help make it better.'

'So you cause me grief then swoop in to save me like a knight in shining armour?'

'I'm no one's knight, *senhorita*. And I prefer Armani to armour.'

He pointedly held out her seat.

Casting a swift glance around, Inez saw that they were attracting attention. Short of causing a scene, there was nothing she could do. Willing her facial muscles to relax into a cordial smile, she slowly sat down and watched as Theo Pantelides folded himself into the seat next to her.

He reached for his champagne at the same time as she reached for her water glass. The brush of his knuckle against her wrist made her jump.

'Relax, *anjo*. I've got this,' came the smooth, deep reassurance.

A hysterical laugh bubbled up her throat, curbed at the last minute by a cough. 'Pardon me if that assurance brings me very little comfort.'

He lifted the glass she'd abandoned and held it out to her. 'Tell me, what's the worst that could happen?'

She took the glass and stared into the sparkling water. The need to moisten her dry throat had receded. 'Believe me, the worst already has happened.'

For a long time she'd hidden from the truth—that her father had his heir, and she was a useless spare part.

Pain writhed through her and her breath grew shaky as her throat clogged with anger and bitterness.

'Get yourself together. Now isn't the time to fall apart. Trust me, Delgado may be a good friend but he has a wandering eye.' The hard bite to his tone cut a path through her emotions.

Setting the glass down, she faced him. 'I have been toyed with enough to last me a century, and I know your business here tonight has nothing to do with me, so do me a favour, *senhor*, and tell me straight—what do you want?' she whispered fiercely. She noted vaguely that her heartbeat was once again on rapid acceleration to sky-high. Her fingers shook and her belly churned with emotions she couldn't have named to save her life.

'First of all, cut out the *senhor* bit. If you want to address me in any way, call me Theo.'

'I will address you how I see fit, Mr Pantelides. And I see that once again you have failed to give me a straight answer.'

'No, I've failed to jump when you say. You need to be taught a little patience, *anjo*.'

She lifted a deliberately mocking brow. 'And you propose to be the one to teach me?'

That wide, breathtaking smile appeared again. Just like that, her pulse leapt then galloped with a speed even the finest racehorse would've strained to match.

What was going on here?

'Only if you ask nicely.'

She was searching for an appropriately cutting response when her father reached the table with the rest of the guests.

He cast her a narrow-eyed glance before his gaze slid to Theo Pantelides.

'Mr Pantelides, I had hoped for a few minutes of your time before the evening started properly,' her father said as he took his seat across the table.

Inez wasn't sure whether she imagined the slight stiffening in the posture of the man beside her. Her senses were too highly strung for her to trust their accuracy. Searching his profile as he stared at her father, nothing in his face gave any indication as to his true feelings.

'I'm all for mixing business with pleasure. However, I draw the line at mixing business with the plight of the poor. Let the *favela* kids have their cause heard. *Then* we will attend to business.'

The firm put-down sent an arctic chill around the table. The Secretary's wife gave a visible gasp and her skin blanched beneath her overdone make-up. Pietro, who'd just approached the table as Theo replied, gripped the back of his chair, anger embedded in his face.

Silence reigned for several fraught seconds. Her father flicked a glance at Pietro, who yanked back his seat and sat down. The hands her brother placed on the table were curled into fists and for a moment Inez wondered if his famous temper was about to be let loose on their guests.

Benedicto smiled at Theo. 'Of course. This cause is extremely dear to my heart. My own mother was brought up in the *favelas*.'

'As indeed you were, no?' Theo queried silkily.

Again, the Secretary's wife gasped. She reached for her wine glass and took a quick gulp. When she went to take another, her husband surreptitiously stayed her hand and sent her a stern disapproving look.

Her father nodded to the waiter, who stood poised with a bottle of the finest red wine. He took his time to savour his first sip before he answered.

'You are quite mistaken, Mr Pantelides. My mother managed to escape the fate most of her lot failed to and bettered her life long before she bore me. But I inherited her fighting spirit and her determination to do what I can for the bleak place she once called home.'

Theo's eyebrow quirked. 'Right. I may have been misinformed, then,' he said, although his dry tone suggested otherwise.

'I assure you misinformation is rife when it comes to the ploys of political opponents. And I have been told more than once that only a foolish man believes everything he reads in the papers.'

Theo slashed a smile that had a definite edge to it across the table. 'Trust me, I know a thing or two about what lengths newspapers will go to achieve a headline.'

'We seem to have lost Alfonso. Would you care to explain his absence, Inez?' Pietro's voice slid through the conversation.

Anger still rippled off him and Inez was acutely aware that he hadn't directly addressed Theo Pantelides.

Before she could speak, the man in question turned to her brother. 'He was called away suddenly. Emergency business elsewhere. Couldn't be helped. Since I was there when he took his leave, your sister offered me his seat and I graciously accepted, didn't you, *anjo*?'

She saw Pietro's eyes visibly widen at the blatant endearment. Just as swiftly, they narrowed and she could almost see the wheels spinning in a different direction as his gaze swung between her and Theo Pantelides.

No! Never! Her fingers curled into fists and she glared at him until he looked away.

'Well, perhaps Delgado's loss is our gain, *sim*?' her father prompted.

Again Theo smiled. Again her heart thudded hard at the sheer magnetism of his smile, even though it sorely lacked any humour.

The man was an enigma. He'd inveigled his way onto the top table, then proceeded to insult his host, just as he'd insulted her.

Inez had little doubt her father would unleash his anger at the slight later.

But right now she was more puzzled by the man next to her. What was his game plan? If he was in a position to acquire a controlling share of their company then clearly he was a man of considerable means. But he wasn't Brazilian. That much she knew. So why was he interested in her father's political ambitions?

She realised she was staring when that proud head turned and gold-flecked hazel eyes captured hers, one eyebrow quirked in amusement.

Hastily averting her gaze, she picked up her glass and took another sip.

Thankfully, the master of ceremonies chose that moment to climb onto the podium to announce the first course and the first speaker.

Inez barely tasted the salmon mousse and the wine that

accompanied it. Nor did she absorb the speech given by the health minister about what was being done to help the poor.

Her hyperawareness of the man beside her interfered with her ability to think straight. The last time she'd felt anything remotely like this, she'd wandered down a path she'd hated herself for ever since. She'd almost given herself to a man who had no use for her besides using her as a pawn.

Never again!

Six more weeks. She needed to focus on that. Once her father was on his campaign trail, she could start her new life.

She'd heard the rumours about her father's ruthless beginnings when she was growing up; a couple of her school friends had whispered about unsavoury dealings her father had been involved in. Inez had never found concrete proof. The one time she'd asked her mother, she'd been quickly admonished not to believe lies about her family.

At the time, she'd assured herself that they weren't true. But the passage of time had whittled away that assurance. Now, with each day that passed, she suspected differently.

'You look as if the world is coming to an end, *anjo*,' the man she was desperately trying to ignore murmured. Again the endearment rolled off his tongue in a deep, seductive murmur that sent shivery awareness cascading over her skin.

'I hope you're not going to ask me to smile again, because—' She gasped as he took her hand and lifted it to his mouth.

Firm, warm lips brushed her skin and Inez's stomach dipped in sensual free fall that took her breath away. Desperately, she tried to snatch her hand back.

'What the hell do you think you're doing?' she snapped.

'Helping you. Relax. If you continue to look at me like you want to claw my eyes out, this won't work.'

'What exactly *is* this? And why on earth should I play along?'

'Your brother and father are still wondering why Delgado

left so abruptly. Do you want to suffer the third degree later or will you let me help you make it all go away?'

She eyed him suspiciously. The notion that there was something going on behind that smooth, charismatic façade didn't dissipate. In fact, it escalated as he stared down at her, his features enigmatic save for that smile that lingered on his wide, sexy mouth.

'Why do you want to help me?' Again she tried to take back her hand but he held on, one thumb smoothing over her inner wrist. Blood surged through her veins at his touch, her pulse racing at the spot that he so expertly explored.

'Because I'm hoping it would persuade you to have lunch with me tomorrow,' he replied.

His gaze flicked across the table. Although his expression didn't change, she again sensed the tension that hovered on the edge of his civility. This man didn't like her family. Which begged the question: what was he doing here investing in their company?

He swung that intense stare back to her and she lost her train of thought. Grabbing it back, she shook her head.

'I'll have to refuse the lunch offer, I'm afraid. I have other plans.'

'Dinner, then?'

'I have plans then, too. Besides, don't you have business with my father tomorrow?'

'Our business won't take longer than me signing on a dotted line.'

'A dotted line that gives you a permanent controlling share in my family's company?'

His eyes gleamed. 'Not permanent. Only until I have what I want.'

CHAPTER THREE

'AND WHAT IS it you want?'

'For now? Lunch. Tomorrow. With you.' Another pass of his thumb over her pulse.

Another roll of sensation deep in her belly. The temptation to say yes suddenly overcame her, despite the warning bells shrieking at the back of her mind.

She forced herself to heed those warning bells. Her painfully short foray into a relationship had taught her that good looks and charm often hid an agenda that would most likely not benefit her or her heart. And Theo Pantelides had metaphorical skull and crossbones stamped all over him.

'The answer is still no,' she replied, a lot sharper than she'd intended.

His lips compressed but he shrugged. As if her answer hadn't fazed him.

And it probably hadn't. He was one of those men who drew women like bees to pollen. He could probably secure a lunch date with half of the women in this room and tempt the other married half into sin should he choose to.

With his dark, exquisite looks and deep sexy voice, he could have any woman he chose to display even the mildest interest in.

The thought that he would do just such a thing punched so fierce a reaction in her belly that she suppressed a shocked gasp.

What on earth is wrong with me? She needed to get herself back under control before she did something foolish—like discard her plans for tomorrow in favour of spending more time with this infuriatingly self-assured, visually stunning man.

Giving herself a fierce pep talk, she pulled her hand from his grasp.

She folded her hand in her lap and wrapped her other hand over her wrist. But suddenly her own touch felt...inadequate.

She was saved from exploring the peculiar feeling when the lights dimmed and the projector started reeling pictures of miles and miles of rusted shingle roofs that formed the world famous Rio *favelas*.

Her father climbed onto the podium to begin his speech.

The tale of despair-driven prostitution, violence, gang warfare and kidnapping of innocents, and the need to do whatever was needed to help was one she'd heard at many fund-raisers and charity dinners.

She clenched her fist. Knowing that half the people in here, dripping in diamonds and tuxedos worth several thousand dollars, would've forgotten the plight of the *favela* residents by the time dessert was served made her silently scream in frustration.

The need to get up, to walk out almost overwhelmed her but she stayed put.

There would be no running. No walking away from the work she'd committed herself to, nor walking away from the formative minds that were depending on her.

Fierce pride tightened her chest at the part she was playing in the young lives under her charge. And the fact that she'd managed to change that part of her own life without her father or brother's interference.

She refocused as her father finished his speech to rousing applause. The projector was shut off and the lights grew brighter.

She reached forward for her glass of wine and noticed that she was once again the focus of Theo's gaze.

'Should I be offended that I'm being so comprehensively ignored?' he asked.

'It's not a state you're used to, I expect?' With her surroundings once more in focus, she noticed the looks he was getting from women on other tables. She didn't delude herself that any of them were interested in his views on politics or world peace. No, each and every one of them would vie for much more personal, much more physical contact with the lean, broad-shouldered man next to her, whose hands casually caressed his wine glass stem in a way that made her think indecent thoughts.

She noticed the young famous actress on the next table where Theo should have been sitting gazing over at him, and again felt the sharp edge of an unknown emotion pierce her insides.

His smile grew hard. 'You'd be surprised.'

Curiosity brought her gaze back to his. 'Would I? How?'

'That question makes me think you've formed an opinion of me.'

'And that answer convinces me that you're very good at deflecting. You may fool others, but you do not fool me.'

He stared at her for a moment before one corner of his mouth lifted. Abruptly, he stood and held out his hand. 'Dance with me, *anjo*, and enlighten me further as to what you think you know about me.'

The demand was silky and yet implacable. In full view of the other guests, her refusal would be extremely discourteous.

Her heart hammered as she slowly slid her hand into his and let him draw her to her feet.

Emotions she was trying and failing to suppress flared up at the warmth and firmness of his grip. Fervently, she prayed for time to speed up, for the evening to end so she could be free of this man. Her reaction to him was puzzling in the extreme and the notion that she was being toyed with unsettled her more with each passing second.

As they skirted the table to head for the dance floor, her gaze met her father's. Expecting approval for accommodating the man whose business he was so obviously keen to garner, she was taken aback when she saw his icy disapproval.

Through the elite Rio grapevine she knew Alfonso Delgado's net worth and knew he couldn't afford to acquire a controlling share of Da Costa Holdings. So why did her father disapprove of a man who was clearly superior in monetary worth to Alfonso?

'You really have to do better with your social skills than this. Or I'll have to do something drastic to retain your attention.' The hard bite to Theo's voice slashed through her thoughts. 'Or were you really that into Delgado?'

'No, I wasn't.'

Her immediate denial seemed to pacify him. 'Then tell me what's on your mind.'

Inez found herself speaking before she could snap at him not to issue orders. 'Have you ever found yourself in a position where everything you do turns out wrong, no matter how hard you try?'

'There have been a few instances.' He pulled her close and slid an arm around her back. Heat transmitted to her skin via the soft material of her dress and flooded through her body. This close, his scent washed over her. Strong but not overpowering, masculine and heady in a way that made her want to draw even closer, touch her mouth to the bronze skin just above his collar.

Deus!

'You think this is one of those occasions for you?'

'I don't think; I know.'

'Why?'

Her laugh grated its way up her throat. 'Because I have a perfectly functioning brain.'

'You're worried because your father and brother are displeased with you?'

'Everything else this evening has gone according to plan except...'

'Delgado. You're worried that your father offered you up on a silver platter because he seems to think you're a prize worth winning and now he'll demand to know what you did wrong.'

Her eyes snapped to his, the insult surprisingly painful. 'What do you mean by *seems to think*? What do you know about my father? Or about me, for that matter?'

Theo forced himself not to tense at the question. Or let the fact that her body seemed to fit so perfectly in his arms impact on his thinking abilities. 'Enough.'

'Do you always go around making unfounded remarks about someone you've just met?'

He let a small smile play over his mouth. 'Enlighten me, then. Are you a prize worth winning?'

'There's no point enlightening you because it will serve no useful purpose. After tonight you and I will never meet again.'

She took a firm step back. Attempted to prise herself out of his arms. He held her easily, willing back the thrum of anger and bitterness that rose like bile in his throat.

'Never say never, *anjo*.'

Her fiery brown eyes glared at him. 'Don't.'

He feigned innocence. 'Don't what?'

'Don't keep calling me that.'

'You don't like it?'

'You have no right to slap a pet name on someone you just met.'

The hand holding hers tightened. 'Calm down—'

'No, I won't calm down. I'm not an angel. I'm certainly not *your* angel.'

'Inez.' A warning, subtle but effective.

Inez's pulse stalled, then thundered wildly through her veins.

'Don't,' she whispered again. Only this time she wasn't sure what she pleaded for.

He leaned closer until his mouth was an inch from her ear. When he breathed out, warmth teased her earlobe. 'Don't use your given name? It's either that or *anjo*. All the other words are only appropriate for the bedroom.'

Heat flamed through her belly as indecent thoughts of rumpled sheets, sweaty bodies and incandescent pleasure reeled through her mind.

She shook her head to dispel the images and heard his low laugh.

When she stared up at him, his eyes blazed down at her with a hunger that smashed through her body. Her nipples slowly hardened and the fire raged higher as his lips parted on another heart-stopping smile. Unable to help herself, her eyes dropped to the sensual curve of his mouth.

'I think it's my turn to say *don't*. Not if you don't want to be thrown over my shoulder and raced to the nearest cave.'

She forced a laugh despite the sensations rushing through her. 'This is the twenty-first century, *senhor*.'

'But what I'm feeling right now isn't. It's very basic. Primeval, in fact.'

He swerved her out of the path of another couple and used the move to draw her even closer. At the fierce evidence of his arousal against her stomach, Inez swallowed hard.

Her confusion escalated.

Constantine had been charismatic and breathtaking in his own right. But he'd never made her feel like *this*, not even in the beginning…before everything had gone disastrously wrong.

Thinking of the man who'd broken her heart and betrayed her so cruelly threw much needed ice over her heated senses. She'd made a fool of herself over one man. Foolishly believed he was the answer to her prayers. She was wise enough now to know Theo Pantelides wasn't the answer to any prayer, unless it was the crash and burn type.

'I believe I've fulfilled my obligatory dance duty to you. Perhaps you'd like to find a more unwitting female to club over the head and drag to your cave?' She injected as much indifference into her voice as possible.

'That won't be necessary. I've already found what I'm looking for.'

Theo watched several emotions chase over her features before Inez da Costa regained her impeccable hostess persona.

Although he silently cursed himself for his physical reaction, he was thankful she realised her effect on him.

Let her think she held the power. Allow her to believe that he could be manipulated to her advantage. Or, rather, her father's advantage.

Her reaction to Delgado's departure had shown him that fulfilling her role as her father's Venus flytrap was most important to Inez da Costa. Or was it something else? Did she hope to bag *herself* a millionaire while serving her father's purpose? She came from a family ruthless in its pursuit of wealth and power. Was that her underlying agenda?

That knowledge demanded that he rethink his strategy. The conclusion he'd arrived at was surprising but easily adaptable.

He had an opportunity to kill a few more birds with one stone. With any luck, he would conclude his business in Rio in a far shorter time than he'd already anticipated if he played his cards right.

Inez tried to wrench herself from his grasp once more. The primitive feelings he'd mentioned so casually a moment ago resurfaced. When she tugged harder, he forced himself to release her. Her soft hand slid from his, leaving a trail of sensation that made his groin pound and his blood heat.

The plan he'd hatched solidified as he gazed down into

her heart-shaped face, saw her fighting to stop her clear agitation from messing with her breathing.

Theo hid a smile.

Either she was offended at his primitive declaration or she was turned on by it. Since she wasn't slapping his face, he concluded that it was the latter.

His gaze dropped lower, and the sight of her tightly beaded nipples against her gown made his own breathing stall in his chest. Lower still, her tiny waist gave way to those tempting hips that his palms ached to explore.

Even as he talked himself into believing his reaction would ultimately serve his purpose, a part of Theo was forced to acknowledge that he hadn't reacted this strongly to a woman in a very long time. Everything about her brought his senses to roaring life in a way only the thought of revenge had for the past decade.

Revenge...retribution over the person who had created such chaos in his life.

He gritted his teeth as the sound of tinkling laughter and animated conversation refocused his mind to his task and purpose.

'Good evening, Mr Pantelides. I hope you enjoy the rest of your evening,' Inez said stiltedly.

She turned and walked off the dance floor before he could reply. Not that he felt like replying. Although he'd mostly kept on track throughout the evening, a large part of him had become far too consumed by her seductive presence.

Inez da Costa was only one part of the game. To keep on track he needed to keep his head in the *whole* game.

He headed for the bar and sensed the moment Benedicto and his son halted their conversation and moved pincer-like towards him.

Dreaded anxiety washed over his senses but he forced himself to breathe through it.

I am no longer in that dark, cold place. I am in light. I am free...

He tersely repeated the short statement under his breath as he tossed back the shot of vodka and set it down with cold, precise care.

He was no longer weak. No longer helpless.

And he most certainly would never be put in a position to beg for his life. Ever again.

By the time they reached him, he'd regained control of his body.

'Senhor Pantelides—'

'We're about to become business partners—' his gaze slid over Pietro's head to where Inez was holding court in a group of guests; the sleek line of her neck and the curve of her body sent another punch of heat straight to his groin '—and hopefully a little bit more than that. Call me Theo.'

The younger man looked a little taken aback, but he rallied quickly, nodded and held out his hand. 'Theo...we wanted to hammer down a time to discuss finalising our agreement.'

He took Pietro's hand in a firm grip. Benedicto started to offer his hand. Theo deliberately turned away. Catching the bartender's eye, he held up his fingers for three more drinks. By the time he faced them again, Benedicto had lowered his hand.

Theo breathed through the deep anger that churned through his belly and smiled.

'Tomorrow. Ten o'clock. My office. I'll have the documents ready for us to sign.'

This time it was Benedicto who looked taken aback. 'I was under the impression that you wanted to iron out a few more details.'

Theo's gaze flicked back to Inez. 'I had a few concerns but they no longer matter. Your campaign funds will be ready in the next twenty-four hours.'

Father and son exchanged triumphant looks. 'We are pleased to hear it,' Benedicto said.

'Good, then I hope the three of you will join me for dinner tomorrow evening to celebrate our new deal.'

Benedicto frowned. 'The three of us?'

'Of course. I expect that, since this is a family company, your daughter would wish to be included in the celebrations? After all, the company was her mother's family's business before it became yours, Senhor da Costa, was it not?' he queried silkily.

The older man's eyes narrowed and something unpleasant slid across his face. 'I bought my father-in-law out over a decade ago but yes, it's a family business.'

Bought out using money he'd obtained by inflicting pain and merciless torment.

The bartender slid their shots across the polished counter.

Theo picked up the nearest shot glass and raised it. 'In that case, I look forward to welcoming you all as my guests tomorrow evening. *Saúde*.'

'*Saúde*,' Benedicto and his son responded.

Theo threw back the drink and this time didn't hold back from slamming it down.

Again he saw father and son exchange looks. He didn't care.

All he cared about was making it out of the ballroom in one piece before he buried his fist in Benedicto da Costa's bony face. The urge to tear apart the man who'd caused his family, caused *him*, so much anguish reared through him.

The sound of his phone vibrating in his jacket pocket brought a welcome distraction from his murderous thoughts.

'Excuse me, gentlemen.' He walked away without a backward glance, gaining the double doors leading out to the wide terrace before activating his phone.

'Heads up, you're about to get into serious trouble with Ari if you don't fess up as to why you're really in Rio,' Sakis, his brother, said in greeting.

'Too late. I've already had the hairdryer treatment earlier this evening.'

'Yeah, but do you know he's thinking of flying down there for a face-to-face?'

Theo cursed. 'Doesn't he have enough on his hands being all loved up and taking care of his pregnant fiancé?' He wasn't concerned about a confrontation with Ari. But he was concerned that Ari's presence might alert Benedicto to Theo's true intentions.

So far, Benedicto da Costa was oblivious as to the connections Theo had made to what had happened twelve years ago. The older man had been very careful to erase every connection with the incident and sever ties with anyone who could bear witness to the crime he'd committed. He hadn't been careful enough. But he didn't know that.

Having another Pantelides in Rio could set off alarm bells.

'You need to stall him.'

'He's concerned,' Sakis murmured. Theo heard the same concern reflected in his brother's voice. 'So am I.'

'It needs to be done,' he replied simply.

'I get that. But you don't need to do it alone. He's dangerous. The moment he guesses what your true intentions are—'

'He won't; I've made sure of it.'

'How can you be absolutely certain? Theo, don't be stubborn. I can help—'

'No. I need to see this through myself.'

Sakis sighed. 'Are you sure?'

Theo turned slowly and surveyed the ballroom. Rio's finest drank and laughed without a care in the world. In the centre of that crowd stood Benedicto da Costa, the reason why Theo couldn't sleep through a single night without waking to hellish nightmares; the reason anxiety hovered just underneath his skin, ready to infest his control should he loosen his grip for one careless second.

Inexorably, his eyes were drawn to the female member of the diabolical family. Inez was dancing with a man whose blatant interest and barely disguised lust made Theo's fist curl over the cold stone bannister.

His stomach churned and adrenaline poured through his system the same way a boxer experienced a heady rush in the seconds before a fight. This fight had been long coming. He would see it through. He had to. Otherwise he feared his demons would never be exorcised.

He'd lived with them for far too long, and they needed to be silenced. He needed to regain complete, unshakeable hold of his life once more.

His other hand tightened around his mobile phone, his heart thundering enough to drown out the music. He spoke succinctly so his brother would be in no doubt that he meant every word.

'Am I sure that I need to bring down the man who kidnapped and tortured me for over two weeks until Ari negotiated a two million ransom for my release? *Hell, yes*. I'm going to make him feel ten million times worse than what he did to me and to our family and I don't intend to rest until I bring all of them down.'

CHAPTER FOUR

'A DOUBLE-SHOT AMERICANO, *por favor*.' Inez smiled absently at the barista while she tried to juggle her sketchpad and fish out enough change from her purse to pay for the coffee.

It was barely nine o'clock and yet the heat was already oppressive, even more than usual for a Thursday morning in February. Normally, she would've opted for a cool caffeine drink but her energy levels needed an extra boost this morning.

She'd slept badly after the fund-raiser last night. And what little sleep she'd managed had been interspersed with images of a man she had no business thinking, never mind dreaming, about.

And yet Theo Pantelides's face had haunted her slumber...still haunted her, if truth be told.

The last time she'd seen him he'd been leaning against the terrace bannister outside the ballroom, his eyes fixed firmly on her. Inez wasn't sure why her attention had been drawn outside. All she knew was that something had compelled her to look that way as she danced with a guest.

Even from that distance the tension whipping through his frame had been unmistakable, as had the blatant dark promise in his eyes as his gaze raked her from head to toe.

More than anything she'd wished she could lip-read when she'd watched his lips move to answer whoever was at the other end of his phone conversation.

That last look plagued her. It'd held hunger, anger and another emotion that she couldn't quite decipher. Brushing it off, she smiled, accepted her coffee and headed outside. She was a little early for her class with the inner city kids but she hadn't wanted to spend another moment at the tension-fraught breakfast table with her father and brother this morning.

In contrast to Pietro's third degree as to what exactly had happened with Alfonso Delgado, her father had been cold and strangely preoccupied. The moment he'd stood abruptly and left the table, she'd made her excuses and walked away.

Even Pietro's reminder that they had a dinner engagement she couldn't recall making hadn't been worth stopping to query. All she'd wanted was to get out of the mansion that felt more and more as if it was closing in on her.

'*Bom dia, anjo.*' The deep murmured greeting brought her thoughts and footsteps to a crashing halt.

Theo leaned casually against a gleaming black sports car, a pair of dark sunglasses hiding his eyes from her. But her full body tingle announced that she was the full, unwavering focus of his gaze. Her breath stalled, her heart accelerating wildly as her pulse went into overdrive.

'What the hell are you doing here?' she blurted before she could stop her strong reaction.

Aside from the devastation his tall, lean suited frame caused to her insides, the thought that he could discover where she was headed or what she did with her Tuesday and Thursday mornings made her palms grow clammy. By lunchtime today, if Pietro were to be believed, Theo would be firmly entrenched as a business partner in her family's company. Which meant constant contact with her family. Which meant he could disclose parts of her life she wasn't yet ready to disclose to her family.

'Are you following me?' she accused hotly as she approached him, her senses jumping with the possibilities and consequences of her discovery.

'Not today. My trench coat and fedora are at the laundry.'

'Keep them there. In this heat, you'd boil to death.'

A smile broke across his face. 'Do I detect a little unladylike relish in your voice, *anjo*?'

'What you detect is high scepticism that you're here by accident and not following me,' she snapped.

'You give me too much credit, *agape mou*. I asked for the best coffee shop in the city and I was directed here. That you're here too merely confirms that assertion. Unless you go out of your way to sample bad coffee?'

Before she could respond, he straightened and reached for the hand wrapped around her coffee. Curling his hand over hers, he brought his lips to the small opening on her coffee lid and tilted the cup towards him.

He savoured the drink in his mouth for a few seconds before he swallowed.

Inez fought to breathe as she watched his strong throat move. The slow swirl of his tongue over his lower lip caused darts of sharp need to arrow straight between her legs.

'Delicious. And surprising. I would've pegged you for a latte girl.'

'Which goes to show you know next to nothing about me,' she retorted.

He slowly raised his sunglasses and speared her with his mesmerising eyes. Although a smile hovered over his sensual lips, some unnameable tension hovered in the air between them. A charged friction that warned her all was not as it seemed.

Hell, she knew that. Theo Pantelides spelled danger. Whether smiling or serious, dallying with him was akin to playing with electricity. Depending on his mood, you could either receive a mild static frizzle or a full-blown electrocution. And she had no intention of testing him for either.

'*Sim*, I don't know enough about you. But I intend to remedy that situation in the near future.'

She shrugged. 'It is your time to waste.'

He merely smiled and turned towards his car.

'I thought you came to get coffee?' she probed, then bit her lip for prolonging a meeting she wanted over and done with. Last night she'd told herself to be thankful that she would never see this man again. And yet, here she was, feeling mildly bereft at the notion that he was leaving.

He paused and his gaze slid over her. Immediately, she became supremely conscious of the white shorts and blue tank top she'd hurriedly thrown on this morning. Her hair was caught up in a ponytail because it helped keep it out of the way during her class. Her face was devoid of make-up except for the light sunscreen and the gloss she'd passed over her lips. All in all, she projected a much different image this morning than the sophisticated hostess she'd been last night.

Catching herself wondering whether he found her wanting now, she mentally slammed the thought down. She didn't care what Theo thought of her.

'I have the kick I need to keep me going. See you tonight.'

'Tonight? Why would you be seeing me tonight?' she demanded.

His smile slowly disappeared as his gaze slid over her again. This time, his hot gaze held an element of possessiveness that made her fight to keep from fidgeting under his keen scrutiny.

Stepping back, he activated a button on his car key and the door slid smoothly upward. She watched, completely captivated, as he lowered his tall masculine frame inside the small space. A touch of a slim finger on a button and the engine roared to life.

'Because I want to see you. And I always get what I want, Inez,' he said cryptically, his tone suddenly hard and biting. 'Remember that.'

I always get what I want.

Another shiver of apprehension coursed down her spine. All through the two art and graphic design classes she taught from ten till midday, the infernal words throbbed through her head as if someone had set them on repeat.

She managed to keep her focus, barely, as she demonstrated the differences between charcoal and pencil strokes to a group of ten-year-olds. Once or twice she had to repeat herself because she lost her train of thought, much to the amusement of her pupils, but the satisfying feeling of imparting knowledge to children who would otherwise have been left wandering the streets momentarily swamped the roiling emotions that Theo had stirred with his unexpected appearance this morning.

The suspicion that he had been following her didn't go away all through her hurriedly taken lunch and the meeting she'd scheduled with the volunteer coordinator at the centre.

Her decision to forge her own path by seeking a permanent position at the centre had solidified as she'd tossed and turned through the night.

Seeking her independence meant finding a paying job. To do that she needed more experience, which she hoped her longer hours spent volunteering would give her.

Thanks to her father's interference, all she had was one semester at university. It wasn't great but, until such time as she could further her education, it was better than nothing. That plus her volunteering was a starting point.

A starting point that was greatly enhanced when the coordinator agreed to increase her hours to three full days.

She was smiling as she activated her phone on the way to her car after leaving the centre.

The first text was from Pietro, reminding her that they were dining out that evening. With Theo Pantelides.

The unladylike curse she uttered won her a severe look of disapproval from an elderly lady walking past. The urge to text back a refusal was immediate and visceral.

After last night and this morning, exposing herself to the raw emotions Theo provoked was the last thing she needed.

And even more than her suspicions this morning, she

had a feeling he'd engineered this dinner. Hell, he'd as much as taunted her with it with his last words to her this morning.

As much as she tried to think positive and hope that the dinner would be quick and painless, a premonition gripped her insides as she slid behind the wheel and headed home.

'Filho da puta.' Her brother's habitual crude cursing wasn't a surprise to her. That it had seemingly come out of nowhere was.

'What's wrong?' She eyed him as they stepped out of the car at the marina of the exclusive Rio Yacht Club just before seven p.m.

She pulled down her box-pleated hem and wished she'd worn something a little longer than the form-fitting mid-thigh-length royal-blue sleeveless dress. The traffic had been horrendous and she'd arrived home much later than planned. The dress had been the nearest thing to hand. Now she stared down at the four-inch black platform heels she'd teamed with it and grimaced at the amount of thigh and legs on show.

The light breeze lifted a few strands of her loose hair as she turned to her brother and saw him jerk his chin towards the largest yacht moored at the far end of the pier. 'Trust Pantelides to rub my nose in it,' he said acerbically.

She looked from the sleek black, gold-trimmed vessel back to her brother. 'Rub your nose...what are you talking about?'

With a sullen look, he strode off down the jetty. 'That's my boat.'

'Yours? When did you buy a boat?'

'I didn't. I couldn't. Not after the mess up with *Pai*'s last campaign. That boat was supposed to be mine!' Dark anger clouded his face.

Her heart jumped into her throat. 'Pietro, a boat like that costs millions of dollars. Besides that very unsubtle hint that

I in any way stood in the way of your acquiring it—which is preposterous, by the way—there's no way you could ever have afforded a boat like that, so—'

'Forget it. Let's go and get this over with. It's bad enough *Pai* pulled out of coming tonight. Now I have to schmooze for both of us. You have to play your part, too. It's clear Pantelides's got a thing for you.'

Disgust and anger rose in her and she snatched her hand away from Pietro when he tried to lead her down the gangplank.

'I won't participate in another of your soulless schemes. So you may as well forget it right now.'

'Inez—'

'No!' Feelings she'd bottled up for much longer than she cared to think about rose to the surface. 'You keep asking me to throw myself at prospective investors so you can fund *Pai*'s campaign. You're his campaign manager and yet you can't seem to function without my help. Why is that?'

Pietro's eyes darkened. 'Watch your mouth, sister.'

'Show me some respect and I'll consider it,' she challenged.

'What the hell has got into you?'

'Nothing that hasn't always been there, Pietro. But you need me to point it out to you so I will. I'm done. If you want me to accompany you as your *sister* to Theo Pantelides's dinner, then I will. If you have another scheme up your sleeve, then you might as well forget it because I am not interested.'

Her brother's lips pursed but she saw a hint of shame in his eyes before his gaze slid away. 'I don't have time to argue with you right now. All I ask, if it's not too much, of course, is that you help me secure this deal with Pantelides, because if we lose his backing then we might as well pack up and head back up to the ranch in the mountains.' He set off down the jetty.

She hurried to keep up, picking her way carefully over

wooden slats. 'But I thought everything was done and dusted this morning?' she asked when she caught up with him.

Anxiety slid over Pietro's face. 'Pantelides cancelled the meeting. Something came up, he said. Except I know it was a lie. I have it on good authority he was parked outside a coffee shop chatting up some girl when he was supposed to be meeting us to finalise the agreement.'

Inez stumbled, barely catching herself from toppling headlong into the water a few feet away.

'*You're having him watched?*' How she managed to keep her voice even, she didn't know.

Petulance joined anxiety. 'Of course I am. And I'd bet my Rolex that he's doing the same to us.'

The thought of being the subject of anyone's surveillance made her skin crawl, even though a part of her had reluctantly accepted the truth: that her father's business dealings weren't always legitimate. But hearing her brother admit it made her stomach turn.

And if that was the way Theo Pantelides conducted his business as well…

She pressed her lips together and looked up as Pietro strode past the potted palm lined entrance to the Yacht Club.

'Aren't we dining in there?'

He shook his head. 'No. We're dining on my…on *his* boat,' he tossed out bitterly.

Inez glanced at the yacht they were approaching.

This close, the vessel was even more magnificent. Its sleek lines and exquisite craftsmanship made her fingers itch for her sketching pad. She was so busy admiring the boat and yearning to capture its beauty on paper that she didn't see its owner until she was right in front of him.

Then everything else ceased to register.

He wore a black shirt with black trousers, his dark hair raked back from his face. Under the soft golden lights spilling from the second deck his sculpted cheekbones and strong jaw jutted out in heart-stopping relief.

At the back of her mind, Inez experienced a bout of irritation at the fact that he captured attention so exclusively. So effortlessly.

Even as he shook hands with Pietro and welcomed him on board the *Pantelides 9*, his eyes remained on her. And God help her, but she couldn't look away.

On unsteady feet, which she firmly blamed on the swaying vessel, she climbed the steps to where he waited. When his eyes released hers to travel over her body, she grappled with controlling her breath. She reached him and reluctantly held out her hand in greeting.

'Thank you for the dinner invitation, Mr Pantelides.'

With a mocking smile, he took her hand and used the grip to pull her close. Despite her heels, he was almost a foot taller than her, easily six foot four. Which meant he had to lean down quite a bit to whisper in her ear, 'So formal, *anjo*. I look forward to loosening your inhibitions enough to dissolve that starchy demeanour.'

Her pulse, which had begun racing when his palm slid against hers, thundered even harder at his words. 'I can see how not having a woman fall at your feet the moment you crook your finger can present a challenge, *senhor*. But you really should learn the difference between playing hard to get and being plainly uninterested.'

His eyebrow quirked. 'You fall into the latter category, of course?' he mocked.

'*Sim*, that is exactly so.'

He looked towards where Pietro had accepted a glass of champagne from a waiter and was admiring the luxuriously decorated deck, at the end of which a multi-coloured lit jet pool swirled and shimmered.

When his gaze re-fixed on hers, there was a steely determination in his eyes that sent a shiver down her spine. All the earlier alarm bells where Theo was concerned clanged loudly in her brain.

'Then I will have to get a little more inventive,' he murmured silkily before dropping her hand.

Inez clenched her fist and fought the urge to rub the tingling in her palm. She didn't want him getting inventive where she was concerned because she had a nasty feeling she wouldn't emerge unscathed from the encounter.

But she kept her mouth shut and followed him onto the deck. The cream and gold décor was the last word in luxury and opulence. Plump gold seats offered comfort and a superior view onto the well-lit marina and the open sea to their right. To their left, the lights of Rio gleamed, with the backdrop of the huge mountain, on top of which resided the world-famous Cristo Redentor.

A sultry breeze wafted through the deck as a waiter served more flutes of champagne. She took a glass as Pietro rejoined them. His glass was already half empty and she watched him take another greedy gulp before he pointed a finger at Theo.

'I wish you'd given me the chance to make you another offer for this boat before you pulled the plug on our sale agreement, Pantelides.'

Theo's jaw tightened before he answered. 'You had several opportunities to make good but you failed to close the deal. So I cut my losses.' He shrugged. 'Business is business.'

Pietro bristled. 'And cancelling our meeting today? Was that for business too, or pleasure?'

Theo's eyes caught and held hers. Inez held her breath, wondering if he was about to give her up. His eyes gleamed with a mixture of danger and amusement. Somehow he'd sensed that he held her in his power. And he relished that power. Her hand trembled slightly as she waited for the axe to fall.

'I'm not in the habit of discussing my other business interests, or my pleasurable ones, for that matter. But, suffice it to say, what kept me away from our meeting was very much worth my time.' His gaze swept down, lingering over her breasts and hips in a blatant appraisal that made her breathing grow shallow. When his eyes returned to hers, Inez was sure all the oxygen had been sucked out of the atmosphere.

'Our business together should be equally worth your time,' Pietro countered.

Theo finally set her free from his captivating gaze. Narrow-eyed, he glanced at Pietro.

'Which is why I rescheduled for this evening. Of course, your father chose not to grace us with his presence. So the song and dance continues, I guess.' The hard edge was definitely in his tone again, prompting those alarm bells to ring louder.

Pietro muttered something under his breath that she was sure wasn't complimentary. He snapped his fingers at the waiter and swapped his empty glass for a full one.

'Well, we'll be there at the appointed time tomorrow. We can only hope that you will not be delayed…elsewhere.'

The upward movement of Theo's mouth could in no way be termed a smile. His eyes flicked back to her. 'Don't worry, da Costa, I intend to hammer out the final points of our agreement tonight. When I turn up to sign tomorrow, it will be with the knowledge that all my stipulations have been satisfied.'

The firm belief that his statement was connected to her wouldn't dissipate all through dinner. As a host, Theo was effortlessly entertaining. He even managed to draw a chuckle from Pietro once or twice.

But Inez couldn't shake the feeling that they were being toyed with. And once or twice she caught the faintest hint of fury and repulsion on his face, especially when her father's name came up.

She shook herself out of her unsettling thoughts when the most mouth-watering dessert was set down before her.

Whatever Theo was up to, it was nothing to do with her. Her father had managed their family business with enough savvy not to be drawn into a scam.

With that comforting thought in mind, she picked up her spoon and scooped up a mouthful of chocolate truffle-topped cheesecake.

Her tiny groan of delight drew intense eyes back to hers. Suddenly, the thought of dishing out a little of the mockery he'd doled out to her tingled through her. Keeping her gaze on his, she slowly drew the spoon out from between her lips, then licked the remnants of chocolate with a slow flick of her tongue.

His nostrils flared immediately, hunger darkening his eyes to a leaf-green that was mesmerising to witness. With another swirl of her tongue, she lowered the spoon and scooped up another mouthful.

His large fist tightened around the after-dinner espresso he'd opted for and she momentarily expected the bone china to shatter beneath his grip. But slowly he released it and sat back in his chair, his eyes never leaving her face.

'Enjoying your dessert, *anjo*?' he asked in that low, rough tone of his.

She hated to admit that the endearment was beginning to have an effect on her. The way he mouthed it made heat bloom in her belly, made her aware of her every heartbeat... made her wonder how it would sound whispered to her at the height of passion. *No!*

'Yes. Very much.' She fake smiled to project an air of nonchalance.

He smiled at her mocking formality. 'Good. I'll make a note of it for the next time we dine together.'

Before she could tell him she intended to move heaven and earth to make sure there wouldn't be a next time, Pietro lurched to his feet. 'I never got the chance to inspect my…this boat before the opportunity to buy it was regrettably taken away. You won't mind if I take a look around, would you?' he slurred.

Theo motioned the hovering waiter over. He murmured to him and the waiter went to the deck bar and picked up a handset. 'Not at all. My skipper will give you the tour.'

A middle-aged man with greying hair climbed onto the deck a few minutes later and escorted a swaying Pietro towards the stairs.

Inez watched him go with a mixture of anxiety and sympathy.

'He's drunk.' Her appetite gone for good, she set her spoon down and pushed the plate away.

'You say that as if it's my fault,' he replied lazily.

'Did you really have to do that?' She glared at him.

He raised a brow. 'Do what, exactly?'

'This was supposed to be Pietro's boat.' No matter how unrealistic that notion had been, her brother didn't deserve to be humiliated like this.

'*Supposed* being the operative word. We had a *gentleman's* agreement.' That hard bite was back again, sending trepidation dancing along her nerve ends. 'He didn't hold out his end of the deal.'

'Regardless of that, do you have to rub his nose in it like this?' she countered.

'As I said before, I'm a businessman, *anjo*. And I currently have a yacht worth tens of millions of dollars that needs an owner. The Boat Show starts next week. I relocated aboard in order to get it in shape for prospective buyers, otherwise our dinner would have taken place at my residence in Leblon and your brother's delicate feelings would've been spared.'

She frowned. 'You're selling the boat?' The thought of the beautiful vessel going to some unknown, probably pompous new owner made her nose wrinkle in distaste. The design was exquisite, unique…sort of like its owner.

As hard as she tried to imagine it, she couldn't see anyone else owning the boat besides Theo. Not even Pietro. Its black and gold contrasts depicted darkness and light in a complementary synergy—two fascinating characteristics she'd glimpsed more than once in Theo.

'Needs must.'

She looked around the beautiful deck, imagined its graceful lines awash with sunlight, and sighed.

Theo's eyes narrowed as he stared across at her. 'You like the boat.'

'Yes, it's...beautiful.'

He watched her for a few minutes then he nodded. 'Let's make a date for Sunday afternoon. We'll take her out for a quick spin.'

She laughed. 'Unless I'm mistaken, this is a four hundred foot vessel. You don't just take her out for a *quick* spin.'

'A long spin, then. I need to make sure it runs perfectly. If you still like it when we return to shore, I'll keep it.'

Her heart lurched then sped up like a runaway freight train. 'You would do that...for me?'

'*Sim*,' he replied simply.

Genuine puzzlement, along with a heavy dose of excitement she didn't want to admit to, made her blurt, 'Why?'

He strolled lazily to where she stood. This close, she had to tilt her head to catch his gaze. *Darkness and light*. He might have been smiling but Inez could almost reach out and touch the undercurrent of emotions swirling beneath his civility. She jumped slightly when he brushed a forefinger down her cheek.

'Because I intend to keep you, *anjo*. And while you will not have a lot of choice in the matter, I'm willing to make a few adjustments to ensure your contentment.'

CHAPTER FIVE

THEO WATCHED HER grapple with what he'd just said. Unlike her brother, she wasn't inebriated—she'd barely touched her glass of the rich Barolo 2009 he'd specially chosen for their dinner.

She shook her head in confusion. 'You intend to *keep* me?'

Her skin, satin-smooth beneath his touch, begged to be caressed. He gave in to the urge and traced her from cheek to jaw. When she withdrew from him, he followed. He stroked the pulse beating in her neck and pushed back the need to step closer, touch his mouth to the spot.

He'd learnt two things last night.

The first was that Benedicto da Costa, for all his cunning and veneer of sophistication, was still a greedy, vicious snake who thought he could con millions of dollars out of an unsuspecting fool like him.

The second was that Inez da Costa could be a key player in the slow and painful revenge he intended to exact for the wrong done to him. It didn't hurt that the chemistry between them burned the very air they breathed.

In the past Theo had made several opportune decisions by switching tactics at the last minute and making the most of whatever situation he found himself him.

With the newfound information at his fingertips, he'd found a way not only to end the da Costas once and for all, but also to make a tidy profit to boot.

He barely stopped himself from smiling as he looked down into Inez's face. She really was stunningly beautiful. With a mouth that begged to be explored.

'Mr Pantelides?'

'Theo,' he murmured, anticipating her refusal to use his first name.

She blew out an exasperated breath. 'Theo. Explain yourself.'

The unexpected sound of his name on her lips sent a pulse of heat through his body. Followed swiftly by a feeling he recognised as pleasure.

With a silent curse he dropped his hand. Pleasure featured nowhere on his mission to Rio. Nor was standing around, gazing into the face that reminded him of the painting of an angel that used to hang in his father's house.

Pain. Reparation. Merciless humiliation. Those were his objectives.

'There's no hidden message in there, *anjo*. For the duration of my stay in Rio I expect you to make yourself available to me, day and night.'

Her genuine laughter echoed around the open deck. When he didn't join in, she quickly sobered. 'Oh, I'm sorry. But I believe you have me confused with a certain type of woman you must encounter on your travels.'

Theo let the insult slide. He'd told his skipper to take his time with the tour, but even his trusted employee couldn't keep Pietro away for ever. And it looked as if he needed to step up this part of his strategy in order to forward his overall objective.

'I was supposed to sign documents that guaranteed your father's campaign funds this morning but I didn't turn up. Aren't you even a little bit curious as to why?'

A touch of confusion clouded her brown eyes but she shrugged one silky-smooth shoulder that shimmered softly under the deck lights. 'Your business with my father is not my concern.'

A little of that control he kept under a tight leash threatened to slip free. 'You don't care where the money comes from as long as you're kept in the style to which you've grown accustomed, is that it?'

Her eyes widened at the acid leaching from his tone. 'You may think you know me but, I assure you, you've got things wrong—'

'Have I? From where I'm standing it's very evident you're the bait he uses to trap weak, pathetic fools into opening their wallets.'

Her ragged gasp accompanied a look of outrage so near authentic Theo would've believed her reaction had he not seen her in action with Delgado last night.

'If it is your intention to be offensive to show your *machismo*, then *bravo*, you've succeeded,' she threw at him and whirled away.

He caught her wrist before she could take a step.

'Let me go.'

'I've yet to outline my plans, *anjo*.'

'I think you've *outlined* enough. I won't stand here listening to your unfounded insults. I'm going to find Pietro. And then we're leaving.' She tried to free herself. He tightened his grip until he could feel her pulse under his fingers. Furious. Passionate.

His groin stirred and he forced himself to ignore the throb of arousal determined to make itself known. 'You're not leaving here until we have this discussion.'

'What we're having is not a discussion, *senhor*. What you're doing is holding me captive, torturing me with—'

She broke off, no doubt in reaction to his hiss of fury and the flash of icy memory that made his whole body go rigid for one long second.

Theo released her, turned away sharply and shoved his hand through his hair. He noted his fingers' faint trembling and willed himself to stop shaking.

'Th...Theo?' Her voice came from far away, filled with confusion and a touch of concern.

He willed away the effect of the trigger words and forced himself to breathe. But they pounded through his brain nonetheless—*captive, prisoner, torture, darkness...*

Fingers closed over his shoulder and he jerked around. '*Don't!*'

She jumped back, snatching back her hand. It took several more seconds for him to recall where he was. He wasn't in some deep, dark hole in a remote farm in Spain. He was in Rio. With the daughter of the man who continued to cause his recurring nightmares.

'What's...what's wrong with you?' she asked with a wary frown.

He drew in a steady breath and gritted his teeth. 'Nothing. I'll get to the point. The agreement was that I'd take control of Da Costa Holdings and keep a fifty per cent share of the profits in exchange for liquidated funds to finance your father's political campaign. However, the papers your father had drawn up contain a major loophole that I can easily exploit.'

Slowly, his panic receded and he noticed she was absently rubbing her wrist. He quickly replayed his reaction to her touch and breathed a sigh of relief when he confirmed to himself that he hadn't grabbed her in his panic.

She continued to rub her skin and slowly another earthy emotion replaced his roiling feelings. He welcomed the pulse of arousal despite the fact that he had no intention of falling prey to the easy wiles of Inez da Costa. No matter how mouth-watering her body or how angelic her face.

'Shouldn't you be telling my father this, give him a chance to fix the loophole before you sign?'

He smiled at her naiveté. 'Why should I? I stand to gain by signing the agreement as it's drawn up.'

Her brow creased. 'Then why tell me about it? What's

to keep me from telling my father about it the moment I leave here?'

'You won't.'

One expertly plucked eyebrow lifted. 'Again, I think you underestimate me.'

He strode to the extensively stocked bar and poured himself a shot of vodka. 'You won't because if you do I won't sign the agreement in any form. And the offer of financial backing vanishes.'

All trace of colour left her face. 'So this is a blackmail attempt. To what purpose?'

'The purpose needn't concern you. All I want you to know is that there is a loophole which I can choose to exploit or leave alone, depending on your cooperation.'

'But what is to stop you from going ahead with whatever you have planned after I've cooperated with...what exactly is it you want from me?'

'That's the simple part, *anjo*. I want to keep you. Until such time as I tire of you. Then you will be set free.'

When the full meaning of his words finally became clear, ice cascaded down Inez's spine. Despite the warm temperature, she shivered.

Oh, how easily he said the words. As if her answer meant nothing to him. But of course it did. He'd been planning this for a while. The meeting this morning outside the coffee shop—which she was now certain hadn't been coincidental—the dinner invitation that he'd probably known her father wouldn't be able to attend due to his long-standing monthly dinner with the oil minister, the invitation to the yacht, which was sure to cause a reaction in her brother, letting Pietro drink far more than he should've so he'd get her alone...

'You planned this,' she accused in a hushed tone because her throat was working to swallow down her rising anger.

'I plan everything, Inez,' he replied simply.

She looked into his face. The indomitable determination stamped on his harsh features sent a wave of anxiety through her.

She started to speak, to say the words that seemed unreal to her and her mouth trembled. His gaze dropped to the telling reaction and she immediately clamped her lips together. Showing weakness would only get her eaten alive.

Not that she wouldn't be anyway. A bubble of hysteria threatened. She swallowed and held his gaze.

'You want me to be your *mistress*?'

He laughed long and deeply. 'Is that what you would call yourself?'

She flushed. 'How else would you describe what you've just demanded of me? This *keeping* me? What you're suggesting is archaic enough to be described as such. Or does *plaything* more suit your pseudo-modernistic outlook?'

'No, Inez. I don't like the term plaything either. I have no intention of playing with you. No, what I foresee for us is much more grown up than that.' The sexual intent behind the statement was unmistakable.

Rather than being offended or shocked, Inez found herself growing breathless. Excited.

No!

'Yes,' he murmured as if he'd read her mind.

'Whatever term you slap on your intentions, I refuse to be a part of it. I'm going to find my brother—'

He slowly sank onto the plush seat, curved his hand along the back of the chair and levelled one ankle over his knee. 'And tell him that you've dashed his hopes of a possible high profile position in your father's administration because you couldn't take one for the team? I don't think you're in a position to refuse any demands I make, *anjo*.'

'Stop calling me that! And I won't be a pawn in whatever game you're playing with my father and brother. Pietro is well aware of that.'

'Really? Since when? Wasn't serving on your father's

campaign the reason you dropped out of university? Clearly, you play a part in your father's political ambitions or you wouldn't have been trying to fleece poor Alfonso. Why stop now when you're so close to achieving your goals? And why claim innocence when it's something you've done before?'

The hurt that scythed through her was deep and jagged. She wasn't aware she'd moved until she stood over him, glaring down at the arrogant face that wore that oh, so self-assured smile.

'I've never wanted to be this...this person you think I am. I was merely trying to help my family. I misjudged the situation and—'

'You mean you fell in love with your mark.'

She swallowed. 'I don't know what you're getting at.' But deep down she suspected.

'I mean you were set a target and you fell in love with your target. Isn't that what happened with Blanco?'

Light-headedness assailed her as he confirmed her suspicion. 'You know about Constantine?'

'I know everything I need to know about your family, *anjo*. But by all means enlighten me as to why you've been so misjudged.'

His cynicism raked her nerves raw. 'I made a mistake, one that I freely admit to.'

'What mistake do you mean, *querida*? I want to hear it.'

'I misjudged a man I thought I could trust.'

'You mean you meant to use him but found out he intended to use you too?' he mocked. 'Some would call that poetic justice.'

Recalling Constantine's public humiliation of her, the names he'd called her in the press, her stomach turned over. 'You're despicable.' She raised her chin. 'And assuming you're even close to being right, won't I be a fool to repeat that mistake again?'

'No.'

'No?'

His eyes fixed on hers. Serious and intense. 'Because this time you know exactly what you're getting. There will be no delusions of love on either of our parts. No pretence. Just a task, executed with smooth efficiency.'

'But you intend to parade me about as your...lover? What will everyone think?'

He shrugged. 'I don't care what everyone thinks. And I don't much think that bothers you either.'

She shivered. 'Of course it bothers me. What makes you think it won't?'

'You're the ultimate young Rio socialite. You have a dedicated following and young impressionable girls can't wait to grow up and be you.' His mockery was unmistakable.

Heat crept up her cheeks. 'That's just the media spinning itself out of control.'

'Carefully fuelled by you to help your father's status. You're always seen with the right offspring of the right ministers and CEOs. You're the attraction to draw the young voters, are you not?'

She couldn't deny the allegation because it was true. Nor did she want to waste time straying away from the more serious subject of the demand he was making of her.

The demand she wouldn't—*couldn't*—consent to.

But there was something about him...a reassurance... and expectation of acquiescence that made the hairs on her nape stand on end.

'What happens if I refuse this...this sleazy proposal?'

'I sign the agreement then use the company as I wish. I could dismantle it piece by piece and sell it off for a neat profit. Or I could just drive down the share price and watch the company implode from the inside out. But that's all boring business. What do you care?'

Her fists clenched. 'I care because my grandfather built that company from nothing.'

'And now your father's willing to hand it over to a complete stranger just so he can further his political career.'

She pursed her lips and fought not to react. She'd been deeply concerned when she'd first heard how her father planned to raise funds for his campaign. Concerns that had been airily brushed away with reassurances of airtight clauses.

Clauses which Theo had apparently easily loopholed.

Maybe it wasn't too late. She could tell him to go to hell and warn her father and brother about the danger their proposed business partner presented and advise them to walk away. Surely that would be better than admitting the lion into their midst and letting him wreak havoc at whim?

Light hazel eyes watched her with a predatory gleam. 'If you're thinking of warning your family, I'd think twice. Remember how easily I dispatched Delgado?'

She stiffened, recalling how a few whispered words had caused one investor in her father's campaign to walk away. 'You don't mean that,' she tried.

He slowly rose from the chair and towered over her. Every protective instinct screamed at her to step back but she stood her ground. Any show of weakness would be mercilessly pounced on.

'Do you want to test me, *anjo*?' The blade of steel that hovered over the endearment sent a shiver down her spine.

She slowly uncurled her fists and forced herself to breathe. 'What do you expect me to do?'

His smile was equally as predatory as the look in his eyes. 'You will inform your father and brother tomorrow that you and I are an item—our meeting last night sparked a chemistry so hot we couldn't *not* be together.'

A tiny sliver of relief eased her constricted chest. 'If that's all you want, I'm sure I can convince them—'

His mocking smile stopped her words.

'After you tell them that, you'll pack your bags and move in with me.'

Shock slammed her sideways. 'Are you serious?'

He gripped her chin and held her pinned under his gaze. 'I've never been more serious in my life.'

'But...why?'

'My reasons are my own. You just need to do as you're told.'

Do as you're told. Constantine had tried to blackmail her with those very words. When she'd refused he'd spread rumours about her in the newspapers.

Anger grew in her belly. But it was a helpless anger born of the knowledge that there was nothing she could do. Once again she was trapped in a hell that came from trying to do what was right for her family.

Only this time she was to truly pay with her body. In a stranger's bed. Her heart tripped before going into fierce overdrive.

She gazed at Theo's face, then his body. A body she would in the very near future become scorchingly intimate with. The horror she'd expected to feel oddly did not materialise.

'How long exactly will I be expected to *do as I'm told*?' she snapped.

'Until after the elections.'

A horrified gasp escaped her throat and she forcibly wrenched herself from his grip. 'But...that's...the elections are *three months* away!'

'*Sim*,' he replied simply.

'*Sim*? You expect me to put my life on hold for the next three months, just like that?' She clicked her fingers.

He raised an eyebrow. 'Do you want me to repeat the part about you not having a choice?'

She searched his face, trying to find meaning behind his intentions. 'What did my father do? Did he best you at a deal? Bad-mouth you to investors? Because I can't see what would make you want to go down this path of trying to get your own back.'

She watched his eyes darken, and his nostrils flare. All

traces of mockery were wiped from his face as he stared down at her. Only she was sure he wasn't really seeing her.

His usual intense focus dulled for several seconds and his jaw clenched so tight she feared it could crack. Whatever memory he was reliving caused volcanic fury to bubble beneath the harsh, ragged breath he expelled and this time she did take that step back, purely for self-preservation.

Voices sounded on the deck below. In a few minutes Pietro and the skipper would return from their tour. Inez wasn't sure whether to be grateful for the disruption or frustrated that her opportunity to find out Theo's reasons for demanding her presence in his bed had been thwarted.

His gaze sharpened, flicked towards the steps and back to her.

'It's time for your answer. Do you agree to my terms?'

She shook her head. 'Not until you tell me— *what are you doing*?' she blurted as he snapped out an arm and tugged her close.

One large bold hand gripped her waist and the other speared through her hair. Completely captured, she couldn't move as he angled her face to his. The unsettling fury was still evident in his darkened eyes and taut mouth. Despite the heat transmitted from his grip, she shivered.

'You seem to think you can talk or question your way out of this, *anjo*. You can't. But perhaps it was a mistake to expect a verbal agreement. Perhaps a physical demonstration is what's best?'

Despite his rhetorical question, she tried to answer. 'No...'

'Yes!' he muttered fiercely. Then his mouth smashed down on hers.

She'd been kissed before. By casual boyfriends in her late teens who she'd felt safe enough with.

By Constantine, in the beginning, before he'd revealed his true ruthless colours.

Nothing of what had gone before prepared her for the power and expertise behind Theo's kiss. Her world tilted beneath her feet as his tongue ruthlessly breached the seam of her lips. Hot, erotically charged and savagely determined, he invaded her mouth with searing passion. Bold and brazen, he flicked his tongue against hers, tasting her once and coming back for more.

The shocked little noise she made was a cross between surprise and her body's stunned reaction to the invasion.

The hand at her waist pressed her closer to his body. Whipcord strength, sleek muscles and his own unique scent brought different sensations that attacked her flailing senses.

Fire lashed through her belly as liquid heat pooled between her thighs. Her breasts, crushed against his chest, swelled and ached, her nipples peaking into demanding points with a swiftness that made her dizzy.

Deus!

Feeling her world careen even faster out of control, she threw up her hands. Hard muscle rippled beneath her fingers. The need to explore slammed into her. Before she could question her actions, she slid her hands over his warm cotton-covered shoulders to his nape, her fingers tingling as they encountered his bare skin.

He jerked beneath her touch, pulled back with a tug on her hair. Breathing harshly, he stared into her eyes for several seconds. Hunger blazed in his, turning them a dark, mesmerising molten gold that stole what little breath she had from her lungs. Then his eyes dropped lower to her parted mouth.

A rough sound rumbled from his throat. Then he was kissing her again. Harder, more demanding, more possessively than before.

Inez pushed her fingers through his hair as arousal like she'd never experienced before bit deep. This time, when his tongue slid into her mouth, she met it with hers. Boldly, she tried to give as much as she got, although she knew she was hopelessly inadequate when it came to experience.

The hand around her waist tightened and she was lifted off her feet. Seconds later, she found herself on the bar stool, her legs splayed and Theo firmly between thighs exposed by her stance. He came at her again, the force of his sensual attack tilting the stool backwards.

She threw out her hands onto the counter to keep from toppling over. Theo growled beneath his breath, his hands moving upward from her waist to cup her breasts. He moulded her willing, aching flesh so expertly she whimpered and arched into his hold. Beneath her clothes, her tight nipples unfurled in eager anticipation when his thumbs grazed over them. The deep pleasurable shudder made him repeat the action, eliciting a soft cry of pleasure from deep inside her.

'*Inez!*'

The rapier-sharp call of her name doused her with ice-cold water. She wrenched herself from Theo's hold…or at least she tried to.

The hands that had dropped from her breasts to her waist at the sound of Pietro's return stayed her desperate flight.

'What the *hell* do you think you're doing?' Pietro growled, no longer looking as drunk as he'd been half an hour ago.

'If you need it explained to you, da Costa, then I'm wondering who the hell I'm getting into business with.'

Her brother flushed in anger. 'I wasn't talking to you, Pantelides. But maybe I should ask you what you're doing, pawing my sister like some mad animal.'

Inez desperately tried to pull her dress down. But Theo stood firmly between her thighs, making the task impossible. Her sound of distress drew his attention from Pietro. He stared down at her for a second before he adjusted his stance. But although he allowed her to close her legs and pull her dress down, his hands didn't drop from her waist.

If anything, they tightened, their hold so possessive she fought to breathe.

'Inez was going to tell you tomorrow. But I guess tonight's as good a time as any.'

Pietro's gaze shifted from Theo's face to hers. 'Tell me what?'

'Do you want to do the honours, *anjo*? Or shall I?' he queried softly.

Her heartbeat accelerated but not with the arousal pounding through her bloodstream. She heard the clear warning in Theo's tone. Anything short of what he'd demanded of her would see her family ruined completely.

She opened her mouth. Closed it again and swallowed hard.

A trace of fear washed over Pietro's face. Despite their strained relationship, there'd been times in the past when they'd been close. She knew how much a political career of his own some day meant to him. How much he was pinning his hopes on what her father's campaign would mean to him personally.

She tried again to speak the words Theo demanded she speak. But her vocal cords wouldn't work.

'Would someone hurry up and tell me what's going on?'

Fierce hazel eyes drifted over her face in a look that spelled possession so potent her breath caught.

Theo curled his arm over her shoulders and pulled her into the heat of his body. He drifted his mouth over her temple in an adoring move so utterly convincing she reeled at his skilful deception.

She was grappling with that, and with just how much of the kiss they'd shared had been an exercise in pure ruthless seduction on his part, when he spoke.

'Your sister and I have become...enamoured with each other. We only met last night but already I cannot bear to be without her.' His voice held none of the mockery from before, sparking another stunned realisation of his skill. He stared down at her and she caught the implacable determination in his eyes.

When his gaze reconnected with Pietro's she stared, mesmerised, at his profile then shivered at the iron-hard set to his jaw.

'Tomorrow she will be moving out of your home. And into mine.'

CHAPTER SIX

'*Like hell you are*,' Pietro repeated for the hundredth time as their chauffeur-driven car stopped outside the opulent Ipanema mansion she'd grown up in.

She quickly threw open the door and hurried up the steps leading to the double oak front doors although she knew escape wouldn't be easy. Pietro was hard on her heels.

'Did you hear what I said?' he demanded.

'I heard you loud and clear. But you fail to realise I'm no longer a child. I'm twenty-four years old—well over the age when I can do whatever the heck I want.'

He slid a hand through his hair. 'Look, I know I may have pushed you into playing a greater part in *Pai*'s fundraising campaign. But...I don't think getting involved with Pantelides is a good idea,' he said abruptly.

Inez's heart lurched at his concern but she couldn't reassure him because she herself didn't know what the future held. 'Thank you for your concern but like I said, I'm a grown up.'

He swivelled on his heel in the vast entrance hall of the villa. 'Are you really that into him? I know what I saw on his deck tells its own story but you only met him last night!'

'I hadn't met Alfonso Delgado before last night either and yet you expected me to charm him.'

'*Charm* him, not move in with him!'

'There's no point arguing with me. My mind is made up.'

Pietro's face darkened. 'Is this some sort of rebellion?'

Inez sighed. 'Of course not. But I'd planned to move out anyway, once you and *Pai* started on the campaign trail.'

'Move out and go where? This is your home, Inez,' he replied.

She shook her head. 'My world doesn't begin and end in this house, Pietro. I intend to rent an apartment, get a job.'

'Then don't start by ruining yourself with Pantelides.'

Her throat clogged. 'My reputation is already in shreds after Constantine. I really have nothing left to lose.'

She turned to head up the grand staircase that led to the twin wings of their villa. Behind her, she could still hear Pietro pacing the hallway.

'This doesn't make any sense, Inez. Perhaps a good night's sleep will bring you to your senses.'

She didn't answer. Because she didn't want to waste her time telling him the decision had already been made for her.

For Theo to have gone to the effort of staging that kiss and paving the way for the lies she had to perpetuate, she knew without a shadow of a doubt that his demands were real.

He'd gone to a lot of trouble to set up tonight's meeting. She would be a fool to bait him to see if he would carry out his threat.

Her heart hammered as she undressed and stepped beneath the shower. Slowly soaping her body, she found her mind drifting back to their kiss. The incandescent delirium of it was unlike anything she'd felt before.

Her fingers touched her lips, and they tingled in remembrance.

Tomorrow she was inviting herself into the lion's den to be devoured whole for the sake of her family.

A hysterical laugh became lost in the sound of the running water.

Pietro was finally showing signs of being the brother she remembered before their mother died. Shame that she'd had to sacrifice herself on the altar of their family's prosperity before he'd come round. As for her father...sadness engulfed her at the thought that even if he knew of her sacrifice, he probably wouldn't lift a finger to shield her from it.

Theo's gaze strayed to his phone for the umpteenth time in under twenty minutes and he cursed under his breath.

He'd called Inez this morning and they'd agreed a time of eleven o'clock, two hours before he was due to sign the documents at her father's office.

It was now eleven twenty-five and there was no sign of her. No big deal. She was probably stuck in traffic. Or she hadn't left her home on time, especially if she was packing for a three-month stay.

Besides, women are always late.

Even as a child he'd known this. His mother had never been on time for a single event in her life.

His mother...

Memory rained down vicious blows that had him catching his breath. His mother, the woman who'd been nowhere in sight, either before or after he was kidnapped and held for ransom by Benedicto da Costa's vicious thugs.

For weeks after he'd been rescued and returned home, broken and devastated by his ordeal, he'd asked for his mother. Ari had made several excuses for her absence. But Theo had been unable to reconcile the fact that the mother who'd once treated him as if he'd been the centre of her world suddenly couldn't even be bothered to pick up the phone and enquire about her mentally and physically traumatised child.

No. She'd been too preoccupied with wallowing in her misery following her husband's betrayal to bother with her own children.

Ari had been the one to hold them together after their family was shattered by the press uncovering their father's many shady dealings and philandering ways.

For a very long time he'd laboured under the misconception that out of the three brothers he was the most special in their father's eyes. That just because he was the miracle baby his parents had never thought they'd have, he was their favourite. His kidnapping and what he'd uncovered since had mercilessly ripped that indulgent blindfold away.

Finding out that his father had known about Benedicto da Costa's escalating threats and that he'd done nothing to warn or protect him had forced the cruellest reality on him.

And his mother's response to all that had been to abandon him, together with her other two children, and go into hiding.

Hearing of his father's eventual death had made him even angrier at being robbed of the chance to look his father in the eye and see the monster for himself.

Because, even now, a pathetic part of him clung to the hope that maybe his father hadn't known the full extent of the kidnapping threat; hadn't known that Benedicto da Costa's reaction to being thwarted out of a business deal would be to kidnap a seventeen-year-old boy, and have his torture photographed and sent to his family to pressure them into finding the millions of dollars owed to him.

His phone rang, wrenching him out of the bitter recollections. Glancing down at the number, a bolt of white-hot anger lanced through him. He forced himself to wait for a couple more rings before he answered it. 'Pantelides.'

'*Bom dia.* I've just had a very interesting conversation with my daughter.' Theo detected the throb of anger in Benedicto da Costa's voice and a grim smile curved his own lips. 'She seems determined to pursue this rather *sudden* course of action where you're concerned.'

'Your daughter strikes me as a very determined woman who knows exactly what she wants,' he replied smoothly.

'She is. All the same, I can't help think that this decision is rather precipitate.' There was clear suspicion in Benedicto's voice now.

'Trust me, it's been very well thought through on my part. Tell me, Benedicto, has she left yet?'

'*Sim*, against my wishes, she has left home,' he replied, his voice taut with displeasure.

A wave of satisfaction swept through Theo. 'Good. I'll await her arrival.'

'I hope this will not delay our meeting,' the older man enquired.

'Don't worry. The moment I welcome your daughter into my home, I'll head to your offices.'

An edgy silence greeted his answer and Theo could sense him weighing his words to perceive a possible threat. Finally, Benedicto answered, 'We should celebrate our partnership once the documents are signed.'

Theo's mouth twisted. Benedicto had already moved on from the subject of his daughter. And he noticed there had been no admonition to treat her well, *or else...*

But the knowledge that Benedicto had intensely disapproved of Inez's intentions and had called him to air that disapproval was good enough for him.

'Great idea. Unfortunately, I'll be busy for the next few nights. Perhaps some time next week Inez and I will have you and Pietro over for dinner.'

The fiery exhalation that greeted his indelicate words made Theo's grin widen.

'Of course. I'll look forward to it. *Até a próxima*,' Benedicto said tightly.

Theo ended the call without responding. He absorbed the pulse of triumph rushing through his bloodstream for a pleasurable second before he exhaled.

His plan was far from being executed. But this was a brilliant start.

He looked out of the floor to ceiling window at the sparkling pool and the beach beyond and tried to push away the images that had visited him again last night and the single hoarse scream that had woken him.

A full body shudder raked his frame and he shoved a hand through his hair. Although he'd long ago accepted the nightmares as part of his existence, he loathed their presence and the helplessness he felt in those endless moments when he was caught in their grip.

The single therapy session he'd let Ari talk him into attending had mentioned triggers and the importance of anxiety-detectors.

He laughed under his breath. Putting himself within touching distance of the man responsible for those nightmares would be termed as foolhardy by most definitions.

Theo chose to believe that exacting excruciating revenge would heal him. *An eye for an eye.*

And if he had to suffer a few side-effects during the process, then so be it.

He tensed as his security intercom buzzed. Crossing the vast sun-dappled room, he picked up the handset.

'*Senhor*, there's a Senhorita da Costa here to see you.'

A throb of a different nature invaded his bloodstream. 'Let her in,' he instructed.

Replacing the handset, he found himself striding to the front door and out onto his driveway before he realised what he was doing.

Hands on his hips, he watched her tiny green sports car appear on his long driveway. The top was down and the wind was blowing through her loose thick hair. Stylish sunglasses shielded her eyes from him but he knew she was watching him just as he was studying her.

She brought the car to a smooth stop a few feet from him and turned off the ignition. For several seconds the only sound that impinged on the late morning air was the water cascading from the stone nymph's urn into the fountain bowl. Then the sound of her seat belt retracting joined the tinkling.

'You're late,' he breathed.

She pulled out her keys and opened her door. 'It took

a while to uproot myself from the only home I've ever known,' she said waspishly.

A touch from a well-manicured finger and the boot popped open. He strolled forward, viewed its contents and his eyes narrowed.

'And yet you only packed two suitcases for a three-month stay?' he remarked darkly. 'I hope you don't think you can run back to *Pai*'s house each time you need a new toothbrush?'

She got out of the car.

From across the width of the open top, she glared at him. 'I can afford to buy my own toothbrush, thanks,' she retorted.

Theo nodded. 'Good to hear it.' Unable to stop himself, his gaze travelled down her body.

Faded jeans moulded her hips and her cream scooped-neck silk top left her arms bare. Its short-in-the-front, longer-at-the-back design exposed a delicious inch of golden, smooth midriff when she turned to shut her door and the air lifted the light material.

Heat invaded his groin, once again reminding him of their kiss last night.

The kiss that had blown him clean away and rendered him almost incoherent by the time her brother had rudely interrupted them.

Hell, she'd been so responsive, so intoxicatingly passionate, she'd gone to his head within seconds. What had set out as a hammering-a-point-home exercise to convince her he meant business had swiftly morphed into something else. Something he'd still been struggling to decipher when she'd been hustled off his boat by her suddenly protective brother.

One thing he'd been certain of was that had Pietro been a few more minutes returning to the top deck, Theo was sure he would've had his hands on her bare skin, exploring her in a more earthy way, propriety be damned.

Luckily, he'd come to his senses. And, from here on in, he intended to focus on his plan and his plan alone.

She went to the boot and bent over to lift the first case. The sight of her rounded bottom made a vein throb in his temple.

He stepped forward, grabbed the cases from her and handed them to his hovering butler. 'I'm running late for my meeting. We should have done this last night like I suggested.'

He'd tried. But she'd stood her ground and he had quickly decided that there was nothing to be gained from getting into a slanging match with Pietro da Costa. That he'd also realised that his change of timing was to do with that kiss and nothing to do with his carefully laid plans had had him sharply reassessing his priorities.

'I'm here now. Don't let me stop you from leaving if you wish to.'

He smiled at the undisguised hope in her voice. 'Now what kind of host would I be if I desert you the moment you turn up?'

'The same as the one who blackmailed me into this situation in the first place?' she replied caustically.

There was a thread of unhappiness in her voice that grated at him.

'This will go a lot easier if you accept the status quo.'

'You mean just shut up and *do as I'm told*?' she snapped bitterly as she slammed the boot shut and walked towards him.

Unease weaved through him. With restless shoulders, he shrugged it away. 'No. You can protest all you want. I just want you to be aware of the futility of it.'

She snorted under her breath, a sound that made his smile widen. She had spirit, and wasn't afraid to bare her claws when cornered. Which made him wonder why she withstood the unreasonable control from her father. Were material benefits so important to her?

The heavy glass front door slid shut behind them and he watched her reaction to his house. It was an architectural masterpiece, and had featured in several top magazines before he'd bought it a year ago and ceased all publicity of the award-winning design.

'Wow,' she breathed. 'This place must have cost you a bomb.'

Theo had his answer. Disappointment scythed through him as he watched her move to the bronze sculpture he'd acquired several weeks back.

'I saw the exhibition on this two months ago. This piece is worth a cool half million,' she gasped in wonder. 'And that one—' she pointed to another smaller sculpture he'd commissioned by his favourite New York artist '—is an exclusive piece, worth over two million dollars.'

His lips twisted. 'Should I be worried that you know the monetary value of every piece of art in my house?'

She whirled to face him. 'Excuse me?'

'I hope we can engage in more meaningful dialogue than how much everything is worth. I find the subject of avarice…distasteful.'

Her gasp sounded genuinely hurt-filled. 'I wasn't…I'm just…that's a horrible thing to say, Mr Pantelides.'

His eyebrow lifted. 'I thought I kissed all the formality out of you last night?'

She flushed a delicate pink that made her skin glow. Her expressive brown eyes slid from his and she turned back to examine the room.

It was then that he noticed the faint bruises on her left arm. He was striding to her and lifting her arm to examine the marks before his brain had connected with his body.

'Who did this to you?' he demanded.

Her surprised gaze snapped from his to her arm. Her flush deepened as she swiftly shook her head. 'I…it doesn't matter; it's nothing—'

He swallowed hard. 'Like hell it is.' The idea that his demands on her might have caused this to happen to her made a thread of revulsion rise in his belly. He forced it down and concentrated on her face. 'Tell me who it was.'

She swallowed. 'My father.'

Pure fury blurred his vision for several seconds. 'Your *father* did this to you?'

She gave a jerky nod.

Why the hell was he surprised? 'Has he done anything like this before?' he bit out.

She pressed her lips together in a vain attempt not to answer. A firm grip of her chin, tilting it to his gaze, convinced her otherwise. 'Once. Maybe twice.'

His vicious curse made her shiver. Theo examined the marks, which would grow yellowish by nightfall, and pushed down the mounting fury. 'That son of a bitch will never touch you again.'

Shock made her gasp. 'That *son of a bitch* is my *father*. And I've given you what you wanted, so I expect you to hold up your end of the bargain.'

He frowned with genuine puzzlement. 'Why do you tolerate this, Inez?' He glanced from the bruises to her face. 'You're more than old enough to live on your own. Hell, if money and a rich lifestyle are what you crave, you're sufficiently resourceful to find some wealthy guy who would—'

She snatched her arm from his grasp. It was then that he realised he'd been caressing her soft skin with his thumb. He missed the connection almost immediately.

'I certainly hope you're not about to suggest what I think you are?'

Keen frustration rocked him into movement. 'I'm curious, that's all.'

'I'm not here to satisfy your curiosity. And perhaps you've been lucky enough to be granted a perfect family but not everyone has been afforded the same luxury. We made do with what we... Did I say something funny?' she snapped.

He cut off the mirthless laughter that had bubbled up at

her words. 'Yes. *You're damned hilarious*. You obviously don't know what you're talking about.'

She stared at him with confusion and a little trepidation. 'No. But how can I? We only met two nights ago. And now I'm here, your possession for the foreseeable future.'

The simple statement twisted like live electricity between them. The look in her eyes said she was daring him to react to it. But the off-kilter emotions swirling through his chest made him back away from it. He shouldn't have dealt with her so soon after speaking to Benedicto. He should've left Teresa, his housekeeper, to see to her needs.

He turned and headed for the door. 'I'll show you upstairs. And then I need to go.'

Striding into the hallway, he started up the grand central stairs that led to the upper two floors of his house. After a few steps, he noticed she wasn't behind him.

Turning, he found her paused on the second step, her gaze once again wide and wondrous as she stared around her.

'What?'

'There are no concrete walls.' She looked up at the all-encompassing glass around her. 'Or ceilings.'

He resumed climbing the stairs. 'I don't like walls. And I don't like ceilings,' he threw over his shoulder.

She hurried after him and caught up with him as they neared the first suite of rooms. She regarded him for a few seconds then bit her lip.

He paused with a hand on the doorknob. 'What?' he asked again, trying and not succeeding in prising his gaze from her plump lips.

'I'm not sure whether to take that as a metaphor or not.'

'*Anjo*, there's no hidden meaning behind my words. I literally do not like concrete walls or ceilings.'

She frowned in puzzlement. 'I don't understand.'

'It's very simple. I don't like being closed in.'

'You're…*claustrophobic*?' She whispered the word as if she wasn't sure how to apply it to him.

He shrugged and hurriedly threw open the door, a part of him reeling at what he'd just admitted. 'We all have our flaws,' he retorted.

'Were you born with it?'

His jaw clenched once. 'No. It was a condition thrust upon me quite against my will.'

'But...you seem...'

'Invincible?' he mocked.

Her lips pursed. 'I was going to say self-assured.'

'Appearances can be deceptive, *querida*. After you.' He indicated the door he'd just opened.

She stopped dead in the middle of the room. From where he stood, Theo could see what she was seeing. With the glass walls and white carpet and furnishings and nothing but the view of the blue sky and sea beyond, the vista was breathtaking.

'*Deus*, I feel as if I'm floating on a cloud,' she murmured with an awe-filled voice.

'That is the primary aim of the property. Light, air, no constrictions.'

He'd learned to his cost that constrictions triggered his anxiety and fuelled his nightmares. Which was why every single property he owned was filled with light.

'It's beautiful.'

The strong pulse of pleasure that washed through him had him stepping back. Things were getting out of hand. He needed to walk away, go to his meeting with Benedicto and remind himself why he was in Rio. This need to bask in Inez's presence, touch her skin, indulge in the urge to taste her sensual lips once more needed to killed. He had to stick to his game plan.

'Make yourself at home. I'll be back later. We're going out this evening. Dinner at Cabana de Ouro, then probably clubbing. Wear something short and sexy.'

Her eyes widened at his curt tone but he was already turning away. He didn't stop until he reached the landing.

On a completely unstoppable urge, he looked over his shoulder. Through the glass walls, he saw her frozen in the middle of her suite, her eyes fixed on him.

She looked lost. And confused. And a little relieved.

With grim determination he turned and headed down the stairs. And he hated himself for needing the reminder that Benedicto da Costa had damaged not just him, but his whole family.

The payback should be equal to the crime committed.

The black satin boy shorts she chose to wear were plenty stylish and sexy. They also moulded her behind much more than she was strictly comfortable with but everything else she'd hastily packed was too formal for dinner at Cabana de Ouro, the trendy restaurant and bar in Ipanema. Coupled with the dark gold silk top, with her hair piled on top of her head and gold hoops in her ears and bangles on her wrist, she looked good enough for whatever club Theo intended to take her to after dinner.

Clubbing wasn't strictly her entertainment of choice. But since, for the next twelve weeks, Theo expected her to obey his every command, the least she could do was learn to pick her battles. And she'd already endured one battle this morning in the form of confrontation with Theo. And found out he was claustrophobic.

He'd been right; she'd secretly imagined him to be invincible. The way he carried himself, the innate authority and self-assurance that seemed part of his genetic make up, she'd had no trouble seeing him best each situation he found himself him.

Hearing him admit to a deep flaw that most grown men would be ashamed of had floored her. Coupled with his concern when he'd seen the marks her father had inflicted when she'd announced she was moving in with Theo, she'd been seriously floundering in a sea of uncertainty by the time he'd left her bedroom.

She examined the marks on her arm now and released a shaky breath to see that they were fading. She was shrugging on the shoulder-padded waist-length leather jacket that went with the outfit when she heard Theo's Aston Martin roar into the driveway.

Her fingers trembled as she fastened the long-chained gold medallion necklace at her nape.

He'd left her so abruptly this morning she hadn't had the time to question him about sleeping arrangements. A closer examination of her suite after he'd left had revealed no presence of another occupant, and after talking to Teresa, his housekeeper, she'd found out that the *senhor*'s suite was directly above hers, taking up the whole glass-roofed top floor of the house.

The fact that she wouldn't be expected to share his bed immediately should've pleased her. Instead she was more on edge than ever. Or maybe that was what he wanted? That she should be kept guessing, kept on a knife-edge of uncertainty like some sort of game?

Deus!

She'd barely spent one day under his glass roof and already she was being driven mad. His response to her admiring his sculptures had been too infuriating for her to explain how she'd come to acquire such knowledge of sculptures—her late mother's talent. If he wanted to believe Inez appreciated beautiful art purely with dollar signs in her eyes, that was his problem.

Her breath caught as she heard distinct footsteps in the hallway. Teresa had shown her how to shroud the bedroom glass for privacy and she'd activated it before she'd gone in to take a shower. It was still shrouded now although she could make out a faint outline of the towering man who knocked a few seconds later.

'Come in.' She cringed at the husky breathlessness of her voice.

The heavy glass swung back and Theo stood framed in the doorway.

Light hazel eyes locked on her with the force of a laser beam for several seconds before they travelled slowly down her body.

Before meeting him, Inez would've found it hard to believe she could physically react so strongly to a look from a man. Constantine, with all his misleading smiles and false charm, had never affected her like this, not even when she'd believed herself in love with him.

With Theo the evidence was irrefutable—in the accelerated beat of her heart, the tightening and heaviness of her breasts and the stinging heat that spread outward from her belly like a flash fire.

She watched his mouth drop open as his gaze reached her shorts and her own mouth dried at the look that settled on his face.

'What the hell are you wearing?'

'What? I'm wearing clothes, Mr Pantelides,' she snapped, once she was able to get her brain working again.

He stepped into the room and the door slid shut behind him. All at once, she became aware of the sheer size of him, of the restriction in her breathing and the fact that her eyes were devouring his magnificent form.

'Let's get one thing straight. From now on you'll address me as Theo. No more *senhor* and no more Mr Pantelides, understand?'

'Is that an order?' She tilted her chin to see his face as he stopped before her.

'It's a friendly warning that there will be consequences if you don't comply.'

'What consequences?' she huffed.

'How about every time you call me *senhor* I kiss that sassy mouth of yours?'

CHAPTER SEVEN

'Excuse me?' Her voice was a little more breathless. With excitement. *Deus*, what was wrong with her? This man was threatening her family, was effectively turning her life upside down for the sake of some unknown grudge. And all she could think of was him kissing her again.

'No, you're not excused. Use my first name or I'll kiss it into you. Your choice. Now tell me what the hell you're wearing.' His gaze dropped back to her shorts, his eyes glazing with hunger so acute, her heart hammered.

'These are shorts. You said "short and sexy".'

His mouth worked for a few seconds before he nodded. 'I said short, but I don't think I meant that short, *anjo*.'

Heat raced up her neck and she barely managed to stop her hand from connecting with his face. 'They are not that bad.'

His rasping laugh made her face flame. 'Trust me, from where I'm standing, they're lethal.'

'I have nothing else to change into. Everything else is too formal for a club.'

Dark eyes rose, almost reluctantly, to clash with hers. 'I find that very hard to believe.'

'It's true. I didn't have enough time to pack properly. Besides, I didn't take you for…'

His eyes narrowed. 'Didn't take me for what?'

She shrugged. 'You don't strike me as the clubbing type.'

One corner of his mouth lifted. 'Have you been forming impressions about me, *anjo*?'

She kicked herself for that revelatory remark. 'Not really.'

He looked down at her shorts one more time and he turned abruptly for the door. 'I'll be ready to go in fifteen minutes. You can tell me what other impressions you've formed about me at dinner.'

Inez exhaled and realised she hadn't taken a full breath since he'd walked into her presence. Her whole body quivered as she shoved her feet into three-inch platforms and made sure her cell phone and lipstick were in the black and gold clutch.

She caught sight of herself in the hallway mirror as she made her way down and cringed at the feverish look in her eyes.

Reassuring herself firmly that it was anger at Theo for his overbearing treatment of her, she made her way to the living room.

Floodlights illuminated the pool and gardens in a stunning display of shimmering light and shrubbery. Like every single aspect of the building, the sight was so breathtaking her fingers itched with the need to draw.

Setting her clutch down, she went to the large duffel bag she'd brought down this afternoon and took out her sketchpad and pencil.

She was so lost in capturing the vista before her, she didn't sense Theo enter the room until his unique scent wrapped itself around her.

She jerked around to see him standing close behind her, his eyes on her picture.

'You draw?' he asked in surprise.

Unable to answer for the loud hammering of her heart, she nodded.

He reached forward and plucked the pad from her nerveless fingers. Slowly, he thumbed through the pages. 'You're very talented,' he finally said.

Expecting a derogatory remark to follow, like his comment on his art this morning, her eyes widened when she realised he meant it. 'You really think so?' she asked.

He closed the pad and handed it back to her, his eyes speculative as they rested on her face. 'I wouldn't say it otherwise, *anjo*.'

Pleasure fizzed through her. 'Thank you.' She smiled as she stood. Crossing over to her duffel bag, she bent to place the pad back into it.

'*Thee mou!*'

She dropped the pad and hastily straightened. 'What?'

'You bend over like that while we're out and I will not be responsible for my actions, understood?' he growled.

Her mouth dropped open at the dark promise in his voice. A shudder ran through her body as hunger further darkened his eyes. She licked her lip nervously as the atmosphere thickened with sensual charges that crackled and snapped along her nerves.

'We...we don't have to go out if what I'm wearing offends you...Theo,' she ventured hesitantly, sensing that he held himself on the very edge of control.

He inhaled deeply, his chest expanding underneath the dark green shirt and black leather jacket he wore with black trousers. 'That's where you're wrong. What you're offering doesn't offend me in the least. But I'm a red-blooded, possessive male who is finding it difficult not to roar out his primitive reaction to the idea of other men looking at you.' He said it so matter-of-factly she couldn't form a decent response. 'But I'll try to be a *gentleman*. Come.' He held out his arm.

With seriously indecent thoughts of Theo fighting to the death for her flitting through her mind, she crossed the room to his side.

He led them out and held the passenger door of his car open. The first few minutes of the ride to Ipanema was conducted in silence. Every now and then, he raked a hand through his hair and slid a glance at her naked thighs. Each time, he exhaled noisily.

A wild part of her wanted to flaunt herself for him, revel in his very physical reaction to her attire. Another part of her wanted to run and hide from the volatile emotions swirling through the enclosed space of the luxurious sports car.

By the time they drew up in the car park of the exclusive restaurant her pulse was jumping with anxiety. She forced the feeling down and followed him into the restaurant. Finding out they were dining in the even more exclusive upper floor led to all sorts of renewed anxiety as she preceded him up the steps.

The moment they were seated, he leaned forward. 'The moment we return home, I'm burning those shorts.'

She glared at him. 'No, you are not, *senhor!* They're my favourite pair.'

'Then frame them and mount them on a wall. But you most definitely will not be wearing them out again.'

That wild streak widened. 'I thought you would be man enough to handle a little...challenge. Are you saying you're not?'

His eyes narrowed. 'Don't bait a hungry lion, *querida*, unless you're prepared to be devoured,' he grated out.

'Did you tell your last girlfriend how she should dress too?' she challenged.

His mouth compressed. 'My last girlfriend was under the misconception that the more frequently she walked around naked the more interested I would be in her. She lasted ten days.'

Inez's curiosity spiked, along with an emotion she was very loath to name. 'How long did your longest relationship last?'

'Three weeks.'

Her breath caught. 'So why three *months* with me?' she asked.

He looked startled for a moment then he shrugged. 'Because you're not my girlfriend. You're so very much more.'

Inez was struck dumb by his reply. A small foolish part of her even felt giddy, until she reminded herself that she was intended to be nothing but his *mistress*. Again unfathomable emotions wrapped themselves around her heart. She cleared her throat and fought to keep her voice even. 'Why *misconception*?'

'Very few women manage to catch and keep my interest for very long, *anjo*.'

'Because you get bored easily?' she dared.

His lashes swept down for a few seconds before they rose again to capture hers. 'Because my demons always win when pitted against the rigours of normal relationships.'

'*Demons?*'

'*Sim, anjo*. Demons. I have a lot of them. And they're very possessive.' A wave of anguish rolled over his face, then it was gone the next instant. He nodded to the hovering *sommelier* and ordered their wine. Another pulse of surprise went through her when she noticed it was the same wine she'd served at the fund-raiser and her favourite.

'The burning is now off the table. Hell, you can even keep the damn shorts. But, for the sake of my sanity, can we agree that you don't wear them outside?' he asked with one quirked eyebrow.

She pretended to consider it. 'What is your sanity worth to me?'

'You think you're in a position to bargain with me, Inez?' he asked, his voice deceptively soft.

'I never pass up an opportunity to bargain.'

He regarded her silently for several minutes. Then he shrugged. 'As long as I achieve my goals in the end, I see no reason why the road to success shouldn't be littered with minor obstacles. Tell me what you desire.'

'Is that what I am, a minor obstacle?'

'Don't miss your opportunity with meaningless questions.'

The need for clarity finally forced her to speak. 'I wish to know exactly what you want of me.'

'Sorry, I cannot answer that.'

She frowned. 'Why not?'

'Because my needs are...fluid.' The peculiar smile accompanying his answer sent a tingle of alarm down her spine.

'So I am to live in uncertainty for the next three months?'

'The unknown can be challenging. It can also be exciting.'

'Is that why you came to Rio? To seek challenge and excitement?'

For several seconds he stared at her. Then he slowly shook his head. 'No, my reason for being in Rio is specific and a well-planned event.'

Inez shivered at the succinct response. 'I can't help but be frightened by your answer.'

Her candid admission seemed to surprise him. 'Why is that?'

'Because I have a feeling it has something to do with my family. Pietro has his flaws but he's never done anything without my father's express approval. Besides, you're much older than him, which makes it unlikely that he's the one you came here for. You're here because of my father, aren't you?'

It took an astonishing amount of control not to react to her simple but accurate summation of the single subject that had consumed him for over a decade.

Thinking back, he realised he'd given her several clues to enable her to reach this conclusion. Somehow, in the mere forty-eight hours that he'd known her, Inez had managed to slip under his guard and was threatening to uncover his true purpose for being in Rio.

He also realised that he'd given her much more leeway than he'd ever intended to when he'd formulated his plan. Inviting her to compromise? Inviting her to state her desires with the knowledge that he was seriously considering granting them?

After his hasty departure this morning he'd realised that he'd let those marks on her arms sway him into going easy on her. *Because he hadn't wanted her to think he was a monster like her father?*

The man who hadn't so much as asked after his daughter when Theo had attended his office to sign the agreement papers?

The man whose eyes had shone with greed and triumph even before the ink had dried on the documents?

No, he was nothing like Benedicto da Costa. He wasn't about to lose any already precious sleep wondering about that little statement.

What he had to be careful of was that his enemy's daughter didn't guess his intentions. He was so very close to having Benedicto right where he wanted him. He couldn't afford to be swayed by a heart-shaped face or the most sinfully sexy pair of shorts he'd ever seen in his life, no matter how acute the ache in his groin.

'Will you please tell me why you're after my father?' she implored softly. The concern on her face appeared genuine and he suddenly realised that, despite Benedicto's treatment of her, Inez cared for her father.

His nostrils flared as bitterness rocked through him. He'd once been in that same position, foolishly believing that the father he'd idolised and loved beyond reason cared just as deeply for him. That he wasn't the fraudster and philanderer the press were making him out to be.

Now, he wanted to rip the blindfold from her eyes, make her see the true monster in the man she called *Pai*. Make her see that her love was nothing but a manipulative tool that would be used against her eventually.

Except he had a strong feeling she already knew, and chose to overlook it. Which made his blood boil even more.

'Why, do you plan to sacrifice yourself to save him?' he taunted.

She gasped, dropping the sterling silver fork she'd been nervously toying with. 'So, it *is* my father!'

He cursed under his breath. 'If you so much as breathe a word in his direction about your suspicions, I'll make sure you regret it for the rest of your life.'

She paled. 'You really expect me to sit back and watch you destroy him?'

'I expect you to hold up your end of the bargain we struck. Live under my roof in exchange for me leaving the loophole in the contract alone. Are you prepared to do that or do I need to plot another plan of action?' he asked, not bothering to hide the threat in his voice.

She stared back at him apprehensively. Her chin rose and her brown eyes burned holes in him but she nodded. 'I'll stick to our agreement.'

When their wine was served, he watched her take a big gulp and curbed the desire to follow suit. He was driving and needed to restrict his drinking. Nevertheless, a sip of the Chilean red went a way to restoring a little order to his floundering thoughts.

Thee mou, he hadn't even fired the first salvo and things were getting out of hand. Why on earth had he shared the presence of his demons with her? And that comment about her being so much more than a girlfriend? He silently shook his head and sucked in a control-affirming breath.

Their dinner progressed in near silence. Theo reminded himself that his main reason for bringing her out hadn't been for conversation. When she refused dessert, he settled the bill quickly and rose to help her out of her seat.

Fire shot through his groin, hard and fierce, as he was once again confronted with the risqué shorts. While they'd been seated, he'd managed to tamp down the effect of those shorts on his raging libido.

Now, as she walked in front of him, he was treated to a mouth-watering sight of her deliciously rounded bottom and stunning legs. With each sway of her hips, he grew harder until he wondered if he had any blood left in his upper extremities that hadn't migrated south.

He was reconsidering his decision not to burn the shorts at the earliest opportunity when he caught a male diner staring in blatant appreciation at her legs.

His growl was low but unmistakable. The man hastily averted his gaze but Theo was still simmering in primitive emotions when they reached the car park.

He followed her to the passenger side but, instead of opening the door for her, he braced his hand on either side of her and leaned in close. With her front pressed against the door, her bottom was moulded into his groin in such a way that she couldn't fail to notice his state of arousal.

Her breathing quickened, but she stayed put. 'What are you doing?'

'Delivering the punishment I promised.'

'Sorry?'

'You called me *senhor* when we were in the restaurant.'

She tried to turn around but he pressed her more firmly against the car. 'I...don't remember.'

'Of course you do. You also thought I wouldn't act on my promise in full view of other diners, didn't you?'

'No, I wasn't—'

'Maybe you were right. Or maybe we both knew I'd want to do more than just kiss you.'

'You're wrong...'

'Am I?'

'Yes...'

'So you'd prefer I let this one slide?' He rocked his hips against her bottom and her breath hitched. 'You won't think me weak?'

Her shocked laugh heated the air around them. 'Only someone foolish would think you weak.'

'I'm not sure whether there's a compliment in there. Is there?'

Her head fell forward, exposing the seductive line of her neck. 'Am I to pander to your ego too, Theo?'

He laughed. 'How can you appear submissive and yet taunt me at the same time?'

She lifted her head and turned to stare at him. Whatever she saw in his face made her squirm harder. Provocatively. Her gaze dropped to his mouth and Theo could no more resist the temptation than he could breathe.

Fingers sliding beneath her knotted hair to hold her still, he caught her mouth in a fierce kiss. Every emotion he'd experienced since waking that morning was delivered in that kiss—passion, arousal, confusion, anxiety and anger. He pinned her against the car so she couldn't move, couldn't put those seductive hands on his body.

Although he missed her touch, a part of him was thankful because, had she had access, he would've lost even more of his mind than he suspected he was losing.

He registered the brief flashes behind his closed eyelids but didn't break the kiss. He suspected Inez had no idea what had just happened. And even if she had, she wouldn't have suspected the true reason behind the paparazzi shots because she was used to being the darling of the press.

Well, she was in for a rude awakening…

She started to open her mouth wider, to return his demanding kiss.

He slowly lifted his head. When she made a tiny sound of protest and tried to recapture his mouth, he forced himself to step away. He'd achieved one part of what he'd set out to do. The second part was a short drive away.

Curving his arm around her waist, he peeled her away from the door, opened it and deposited her inside, all the time trying not to stare down at her legs and imagine how they would feel wrapped around his waist.

He swallowed hard as he rounded the hood and slid behind the wheel.

'Time to head to the club before I give in to the urge to deliver more punishment.'

Her eyes dropped to his mouth and he barely suppressed a groan as she licked her lips.

'For your mercy, I will teach you how to samba like a true Brazilian,' she replied huskily.

Inez lay among the white sheets the next morning, trying hard not to relive the events of the night before but it was as futile as trying to stop a tidal wave.

They'd eventually emerged from the nightclub at two in the morning. She'd been flushed and sweaty from being plastered to Theo's superb body for three straight hours. But the wild racing of her heart had nothing to do with her exertions on the dance floor and everything to do with the man who'd focused on her as if she was the only woman in the whole club.

And *Deus*, had he danced like a dream? Far from tutoring him on the correct steps of her native dance, she'd found herself following his lead as he'd moved expertly on the dance floor.

When he'd caught her to him, her back to his front and replayed the scene in the car park, but this time to music, she'd seriously feared her heart would beat itself to expiration.

In that moment, she'd forgotten that there was a sinister purpose to Theo's plan; that he'd all but admitted she was being used as a pawn in some deadly game he was playing with her father. When he'd laid his stubbled jaw against her cheek and hummed the sultry samba music in her ear, she'd closed her eyes and imagined what it would be like to belong—truly belong—to a man like Theo.

Turning over in bed, she groaned in disbelief at how

susceptible she'd been to his hard body and magnetic charisma. *Santa Maria*, she'd been all but putty in his hands.

Luckily, the fresh air and the long drive back had hammered some sense into her. The moment they'd returned, she'd bidden him a curt *boa noite*, left him standing in the hallway and retreated as fast as her sore feet would carry her.

And she intended to carry on like that. She might not know what his end game was, but she refused to be a willing participant in his campaign.

The last thing she wanted to do was to fall for another manipulator like Constantine.

She was here only because she had no choice but she didn't intend to idle away her time in this house. Theo expected her to stay here for three months, which meant whatever he had planned was not to be executed immediately. Perhaps she could convince him to change his mind in that time.

Yeah, and fairy tales really did come true...

Or she could find out exactly what his intentions were.

She'd seen the look in his eyes when he spoke about her father. Whatever vendetta he'd planned, he intended to see it through.

Helplessly, she rolled over in bed and her eyes lit on the bedside clock. She jerked upright and threw the sheet aside. She might not have anywhere to be on this Saturday morning but lazing about in bed past ten o'clock wasn't her style.

She jumped into the shower, shampooed her hair and washed her body with quick, regimented movement ingrained in her from her time at the Swiss boarding school her father had sent her to just to impress his friends.

Leaving her damp hair to dry naturally, she pulled on an aqua-coloured sundress and slipped her feet into low-heeled thongs. Smoothing her favourite sunscreen moisturiser over her face and arms, she left her room and headed downstairs.

Teresa was crossing the hallway carrying a *cafetière* of freshly made coffee and indicated for Inez to follow her.

She led her out to the terrace that overlooked the immense square infinity pool. Light danced off the water but her attention was caught and held by the man seated at the cast iron oval breakfast table.

His white short-sleeved polo shirt did amazing things to his eyes and olive-toned skin. And loose green shorts exposed solid thighs and lightly hair-sprinkled legs that made her mouth dry before flooding with moisture that threatened to choke her.

'*Bom dia, anjo*. Are you going to stand there all morning?' he mocked.

She forced her legs to move and took the chair he indicated to his right.

'Coffee?' he asked, his voice deep and low.

'Yes, please.' Her voice had grown husky and emerged barely above a whisper.

He nodded to Teresa who smiled, filled her cup then made herself scarce.

Inez sipped the hot brew just as a delaying tactic so she didn't have to look at him.

So far she'd seen Theo in formal evening wear and smart casual and each look had threatened to knock her sideways. But seeing him now, with so much of his vibrant olive skin on show, threatened to topple her completely. She took another hasty sip and choked as the liquid scalded her mouth.

Grabbing the napkin to stop herself from dribbling like an idiot, she looked up and caught his mocking smile. 'You'd rather blister yourself than converse with me?'

She swallowed and fought to present a passable smile. 'Of course not. I was just enjoying the...view.' She indicated beyond his shoulder, where the garden extended beyond the pool and sloped down to the sandy white beach and sparkling ocean.

With a disbelieving smile, he picked up the paper next to his plate and shook it out. 'If you say so—'

Her horrified gasp made him lower the newspaper. 'Something wrong?'

'Is that a picture of *us*?' she demanded through a severely constricted throat. The question was redundant because the picture taking up the whole of the front page was printed in vivid Technicolor.

He'd already seen it, of course, so he didn't bother to glance where her appalled gaze was riveted. 'Yes. Fresh off the morning press.'

'*Meu deus!*' She reached out and snatched the broadsheet out of his grasp. It was even worse up close. 'It looks as if…as if—' Disbelief caught in her throat, eating the rest of her words.

'As if I'm taking you from behind?' he supplied helpfully.

Humiliating heat stained her cheeks. '*Sim*,' she muttered fiercely. 'With your jacket covering me that way it looks as if I'm wearing nothing from the waist down! It's…it's disgusting!'

He plucked the paper from her hand and studied the picture. 'Hmm, it certainly is…*something*.'

'How can you sit there and be so unconcerned about it?' The picture had been taken with a high-resolution camera but, with the low lighting in the car park, the suggestiveness in the picture could be misinterpreted a thousand ways. None of them complimentary.

'Relax. We weren't exactly having sex, were we?'

'That's not the point.' She grabbed the paper back and quickly perused the article accompanying the gratuitous picture, fearing the worst. Sure enough, her father's political campaign had been called into question, along with an even more unsavoury speculation on her private life.

If this is what they do in public we can only imagine what they do in private…

Her hands shook as she threw the offending paper down. 'I thought this was a reputable paper.'

'It is.'

'Then why would they print something so...offensive?'

'Perhaps because it's true. We were kissing in the car park. And you were pushing your delectable backside into my groin as if you couldn't wait till we got home to do me.'

She surged to her feet, knocking her chair aside. Her whole body was shaking with fury and she could barely grasp the chair to straighten it.

'We both know I was not!'

'Do we? I told you those shorts were a bad idea. Do you blame me for getting carried away?'

'Oh, you're *despicable!*'

'And you're delicious when you're angry,' he replied lazily, picked up the paper and carried on reading.

The urge to drive her fist through the paper into his face made her take another hasty step back.

She abhorred violence. Or at least she had before she'd met Theo Pantelides. Now she wasn't so sure what she was capable of...

'Aren't you going to eat, *anjo*?' he asked without taking his eyes off the page.

'No. I've lost my appetite,' she snapped.

She fled the terrace to the sound of his mocking laughter and raced up to her room, her face flaming and angry humiliation smashing through her chest.

He found her on the beach an hour later. She heard the crunch of his feet in the warm sand and studiously avoided looking up. She carried on sketching the stationary boat anchored about a mile away and ignored him when he settled himself on the flat rock next to her.

He didn't speak for a few minutes before he let out an irritated breath. 'The silent treatment doesn't work for me, Inez.'

She snapped her pad shut and turned to face him. His

lips were pinched with displeasure but his eyes were focused, gauging her reaction...almost as if her reaction mattered.

'Having my sex life sleazily speculated about in the weekend newspaper doesn't work for me either.' She blinked to dilute the intense focus and continued. 'I agree that perhaps those shorts were not the best idea. But I saw the other diners in that restaurant. There were people far more famous than I am. But still the paparazzo followed us into the car park and took our picture.'

Inez thought he tensed but perhaps it was the movement of his body as he reached behind him and produced a plate laden with food. 'It's done. Let's move on.'

She yearned to remain on her high horse, but with her exertions last night, coupled with having eaten less than a whole meal in the last twenty-four hours, it wasn't surprising when her stomach growled loudly in anticipation.

He shook out a napkin and settled the plate in her lap. 'Eat up,' he instructed and picked up her sketchpad. 'You have an hour before the stylist arrives to address the issue of your wardrobe.'

She froze in the act of reaching for the food. 'I don't need a stylist. I can easily go back home and pack up some more clothes.'

'You'll not be returning to your father's house for the next three months. Besides, if your clothes are all in the style of heavy evening gowns or tiny shorts, then you'll agree the time has come to go a different route?'

She mentally scanned her wardrobe and swiftly concluded that he was probably right. 'There really is no need,' she tried anyway.

'It's too late to change the plan, Inez.'

And, just like that, the subject was closed. He tapped the plate and, as if on cue, her stomach growled again.

Giving up the argument, she devoured the thick sliced beef sandwich and polished off the apple in greedy bites.

She was gulping down the bottled water when she saw him pause at her sketch of a boat.

'This is very good.'

'Thank you.'

He tilted the page. 'You like boats?'

'Very much. My mother used to take me sailing. It was my favourite thing to do with her.'

He closed the pad. 'Were you two close?'

'She was my best friend,' she responded in a voice that cracked with pain. 'Not a day goes by that I don't miss her.'

His fingers seemed to tighten on the rock before they relaxed again. 'Mothers have a way of affecting you that way. It makes their absence all the harder to bear.'

'Is yours...when did you lose yours?' she asked.

He turned and stared at her. A bleak look entered his eyes but dissolved in the next blink. 'My mother is very much alive.'

She gasped. 'But I thought you said...'

'Absence doesn't mean death. There are several ways for a parent to be absent from a child's life without the ultimate separation.'

'Are you talking about abandonment?'

Again he glanced at her, and this time she caught a clearer glimpse of his emotions. Pain. Devastating pain.

'Abandonment. Indifference. Selfishness. Self-absorption. There are many forms of delivering the same blow,' he elaborated in a rough voice.

'I know. But I was lucky. My mother was the best mother in the world.'

'Is that why you're trying to be the best daughter in the world for your father, despite what you know of him?'

His accusation was like sandpaper against her skin. 'I beg your pardon?'

He shook his head. 'Don't bother denying it. You know exactly what sort of person he is. And yet you've stood by him all these years. Why—because you want a pat on the head and to be told you're a good daughter?'

The truth of his words hit her square in the chest. Up until yesterday, everything she'd done, every plan of her father's she'd gone along with had been to win his approval, and in some way make up for the fact that she hadn't been born the right gender. She didn't want to curl up and hide from the truth. But the callous way he condemned her made her want to justify her actions.

'I'm not blind to my father's shortcomings.' She ignored his caustic snort. 'But neither am I going to make excuses for my actions. My loyalty to my family isn't something I'm ashamed of.'

'Even when that loyalty meant turning a blind eye to other people's suffering?' he demanded icily.

She frowned. 'Whose suffering?'

'The people he left behind in the *favelas* for a start. Do you know that less than two per cent of the funds raised at those so-called charity events you so painstakingly put together actually make it to the people who need it most?'

She felt her face redden. His condemning gaze raked over her features. 'Of course you do,' he murmured acidly.

'It happened in the past, I admit it, but I only agreed to organise the last event if everything over and above the cost of doing it went to the *favelas*.' At his disbelieving look, she added, 'I do a lot of work with charities. I know what I'm talking about.'

'And did you ensure that it was done?'

'Yes. The charity confirmed they'd received the funds yesterday.'

One eyebrow quirked in surprise before he jerked to his feet. Thrusting his hands into his pockets, he turned to face her. 'That's progress at least.'

'Thank you. I don't live in a fairy tale. Trust me, I'm trying to do my part to help the *favelas*.'

'How?'

She debated a few seconds before she answered. 'I work at an inner city charity a few times a week.'

His gaze probed hers. 'That morning outside the coffee shop, that was where you were going?'

'Yes.'

'What does your father think?'

She bit her lip. 'He doesn't know.'

His mouth twisted. 'Because it will draw attention to his lies about his upbringing? Everyone knows he was born and raised in the *favelas*.'

'It's part of the reason why I didn't tell him, yes. But he denies his *favela* upbringing because he's...ashamed.'

'And yet he doesn't mind anyone knowing about his mother?'

'He thinks it gives him a little leverage with the common man to be indirectly associated with the *favelas*.'

'So he likes to rewrite his history as he goes along?'

'Perhaps. I don't delude myself for one second that my father doesn't bend the rules and the truth at times.'

His harsh laugh made her start. 'Right. Are you talking about, oh, let's see...doing ninety on a sixty miles per hour road, or are we talking about something with a little more...teeth?'

That note she'd heard before. The one that sent a foreboding chill along her spine, that warned her that something else was going on here. Something she should be running far and fast from. 'I...I'm not sure what you're implying.'

'Then let me spell it out for you. Are we talking about harmless anecdotes or are we talking about actual deeds? You know—broken kneecaps? Ruptured spleens. *Kidnap for ransom*?'

Her hand flew to her mouth. 'What the hell are you talking about?'

'Come on, you know what your father is capable of. Do

I need to remind you of what he did to you when you displeased him?'

She followed his gaze to the marks on her arm and slowly shook her head. 'I don't excuse this but I refuse to believe he's the monster you describe.'

His mouth twisted. 'I'll let you enjoy your rosy outlook for now, *querida*. I, too, felt like that once about my own father.'

'Is that what you're going to do to my father? Make him accountable for the things he's done?'

For several heartbeats she was sure he wouldn't answer her, or would change the subject the way he'd done in the past. But finally he nodded.

'Yes. I intend to make him pay for what he took from me twelve years ago.'

Her breath froze in her lungs. 'What did he take from you?'

He turned abruptly and faced the water, his stance rigid and forbidding. But Inez found herself moving towards him anyway, a visceral need driving her. She reached out and touched his shoulder. He tensed harder and she was reminded of his reaction to her touch on his boat. 'Theo?'

'I don't like being touched when my back's turned, *anjo*.'

She frowned. 'Why not?'

'Part of my demons.'

Her gut clenched hard at the rough note in his voice. 'Did…did my father do that to you?'

'Not personally. After all, he's an upright citizen now, isn't he? A man the people should trust.' He whipped about to face her.

'But he had something to do with your claustrophobia. And this?'

'Yes.'

'Theo—'

'Enough with the questions! You're forgetting why you're here. Do you need a reminder?'

She swallowed at the arctic look in his eyes. All signs of the raw, vulnerable pain she'd glimpsed minutes ago were wiped clean. Theo Pantelides was once again a man in control, bent on revenge. Slowly, she shook her head. 'No. No, I don't.'

CHAPTER EIGHT

THEIR CONVERSATION AT the beach set a frigid benchmark for the beginning of her stay at Theo's glass mansion.

The next two weeks passed in an icy blur of hectic days and even more hectic evenings. They'd quickly fallen into a routine where Theo left after a quick cup of coffee and a brief outline of when and where they would be dining that evening.

On the second morning when she'd told him she was heading for the charity, he'd raised an eyebrow. 'What sort of work do you do there?'

'Whatever I'm needed to do.' She'd been reluctant to tell him any specifics in case he disparaged her efforts as a rich girl's means of passing the time till the next party.

He'd returned to his coffee. 'Your time is your own when I'm not around. As long you're back here when I return, I see no problem.'

That had been the end of the subject.

After repeating his warning not to mention anything to her father he'd walked away. The man who'd shown her his pain and devastation had completely retreated.

His demeanour during their time indoors was icily courteous. However, when they went out, which they did most evenings, he was the attentive host, touching her, threading his fingers through her hair and gazing adoringly at her.

It was after the fifth night out that she realised he was

pandering to the paparazzi. Without fail, a picture of them in a compromising position appeared in the newspapers the very next morning.

But while she cringed with every exposing photo, he shrugged it off. It wasn't until her third weekend with him, when the newspapers posted the first poll results of the mayoral race, that she finally had her suspicions confirmed.

He was swimming in the pool, his lean and stunning body cutting through the water like the sleekest shark. The byline explaining the reasons behind the voters' reaction had her surging to her feet and storming to the edge of the pool.

'Is this why you've been taking me out every night since I moved in? So I'd be labelled the slut daughter of a man not fit to be mayor?' She raised her voice loud enough to be heard above his powerful strokes.

He stopped mid-stroke, straightened and slicked back his wet hair. With smooth breaststrokes he swam to where she stood barefoot. Looking down at his wet, sun-kissed face, she momentarily lost her train of thought.

He soon set her straight. 'Your father isn't worthy to lead a chain gang, never mind a city,' he replied in succinct, condemning tones. 'And before I'm done with him, the whole world will know it.'

Despite seeing the evidence for herself two weeks ago at the beach, despite knowing that whatever her father had done to him had been devastating, she staggered back a step at that solid, implacable oath.

He planted his hands on the tiles and heaved himself out of the water. It took every ounce of her self-control not to devour him with hungry eyes. But not looking didn't mean not feeling. Her insides clenched with the ever-growing hunger she'd been unable to stem since the first night he'd walked into her life. And, with each passing day, she was finding it harder and harder to remain unaffected.

It seemed not even knowing why she was here, or the full extent of how Theo intended to use her to hurt her father, could cause her intense emotional reaction to his proximity to abate.

Which made her ten kinds of a fool, who needed to pull her thoughts together or risk getting hurt all over again.

'So you don't deny that you used me as bait to derail my father's campaign?'

Hazel eyes, devoid of emotion, narrowed on her face. 'That was one course of action. But you haven't been labelled a slut. I'll sue any newspaper that dares to call you that,' he rasped.

Her laughter scraped her throat. 'There are several ways to describe someone without using the actual derogatory word, Theo.'

He paused in drying his hair and looked at her. Slowly, he held out his hand. 'Show me.'

She handed the paper over. He read it tight-jawed. 'I'll have them print a retraction.'

Dismay roiled through her stomach, along with a heavy dose of rebellious anger.

'That's not the point, though, is it? The harm's already done. You know this means I'll have to stop volunteering, don't you? I can't bring this sort of attention to the charity.'

He frowned and she caught a look of unease on his face. 'I'll take care of this.'

'Forget it; it's too late. And congratulations; you've achieved your aim. But I won't be paraded about and pawed in public any more, so if you're planning on another night on the town you'll have to do it without me.'

His gaze slowly rose to hers and he resumed rubbing the towel through his hair. 'Fine. We'll do something else.' He threw the paper on the table.

She regarded him suspiciously. 'Something like what?'

'I promised you a trip on the yacht. We'll sail this evening and spend tomorrow aboard. Would you like that?'

At times like these, when he was being a courteous host,

she found it hard to believe he was the same man who was hell-bent on seeking revenge on her father for past wrongs.

She'd given in to her gnawing curiosity after his revelations on the beach and searched the Internet for a clue as to what had happened to him. All she'd come up with were scant snippets of his late father's dirty dealings before Alexandrou Pantelides had died in prison. As far as she knew, there was no connection between Theo's family and hers. The Pantelides brothers, one of whom was married and recently a parent, and the other engaged to be married, were a huge success in the oil, shipping and luxury hotel world. Theo's job as a troubleshooter extraordinaire for the billion-dollar conglomerate meant he never settled in one place for very long. An ideal job for a man whose personal relationships were fleeting at best.

And a man tormented by a horde of demons.

She looked closer at him, tried to see the man behind the wall, the man who'd bared his soul for a brief moment when he'd spoken of his mother's abandonment.

But that man was closed off.

'What does it matter what I want? Frankly, I'm surprised my father hasn't been in touch about this.'

'He has. I refused to take his calls.'

'I didn't mean you. Since I was also the subject in these photos, I'm surprised he hasn't called me to vent his anger.'

His eyelids swept down and shielded his gaze from her. Apprehension struck a jagged path through her. 'He has, hasn't he?'

'He tried. I suggested that perhaps he refrain from contacting you and concentrate on kissing babies and convincing little old ladies to cast their ballot in his favour.'

Shock rooted her to the ground. 'How dare you take control of my life like this?'

'Would you rather I gave him access so he airs his disappointment?'

'What do you care? It's a little late to protect me, don't you think?'

His jaw tightened. 'For as long as you remain under my roof, you're under my protection.'

'*Meu deus*, please don't pretend you care!'

She realised how close she was to tears and swallowed hard. Fearing she would break down in front of him, she whirled round, intent on heading for her room. She made it two steps before he stopped her.

Flinging away the towel, he cupped her cheeks with both hands. 'Stop getting yourself distressed about this.'

'Is that another command?'

His eyes narrowed. 'You're angry.'

'Damn right I am. I wish I'd never set eyes on you. In fact I wish—'

His mouth slanted over hers, hot, hungry and all consuming. Her groan of protest was less than heartfelt and devoured within a millisecond.

A part of her was furious that he'd resorted to kissing her to shut her up. But it was only a minuscule part. The rest of her body was too busy revelling in the feel of his warm bare back and the fine definition of muscles that rippled beneath her caress.

His hands speared into her hair, imprisoning her for the invasion of his tongue as he took the kiss to another level.

His first kiss over two weeks ago had been a pure threat and the two that followed a show of mastery. This kiss was different. There was hunger and passion behind it, but also a gentleness that calmed her roiling emotions and slowly replaced them with a different sensation. Need clamoured inside her; a need to be closer still to his magnificent body; a need to dig her hands into his back and feel him shudder in reaction.

His groan was smothered between their melded lips as she dug her fingers even deeper. Power surged through her when he jerked again.

One hand dropped to her bottom and yanked her lower body into his groin. His erection was unmistakable. Bold, thick and hot, it pressed against her belly with insistent power that made her heartbeat skitter out of control.

She wanted him. Above and beyond all sense, she wanted this man. Her willpower, when it came to the chemistry between them, was laughably negligible.

But she couldn't give in. *Couldn't...*

The gentleness she'd sensed in him was false, she reminded herself fiercely. The bottom line was that in a few short weeks he would walk away. Leave her and her family devastated.

'I'm losing you. Come back, *anjo*,' he murmured seductively against her mouth. He ran his tongue over her lower lip and her knees weakened.

When he cupped her bottom and squeezed, she desperately summoned all her resolve and pushed against his chest. 'No.'

He raised his head and she saw behind the wall. He was as caught in this insane chemistry as she was. A little part of her felt better.

'I can change your mind, Inez. Regardless of what I intend for your father, what is between us is undeniable.'

'Do you hear yourself? You think I should forget everything else and sleep with you just because you made me feel a certain way?'

'That's generally the reason why men and women have sex.'

'But we're not just any man and any woman, Theo, are we?'

He stiffened, and a hard look entered his eyes. 'Are you saying that you've been in love with every man you've slept with?' he queried.

She froze and prayed her humiliation wouldn't show on her face as she tried to stem the memory of Constantine's treatment of her.

His cruel rejection was still an ache beneath her breastbone.

'Inez?' Theo interjected harshly.

'My past relationships are none of your business.'

His slightly reddened mouth twisted. 'Far be it for me to request to be lumped in with your other lovers, but isn't it a touch hypocritical to apply one criteria to me that you haven't done with one of your lovers, in particular?'

'If you're referring to Constantine, let me assure you that you have no idea what you're talking about.'

His hand tightened around her waist. 'Then enlighten me. Why did he dump you?'

Inez broke free. 'We weren't compatible.'

'Or he found out the true reason you were with him and wanted nothing to do with you?'

'No. That wasn't why...' She screeched to a stop as the words stuck in her throat.

'So what was it? Did you really love him or did you convince yourself you did in order to achieve your aims?'

She bit her lip as he shone a light on the stark question. Had she blown her feelings out of proportion? Constantine had been charismatic, yes, but he'd never created the decadent chaos that Theo created in her.

When she'd imagined love, she'd always imagined passion, hunger and a keen pleasure even the slightest thought of that special someone brought. She'd believed herself in love with Constantine and yet she'd never experienced those emotions.

Well, she most definitely wasn't feeling them now.

'I believed my emotions were genuine at the time. But he didn't. He believed I was using him to further my father's campaign.'

'What did he do?' he asked. She looked into his eyes and fooled herself into thinking she saw a thawing of the hardness there.

'He made painful digs at me whenever he gave interviews. He made the tabloids call my character into question...much the same way you're doing now.'

He dropped his hand. 'It's not the same—'

'Yes, it is. Look Theo, I just want to be left alone to do my time.'

He paled. 'You're not in prison, Inez.'

She put much needed distance between them. 'Am I not? How else would you describe my presence here?'

Theo watched her walk away and curled his fists at his sides. The urge to call her back was so strong he forced himself to exhale slowly to expel the need. Her reference to her presence under his roof as a prison sentence had stung badly.

But hell, the truth was irrefutable. He'd forced her to make a choice, and no amount of dinner dates or designer shopping sprees would gloss over the fact that he'd set the tabloids on her as a way to dismantle her father's campaign.

Witnessing her clear distress just now had made his chest ache in a way that confused and irritated him.

Perhaps he needed to step up his agenda, end this dangerous game once and for all and move on with his life.

His brothers would certainly agree. He'd been avoiding their calls for the best part of a fortnight, replying only by email and with curt one-liners that he knew would only go so far before something gave.

He gritted his teeth against the prompt to deliver a swift killing blow to Benedicto da Costa.

His own ordeal hadn't been swift. It'd been long and tortuous. The punishment should fit the crime. Any hesitation on his part now merely stemmed from the afterglow of the chemistry between him and Inez. He freely admitted that theirs was a strong and potent brand, more intense than anything he'd ever experienced before.

It was messing with his mind, the same way the thought of her ex-lover had made him see red for several long seconds. But there was no way he was letting it impede his goal.

Which meant he had to come at this problem from another angle.

He swallowed the acrid taste in his mouth at the thought that Inez had put him into the same class as Constantine Blanco.

Slowly walking back indoors, he turned over the dilemma in his mind. By the time he reached his suite and changed out of his swimming trunks, a smile was curving his lips.

An hour later, he watched her descend the stairs, her duffel bag slung over her shoulder and an overnight case in her hand.

'Did Teresa tell you to pack your swimming gear?'

She regarded him warily. 'Yes. But I thought we were just taking the boat out?'

He shrugged. 'I thought you would welcome the opportunity to sunbathe away from the prying lenses of the paparazzi? There are several decks on the yacht that you can sunbathe on. Or we can swim in the sea, dine alone under the stars. Would you like that?' he asked, then felt a jolt at how much he wanted her to answer in the affirmative. In the past, he'd never taken the time to seek out what pleased his girlfriends beyond the usual gifts and fine dining. It was why he operated his relationships on a strict short-term basis with as little maintenance as possible.

Inez was far from low maintenance. And yet he found himself even more drawn to her.

She glanced pointedly over his shoulder. 'I'll think about it and let you know.'

His unsettled feelings escalated. He reminded himself that they were heading for his boat. She liked his boat. Perhaps she would relent enough to forget that she was angry with him. Forget about Blanco and forget that she was being blackmailed.

Theo was still debating why her feelings meant so much to him when he pulled up at the marina.

***

'You've been smiling ever since we set sail.'

Her voice was full of heavy suspicion. Theo's smile widened as he tilted his face up into the sunshine. 'Have I? It must be the weather.'

'The weather has been the same for the last month,' she replied sourly.

He slowly lowered his head and captured her gaze with his. 'Then it must be the company.'

A delicate wave of heat surged up her neck into her cheeks, making him wonder, as he had more than once these past two weeks, how she could have been involved with someone like Blanco and still blush like a schoolgirl.

Theo had looked into Constantine Blanco and had not been surprised to find that he was cut from the same cloth as Benedicto. It was perhaps why Da Costa had chosen to ally himself with the younger man politically. He'd sent his daughter to spy on Blanco and had been double-crossed in the bargain.

Theo's smile slipped as he recalled her hurt when he'd thrown her relationship with Blanco at her. He reached for the glass of wine that had accompanied their late afternoon meal and took a large gulp.

The guilt tightening in his chest since her accusation at the pool squeezed harder.

What the hell was going on with him?

'Have you decided whether you're selling the boat or not?' she asked.

In the sunlight, her black hair gleamed like polished jet, making him burn to feel its silkiness beneath his fingers.

He stared into his drink. 'Maybe. I'll have to weigh up practical usage versus the desire to hang on to something beautiful.'

'But you're a billionaire. Isn't collecting toys part and parcel of your status?'

'I wasn't always a man of means. In fact my brothers and

I worked our backsides off to achieve the level of success we enjoy now.' His smile felt tight and strained.

'Your brothers...Sakis and Arion...'

He looked up in surprise. 'You've been playing around on the Internet, I see.'

She raised her chin. 'I thought it wise to learn a little bit more about my enemy.'

The label grated. Badly. 'What else did you try to discover while you were rooting around my family tree?'

'Your brother Sakis had some trouble with a saboteur on one of his oil tankers.'

He nodded. 'We dealt with that quite satisfactorily.'

'And now your brother Ari is engaged to the widow of the man who tried to throw your company into chaos?' She frowned.

A reluctant grin tugged at his mouth. 'What can I say; we thrive on interesting challenges.'

'You also seem to make enemies with the people you do business with. So far you've led me to believe it was my father who wronged you. How do I know it's not the other way round? That you're not here because you deserved everything you got?'

The stem of the wine glass snapped with a sickening crack. Even then it took the cold wine seeping into his shirt to realise what he'd done.

The top part of the glass landed on the table, rolled off and smashed onto the deck.

Inez gasped. 'Theo, you're bleeding!' She surged to her feet and sprang towards him.

'Stop!'

'But your finger...'

'Is nothing compared to what will happen to your foot if you take another step.'

She glanced down at the broken glass an inch from her bare foot and glanced back at his bleeding forefinger. Anguish creased her pale features.

'Sit down, Inez,' he instructed tersely.

'Please, let me help,' she implored.

Gritting his teeth, he grabbed a napkin and formed a small tourniquet around the gaping wound. 'It's not deep but will need to be cleaned properly. There's a first aid kit behind the bar.'

She nodded, slipped on her sandals and dashed for the bar. Theo stood and moved from the dining table to the wraparound sofa to give the crew member who'd arrived on deck room to sweep up the broken glass. He glanced up as Inez rushed back and set the kit on the coffee table.

Her eyes were turbulent with worry as she glanced from his face to the blood-soaked napkin.

'Are you going to stand there staring at me all evening? I'm bleeding to death here.'

With a hoarse croak, she jerked into action. She carefully cleaned the wound with antiseptic and applied gauze before securing it with a plaster. All through the procedure, she darted quick, apologetic glances at him.

As he stared at her, he felt a different sort of jolt run through him. One he hadn't been aware he was missing until he felt it.

Care. Concern. Fear for him.

When was the last time anyone besides Ari and Sakis had felt like that about him? When was the last time his own mother lavished such attention on him? Inez slid him another worried glance and his breath shuddered out.

'Calm yourself, *anjo*. I'll live. I'm sure of it.'

She exhaled noisily and her agitated pulse pounded at her throat. '*Sinto muito*,' she said in a rush.

'Don't apologise. It wasn't your fault.'

'But...if I hadn't accused you of...'

'You're operating in the dark and want to find out the truth. I respect that. But I can't tell you what my business with your father is until I'm ready. You have to respect that.'

'But...this...' She glanced down at his finger and shook

her head. 'Your reaction…the claustrophobia and the touching thing…I can't help but fear the worst, Theo,' she whispered.

Against his will, his chest constricted at the anguish in her voice. He wanted to comfort her. Wanted to take that look of anticipated pain from her face. He wanted to kiss her until they both forgot why she was his prisoner and why he was beginning to dread the day he had to set her free.

He swallowed hard.

'Let's make a deal. For the next twenty-four hours, no talk of your father or the reason why I'm in Rio. Agreed?'

Her mouth wobbled and her teeth worried her bottom lip as she glanced back at his finger. Her eyes were no less turbulent when they rose to his but he saw determination flare in their depths. 'Agreed.'

Theo stood at the railing on the third floor deck and watched her swim in the pool on the second deck the next morning. She moved like a water nymph, her long black hair streaming down her back as she scissored her arms and legs underwater.

He gripped the rail until his knuckles turned white but still he couldn't take his eyes off her.

'I'm waiting for an answer, Theo,' came the weary voice at the end of the line.

Theo sighed. 'Sorry, remind me again what the question was.'

Ari grunted with annoyance. 'I asked you why I couldn't have one peaceful breakfast without opening the papers to find you wrapped around some poor girl. Seriously, my digestive system has sent me a stern memo. Either I treat it better and not subject it to such images or it goes on permanent vacation.'

Theo heard Perla, his soon-to-be sister-in-law, laughing in the background.

'The answer is simple. Don't read the papers.'

Ari sighed. 'How long is this going to go on for?'

'Everything should be signed, sealed and delivered in a week or two,' he responded, rolling his shoulders to ease the tension tightening his muscles. Another sleepless night, plagued with nightmares. He'd given up on sleep somewhere around three a.m.

'You sound very sure.'

His grip tightened around the phone. As he'd lain awake he'd briefly toyed with the idea of ending this vendetta sooner. And he'd been stunned when the idea had taken firm hold. 'I am.'

'And nothing you're doing down there will affect the wedding? Don't forget it's in two weeks. If you can prise yourself away from that piece of skirt for long enough—'

'She's not a piece of skirt,' he snarled before he could catch his response. Ari's silence made him hurry to speak. 'I'll be at your wedding.'

'Good, since you've missed most of the rehearsals, I'll send you the video of what you need to do. Make sure you get it right; we'll do a quick rehearsal when you get here. I'm not having you mess things up for Perla.'

'Sure. Fine,' he murmured.

He followed the curvy, sexy shape underneath the water and held his breath as Inez broke the surface and rose out of the pool. Dripping curves and sun-kissed skin made his body clench unbearably. He wanted to trace every single inch of her with his hands, his mouth, his tongue. 'Oh, and tell Perla I'm bringing a guest.'

His brother muttered a curse and relayed the message. Theo heard Perla's whoop of delight. 'The love of my life grudgingly agrees but suggests that perhaps, next time, you could be courteous enough to give us a heads-up sooner?'

'Next time? You mean you'll be getting married for a third time?'

He hung up to more pithy curses ringing in his ears and found himself smiling. Without taking his eyes off the figure below, he descended the spiral staircase and walked towards the bikini-clad goddess reaching for the towel on the shelf next to the pool.

Her back was turned and he slowed to a stop as the sight of her tiny waist and curvy hips made blood rush through his veins. Lust twisted through his gut, hard and demanding.

Hell, this was getting unbearable.

He threw his cell phone on the breakfast table and watched her jerk around to face him. The towel she was holding to her hair stilled.

'Hi.'

'Good morning. Enjoy your swim?'

'It was very refreshing,' she replied huskily, her eyes following him warily as he strode towards her. 'So, what's the plan for today?' she asked.

I want to haul you off to my bed and keep you underneath me until we both pass out from the pleasure overload.

He wrenched his gaze from her full breasts, lovingly cupped by damp white triangles, and concentrated on breathing. 'We're headed for Copacabana. We'll stop for something to eat then head back tonight. Or if you want we can stay on the boat and leave in the morning?'

She thought about it for a second and nodded. 'I'd love to draw the boat in the moonlight.'

'Then that's what you shall do.'

Her gaze turned puzzling, weighing.

'What's on your mind?' he asked.

She shook her head slightly and slowly folded the towel. 'Sometimes I feel as if I'm dealing with two people.'

Something hard tugged in his chest. 'Which one do you prefer?'

'Are you joking? The person you are now, of course.'

He froze as the tug tightened its hold on him. His breath came in short pants as he closed the distance between them. 'I thought we weren't going to delve into our issues today.'

'You asked me what was on my mind.'

He nodded. 'I guess I did.' He stared into the pure, make-up-free perfection of her face and something very close to regret rose in his gut.

'Now it's my turn to ask you what's on your mind, Theo,' she murmured thoughtfully.

'It's completely pointless, of course, but I'm wishing we'd met under different circumstances.'

Her mouth dropped open. 'You are?'

The urge to touch grew, and he finally gave in. He traced his thumb over her lips and felt them pucker slightly under his touch. 'As I said, it's pointless.'

'Because you would've been done with me within a week?' she ventured.

'No. I would've kept you for much longer, *anjo*. Perhaps even for ever.'

He forced himself to step away. Once again she'd slid so effortlessly under his skin, opened him up to wishes and possibilities he'd forced himself never to entertain after what their respective fathers and his mother had done to him. She was making him believe in impossible dreams, feelings he had no business experiencing.

He strode quickly towards the pool. A cold dip would wash away the fiery need and alien emotions tearing his insides to shreds. He hoped.

He emerged twenty minutes later to find her polishing off the last of her scrambled eggs and coffee. Over the past fortnight he'd noticed that she ate with a gusto that triggered his own appetite. Or *appetites*.

As he poured his coffee and helped himself to fruit, she reached for the ever-present duffel bag and pulled out her sketchpad.

'Have you thought of doing something with your talent?' he asked.

A shadow passed over her face before she tried to smile through it, but he guessed the reason behind it. Her father.

'I will once I resume my education. I put pursuing my degree on hiatus for a while.'

He didn't need to ask why. 'Until when?'

She shrugged and searched for a fresh page in her pad. 'I haven't decided yet.'

Theo tried not to let his anger show. They'd called a truce for twenty-four hours.

'What will you study when you return?'

'I love buildings and boats. I may go into architecture or boat design.'

He glanced from her face to the pad. 'Boat design, huh?'

She nodded.

He picked up his coffee and regarded her over the rim. 'Why don't you design me one?'

'You want me to design a boat for you?'

'Yes. I'm sure your research showed you what sort of designs we specialise in. It has to be up to the Pantelides standard. But use your own template. Make it state-of-the-art, of course.'

'Of course,' she murmured but he could see the gleam of interest in her eyes as she stared down at her pad.

Her pencil flew across the paper as he devoured his breakfast. She didn't look up as he rose and rounded the table to where she sat. He didn't glance down at her drawing; he was too absorbed with the sheer joy on her face as she became immersed in her task.

Even when his finger drifted down her cheek to the corner of her mouth she barely glanced up at him. But her breath hitched and she jerked a tiny bit towards his touch before he withdrew his hand.

As he walked away, Theo marvelled at how light-hearted he felt.

CHAPTER NINE

THEY DROPPED ANCHOR about a mile away from Copacabana Beach and took a launch ashore.

Inez looked to where Theo stood, legs braced, at the wheel of the launch. The wind rushed through his dark hair, whipping it across his forehead. Stupid that she should be jealous of the wind but she clenched her fingers in her lap as they tingled with the need to touch him.

I would've kept you for much longer, anjo. *Perhaps even for ever.*

Try as she had for the last few hours, she couldn't get his words out of her head. They struck her straight to the heart in unguarded moments, made her breath catch in ways that made her dizzy. Every time she pushed the feeling away. But, inevitably, it returned.

She was in serious trouble here...

A shout from nearby sunbathers drew her attention to the fact that they were not alone any more.

She watched the surge of people and the noise of tourists enjoying a Sunday stroll along the beach roads and suddenly felt as if she was losing the tenuous connection she'd made with Theo last night and this morning. Which was silly. There was no connection. Just a precarious truce.

And an exciting task designing a Pantelides boat, which had made joy bubble beneath her skin all day.

He brought the launch to a smooth stop at the pier and

turned off the engine. Jumping out with lithe grace, he held out his hand to her, the smile on his face making her breath stutter in her chest as she slipped her hand into his.

'I'm in the mood for some traditional food and I know just the place for it. You happy to trust me?'

Safely on solid ground, she glanced up and found herself nodding. 'Yes.'

His eyes darkened. 'It's a bit of a walk.' He glanced at her high-heeled wedges with a cocked eyebrow.

'Don't worry about me. I was born in heels.'

'Then I pity your poor *mãe*.'

She laughed and saw his answering smile.

Gradually they fell silent and his gaze drifted over her face, resting on her mouth for a few seconds before he tugged on her hand. 'Come on, *anjo*.'

He led her along the pier and towards the streets. Ten minutes later, she stared in surprise when they stopped outside a door with a faded sign and a single light bulb above it.

'I hear they serve the best *feijoadas* in Rio,' he said, his gaze probing her every expression.

Inez forced the lump in her throat down as she stared at the sign that had been very much part of a long ago, happier childhood. 'It's true. I…how do you know about this place?'

The hand he'd captured since they alighted from the boat meshed with hers, causing her heart to flutter wildly as he brought it to his lips and kissed the back of it. 'I made it my business to find out.'

Again tears choked her and she couldn't speak for several moments. 'Thank you.'

He nodded. 'My pleasure.'

They stopped in the doorway to allow their eyes to adjust to the candlelit interior.

'*Pequena estrela!*' A matronly woman in her late forties approached, her face lit up with a smile.

After exchanging hugs, Inez turned to introduce Theo.

'Camila and my mother were best friends. I used to have supper here many times after school when I was a kid.'

Theo responded to the introduction in smooth, charming Portuguese that had the older woman blushing before she led them to a table in the middle of the room.

'You want the usual?' Camila asked after she'd brought over a basket of bread and taken their wine order.

Inez glanced at Theo. 'Will you let me choose?'

He sat back in his chair, his gaze brushing her face. 'It's your show, *anjo*.'

She rattled off the order and added a few more dishes that had Camila nodding in approval before she bustled off.

Alone with Theo, she tried to calm her giddy senses. Not read too much into why he'd brought her here of all places. But her emotions refused to be calmed.

He was making her feel things she had no business feeling, considering their circumstances. Her heart was very much in danger of being devastated. And this time the danger signs were not disguised as they'd been with Constantine. She was walking into this with her heart and eyes wide open...

'You're frowning too hard, *querida*.'

Plucking a piece of bread from the basket, she fought to focus on not ruining their truce. 'I think I may have ordered too much food.'

'You have a healthy appetite. Nothing wrong with that.'

'It's that healthy appetite that keeps me on the wrong side of chubby.'

'You're not chubby. You're perfect.'

Her hand stilled on the way to her mouth. In the ambient light, she witnessed the potent, knee-weakening look of appreciation on his face. The look slowly grew until hunger became deeply etched into his every feature.

Desire pounded through her, sending radial pulses of heat through her body to concentrate on that needy place between her legs. '*Obrigado*,' she murmured hoarsely.

He nodded slowly, leant forward and took the piece of bread from her hand. Tearing off a piece, he held it against her mouth. When she opened it, he placed it on her tongue and watched her chew.

Then he sat back and ate the remaining piece.

She eventually managed to swallow and cast around for a safe topic of conversation that didn't involve her father or the dangerous emotions arcing between them.

Whether he noticed her floundering or not, she smiled gratefully when he asked, 'Did your mother grow up around here?'

'No, both she and Camila grew up near the Serra Geral, although she spent part of her childhood in Arizona where my grandmother was from. Their fathers were ranch-owning *gauchos* and neighbours but after they both married they moved to Rio and stayed in touch. Camila is like a second mother to me...'

'Da Costa Holdings isn't a cattle business, though,' he replied, then stiffened slightly.

She smiled quickly, wanting to hold onto the animosity-free atmosphere they'd found. 'No, after my grandfather died, my mother sold the ranch and let my father expand the company instead.' She breathed in relief when Camila returned with their wine and first course.

The older woman's warm smile and effusive manner further lightened the mood. By the time she took her first sip of the bold red wine the slightly chilly interlude had passed.

Theo complimented her on the food choice and tucked into the grilled fish starter. The conversation returned to safer topics and eventually turned to his previous career as a championship-winning rower.

'Why did you stop competing?'

He shrugged. 'I tried a few partners after Ari and Sakis retired. The chemistry was lacking. In a sport like that chemistry is key.' He topped up her wine and took a sip of his own.

'You've been lucky to have had the opportunity to do something you loved,' she replied wistfully.

His smile looked a little taut around the edges. 'Luck is a luxury that normally comes along as a result of hard work.'

She glanced down into her wine. 'But sometimes, no matter how hard you try, fate has other ideas for you.'

His eyes narrowed into sharp laser-like beams. 'Yes. But the answer is to turn it to your advantage.'

'Or you can walk away. Find a different option?'

One corner of his mouth lifted. 'Walking away has never been my style.'

She slowly nodded. 'You wouldn't have won championships if you were a man who walked away.'

His expression morphed into something that resembled gratitude. She couldn't claim she understood all his motives but she was beginning to grasp what made Theo tick. As long as he could see a problem in any area of his life, he would not walk away until it was resolved. It was why he was the troubleshooter for Pantelides Inc.

She'd watched footage of him rowing. His grit and determination had held her enthralled throughout the feature and she would be lying now if she didn't admit it was a huge turn-on.

'But there's also strength in walking away. You walked away from rowing rather than risk partnering up with the wrong person.'

He stiffened. 'Inez...'

She fought the urge to back down. 'I don't want to mess up our truce but I want you to just think about it. There's no shame in forgiving. No shame in letting the past *stay* in the past.'

His eyes grew dark and haunted. 'What about my demons?'

'Do you have a cast-iron guarantee that they will be vanquished by the path you've chosen?'

He frowned for several seconds before his eyes narrowed. 'You're right. Let's not mess up the truce, shall we?'

'Theo...'

'*Anjo*. Enough. Have some more wine.' He smiled.

And, just like that, her pulse surged faster. Hell, everything he did made her pulse race. She took a sip and licked her lips as the languorous effect of the wine and the captivating man sitting opposite her took hold.

She really needed to stop drinking so much. She pulled her gaze from the rugged perfection of his face as Camila returned to offer them coffee.

Inez declined and looked over to see his eyes riveted on her.

'I think we need to get you back to the boat.'

Laughter that seemed to be coming easier around him escaped her throat. 'You make me sound as if I've been naughty,' she said after Camila collected their empty plates and left.

'Trust me, I would tell you if you'd been.'

'Well, the night is still young and I'm not ruling anything out.' She laughed again.

His mouth curved in one of those devastating smiles as he reached for his wallet and extracted several crisp notes.

'I say it's definitely time to get you back and into bed.'

Her breath caught. He didn't mean what she thought he meant. Of course he didn't. But images suddenly bombarded her brain that had her blushing.

As she said goodbye to Camila and headed outside, she prayed he wouldn't see her reaction to his words.

'Hey, slow down, you'll break your ankle rushing in those heels.' He caught up with her outside and slid a hand around her waist.

The warmth of his body was suddenly too much to bear. 'It's okay, I'm fine.' Her voice emerged a touch too forceful and he glanced sharply at her.

'What's wrong?'

She raked an exasperated hand through her hair and tried to stem the words forming at the back of her mind. They came out anyway. 'You're supposed to be my enemy. And yet you brought me to one of my favourite places in the world. You're being so kind and attentive and I can't help… I…I want you.'

The transformation that occurred sent her senses reeling. From the charming, desirous dinner companion, Theo turned into a hungry predatory beast in the space of a heartbeat.

He pulled her into a dark alley between two high-rises. Her heart hammered as he held her against the wall and leaned in close.

'You don't want to say things like that to me right now, Inez,' he grated harshly.

His mouth was so tantalising close, she shut her eyes to avoid closing the gap between them and experiencing another potent kiss. 'I don't want to be saying them either. I can't seem to stop myself because it's the truth.'

'That's just the wine talking,' he replied.

She nodded then groaned when he leaned in closer. Heat from his body burned hers and his breath washed over her face. When his stubbled jaw brushed her cheek, she bit hard on her lower lip to stop another groan from escaping.

'Open your eyes, Inez.'

She shook her head. '*Nao…por favor…*'

'What are you begging me for?' he whispered in her ear.

A deep shudder coursed down her spine. 'I don't know…' She stopped and sucked in a desperate breath. 'Kiss me,' she pleaded.

With a dark moan, he touched his mouth to the corner of hers. Fleeting. Feather-light. Barely enough.

Her hands gripped his waist and held on tight. '*Please,*' she whispered.

'*Anjo*, if I start I won't be able to stop. And neither of us wants to spend the night in jail for lewd behaviour.'

She finally opened her eyes. He stood, tall, dark, devastatingly good-looking and tense, with a hunger she'd never seen in a man's eyes. That it was directed at her made her pulse race that much harder.

'Theo.' Her fingers crept up to his face, dying to touch his warm olive skin. 'Let it go. Whatever my father did, revenge would only bring you fleeting satisfaction.'

His jaw tightened but he didn't look as forbidding as he'd looked before. 'It's the only thing I've dreamed about for the last twelve years.'

Her hand crept up to settle over his heart. 'Have you stopped to think that obsessing about it may just be feeding the demons?'

One large hand settled over hers and he stared fiercely down at her. 'Are you offering me another way to quiet them, *anjo*?'

'Maybe.'

He captured her hand and planted a kiss in her palm. When he glanced down at her, a feverish light burned in his molten eyes. 'He doesn't deserve to have you as a daughter.'

'I can say the same about your parents but we play the hand that is dealt us the best way we can. And when it gets really bad I try to remember a happier time. Surely you must have some happy memories with your mother? And was your father really all bad?'

His mouth tightened. Then, slowly, he shook his head. 'No. It wasn't always bad.'

'Tell me.'

He frowned slightly. 'They thought Sakis would be their last child. I came as a surprise, or so my mother tells me. She used to call me her special boy. My father...he took me everywhere with him. He had a sports car—an Aston Martin—that I loved riding in. We'd take long drives along the coast...' He stopped and his eyes glazed over.

She kept silent, letting him relive the memories, hoping that he would find a way to soften the hard ache inside him. But when his eyes refocused, she saw the raw pain reflected in them.

'I'm not a father, and I probably never will be. But even I know those things are easy to do when life's a smooth sail. The true test comes when things get rough. I find it hard to believe that my brothers and I were ever in any way special to our parents when they turned their backs on us when we needed them most. He could've saved me, Inez—' He stopped abruptly and her heart clenched with pain for him.

'How?'

'One simple phone call to warn me and I wouldn't be here...I wouldn't be afraid of going to sleep each night because of hellish nightmares...' A deep shudder raked his tall frame.

'Oh, Theo,' she murmured. He leaned into the hand she placed on his cheek for several seconds then he pulled away and tilted her chin up.

The vulnerable man was gone. 'This changes nothing. I am what I am. Do you still want me?'

She swallowed. 'Yes.'

Something resembling relief swept through his eyes. 'You have half an hour and a lot of head-clearing air before we're back on the boat. I suggest you use that time to think carefully about whether you want this to go any further. Because, once we cross the line, there won't be any going back.'

CHAPTER TEN

THEO THREW THE reins of the launch to the waiting crew member and turned to help her out. Her bare feet hit the landing pad and she swayed a little when the boat rocked.

Contrary to her thinking he would rush her back to the boat after his pronouncement, Theo had taken his time walking her back down the streets to the promenade and onto the beach that led to the pier.

Hell, he'd even taken the time to help her out of her shoes so they could walk along the shore.

But the plaguing doubt that perhaps he didn't want her as much as her screaming senses craved him evaporated the moment she looked into his eyes.

Burnt a dark gold by volcanic desire, he stared down at her for several seconds before he demanded in a hoarse voice, 'Well?'

She licked her lips and watched his agitated exhalation. 'I still want you.'

'Are you sure? There will be no room for regret in the morning, Inez. I won't allow it.'

'I'm not drunk, Theo. Besides, I wanted you this morning and I wasn't drunk then. Or last week, or the first night we met.'

His nostrils flared as he dragged her close on the deserted lower deck. 'That first night, you felt what I felt?'

An impossible attraction that had no rhyme or reason? 'Yes,' she answered simply.

He swung her up in his arms and strode into the galley and down the steps into his large, opulent suite. Somewhere along the line, her shoes fell from her useless hands. She knew they had because her fingers were buried in his hair, and her mouth was on his by the time he kicked the door shut behind them.

Their tongues slid erotically against each other as they explored one another, his forceful, hers growing bolder by the second. Because she knew he liked it, she nipped his bottom lip with her teeth.

His deep growl echoed inside her before he pulled away. Eyes on hers, he slowly lowered her body down his sleek length. Hard muscles and firm thighs registered against her heated skin and even after her feet hit the plush carpet she held onto him, fearful she'd dissolve into a pool of need the moment she let go.

'I need to undress you,' he said raggedly.

Unable to look away from him, she nodded. The dark purple knee-length dress was form-fitting and secured by a side zip. After a couple of minutes of frustrated searching, she laughed and pointed to the hidden zip beneath her arm.

With a dark curse, he lowered it and tugged the dress over her head.

He dropped the dress. He swallowed. Then he stared so hard she stopped breathing.

'*Thee mou*, you're so beautiful,' he groaned.

The feeling suffusing her was different from her reaction to the incandescent hunger in his eyes. It was pleasure that he liked what he saw, that he might well pardon her for her inexperience.

Eager to experience more of the feeling, she reached for her bra clasp.

'No,' he commanded. He grabbed her hands and placed them on his chest. 'That's my job. *You* don't move.'

He drifted his fingers up her sides, eliciting a deep shiver that brought a satisfied smile to his lips. Her bra came undone a second later and he glanced down at her heavy breasts.

'Do you know how long I've waited to taste these?' He cupped one globe in his hand, lowered his head and flicked his wet tongue repeatedly over her nipple.

Fire scorched through her veins and her head fell back as pleasure surged high.

'Theo,' she gasped as he delivered the same treatment to her other nipple. Caught in the maelstrom of sensation, she wasn't aware her nails were digging into his pecs until he hissed against her skin.

'Take my shirt off, *querida*. I want to feel those nails on my bare skin.'

Fingers trembling, she complied with his demand, pulling the shirt off his broad shoulders and down his arms before giving in to the need to caress his bronzed skin. Heated and satin-smooth, his muscles bunched beneath her touch as she explored him.

But, much too soon, he was pulling her hands away, catching her around the waist and striding to the bed.

Depositing her in the middle of the king-sized bed, he stood staring down at her, one hand on his belt. The power and girth of him knocked the breath out of her lungs and a momentary unease sliced across her pleasure.

So far, Theo hadn't commented on her inexperience but the evidence would become glaringly apparent in a few minutes. She opened her mouth to tell him but he was crawling over the bed towards her, his intense focus paralysing her to everything but the pleasure his eyes promised.

He kissed her again, deeper, more forceful than all the times before. She gave in to her need and buried her hands in his hair, scraped her nails along his scalp and won herself a deep groan of pleasure from him. His lips moved along her jaw to nip her earlobe before going lower to explore her neck and lower.

Once again, he suckled her breasts and once again she lost the ability to think straight.

'You love that, don't you?' he observed huskily when he raised his head.

'*Sim*,' she groaned.

'There are many more pleasures, *anjo*. So many more.'

His lips trailed down her midriff…he kissed his way to the top of her panties before he gripped the flimsy material in his hands. Expecting them to be ripped off—a notion that made her wildly breathless—she was surprised when he slowly and gently lowered them down her legs and drew them off.

Equally slowly, taking his time to savour her, he kissed her from ankle to inner thigh. When his mouth skated over her secret place, her hips arched off the bed in delirious anticipation.

She'd never imagined she'd want a man to go down on her but now she couldn't imagine *not* feeling Theo's mouth on her heated core.

At the touch of his mouth, she cried out, her body twisting as pleasure scythed through her. He tasted her so very thoroughly, his tongue, teeth and lips working in perfect harmony to drive her straight out her mind.

She slid ever closer to breaking point, both fearing and yearning for what lay ahead.

Theo slipped his hands beneath her bottom and pulled her even closer to his seeking mouth. With quick expert flicks of his tongue, he sent her careening over the edge.

Her scream was an alien sound, hoarse and pleasure-ravaged, her grip on the sheets tight as she was buffeted by blissful sensation.

He continued to kiss her until she calmed, then kissed his way up her body to seal her mouth with his.

The earthy taste of her surrender seemed to trigger an even more primitive reaction in him. By the time he lifted his head, his eyes were almost black with hunger.

'Did Blanco make you feel like this?' he grated.

She shook her head. 'No.'

Satisfaction gleamed in his eyes. 'By the time I finish making you mine, you will not remember anyone else who came before me.'

Knowing he would discover her inexperience in a matter of minutes, she took a sustaining breath and blurted, 'I never slept with Constantine. Theo, I'm a virgin.'

He froze in the act of reaching for a condom. Several expressions raced over his face before he spoke. 'So I'm to be your first lover?'

She gave a jerky nod. 'Yes.'

Theo absorbed the news and tried to weigh which was the greater emotion swirling through him—shock or elation. The shock was understandable. But the elation, the fact that he was *pleased* he was to be her first? It'd never crossed his mind that she would be a virgin. But suddenly a few things fell into place. Her blushes, her furtive innocent looks, her surprise at his demanding kisses.

Another feeling rose to curl itself around his chest. Possessiveness.

The fact that he was to be her first made him want to beat his chest like a wild jungle animal. He ripped the condom packet open and stared down at her.

The look of apprehension forced him to slow down. He was moving too fast, possibly scaring her. Time to turn it down a notch.

'I'll go as slow as you want, *querida*, but I won't stop,' he warned. He couldn't. He'd come too far. He wanted her too much.

I would've kept you... Perhaps even for ever.

His own words echoed in his head and yet another emotion swept over him. If they'd met in another time, would she be the one? The idea of Inez as his wife, the mother of his children if he'd been normal, washed over him. His heart raced as he stared down at her, so beautiful, so giving.

Thee mou, what the hell was he doing wishing for the impossible? He wasn't normal...

'I don't want you to stop,' she replied. Then she performed one of those actions that illuminated her inexperience. Her gaze flicked down to his groin and she bit her lip. She had no idea how hot that little gesture made him.

A groan ripped from his chest and effectively wiped away the useless yearning.

Planting his hands on either side of her, he parted her thighs with his and settled himself at her entrance.

'Hold onto me, and feel free to dig your nails into my back if it all gets too much.' He attempted a smile and felt a touch of relief when she returned it.

The seductive bow of her mouth called to him and, leaning down, he drove his tongue between her lips. Gratifyingly, she opened up to him immediately. He deepened the kiss and swallowed her groan.

Carefully, he nudged her entrance, fed himself slowly into her wet heat.

He froze as she tensed. 'Easy, *anjo*. Relax,' he murmured soothingly against her mouth.

With a rough little sound she complied. Except now the tension was channelled into him. The feel of her closing around him threatened to tear him apart. Lying in the cradle of her hips, a sense of wonderment stole over him he'd never felt before. And he wasn't afraid to admit it scared the hell out of him.

'Theo.' She said his name with a touch of imploration and frustration that ramped up his tension. Never had he wanted to make it more right for a sexual partner.

He pushed deeper and felt the resistance of her innocence. Those nails dug in. Pleasure roared through him as he pulled back and looked into her beguiling face.

A face that held a touch of apprehension and breathless anticipation.

'Please, Theo. I want you.'

Her husky entreaty was the final straw. With a hoarsely muttered apology, he breached the flimsy barrier and buried himself deep inside her.

She made a sound of pain that pierced his heart then her head was rolling back on a long moan that echoed around the room. He waited until she had adjusted to him. Then he pulled out and rocked back in.

'*Meu deus*,' she voiced her wonder.

'Inez...' he waited until her glazed eyes focused on him, then he repeated the move '...tell me how you feel.'

'*Fantastico*,' she groaned, and Theo was sure she didn't realise she spoke her native tongue.

Her fingers spiked into his hair and when he thrust into her, she met him with a bold thrust of her own. His breath hissed out.

'You're a fast learner, *querida*.' He increased the tempo and gritted his teeth for control when she immediately matched his pace.

All too soon her back arched off the bed, her chest rising and falling in agitation as she neared her climax. Hot internal muscles rippled along his length and he shut his eyes for one split second to rein in his failing grip on reality. Leaning lower, he took one tight nipple and rolled it in his mouth. Her cry of pleasure was music to his ears. He treated its twin to the same attention then lowered himself on her. Sliding his arms under her shoulders he brought her flush against him and thrust in fast, deep movements.

She screamed once before her teeth closed over the skin on his shoulder. Deep shudders rocked through her as her bliss pulled her completely under.

She bit him harder, her nails scouring his back as she rode the unending wave.

When her head fell back towards the pillow, he raised his

head and looked at her face. The expression of wonder and ecstasy sheening her eyes finally sent him over the edge.

With a roar torn from deep inside him, he gave into the shattering release.

He clamped his mouth shut as new, confusing words threatened to burst free. Praise? Gratitude? Hell, *adoration*? When had he ever felt those emotions in connection to a woman he'd just bedded?

He buried his face in her neck and let the ripples of pleasure wash him away in silence. Until he could fathom just what the hell was going on beyond the chemical level with Inez, he intended to keep his mouth shut.

Inez slowly caressed her hands down his back, not minding at all that she was pinned to the bed by his heavy, muscled weight. Right at that moment, she couldn't think of a better way to suffocate to death. The thought made her giggle.

Theo turned his head and nuzzled her cheek. 'Not the reaction I expect after a mind-blowing orgasm but at least it's a happy sound.'

Immediately her mind turned to the dozens of women he'd pleasured before her. Hot green jealousy burned through her euphoric haze and her hands stilled.

'Hey, what did I say?' His voice rumbled through her. When she didn't immediately answer, he raised his head and stared down at her. 'Inez?'

'It's nothing important,' she replied. And it wasn't.

Earlier this evening, she'd tried to make him see a different way. But he'd refused. This thing between them would last until his vendetta with her father was satisfied. She had no business thinking about what women had come before her or who would replace her once he was done with her family and with Rio.

She endured his intent gaze until he nodded and rose. The feeling of him pulling out of her created a further emptiness inside that made her heart lurch wildly.

Deus, she needed to get a grip. Her hormones were a little askew because she had experienced her first sexual act.

No need to descend into full melt-down mode.

She watched him leave the bed, his body in part shadow in the lamp-lit room. He entered the bathroom and returned a minute later with a damp towel. When she realised his intention, she surged up and tried to reach for the towel.

'No,' he murmured softly. 'Lie back.'

Her face heating up, she slowly subsided against the pillows and allowed him to wash her.

Incredibly, the hunger returned as he gently saw to her needs and when he finally glanced back at her his nostrils were flared, a sign she'd come to recognise as a control-gathering technique.

Her nipples puckered and her body began to react to the look on his face.

'You need time to recover.'

Her body refuted that but her head knew she needed to take time to regroup. When she nodded, he looked almost disappointed. He returned the towel to the bathroom but left the light on as he came back to bed. Getting into bed, he pulled the covers over their bodies and pulled her into his arms.

She settled her hand over his chest and felt his steady heartbeat beneath her fingers. They lay there in silence until another giggle broke free from her jumbled thoughts.

'I'm beginning to get a complex, *anjo*.' He brushed his lips over her forehead.

'I believe this is the part where we make small talk after sex but I can't come up with a single subject.'

She felt his smile against her temple. 'Wrong. Normally this would be the part when I either leave or do what I just did to you all over again.'

Her heart caught. 'And?'

'I'm trying to rein in my primal instincts and not flatten you on your back again.'

Feeling bolder than was wise, Inez opened her mouth to tell him that he needn't hold it back for much longer. Instead a wide yawn took her unawares.

It was his turn to laugh. 'I think the decision on small talk has been shelved in favour of sleep.' He turned her face up to his and pressed his mouth to hers. Within seconds the kiss threatened to combust into something else. He pulled back with a groan and tucked her against him. 'Sleep, Inez. Now,' he commanded gruffly.

With a secretly pleased smile, she slid her arm around his waist, already feeling the drowsy lure of sleep encroaching.

She woke to moonlight streaming through the windows. The bedside lamp glowed and she judged that she'd been asleep for a few hours.

Beside her, Theo lay on his side, tufts of sleep-ruffled hair thrown over his forehead. In the soft lighting he looked younger and peaceful but still so damn sexy her breath caught just looking at him.

She suddenly needed to commit his likeness to paper. Her pad was next door in her suite. Slowly extracting herself from the arm he'd thrown over her, she pulled on his shirt and went to retrieve it.

Returning just as quietly, she settled herself cross-legged at the foot of the bed and began to draw. Every now and then she paused and took a breath, unable to fathom the circumstances she found herself in.

She was in bed with a man who was bent on destroying her family. And yet the overwhelming guilt she expected to feel was missing. Instead she yearned to save him from the demons that she'd glimpsed in his eyes when he spoke of his nightmares.

She swallowed as a well of sadness built inside her. Despite his outward show of invincibility she'd seen his battle. A battle he believed only revenge would win for him…

She froze as Theo made a sound. It was somewhere between a moan of pain and the bark of anger. His hand jerked out and then closed into a tight fist.

His whole body tensed for a breathless second before his chest started to rise and fall in agitated pants.

She dropped the sketchpad. 'Theo?'

'No. No! No! Thee mou, no!' The words were hoarse pleas, soaked with naked fear.

Both hands shot out in a bracing position and his head twisted from side to side.

'Theo!' She rose to her knees, unsure of what to do.

'No. Stop! *Arghh!*' With a forceful lunge, he jolted upright with a blood-curdling cry. Sweat poured down his face and he sucked in huge gulping breaths.

'*Deus*, are you okay?' The question was hopelessly inadequate but it was all she could manage at that moment. Because her heart was turning over with pain for what she'd just witnessed him go through.

She reached out and he jerked back away from her. 'Don't touch me!'

'Theo, it's me. Inez.' Tentatively, she reached out and touched his arm.

He shuddered violently and lurched away from her, staring blankly at her for several seconds before his face grew taut and haunted.

'Inez,' he said with a dark snarl. 'I fell asleep?' There was self-loathing in the question, as if he hated himself for having lowered his guard enough to let the demons in.

Her stomach flipped and her fingers curled into her palm. 'Yes. You...you had a nightmare.'

His mouth twisted with a cruel grimace. 'No kidding. What the hell are you doing here?' he snapped, looking around the room with unfocused eyes.

She frowned. 'We...um, we fell asleep together after...' She stopped as heat rushed up her face.

He turned back to her and his gaze slowly travelled over her. He brushed the hair out of his eyes and gradually the dull green lightened into golden hazel. 'We had sex. I remember now.'

She flinched and watched him with wary eyes.

With sure, predatory moves, he lifted the tangled sheet off his body and prowled to where she was poised on her knees. He stopped a hairsbreadth from her.

'Can I...can I touch you?' she asked, unwilling to have him pull away from her, but a part of her longed to soothe the turbulent blackness in his eyes.

His mouth pinched and he took several steadying breaths before he spoke. 'You want to comfort me?'

'If you'll let me.'

Another deep shudder and he closed his eyes. His head lowered until his forehead rested between her breasts. His arms closed around her and tightened so hard she couldn't move. They stayed like that until his breathing steadied.

'Theo?'

'Hmm?'

'Tell me about your dream.'

He tensed immediately and she bit her lip. He raised his head and stared at her.

'Take my shirt off,' he commanded, his voice hardly above a tortured whisper.

Concern spiked through, despite the heat his words generated. 'Theo, you just had a nightmare—'

'One I want to forget.' His hands were on the back of her thighs, hard and demanding as they caressed up to her bottom. He cupped the globes with more roughness than before but there was no pain in the caress. 'Inez, if you want to help me, do it.'

She drew the shirt over her head and dropped it. His eyes devoured her breasts and his tongue darted out to rest against his bottom lip.

Between her legs, liquid heat dampened her folds and he groaned in dark appreciation as his seeking fingers found her core.

'So ready. So tight,' he rasped. With almost effortless ease, he picked her up, pivoted off the bed and sat on the side. Grabbing a condom, he slipped it on and positioned her legs on either side of him.

'You will *make* me forget.' The words were almost a plea but with a promise of things to come. 'Yes?'

Before she could do so much as nod, he pressed her down on top of him. She cried out as he filled her with his hot, heavy length. His hard grip on her hips controlled the rhythm, which grew more frantic with each thrust.

'Theo,' she gasped as pleasure scalded her insides and rushed her towards ecstasy.

'Shh, no talking,' he instructed.

Biting her lip, she stared into his face.

Torment, anger, pleasure and more than a dose of anxiety mingled into an oddly fascinating tableau. He was still caught up in the hell of his nightmare and her heart broke over his anguish.

She tried to catch his gaze, to transmit a different sort of comfort from the carnal that he clearly sought but he avoided her eyes. Instead he buried his face between her breasts and mercilessly teased her nipples until she whimpered at the torture.

He increased his thrusts, bouncing her on top of him with almost superhuman strength that had her reeling.

Her orgasm crashed into her, flattening her under its fierce onslaught before proceeding to completely drown her.

Through the thunderous rush in her ears, she heard his guttural roar as he achieved his own ruthless release.

Sweat slicked their skin and their breaths rushed in and out in frantic pants. This time, though, there were no pleasurable caresses and giggling was the last thing she felt like doing.

With lithe grace, he twisted around and deposited her on the bed. Without speaking, he strode into the bathroom.

Inez lay on the bed, grappling with what had just happened. In the last twenty-four hours she'd glimpsed the man tortured by his nightmares, had seen a side to Theo she was certain very few people saw. Instead of guarding her own heart, she wanted to open herself up even more to him, find a way of taking away his pain and torment.

Had she not learnt her lesson with Constantine?

No, Theo was nothing like that man who'd taken delight in humiliating her. The retraction Theo had promised had appeared in the online evening edition of the newspaper and she was sure she'd seen a look of contrition in his eyes when he'd watched her read it.

Darkness and light.

She was deeply, almost irreversibly attracted to both. Again her heart twisted and she looked towards the bathroom.

A crash came a second later, followed by a pithy curse. She was off the bed and running into the bathroom before she could think twice.

'I'm fine!' he ground out.

She hesitated in the doorway and watched him. His fingers were curled around the marble sink and his head was bent forward. 'What's wrong, Theo?'

'Dammit, woman, I'm not made of glass. And I've been grappling with my nightmares long before you came along, so leave me alone!'

Hurt shredded her inside. 'Don't push me away.'

He locked eyes with her in the mirror and sighed. 'You're too stubborn for your own good, you know that?'

'Maybe, but before you throw me out I need the bathroom,' she lied.

'Fine; it's all yours.'

He started to turn. That was when she saw his scars. '*Meu deus*, what happened to you?' she whispered raggedly.

His glance ripped from her face to where she pointed to his left hip. The marks were puckered and too evenly spaced and shaped to be an accident. But still her mind couldn't grasp the idea that someone had deliberately inflicted pain on him.

'You mean you haven't guessed already, *querida*? *Your father* happened.'

CHAPTER ELEVEN

INEZ STAGGERED BACKWARDS until her legs hit the vanity unit and she collapsed onto it. 'I don't...you're saying my *father* did this to you?' She shook her head in fierce disbelief.

Theo's mouth twisted. 'Not personally, no. He hired thugs to do it.'

She felt the blood drain from her head. Had she not been seated, she would've swayed under the unbelievable accusation.

'But...why?'

He grabbed a towel and secured it around his waist. 'You did your research on my family. You know what happened to my father.'

She nodded. 'He was indicted for fraud, bribery and embezzlement.'

'Among other things. He was also involved with some extremely shady people.'

He turned and strode from the bathroom.

She followed him, the fear she'd harboured for a long time blooming in her chest. 'And my father was one of these shady people?'

Theo turned and watched her. Shocked knowledge flared in her eyes. For a brief moment, he sympathised with what she was going through. Having the truth blown up in front of you wasn't easy.

In his deepest, darkest moments he still couldn't believe how painfully raw he felt at his father's abandonment.

'My father owed him a lot of money on some crooked scheme they were working on when he was arrested and all our assets were frozen. Your father took exception to being out of pocket. When he realised he wouldn't be paid, he decided to pursue a different route.'

Her haunted eyes dropped to the scars covered by the towel and quickly looked away.

'So I'm here to pay for my father's sins,' she whispered raggedly.

That had initially been his plan. Somewhere along the line that particular plan had become questionable. But he'd be damned before he'd admit that.

'Your father made me pay for my father's. Money and power were his bottom line, and he wanted payback. Nothing else mattered to him, not even the tortured screams of a frightened boy...'

He compressed his lips as her mouth dropped open and anguish creased her face. 'How old were you?'

He raked a hand through his hair. Even as a voice shrieked in his head to stop baring his raw wounds, he was opening his mouth.

'I was seventeen. I was returning from a night out with friends when his goons grabbed me. He had me smuggled from Athens to Spain and threw me into a hole on some abandoned farm in Madrid. Ari found me there two weeks after I was taken. After he damned near bled every single cent he could find from every relative and casual acquaintance in order to stump up the two million dollars ransom that your father demanded.'

Her hands flew to her head, her fingers spiking through the long tresses to grip them in a convulsive stranglehold. 'Please tell me when you say a *hole*...you don't mean that *literally*?' The words were a desperate plea, as if she didn't want to believe how real the monster that was her father.

His smile cracked his lips. 'Oh, yes, *anjo*. A twelve-foot-deep *literal* hole in the ground with vertical sides and no hand or footholds. No light. No heat. One meal a day with a bucket for my necessaries.'

'No...'

'*Yes!* And you know what his men did for *fun* when they were bored?'

She shook her head wildly, her eyes wide and horror-struck as he loosened the towel from around his waist and exposed his puckered skin. 'Cigar tattoos, they called them.'

Tears welled in her eyes and fell down her cheeks. Still shaking her head, she walked to the bed and sank down on it. She buried her face in her hands and a gut-wrenching sob ripped from her throat. After the first one, they came thick and fast.

His chest tightened with emotions he was very loath to name. Each sob caught him on the raw, until he couldn't bear to hear another one.

'Inez! Stop crying,' he instructed hoarsely after five minutes.

She shook her head and sniffled some more.

'Stop it or I'll throw you overboard and you can swim to shore.'

That got her attention. She brushed her hands across her cheeks and speared him with wide, imploring eyes.

'If the only people you saw were his men, how did you know it was my father?'

He couldn't fault her for trying to find a different reality to the one he'd smashed her world with. Hell, he'd done that for a long time after his father had been indicted. 'I followed the money.'

She frowned. 'What?'

'I traced the ransom my brother paid through dummy corporations and offshore accounts. It took a few years but I finally found where it ended up.'

'In my father's account?'

'Yes. And since then I've made it my business to find out how every single cent was spent.'

Her shoulders slumped and tears welled again. He could tell the ground had well and truly shifted beneath her feet.

After several seconds, she raised her head.

'Okay. I'll do whatever you want. For however long you want.'

It was his turn to feel the ground shift under his feet. Shock slammed through him as he realised just how much he wanted to take her. To hang onto her.

But not for the sake of revenge. For an altogether different reason; because he wanted her. Not for her father but *for her*.

He shook his head. 'Inez...'

'I can never buy back those two weeks that were taken from you or the horror you've had to live with. But I can try and find a way to make up for what was done to you.'

'How? By giving me your body whenever and wherever I ask for it?'

She paled a little. But the brave, spirited woman he'd come to see underneath all that false gloss raised her chin. 'If that's what you want.'

His mouth twisted. 'I don't want a damned sacrificial lamb. And I sure as hell don't want you throwing yourself on your sword for that bastard's sake!'

'Then what do you want? You have his company. His campaign is falling apart. He will be left with nothing by the time you're done with him. How much more suffering do you need before you let go of this anger? When will you feel pacified?'

Theo started to answer, then realised he had no answer. The satisfaction he'd thought he'd feel was hollowly absent, as was the deep-seated sense of triumph he'd always thought he would feel when this moment came.

Looking into her face, he saw the pain and confusion reflected there and his puzzlement increased. The ground was still tilting beneath his feet but he'd been on this path for too long to let go.

Hadn't he?

He forced his gaze to meet hers.

'I will let you know when I'm adequately appeased.'

Over the next week, she watched as he slowly dismantled her father's campaign piece by piece. Allegations of impropriety surfaced, triggering an investigation. Although nothing was found to indict Benedicto, his credibility suffered a death blow and any meaningful points he'd managed to retain in the polls dropped to nothing.

On the Monday morning after returning from their sailing trip, the calls to her cell phone started. Both her father and Pietro bombarded her with messages and texts, demanding to know what was going on.

She hadn't needed Theo to warn her not to take their calls. After his revelation, each time she saw her father's name pop up on her screen, her stomach churned with pain and disgust.

Although she'd long suspected that her father's business dealings weren't as pure as the driven snow, she'd never in her wildest dreams entertained the idea that he would condone the brutality that Theo had described. Each time she saw his scars—and she'd seen them every night since their return, when he'd moved her into his suite—a merciless vice had squeezed her heart.

And that vice had tightened every time he'd cried out in the middle of the night after another nightmare.

She'd been surprised that first night after their return when he'd pulled her close after a fiery lovemaking and instructed her to go to sleep.

When he kept her with him the following night, she'd boldly asked him why.

'I don't want to be alone,' he'd stated baldly. And each time he'd come awake he'd reached for her, wrapping his trembling body around her and holding on tight until his nightmare receded and his breathing returned to normal.

More and more, her foolish heart had begun to believe that her presence was making the nightmares, if not any less horrific, then at least tolerable.

Or she could just be living in a fantasy land where her mind and heart had no idea what language the other was speaking. Because she was beginning to believe that her heart was more involved in Theo's welfare than was wise. And yet she couldn't control it enough to make it stop wrenching in pain when he suffered another nightmare, or soar with joy when he took her to the heights of ecstasy. Even the knowledge that some time in the very near future, after his goal to destroy her father was achieved, Theo would pack up his bags and leave Rio for good, made her heart ache in a way that was almost a physical pain.

Santa Maria, she was losing her mind—

'There you are. Teresa told me you're still here. I thought you'd be at the centre by now.' She'd shared more details of her volunteer work with him during the times when he'd been *Normal Theo*, not *Revenge Theo*. And she'd been ridiculously thrilled when he hadn't been judgemental or condescending.

She looked up as he entered the living room and crossed to where she sat, applying finishing touches to the sketch she'd been working on since breakfast an hour ago. She'd thought he'd left for the day but obviously she'd been mistaken.

Glancing up at his lean, solid frame and gorgeous face, her heart performed that painfully giddy flip again and she glanced away. 'I took a day off. I'm…I'm still thinking of resigning.'

He stilled then dropped to his haunches in front of her. 'Why?'

She struggled to breathe as his scent surrounded her, making her yearn to lean in closer. 'This whole thing with my father has brought unwanted attention to people who are already struggling with life's difficulties. I don't think it's fair on the children.'

A look resembling regret passed through his eyes before he blinked it away. After a full minute, he murmured, 'No, it's not. But you won't resign.'

Her heart caught. 'Why not?'

'Because I won't allow you to give up something you love doing. The publicity about your father will go away. I'll make sure of it.'

She met mesmerising hazel eyes. 'Why are you doing this?'

He shrugged. 'Perhaps I'm beginning to realise that I was mistaken about how much collateral damage I was prepared to accept.'

Collateral damage. She was grappling with that when he spoke again.

'I have something for you.'

She glanced warily at him. 'Beware of Greeks bearing gifts. I'm sure I've read that warning somewhere.'

His smile held a certain chill but was heart-stopping nonetheless. 'For the most part, I'd urge you to heed that warning. But this one is completely harmless.' He pulled something from his back pocket and presented it to her. The look in his eyes made her stomach flip as she glanced from his face to the box.

'What is it?' she asked.

'Open it and see.'

She opened the velvet case and gaped at the platinum-linked, three-tiered diamond choker nestling between the two catches.

'Are you trying to make some sort of *macho* statement?'

He shook his head in confusion. 'Sorry, *anjo,* you've lost me.'

'This is a *choker.* You want everyone to see that you own me?'

He frowned. 'What the hell are you talking about?'

'Why a choker? Why not a simple diamond pendant?'

'I asked my jeweller to send a few pieces. I liked the look of that one. So I chose it. No big deal, no mind games. I thought you'd like it,' he finished tersely.

She bit her lip and wondered if she was reading too much into it. Much like she was reading far too much into her feelings for Theo and what would happen when things ended.

'It's a beautiful piece of jewellery. But frankly it's a bit ostentatious for my taste.' She snapped the box shut and held it out to him. 'Besides, since my role as paparazzi bait is over, I don't see where I would wear something like that.'

His jaw tightened and he pushed the box back at her. 'I was just coming to that. Ari is getting married next weekend. You're coming with me as my plus one.'

She couldn't stop her mouth from gaping open any more than she could stop breathing. 'You want me to drop everything and fly to Greece with you?'

'I'm sure you can work something out with the charity. I'm happy to make a donation to cover your absence if you like.'

'I…'

'And we're not going to Greece. Ari and Perla are getting married at their resort in Bermuda.'

'Different continent, same response.'

His eyes narrowed. 'Do I need to remind you that we're only three weeks into our agreement?'

Her fingers trembled and she threw the box down on the sofa. 'No, you don't need to remind me. Call me foolish, but I thought we were getting beyond that.'

'I'm trying to, Inez.'

'Then ask me nicely. For all you know, I may be busy next weekend and would need to rearrange my plans for you.'

He raised an eyebrow. 'Busy doing what?'

'Splitting the atom. Shaving my legs. Rehearsing to join a

circus troupe. What does it matter? You didn't bother to ask. You only brought me trinkets and ordered me to be ready to fly off to Bermuda.' Her mouth trembled and she firmed it.

'You're angry.'

'You're very observant.'

'Tell me why.'

She laughed. Even to her ears it sounded as if it could've easily cut glass. His eyes narrowed as she shook her head. 'What would be the point?'

'The point would be that I would listen.'

She placed her feet on the carpet and tried to stand. He caught her hips and kept her seated in front of him.

This close she could see the hypnotic gold flecks in his eyes. She wanted to drown in them. Wanted to drown in him. She tried to calm her racing pulse.

His gaze dropped to her mouth, then down to her chest and a different sort of fever took hold of her.

'That necklace—'

'Is just a necklace. I thought I'd give it to you now so you could get an outfit to match for the wedding.'

'And the trip?'

'I need a plus one. I need *you*. And you can hate me if you want but I'm not prepared to leave you here so Benedicto can hound you.'

'I can take care of myself.'

His eyes narrowed. 'I don't doubt that. But can you tell me that he won't view your refusal to take his calls this last week as a betrayal?'

Her heart skittered. 'And you think he'll harm me in some way?'

He glanced meaningfully at her arm, then back to her face. 'Sorry, *anjo*, I'm not prepared to take that chance.'

Darkness and light. Tenderness and ruthlessness. It was what kept her emotions on a knife-edge where this man was concerned.

'Will you come to Bermuda with me? Please?'

She glanced at the velvet box. 'I will. But I'm not wearing that necklace.'

'Fine. We'll find you something else.'

'I don't need anything—' Her argument died on her lips when he picked up her sketchpad. She grabbed at it but he held it out of her reach. 'Theo, hand it over.' She breathed a secret sigh of relief when her panic didn't bleed through her voice.

'You're supposed to be designing me a boat.'

'I'm still working on it. I'll show it to you when it's done.'

His gaze brushed her face and settled on her mouth. The intensity of it made her insides contract. After a minute he handed the pad over and rose. 'I look forward to it. We're dining in tonight. I'm in the mood for an early night.'

He left the room just as silently as he'd entered. She realised her fingers were clamped white around her sketchpad and slowly relaxed them.

She flipped through the pages until she came to the one she'd been drawing. It was one of many featuring Theo asleep. She stared at it, seeing the vulnerability and gentleness in his face that he covered up so efficiently when he was awake. When he was asleep he was all light, no darkness. There was a boyishness about him that she only caught rare glimpses of during the day.

Darkness and light. Unfortunately, her heart refused to be picky about which it preferred because, awake or asleep, Theo had captured her emotions so efficiently she was beginning to fear she was falling in love with him.

The nightmare started the way it always did. A glow of light signalled the men's arrival. Followed by the rope ladder and the heavy descent of thick boots, tree trunk thighs and towering thugs.

Each time he'd fought back. A few times he'd landed blows of his own. But each time they'd eventually overpowered him. The tallest, toughest one, the one who favoured those smelly cigars, always laughed. It was the laughter not the pain that triggered his screams. It was a never-ending grating sound that churned through his gut and tripped his heart rate into overdrive.

He felt the scream build in his throat and readied himself for the roar.

Gentle but firm hands shook him awake.

'Theo...*querido!*'

He kept his eyes shut and reached for her, holding on tight as the images receded. The irony of it wasn't lost on him, the thought of how much he now needed the daughter of the man who was responsible for reducing him to a helpless wreck night after night for the last twelve years.

As he held on to her the thought that had plagued him for several days now took hold. He no longer wanted to pursue this vendetta. Yesterday, he'd found himself requesting that the board vote a different way to what he'd originally planned. They'd been stunned. He'd been twice as stunned.

He'd mentally shrugged and told himself there was no reason to turn his back on a healthy profit but he'd known he'd changed his mind for a different reason.

Benedicto was all but finished.

But ending it now would mean Inez would be free to walk away from him. And the very thought of that made him break out in a cold sweat.

He'd managed to buy himself a little more time by persuading her to come with him to Ari's wedding.

After that...

His insides churned as he lay in the darkness and felt her soft hands soothe him.

He pushed away thoughts he wasn't brave enough yet to truly examine.

'*Querido*, are you awake?' she breathed softly.

His heart flipped and his arms tightened convulsively around her soft, warm body. 'I'm awake, *anjo*.'

'I'm not an angel, Theo.'

'You are.'

'If I were an angel, I'd have the power to banish your nightmares,' she replied in a voice fraught with pain.

It took several seconds to realise she ached for him.

Pulling back, he stared into her face.

'You didn't do this to me, Inez.'

Her eyes clouded. 'I know. But that doesn't mean I don't wish you healed.'

His smile felt skewed. 'There's no cure for me, sweetheart,' he said, although he was beginning to doubt that. Just as he was beginning to think that the answer lay right there in his arms. If only there was a way...

'Are you sure? There's therapy—'

'Tried it. Didn't work,' he replied. When he heard the curtness in his voice he soothed an apologetic hand down her back.

She relaxed against him and he buried his face in her hair and breathed her in.

'What happened?'

'What, with the therapy?'

She nodded.

He slowly opened his eyes and stared into the middle distance. 'They spoke about triggers, breathing techniques and anxiety-detectors. There was mention of electro-shock therapy or good old-fashioned pills. I never went back for a second session.'

Her head snapped up. 'You mean all that was at your first session?'

He smiled and kissed her gaping mouth. 'I believed what was wrong with me couldn't be fixed by therapy.'

'*Believed?*'

He realised what he'd said and his breath caught. Was he grasping at straws where there were none?

'I'm beginning to think things aren't as hopeless for me, *anjo*.'

She paled a little but continued to hold his gaze. Slowly,

she nodded. Her luxuriant hair spilled over her shoulder onto his chest as she stared into his eyes. 'I really hope you find closure one day, Theo.'

Simple, frank words, said from the heart. But they froze his insides as surely and as swiftly as an arctic wind froze water.

Because he was seriously doubting that he would ever find peace without this woman in his arms.

CHAPTER TWELVE

THEY BOARDED THEO'S private jet late the next Friday. The moment they stepped on board, Inez sensed something was wrong.

Theo paced up and down, his agitation growing the closer they got to take-off.

When the pilot came through, Theo sent a piercing glance at him and the man hurried into the cockpit.

'Theo, sit down. You're making your pilot nervous.'

He barked out a short laugh and threw himself into the long sofa opposite her chair. His fingers drummed repeatedly on the armrest. 'Don't worry; he's used to it.'

'Used to what?'

'My aversion to enclosed spaces,' he answered tersely.

'Your claustrophobia.' Her heart squeezed as she watched his fingers grip the armrest and the skin around his mouth pale.

Unbuckling her seat belt, she crossed to the sofa and sat down next to him. A sheen of sweat coated his forehead and when his eyes sought hers she read the anxiety in them. Reaching around him, she secured his seat belt then took care of her own as the plane taxied onto the runway.

Taking the arm closest to hers, she pulled it over her shoulder and settled herself against him. He tugged her close immediately, his breathing harsh and uneven.

She hugged him harder, and when he tilted her face up to his she went willingly.

He kissed her with a desperation that tore through her soul. For long, anxiety-filled minutes, he took what she offered, until the need for air drove them apart.

'You get that we cannot kiss all the way to Bermuda, don't you?' she said, laughing.

'Is that a challenge? Because I bet I can,' he threw back with a heart-stopping smile.

Inez noticed that his breathing was no longer agitated and breathed a sigh of relief.

'No, it's not a challenge.' She rested her head on his shoulder and caressed his hard jaw. 'How do you normally get through flying?'

His jaw tightened for a second before he relaxed. 'Mild sleeping pills before take-off normally does the trick.'

'Why not today?'

'You're here,' he said simply. After a minute, he asked, 'Why are you helping me?'

'I cannot forget that my father did this to you. And no, I'm not offering myself as a sacrificial lamb. But I don't want to see you suffer either. I want to help any way I can.'

The reminder that her father loomed large between them grated more than he wanted to admit. 'For how long?' Theo demanded more harshly than he'd intended.

She stiffened. 'Sorry?'

'Are you counting the days until I set you free?' he pressed.

Her eyelids swooped down, concealing her expression. 'I...we have an agreement—'

'Damn the agreement. If you had a choice now, today, would you stay or would you leave?'

'Theo—'

'Answer the question, Inez.'

'I'd choose to stay...'

The bubble of joy that started to grow inside him burst when he registered her flat tone. 'But?'

'But... this could never go anywhere.'

A sense of helplessness blanketed him. 'Why not? Because I blackmailed you?'

She shook her head. 'No. Because a relationship between us would be impossible.'

Theo's vision blurred at her words. He'd pushed her too far. Hung onto his vendetta for too long. His mouth soured with ashen hopelessness. 'I guess we both know where we stand.'

When she moved away, he fought not to pull her back. She stayed close—out of pity? His mouth curled. He told himself he didn't care but the voice in his head mocked him.

He cared, much more than he'd bargained for when he'd forced her to make that stupid choice. The idea of her walking away from him made his insides knot with a pain far greater than he'd ever known.

The plane hit a pocket of turbulence, throwing her against him. When she stayed close, he let her. Forcefully, he reminded himself of one thing.

He'd never meant to keep her for ever.

The Pantelides Bermuda resort was a breathtaking jewel set amid swaying palm trees and sugar-white sand. The sun beat down on them as Theo drove the open-top Jeep towards their villa.

Stunning buildings connected by dark wooden bridges under which the most spectacular water features had been constructed made for a visual masterpiece. All round them bold colour burst free in a heady mix of blues, greens and yellows that begged to be touched.

Their sprawling whitewashed villa featured high ceilings, cool tiled floors and a four-poster bed that dominated the master bedroom.

A tense Theo who hadn't said more than a dozen words

to her since they landed, instructed the porter to place their cases in the master bedroom and tipped the man before walking outside onto the large wooden deck.

'There's a barbecue later this afternoon. Perla thought we might want to rest before then. You can go ahead and rest if you want to. I'll go and catch up with Sakis and Ari.'

He walked away from her and headed out of the door.

The clear indication that she wasn't welcome stung, although why she was surprised was beyond her.

He'd held ajar the possibility of continuing this thing between them and she'd slammed the door shut.

A small part of her was proud she hadn't grasped the suggestion with both hands, while the larger part, the part that had fallen head over heels in love with Theo in spite of all the chaos surrounding them, reeled with heart-wrenching pain at what the future held.

But, as she'd told herself over and over again on the plane as he'd shut his eyes and surprisingly dozed off, she was taking the right steps now to prevent even more heartache later.

Because there was no way Theo would ever reconcile himself to having her as a constant reminder. Certainly not enough to love her.

The reality was that they'd fallen into bed as a result of some crazy chemistry. Chemistry fizzled out. Eventually, the constant reminder that a part of her was responsible for his inner demons and outer scars would grate and rip at whatever remained after the chemistry was gone.

He was better off without her.

Her heart protested loudly at that decision. Ignoring it, she went into the bedroom and lifted her case onto the bed. The cream sheath she'd bought for the wedding needed to be hung out before it creased beyond repair.

Unzipping her case, she opened it and froze. A red velvet box, similar to the black one Theo had presented her with a few days ago lay on top of her clothes.

With shaky hands she picked it up and opened it. The stunning necklace sparkling in the sunlight made her gasp.

The platinum chain had a small loop at one end, with a large teardrop diamond at the other that slipped easily through the hoop. The design was simple and elegant. And so utterly gorgeous she couldn't stop herself from caressing the flawless stone.

Swallowing a lump in her throat at the thoughtfulness behind the necklace, she jumped when a knock came at the door. Thinking it was Theo who'd forgotten to take a key, she opened the door with a smile.

Only to stop when confronted by two stunningly beautiful women, one of whom was heavily pregnant, while the other carried a small baby in her arms.

'Sorry to descend on you like this, only Theo was a bit vague about whether you were actually resting or if you were up for a visit.' The women exchanged glances. 'I've never seen him so scatty, have you?' the pregnant redhead asked the blue-eyed blonde.

'Nope, normally he's quick off the mark with those hopeless one-liners. Today, not so much. Anyway, we thought we'd come on the off-chance that you were *not* resting and say hello…oh, my God, that necklace is gorgeous!' The redhead reached out and traced a manicured forefinger over the diamond.

Then she looked up, noticed Inez's open-mouthed gaze and laughed. 'Sorry, I'm Perla soon-to-be Pantelides. This is Brianna Pantelides, Sakis's wife. And this little heartbreaker is Dimitri.'

'I'm Inez da Costa. I'm a…' she paused, for the first time holding up her relationship with Theo to the harsh light of day and coming up short on explanations '…business associate of Theo's.'

The two women exchanged another glance and she rushed to cover the awkward silence. 'Please, come in.'

Brianna paused. 'Are you sure?'

'*Sim*...yes, I'm sure. I was just unpacking...' she started and noticed Perla's frown.

'Why are you doing that yourself? We have two butlers and three villa staff attached to each residence.'

'I think Theo sent them away,' she said, then bit her lip as Perla's eyebrows shot upward.

'Did he? Ari did that once too, when we first arrived here four months ago. Then we proceeded to have an almighty row.' She smiled at the memory and placed her hand lovingly over her swollen belly.

Brianna laughed and walked to the sofa. Settling herself down, she opened her shirt and adjusted her son for a feed.

Perla sat on the sofa too and they both stared back at her. Their open curiosity made her nape tingle.

'We won't keep you long. I just wanted to run the itinerary by you because, frankly, I don't trust the men with the information. We have a casual dinner tonight, followed by a quick rehearsal. Most of the guests arrive in the morning and the wedding is at three o'clock, okay?'

'Okay.' She ventured a smile and Brianna's eyes widened.

'Gosh, you're stunning! How did you meet Theo again?'

'Brianna!' Perla admonished with a laugh.

'What?'

Inez fiddled with the clasp of the velvet box and pushed down the well of sadness that surged from nowhere. These two women were not only almost family, they were friends too. Whereas her family was in utter chaos and she had no friends to speak of.

She forced another smile. 'He had some business in Rio. I was...am helping him out with it.'

'Right. Okay.' Perla struggled upright and nudged Brianna. 'We'll leave you alone. I think the guys are rowing in about an hour. It's an experience you don't want to miss if you've never seen it before.'

Brianna gently dislodged her drowsy baby from her

breast and laid him on her shoulder, gently patting his back as she stood.

The door opened as they neared it and Theo's large frame filled the doorway.

His gaze zeroed in on her, then dropped to the box still clutched in her hand before coming back up. Her throat dried at the sight of him and the ever present tingle that struck her deep within flared heat outward.

'Um, Theo?' Perla ventured.

'What?' he snapped without taking his eyes from Inez.

'You need to move from the doorway so we can leave.'

He snorted under his breath and entered the villa. He turned with his hand on the door, causing Brianna to roll her eyes. 'We've given Inez the schedule so you have no excuse to be late.'

'I'm never late.'

'Yeah, right. You were almost two hours late for Perla's engagement party and an hour late for Dimitri's christening.'

'Which therefore means I'll only be half an hour late for this wedding. Now, please go and pester your other halves and leave me alone.'

The women grumbled as they left. He turned from the door with a smile on his face but it slowly dimmed as his gaze connected with hers.

'Did they harass you?' he asked, a touch of wary concern in his eyes.

She shook her head. 'No. They were lovely.'

'I don't know about lovely but I tolerate them.' Contrary to his words, his voice held a fondness that made her chest tighten.

Theo understood family. Enough that he'd been devastated when his had been broken. And yet he'd wanted to rip hers apart.

Despite understanding the reason behind his motives, the thought still hurt deeply.

'Inez?'

She turned sharply and headed back to the bedroom. He followed and grabbed her wrist as she reached out to set the box down.

'What's wrong?'

Her throat clogged. 'What *isn't* wrong?'

His eyes narrowed. 'If Brianna or Perla said something to upset you—'

'No, I told you they were wonderful! They were kind and funny and...and incredible.' Tears threatened and she swallowed hard.

'You only met them for twenty minutes.'

'It was enough.'

'Enough for what?'

'Enough to know that I want what they have. And that I'll probably never have it. So far my record has been beyond appalling.'

He frowned. 'You don't have a record.'

'Constantine used me to get dirt on my father and—'

'I don't want you to say his name in my presence,' he interrupted harshly.

'And what about you? You make me hope for things I have no right to hope for, Theo. What sort of fool does that make me?'

'No, you're not a fool. You're one of the bravest, most loyal people I know.' He said the words gravely. 'It is I who is the fool.'

Theo's words echoed through her mind as she watched the brothers row in perfect harmony across the almost still resort water a short while later.

He took the middle position with Sakis in front and Ari at the back. She watched, spellbound, as his shoulders rippled with smooth grace and utmost efficiency.

'Aren't they something to watch?' Perla sighed wistfully.

'*Sim*,' she agreed huskily.

'I think they do that just to get us girls all hot and bothered,' Brianna complained but Inez noticed that she didn't take her eyes off her husband for one second.

When the men eventually returned to shore, the two women joined them and were immediately enfolded into the group.

Theo glanced her way, a touch of irritation in his eyes. Seconds later, he broke away from the group and came towards her.

'I didn't expect you to be down here. You should be resting.'

'I was invited. I hope I'm not intruding.'

'If you were invited then you're not intruding. Come and join us.' He grabbed her hand and led her to where Ari and Sakis were turning over the boat to dry the underside.

The two brothers gave her cursory glances but barely spoke to her. When Ari abruptly asked Theo to accompany him to the boat shed, her stomach fell.

Perla organised a Jeep to take her back to their villa and when Theo returned half an hour later, his jaw was tight and his movements jerky as he swept her off her feet and strode into the bedroom.

He made love to her with a fierce, silent passion that robbed her of speech and breath before he clamped her to his side and slid into sleep.

Her eyes filled with tears and she hurriedly brushed them away. It was no use daydreaming that things would ever magically turn rosy between her and Theo.

As much as she wanted to wish otherwise, they were on a countdown to being over for good.

The wedding was beautiful and quietly elegant in a way only an events organiser extraordinaire like Perla could achieve despite being seven months pregnant. Inez watched the bride and groom dance across the polished floor of the casino, transformed into a spectacular masterpiece that stood directly on the water, and fought the feelings rampaging through her.

Theo would never be hers. She would never have a wedding like this or have him gazing at her the way Ari was gazing at his new wife.

She would never feel the weight of his baby in her belly or have it suckle at her breast.

Despair slowly built inside her, despite knowing deep down that Theo had done her a favour by bringing her here. He didn't need her to save him from whatever nightmares plagued him. He had a family that clearly adored him, who would be there for him when he chose to let them in.

She needed to stop moping and get on with her life.

Her time in Theo's house and his bed was over. In retrospect, she was thankful she'd let him talk her into keeping her volunteer position. It was a lifeline she was grateful for in a world skidding out of control. The things she couldn't control she would learn to live without.

A tall figure danced into her view and her eyes connected with the man who occupied an astonishingly large percentage of her mind. In his arms was an elegantly dressed woman with greying brown hair and a sad expression. She said something to him and he glanced down at her. His smile was gentle but wary and Inez saw her sadness deepen.

Inez heard the soft gurgle of a baby over the music and turned to see Brianna next to her. 'That's their mother.' She nodded to Theo's dance partner. 'Their relationship has been fraught but I think they're all finding their way back to each other.' She glanced at Inez with a smile. 'I hope that you two find your way too.'

Inez shook her head. 'I'm afraid that's impossible.'

Brianna laughed. 'Believe me, I've seen the impossible happen in this family. I've learned not to rule anything out.' She smiled down at her child and danced away with him towards her husband.

Tears stung her eyes as she watched Sakis enfold his wife and son in his arms.

'What's wrong now?' Theo's deep voice sounded in her ear.

She blinked rapidly and pasted a smile on her face. 'Nothing. Weddings...they make me emotional. That's all.'

His eyes narrowed speculatively on her face before he took hold of her elbow. 'Dance with me.'

He led her to the dance floor and pulled her close.

'You have a big family,' she said, more for something to fill the silence.

'They can be a pain in the rear sometimes.'

'Regardless, you all seem to watch out for each other.'

He shrugged. 'Force of habit.'

'No, it's not. Does Ari know who I am?'

His mouth tightened. 'He suspects. I didn't enlighten or deny because it's none of his business. He's welcome to draw his own conclusions. Why do you ask?'

'Because he's been watching me like a hawk since we got here and he hasn't spoken more than two words to me. That's what I mean. What you have with your brothers isn't habit. It's love.'

His mouth twisted in a way that evidenced his dark pain.

'*Love* hasn't conquered the nightmares that have plagued me for all these years, Inez.' The raw pain in his voice made her throat clog. She forced a swallow.

'Because you haven't allowed it to. You resisted any attempt at help because you thought you had to face this demon alone, do things your way.'

The honest barb struck home. He was silent for the rest of the song. Then abruptly he spoke. 'I didn't want to appear weak. I hated myself every time I couldn't walk into a dark room or down an unlit street. I haven't been able to cope with the smell of cigars without breaking out in a cold sweat. Do you know what that feels like?' he asked in a harsh undertone.

She shook her head. 'No, but I know it will never go away if you keep it buried.'

Her warmth, her strength hit him hard and he wanted to reach for her with all he had. Suddenly, everything he'd ever craved, ever wished for seemed coalesced in the woman before him.

'It's no longer buried. A month ago I was still the messed-up boy Ari dug up from that hole twelve years ago. But you did something about that.'

'No, I'm not responsible for that.'

His hand cupped her nape and he whispered fiercely in her ear. 'You are. You've seen me, Inez. I can't sleep with the lights off. I used to panic whenever someone shut a door behind me. That's why I surrounded myself with glass. With you by my side I flew here with no need for sleeping pills.'

'Even though you refused to speak to me for hours.'

He exhaled. 'Things are upside down and inside out right now. Let's just…we'll get through this wedding and head back to Rio. And we will damn well fix this thing between us. Because I'm not prepared to let you go yet.'

CHAPTER THIRTEEN

'I TOLD YOU, you're so much better than a damn sleeping pill.'

Inez laughed as Theo tugged her dress down and lifted her out of it. Leaving it on the floor of the master cabin bedroom, he waited for her to kick her shoes off before he crossed over to the bed. The diamond pendant he'd looked incredibly pleased that she'd worn lay nestled between her breasts.

'Keep that on,' he instructed, just as the plane jerked through turbulence and they fell onto the bed together, a tangle of hard and soft limbs and hot, needy kisses.

'I'm glad I have my uses,' she said, laughing, when he let her up for air.

His face grew serious as he stared down at her. 'You've attained the ultimate purpose in my life, *querida*. Now more than ever you're my saviour: *my* angel.' He cradled her head as he kissed her.

Inez closed her eyes and imagined that she could feel his soul through his reverent kiss. She studiously ignored the voice that mocked that she was deluding herself.

When he finished undressing her with gentle hands, she tried to stem her tears as he made love to her with a greedy passion that touched her very soul.

Afterwards she held him in her arms as he fell asleep. Unable to sleep, her mind drifted back to the wedding.

Theo had introduced her to his mother and again she'd witnessed the sadness in her eyes. When he'd hugged her at the end of the evening and murmured gently into her ear, his mother had burst into tears. Inez had watched as the brothers closed around her and soothed her tears.

She was still watching them when Ari had glanced her way. His measured smile and thoughtful nod in her direction had made her swallow. It hadn't been acceptance but it hadn't been the chilly reception he'd given her either.

As they'd packed to leave, Inez had asked Theo about what had happened with his mother.

'She fell apart completely after my father was arrested. She left Athens and locked herself away at our house in Santorini,' he'd replied in an offhand manner, but Inez had seen his anguish.

Recalling his words about abandonment, she'd gasped, 'She wasn't there when you were kidnapped, was she?'

Heart-shredding pain washed over his face, but a moment later it was replaced by a look even more soul-shaking. Forgiveness. 'No. She wasn't. But I had Ari and Sakis. They were strong for me. And they were that way because of her. I told her that tonight because I think we both needed to hear it.'

His words had resonated deep inside her. But most of all it had been his statement on the dance floor that continued to flash across her mind. *I'm not prepared to let you go yet.*

Her heart lurched. He meant to keep her in his bed for a while yet. Like a trophy he wasn't prepared to relinquish. And her foolish heart performed a giddy little samba at the thought of having a few more moments with him.

She woke to kisses on her forehead and her cheek and opened her eyes to bright sunshine.

'Good, you're awake. We just landed.'

She yawned widely. 'Already? I feel as if I just fell asleep.'

He laughed. 'It's three o'clock in the afternoon. And we have much to do before tonight.'

She stared at his wide grin and her heart lifted with happiness. 'You seem in very good spirits, *querido*,' she commented.

He gathered her close in his arms and gazed down at her. 'There is a reason for that.'

'Tell me,' she murmured softly.

His face turned serious, his eyes fierce as he watched her. 'For the first time in twelve years, I slept through the night without a nightmare,' he muttered hoarsely.

Theo watched her face light up with shocked pleasure before she reached up to clasp his face. Her kiss was gentle and sweet. 'Oh, Theo. I'm so happy for you.'

'I'm happy for *us*,' he replied. With another kiss, he got up and started dressing. 'Get a move on, sweetheart, unless you wish to give the customs guy an eyeful when he boards.'

With a yelp she got up and pulled her clothes on.

Theo's phone started ringing the moment they stepped off the plane. And it wasn't until they were back home that she remembered what he'd said on the plane.

'What did you mean—"we have much to do before tonight"? We're not going out, are we?' She groaned.

He took the phone from his pocket and checked it as another text message came through. She waited impatiently for him to finish.

'No, we're not going out. But we have a guest coming.'

'A guest? Who?'

'I've invited your father to dinner.'

Inez staggered as if a bucket of ice had been poured over her.

'My father is coming here?'

'Yes.'

'And you didn't think to inform me of this? What makes you think I want to see him?'

'We have to. It's time to get this thing over and done with, once and for all.'

'And you don't care how I feel about it?'

'I thought we agreed to fix things when we return to Rio?' he asked with a frown.

'Yes, but when you said *we*, I thought you meant us, you and me. More fool me. Because there is not me without my father, is there?'

'What are you talking about? Of course there is.'

'Then why would you go behind my back to arrange this?'

A tic started in his temple. 'Because it's my fault you're in the middle of all this.' He sighed and clawed a hand through his hair. 'I got a chance to fix things with my mother in Bermuda. We may never get back what we had but I'll take that over nothing. Whatever relationship you choose to have with your own father from here on in is up to you. But this is a hardship I caused in your life and one I have a duty to fix.'

The fight fizzed out of her but the fear that something had gone seriously wrong between the airport and home wouldn't go away.

At seven on the dot, the doorbell rang. She passed her hand over her black jumpsuit and tucked a lock of hair nervously behind her ear as she stood by Theo's side.

The butler entered the living room, followed by her father.

Benedicto da Costa drew to a halt. His narrowed gaze slid from Theo to her, his face a mask of dark anger and cold malice she'd forced herself to overlook in the past.

Now she saw him for who he really was. Images of Theo's scars flashed through her mind and her hands fisted at her side.

'I won't shake your hand because this isn't a social visit,' he rasped icily to Theo. 'And I won't be dining with you, either.'

'Perfectly fine by me. Frankly, the quicker we get this over with the better. But let me remind you that you're here only because of Inez. She may be your daughter but she's under my protection now. I suggest you don't lose sight of that fact. What business you and I have will be finished by week's end.'

Her father's gaze swung back to her. 'Are you just going to stand there and let him speak to your father that way? You disappoint me.'

'That's no surprise. I've been a disappointment from the moment I was born a girl, *Pai*.'

'Your mother will be rolling in her grave at your behaviour.'

She raised her chin. 'No, actually. *Mãe* told me every day she was proud of me. She also encouraged me to follow my dreams. She wanted to be a sculptor. Did you know that?'

'What's your point?'

'She was talented, *Pai*. But she gave it up for you. It was her, not you, who taught me what loyalty and family meant. You were only focused on exploiting that loyalty for your own selfish needs.'

His face tightened and his eyes flickered to Theo, who'd been standing by her with his arms folded, a half smile on his face.

'Is this what I came here for? To be lectured by an ungrateful child?'

Theo shrugged. 'I'm finding it quite entertaining.'

Benedicto growled and shot to his feet. 'If there is a point, *son*, I suggest you get to it.'

Theo grew marble-still, his smile disappearing in the blink of an eye. Pure rage vibrated off his body and Inez watched his nostrils flare as he sucked in a control-sustaining breath.

'*I am not your son*. And you are not worthy to be a father. It's a shame you didn't learn how to be a better parent from the mother who gave birth to you in that *favela* you deny you grew up in. And don't bother denying it again. I know everything there is to know about you, da Costa.'

For the first time since he'd walked in, Benedicto grew

wary. He strolled to the drinks cabinet and took his time examining all the expensive spirits and liqueurs displayed.

Without asking, he poured a measure of single malt whisky and took a bold sip. 'So I bent the truth a little. So what? You've already discredited my campaign. What do you want? My company? Is that your end game? You want to pick up the shares for Da Costa Holdings for peanuts? Well, over my dead body.'

Theo's laugh was menacing enough to cause her skin to tingle in alarm. 'Trust me, a few weeks ago it would've been my pleasure to grant you your wish. But you're wrong on that score. Your company is of no interest to me.'

His wariness increased. 'What's changed?'

Theo's eyes flicked to her and her heart thudded. 'Your daughter.'

'Really?'

Inez shook her head in astonishment. 'Do you really not know who he is, *Pai*?' she asked.

Theo's mouth curved in a mirthless smile. 'Oh, he knows who I am. He's just hoping that *I* don't know what he did twelve years ago.'

Benedicto swallowed, his gaunt face growing pale until he looked ashen. 'I have no idea what you're talking—'

She rushed towards him, anger, pain and disappointment coiling like poisonous snakes inside her. 'Don't you dare deny it. *Don't you dare!*' Her voice cracked and a sob broke through her chest. 'You had a boy kidnapped and tortured! For money. How could you?'

Eyes she'd once thought were like her own turned black with sinister rage. 'How could I? I did it for you. The fancy clothes you strut about in and that fancy car you drive? Where do you think the money came from? I needed it to save the company. Anyway, it was my money. Why did I have to go back to farming just because Pantelides couldn't keep it in his pants or stop his bit on the side from blowing the whistle on him?'

Inez's hand flew to her mouth, her insides icing over. '*Santa Maria*, you truly are a monster.'

Her father's jaw tightened and he addressed Theo. 'Is this the point where you hand whatever file you've gathered on me over to the authorities?'

Theo's mouth twisted. 'So you can bribe your way out of jail? No.'

Benedicto frowned. 'Then what the hell do you want?'

Theo glanced over at her and a look of almost relief washed over his face, as if a weight had been lifted off his shoulders. 'That's up to Inez. And only her. I'm done with you.'

Inez raised her suddenly heavy head and looked from one man to the other.

One stood tall, proud and breathtaking. A man she'd been so determined not to let in. But whose tortured vulnerability had drawn her to him, made her see beneath his skin to the frightened child who was desperately seeking answers.

Choking tears filling her eyes, she turned to the monster who was her father. 'I have nothing else to say to you. I don't want to see you ever again. Goodbye.'

Turning sharply from both men, she rushed out of the room and fled up the stairs.

Theo wasted no time in throwing Benedicto out once Inez left the room. He'd meant what he said—he was done with seeking retribution…had been done almost from the moment he'd met Inez.

Perhaps unwisely, he'd thought the meeting with Benedicto would be swift and cathartic. Instead, he'd brought Inez even more anguish.

He slashed his fingers through his hair as he vaulted up the stairs that led to his third floor suite. Perhaps she'd been right. He'd ambushed her in his rush to get this situation sorted between them.

But he would make it right for her. They would get

through this. They had to. The feelings he'd tried hard to smother had blown up in his face when he'd woken on the plane this afternoon. With the absence of anxiety and fear, the purest reason why he wanted to wake up each morning with Inez had shone through.

The feelings had been so intense he'd almost blurted it out. But he'd decided to wait until she'd confronted her father.

Now he wished he hadn't. He was wishing he'd provided her with that additional support of knowing how much she meant to him before he'd let her father loose on her.

Pursing his mouth in determination, he pushed the bedroom door open. 'Inez, I'm sorry for—'

The sight that confronted him silenced his words and turned his feet to clay. She stared at him, eyes red-rimmed with freshly shed tears.

Because of him. But even that pulse of deep regret couldn't erase the sight before him.

'What are you doing?' he asked, although the part of his brain that hadn't frozen along with his feet could work it out.

Two suitcases were open on the bed, one filled with her clothes. *She was packing...*

The silk top in her hand trembled before she turned and threw it in her case. Then her fingers curled around the edge of the lid.

When she looked at him again, more tears filled her eyes.

'Thank you for opening my eyes to what he truly is,' she murmured huskily.

'Shelve the thanks and tell me what you're doing,' he replied tersely.

One hand swiped at her cheek. 'I'm leaving, Theo.'

'You're what?' His voice rang with disbelief. 'You're going back to your father's house?'

She shuddered from head to toe. 'No. I could never live there again.'

He frowned. 'Then where are you going?'

She gave a tiny shrug. 'I'll stay with Camila.'

He finally got his feet to work and paced to where she stood. When she grabbed her shorts, he ripped them from her hand and threw them on the bed. 'I seem to be missing a link somewhere, sweetheart. Why don't you take a beat and fill me in?'

'I can't stay here.'

A merciless vice squeezed his chest. 'Why not?'

Her face creased in fresh anguish. 'Because he is right. The food he put on our table; the clothes on my back; our fancy education. They *all* came from your suffering.'

'For God's sake—'

She carried on raggedly. 'I never stopped to think about it but I remember the day he came home twelve years ago and told my mother our troubles were over. We weren't exactly poor before then, but after he pressured my mother into selling the ranch he made some bad investments and the company suffered for it. They argued a lot and I used to go to bed every night praying for a miracle just so they'd stop arguing. Can you imagine how I felt when my prayers were answered? And now, all these years later, I find out that what I'd prayed for came at the cost of your—' She choked to a stop, then frantically threw more clothes into the case.

Theo couldn't find an answer as desperately as he tried. He was watching her torture herself and he could do nothing to stop it. '*Anjo*—'

'No. I'm *not* an angel, Theo. I'm a child of the monster, a heartless devil who tortures children and doesn't feel an ounce of regret for it. How can you even bear to look at me?'

'Because you're *not* him!' he interjected fiercely. He took her hands and forced her to face him. 'You're not responsible for his actions. Stay, Inez. We said we would talk about us once we were done with him.'

'But there is no us, is there? We...we just fell into bed because of the circumstances that brought us together. If it hadn't been for my father you'd never have set foot in Brazil.'

'So you're walking away because you think we were never meant to be?' He watched her, forced himself to think how he would feel if she walked away from him. The realisation of what was happening washed over him and ashen despair filled his chest.

'I'm walking away because you need to put everything and everyone associated with your ordeal behind you. Otherwise you will never heal properly.'

He dropped her hand and stared down at her. The ice that had started to build inside him since he'd walked into the room hardened. It crept around his heart and Theo swore he heard it crack. His eyes scoured her beautiful tearstained face, looking for a tiny chink. A tiny ray of hope that would offer deliverance from the quicksand of devastation he could feel himself sinking into.

'So that's it? That's your final decision. You're doing this for my sake but I have no say in the matter?' He couldn't stop the bitterness from lacing his voice.

Her answer was to step back and gather up the last of her clothes. With trembling fingers, she zipped up the cases and lifted them off the bed.

'Inez, answer me!'

She stilled at the door. '*Adeus*, Theo.'

'Go to hell!' he snarled back.

'Table Four need a second helping of *feijoadas*. And a bottle of Rioja.' Camila bustled into the kitchen, checked on the bubbling pot Inez was stirring and nodded in approval. '*Fantastico*. I'll be back in a minute for that order.' She sailed back out on a giddy whirlwind.

Inez wiped her sweating brow and looked over her shoulder. 'Pietro, you grab the bottle; I'll serve up the *feijoadas*.'

Her brother rolled his eyes. 'Who made you queen of the kitchen?'

'I did, when I won the coin toss earlier.'

Her grin came easier today—much easier than it had for far longer than she wanted to dwell on. She still couldn't go for more than ten seconds without thinking of Theo but if she could joke with her brother, that was a good sign that this hollow, half-dead devastation she carried inside her would eventually ease. Right?

'I still think you cheated,' Pietro grumbled.

She lifted one shoulder. 'I'll let you explain to Camila, then, why the Rioja isn't here when she returns, *sim*?'

'Tomorrow, I'm tossing the coin.' He sauntered down the stairs into the basement that served as the restaurant's larder and wine cellar. The smell of the cheese Camila kept in the small space could be overpowering and she smiled again as Pietro made gagging noises.

If there was a bright side to be seen, it was that, amid all the chaos and heartache, somehow she and her brother had grown closer than she'd ever dreamed possible.

They both were yet to decide what they wanted to do with their lives after choosing to walk away from their father and the company, but Camila had encouraged them to take their time. To heal. To reconnect.

When her mother's childhood friend had offered them a job in her restaurant they'd both jumped at it. She'd worked it around her volunteer work and, between the two jobs, it kept her plenty busy.

Keeping herself occupied stopped the tight knot of pain inside her from mushrooming into unbearable agony. In the dark of the night when she lay wide awake and aching was time enough to suffer through the hell of wondering if she was doomed to heartache for ever.

Of wondering if Theo had left Rio in the three weeks since their final bitter encounter. Of wondering if his nightmares were gone for good or if her brief presence in his life had made them worse.

Her hand trembled and she immediately curled it into a fist. Theo was strong. He would survive...

Yes, but he called you his saviour. His angel. And you walked away from him.

'No,' she breathed through the pain ripping through her. She'd done the right thing—

'No what? If you tell me I've got the wrong wine, you'll have to go and get it yourself.'

She shook her head blindly and turned gratefully to the door as Camila walked in. Her quick but assessing glance at her made Inez frown.

'We have a new booking. Table One. And an order of *feijoadas* for one.'

'Wow, you're on fire tonight, sis.'

She ignored Pietro. 'Okay, I'll serve it up and—'

'No, I didn't take a drink order. And I think they want an appetiser first too. Can you go take care of it?'

Inez's eyebrow shot up. 'Me? But I'm not dressed to serve.'

'Pfft. This isn't the Four Seasons, *meu querida*. Besides, it's time you took a break from that hot stove. Tidy your hair a bit and go and take the order.'

Inez looked down at her black skirt and grey T-shirt. It wasn't standard waitress attire but, as Camila had said, this wasn't the Four Seasons. She tucked a strand of hair behind her ear and caught the worried look in the older woman's eyes. It was an expression she'd spied a few times and she reached out and shook her head before the concern could be voiced.

'I'm fine.'

Camila's mouth pursed. 'Good. Then go and attend to Table One.'

With a weary sigh, she washed and dried her hands on her apron. Unfastening it, she hung it on the hook and avoided her image in the small mirror by the door. Her red face from manning the stove for the last three hours would depress her even more.

Plucking a pencil, notebook and menu from the kitchen stand, she nudged the swinging doors with her hip and turned towards Table One.

'You...' she choked out.

Through the drumming in her ears she heard the items in her hand clatter to the floor. A couple of diners glanced her way. Someone picked up the scattered items and placed them in her numb hands. She opened her mouth to thank them but no words emerged.

Every atom in her body was paralysed at the sight of Theo Pantelides.

She heard movement behind her. 'You can't stand here all night, *pequena*. Life will pass you by that way,' Camila said solemnly.

She exhaled shakily and forced herself to move.

Those light hazel eyes never left her as she approached his table. He looked as powerful and as magnificent as ever, even if his cheekbones seemed to stand out a little more than she remembered. His hair had grown a little longer and looked a little dishevelled.

'Sit,' he rasped.

Her heart lurched at the sound of his voice. Licking her dry lips, she shook her head. 'I can't. I'm working.'

'I've received special dispensation from Camila. Sit,' he commanded again.

She sat. He stared at her for a full minute, his eyes raking over her face as if he had been starved of her... Or he was committing her face to memory one last time?

White-hot pain ripped through her. 'Why are you here, Theo?' she blurted.

His eyes rose from her mouth to connect with hers. The breath he took was deep and long. 'I was clearing out the house and I found something you left behind.' He reached down near his feet and laid her sketchpad on the table.

She stared at it, drowning beneath the weight of her despair. 'Oh, thank you.' She paused a second before the words were torn out of her. 'So you're leaving Rio?'

He shrugged. 'There's nothing left for me here.'

Tears burned her eyes as her heart shredded into a million useless pieces. 'I...I wish you well.'

He made a rough sound under his breath. 'Do you?' he asked sarcastically. She glanced up sharply but he wasn't done. 'Problem is, I'd believe those blithe words from the woman sitting across from me. But the woman who drew these...' he flicked over the pages of the sketchpad a few times before he stopped and pointed '...this woman has guts. She was brave enough to draw what was in her heart; what cried out from her soul. Look at her.'

She kept her eyes on his face, her whole body trembling wildly as she gave a jerky shake of her head.

'Look at her, dammit!'

She sucked in a breath. And looked down. The first sketch was the one she'd made of him after they'd made love that first time on the boat. The ones that followed were variations of that first sketch. She'd captured Theo in various poses, each one progressively more lovingly detailed until the final one of him with his brothers, laughing together at the wedding. She'd drawn that from memory on their final night in Bermuda. Staring at the finished picture had cemented her feelings for him.

He turned the page and the image of Brianna and Sakis's baby stared back at her. Dimitri already bore the strong, captivating mark of the Pantelides family. It was that template that she'd used in the following sketches, when capturing her own secret yearning of what her and Theo's baby would look like on paper had been too strong to resist.

'You must think I'm some sort of crazy stalker.'

'There is no stalking involved when the subject is just as crazy about the stalker,' he rasped in a raw undertone.

Her heart flipped into her belly and her whole body trembled. 'You can't be. Theo, I'll ruin your life.'

'I thought my life was ruined before I met you. I was consumed by rage and a thirst for revenge. I let the need for revenge swallow me whole, blinding me to what was important. Family. Love. I thought there was nothing else worth fighting for. But I was wrong. There was you. My life *will* be ruined. But only if you're not in it.'

The tears she'd tried to hold back brimmed and fell down her cheeks. Theo cursed and looked around. 'What's through there?' he asked.

'It's a room, for private parties.'

'Is there a party tonight?'

Before she'd finished shaking her head he was standing and tugging her after him. He kicked the door shut and turned to her.

'Listen to me. You told me I would never see you as anything but the child of a monster. But you forget you're also the child of a loving mother who celebrated every day the special person you are. How do you think she would feel to see you buried here, punishing yourself for what your father did?'

She shut her eyes but the tears squeezed through anyway.

'Open your eyes, Inez.'

She sniffed and complied, staring up at him with blurred vision. 'Now, truly open your eyes and see the wonderful person you are. See the person I see. The brave, talented person who drew those pictures.'

'Oh, Theo,' she cried.

'You have a dream. A dream I want to be a part of.' His hands shook as they traced her face.

'I want that dream to become reality so badly.'

'Then please forgive me for blackmailing you and give us that chance.'

She pulled back. 'Forgive you? There is nothing to forgive. If anything, I should be thanking you for shaking me out of my bleak existence. Even before I truly knew you, you empowered me to fight for what I wanted.'

'So will you fight for us? Will you give me the chance to prove to you that I'm worthy of your love and let me show you how much you mean to me?'

She touched his face and inhaled shakily when he turned to kiss her palm. '*Meu querido,* I fell in love with you so ridiculously soon after meeting you, I swear I'll never confess to you when it happened.'

His stunned laugh brought a wide smile to her face. '*Anjo…*' When her smile dimmed, he shook his head. 'Don't bother to argue with me. I love you with every breath I take. You're my angel and I'll keep repeating it until you believe it.'

'We're not going to have a very smooth-sailing future, are we?'

'No,' he concurred with a laugh then kissed her until her head swam with delirious pleasure. 'But that will be part of our story. And, speaking of smooth sailing…'

'*Sim?*'

'I sent a couple of your sketches to our design guys in Greece. They're interested in talking to you about them. If you're up for it?'

Her mouth dropped open. She waited until he'd kissed it shut before she tried again. '*Really?*'

'Really. And I should bring you good news more often. That happy wriggle does incredible things to my—'

She clamped her hand over his mouth and glanced, alarmed, over his shoulder, just as two text messages beeped in quick succession. He groaned and was about to activate them when a knock sounded on the door.

'*Hell*, I knew I should've found a quieter place for this.'

The door opened and Pietro entered with a bottle of champagne and two glasses.

Theo's expression grew serious as he watched him approach.

Pietro set the bottle and glasses down and stared back at Theo. 'You took care of my sister when I was too much of a *burro* to do so. I'll be for ever in your debt.' He held out his hand.

After several seconds, Theo shook it. 'Don't mention it. Any man who's not afraid to call himself an ass is all right in my book.'

With a self-conscious laugh, Pietro turned to leave.

'Thanks for the drinks,' Theo said. 'But how did you know?'

Inez suppressed a giggle. Pietro rolled his eyes and nodded to the far wall. 'There's a partition to the kitchen. Camila's been spying on you since you came in.'

Theo glanced behind him as the partition widened and Camila beamed at them. Her gaze rested on Inez. 'Your *feijoadas* are good enough, but I always believed your destiny lies elsewhere.' She blew a kiss and shut the partition.

Pietro left and Theo stared down at her. 'Are you ready to start our adventure, *agape mou*?'

'What does that mean?'

'It means *my love*.' His smile dimmed. 'I learnt to speak Portuguese for the wrong reasons. I will teach you Greek for the right ones.'

Her grip tightened on his shirt. 'Were you really planning to leave Rio?'

'Yes. After I persuaded Benedicto to sign over the company into your and Pietro's names, I was done with that soulless vendetta. The thought that I'd lost you in the process nearly killed me.'

'I...what? You got him to sign over the company to us? Theo, we don't want it!'

'It was your grandfather's, then your mother's. It's right that it should be yours and Pietro's. If you don't really want it, I'm sure you'll find a beneficial way to dispose of it.'

She nodded. 'It would go a long way to help the inner city centre and the *favela* kids.'

'Great, we'll make it happen.'

Her heart contracted as she stared into his warm eyes. 'I love you, Theo. Thank you for coming back for me.'

'I couldn't not return, *anjo*, because without you I'm lost.'

She lifted her face to his and he slanted his mouth over hers in a deep, poignant kiss that brought fresh tears to her eyes.

'We need to talk about these tears,' he said drily, then huffed in irritation as his phone beeped again.

'Your brothers?' she guessed.

'And their wives. Ari wants to know if I'm still alive. Sakis wants to know if he can hire you to design his next oil tanker.'

She laughed. 'And their wives?'

He glanced down at the screen and back at her. 'They want to know if they can start planning our wedding.'

She took the phone, flicked the off switch and slipped it into his back pocket. Gripping his waist, she raised herself on tiptoe and leaned close to his ear.

'We will reply to each one of them in the morning. Right now, I want you to take me back to the boat and make love to me, make me yours again. Is that okay?'

'It's more than okay, my angel. It's what I plan to do for the rest of our lives.'

The look of love and adoration in his eyes as he took her hand and walked her out of the room was forever branded on her heart.

* * * * *

WEDDING NIGHT WITH HER ENEMY

MELANIE MILBURNE

To Laura Melania Kacsinta Bernal.
Thanks for being such a lovely fan.
This one is for you! Xx

CHAPTER ONE

ALLEGRA KALLAS WASN'T expecting a fatted calf or a rolled-out red carpet and a brass band. She was used to coming home to Santorini with little or no fanfare. What she expected was her father's usual indifference. His polite but feigned interest in her work in London as a family lawyer and his pained expression when she informed him that, yes, currently she was still single. A situation for a Greek father of a daughter aged thirty-one that was akin to having a noxious disease for which there was no known cure.

Which made her wonder why there was a bottle of champagne waiting on a bed of ice in an ice-bucket with the Kallas coat of arms engraved on it and a silver tray with three crystal glasses standing nearby, and why he was gushing about how wonderful it was to have her home.

Wonderful?

Nothing about Allegra was wonderful to her father. Nothing. What was wonderful to him now was his young wife Elena—only two years older than Allegra—and their new baby Nico, who apparently weren't expected back from Athens until later that evening as Elena was visiting her parents. And since little Nico's christening wasn't until tomorrow...

Who was the third glass for?

Allegra slipped her tote bag off her shoulder and let it drop to the leather sofa next to her, the fine hairs on the back of her neck standing up. 'What's going on?'

Her father smiled. Admittedly it didn't go all the way to his eyes, but then the smiles he turned her way rarely did. He had a habit of grimacing instead of smiling at her. As though he was suffering some sort of gastric upset. 'Can't a father be pleased to see his own flesh and blood?'

When had he ever been pleased to see her? And when had she ever felt like a valued member of the family? But she didn't want to stir up old hurts. Not this weekend. She was home for the christening and then she would fly back to her life in London first thing Monday morning. A weekend was all she was staying. She found it too suffocating, staying any longer than that, and even that was a stretch. She glanced at the champagne flutes on the tray. 'So who's the third glass for? Is someone joining us?'

Her father's expression never faltered but Allegra couldn't help feeling he was uneasy about something. His manner was odd. It wasn't just his overly effusive greeting but the way he kept checking his watch and fidgeting with the cuff of his sleeve, as if it was too tight against his wrist. 'As a matter of fact, yes. He'll be here any moment.'

Something inside Allegra's heart kicked against her chest wall like a small cloven hoof. 'He?'

Her father's mouth lost its smile and a frown brought his heavy salt-and-pepper eyebrows into an intimidating bridge. 'I hope you're not going to be difficult. Draco Papandreou is—'

'*Draco* is coming here?' Allegra's heart kicked again but this time the hoof was wearing steel caps. 'But why?'

'Elena and I have asked him to be Nico's godfather.'

Allegra double blinked. She had thought it a huge compliment when her father and his wife had asked her to be their little son's godmother. She'd assumed it was Elena's idea, not her father's. But she hadn't realised Draco was to be Nico's godfather. She'd thought one of her father's older friends would have been granted the honour. She hadn't realised he considered Draco a close friend these days, only a business associate—or rival, which seemed more appropriate. The Papandreou and Kallas names represented two powerful corporations that had once been close associates, but over the years the increasingly competitive market had caused some fault lines in the relationship.

But Allegra had her own issues with Draco. Issues that meant any meeting with him would be fraught with amusement on his part and mortification on hers. Every time she saw him she was reminded of her clumsy attempt as a gauche teenager to attract his attention by flirting with and simpering over him and, even more embarrassingly, the humiliating way in which he had put a stop to it. 'Why on earth did you ask *him*?'

Her father released a rough-sounding sigh and reached for the shot of ouzo he'd poured earlier. He tipped his head back, swallowed the drink and then placed the glass down with an ominous thud. 'The business is in a bad way. The economic crisis in Greece has hit me hard. Harder than I expected—much harder.

I stand to lose everything if I don't accept a generous bailout merger from him.'

'Draco Papandreou is…is *helping* you?' Every time Allegra said his name a sensation scuttled down her spine like a small sticky-footed creature. She hadn't seen Draco since she'd run into him at a popular London nightspot six months ago where she'd been meeting a date—a date who had stood her up. A fact Draco had showed great mirth in witnessing. *Grr.*

She loathed the man for being so…so *right* about everything. It seemed every time she made one of her stupid mistakes he was there to witness it. After that embarrassing flirtation on her part when she'd been sixteen, she had quickly transferred her attention to another young man in her circle. Draco had warned her about the boy and what had she done? She'd ignored his warning and got her heart broken. Well, not broken, exactly, but certainly her ego had got knocked around a bit.

Then, when she'd been eighteen, Draco had found her helping herself to the notoriously potent punch at one of her father's business parties she was supposed to have been helping him host and had lectured her about drinking too much. Another lecture she'd wilfully ignored…and, yes, he'd been there to see her coughing up her lungs a short time later. Double *grr*. Admittedly, he'd been rather handy with a cool face cloth and had gently held her hair back from her face…

But it hadn't stopped her hating him.

Not one little bit.

Even in all the years since, when she ran into him he had an annoying habit of treating her as if she was still that gauche teenager and not a grown woman with a high-flying legal career in London.

'Draco has offered me a deal,' her father said. 'A business merger that will solve all my financial problems.'

Allegra gave a disdainful snort. 'It sounds too good to be true, which usually means it is. What does *he* want out of it?'

Her father didn't meet her gaze and turned slightly to pour another drink instead. She knew her dad well enough to know he only drank to excess in one of two states: relaxed or stressed. Stressed seemed to be the ticket this time. 'He has some conditions attached,' he said. 'But I have no choice but to accept. I have to think of my new family—Nico and Elena don't deserve to be punished for my misfortune. I've done all I can to hold off the creditors, but it's at crisis point. Draco is my only lifeline…or at least the only one I'm prepared to take.'

His new family. Those words hurt her more than she wanted to admit. When had she ever felt part of his *old* family? She'd been a 'spare part' child. A rescue plan, not a person. Her older brother Dion had contracted leukaemia as a toddler, and back in those days parents had been encouraged to have another child in case the new baby was a bone-marrow match. Needless to say, Allegra hadn't come up with the goods. She had failed on both counts. Not a match. Not male. Dion had died before Allegra was two years old. She didn't even remember him. All she remembered was she had been brought up by a series of nannies because her mother had been stricken with unrelenting grief. A grief that had morphed into depression so crippling, Allegra had been sent to boarding school to 'give her mother a break'.

Her mother had 'accidentally' taken an overdose of sleeping tablets the day before Allegra was to have come home for the summer the year she turned twelve. No one had said the word 'suicide' but she had always believed her mother had intended to end her life that day. The hardest part for Allegra was the sad realisation she hadn't been enough for her mother. Her father hadn't even bothered to hide his disappointment in having a female heir instead of the son he had worshipped. Hardly a day had gone by during her childhood and adolescence when Allegra hadn't felt the sting of that disappointment.

But now her father had moved on with a new wife and a new baby.

Allegra had never belonged and now even less so.

'Draco will tell you about our agreement himself,' her father said. 'Ah, here he is now.'

Allegra whipped around to see Draco's tall figure enter the room. Her eyes met his onyx gaze and a strange sensation spurted and then pooled deep and low in her belly. Every time she looked at him she had exactly the same reaction. Her senses jumped to attention. Her pulse raced. Her heart flip-flopped. Her breath hitched as though it were attached to strings and someone was jerking them. Hard.

He was wearing casual clothes: sandstone-coloured chinos and a white shirt rolled past his strong, tanned forearms, which took nothing away from his aura of commanding authority. When Draco Papandreou walked into a room every head turned. Every female heart fluttered...as hers was doing right now, as though there were manic moths trapped in her heart valves. He oozed sex appeal from every cell of his six-foot-three frame. She could feel it calling out to her feminine hormones like an alpha wolf calling a mate. No other man had ever made her more aware of her body than him. Her body seemed to have a mind of its own when he came anywhere near.

A wicked mind.

A mind that conjured up images of him naked and his long, hair-roughened legs entwined with hers. The only way she could disguise the way he made her feel was to hide behind a screen of sniping sarcasm. He thought her a shrew, but so what? Better that than let him think she was secretly lusting after him. That the embarrassing crush she had foolishly acted on when she'd been sixteen had completely and utterly disappeared. That her dreams didn't feature him in various erotic poses doing all sorts of X-rated things with her. She would rather be hanged and quartered and her body parts posted to the four corners of the earth than admit the only sex she'd had in the last year or so had been by herself, with him as her fantasy.

That—God help her—the last time she'd had sex with a partner it had been Draco she had thought of the whole time.

'Draco, how nice of you to gate crash a private family celebration. No hot date tonight with one of your bottle-blonde bimbos?'

His mouth lifted at one corner in his signature half-cynical, half-amused smile. 'You're my date, *agape mou*. Hasn't your father told you?'

Allegra gave him a look that would have snap-frozen a gas flame. 'Dream on, Papandreou.'

His dark eyes glinted as if the thought of her saying no to him secretly turned him on. That was the trouble with having had a crush on a man since you'd been a pimple-spotted teenager. They *never* let you forget it.

'I have a proposal to put to you,' he said. 'Would you like your father present or shall I do it in private?'

'It's immaterial to me where you do it because nothing you propose to me would ever in a thousand, million, squillion years evoke the word "yes" from me,' Allegra said.

'Er... I think I can hear one of the servants calling me,' her father said and left the room with such haste it looked as though he were running from an explosion. But then, whenever she and Draco were left alone together the prospect of an explosion was a very real possibility.

Draco's gaze held hers in a tether that made the base of her spine shiver. 'Alone at last.'

Allegra broke the eye contact, walked over to the drinks tray and casually poured a glass of champagne. Or at least she hoped it looked casual. She wasn't a big drinker but right now she wanted to suck on that bottle of champagne until it was empty. Then she wanted to throw the bottle at the nearest wall. Then the glasses, one by one, until they shattered into thousands of shards. Then every stick of furniture in the room.

Smash. Bash. Crash.

Why was he here? Why was he helping her father? What could it possibly have to do with her? The questions tumbled through her brain like the champagne tumbling into her glass. Her father's business was hanging in the balance? How could that be? It was one of the most well-established businesses in Greece, and had operated for several generations. Other business people looked up to him, in awe of all he had achieved.

Her father had always brandished his wealth like it was a ten-thousand-strong flock of golden-egg-laying geese. How had it come to this?

Allegra turned and gave Draco a sugar-sweet smile. "Can I offer you a drink? Weed killer? Liquid nitrogen? Cyanide?'

He gave a deep rumble of a laugh that did strange things to her insides. Things they had no business doing. Not for him. 'Under the circumstances, champagne would be perfect.'

She poured a glass and handed it to him, annoyed her hand wasn't quite steady. He took the glass but in doing so his fingers brushed against hers. It was like being touched with a live current. The shock of it sent a jolt through her entire body, making her hormones sit up and beg for more. She snatched her hand back and then wished she hadn't. He had an uncanny ability to read her body language like a cryptographer reading code.

Everything about him unsettled her. Made her feel things she didn't want to feel. But no matter how hard she fought it she couldn't take her eyes off him. It was as though magnets were attached to her eyeballs and he was true north. She had seen a lot of beautiful men over the years but no one came close to having Draco's pulse-tripping features. Ink-black hair with just enough curl to make her want to run her fingers through it and straighten out those sexy kinks. A mouth that was not just sensual but sinfully sculpted. A mouth that made her think of long, drugging kisses. The mere thought of his hard male mouth crushing hers was enough to make her get all hot and bothered and breathless.

She had felt that mouth on hers. Once. Had felt it and

had responded to it, only to have him push her away with an ego-crushing comment about how a silly little girl like her could never satisfy a man like him. For years that cruel put-down had savaged her self-esteem. It had ruined her sexual confidence—not that she'd had much to begin with. Damn him for being so darned attractive. Why couldn't she stop gawping at him as if she were still that stupid, star-struck kid with a crush?

He had shaved but the potent male hormones surging around his body would be enough to defeat any decent razorblade. Dark stubble was peppered along his lean jaw and around his mouth.

Dear God, she had to stop looking at his mouth.

She picked up her glass of champagne but before she could take a sip he held his glass within reach of hers. 'To us.'

Allegra pulled her glass back before it could touch his, sloshing the champagne down the front of her blouse. Of course, she was wearing silk. The saturating liquid made her right breast stand out even though it was inside a lace bra. Why was she so ridiculously clumsy around him? It was mortifying. She brushed off the excess liquid with her hand but it only made the dampness worse, making the upper curve of her breast cling to the fabric as though she were in a wet T-shirt competition.

Draco handed her a clean white handkerchief. Of course he would be carrying a clean white handkerchief. 'Would you like me to—?'

Allegra snatched the square of cloth off him before he could finish the sentence. No way was she letting him touch her breast even if it was through four folds of cotton. She couldn't guarantee a suit of armour and

Kevlar vest would keep her from responding to his touch. She dabbed at her wet breast and never had such a task seemed so erotic. Even her breast thought so. It was tingling and her nipple peaking...but maybe that was because Draco's dark obsidian gaze was following her every movement over it. She screwed the handkerchief into a tight ball and tossed it to the coffee table. 'I'll have it laundered and returned to you.'

'Keep it as a souvenir.'

'The only souvenir I want from you is the word "goodbye".'

His eyes held hers again in a spine-shuddering, resolve-melting lock. 'The only way that's going to happen is if I pull out of this business merger.'

'I don't care about the merger.'

'Maybe not, but you should. It rests solely on your compliance with the terms of the deal.'

Terms? What terms?

Allegra disguised her unease by shaking her loose hair back behind her shoulders in a gesture of indifference. But she was far from indifferent. Something about his unwavering gaze made her feel he was toying with her, like a cat with a mouse it had cleverly cornered. What on earth could he want her compliance over?

Since *that kiss* years before, there had always been a climate of tension between them. A tug of war of wills. A power struggle that crackled the air when they were in the same room together. He was her enemy and she didn't care who knew it. Hating him made it easier for her to forget how much she'd wanted him. Hating him kept her safe from her own traitorous hormones that were annoyingly, persistently, immune to every other man but him. 'My father's business affairs are of no concern to me. I am completely independent of him and have been for the last ten or so years.'

'Independent financially, maybe, but you're his only daughter. His only child. He paid for your stellar education. He gave you everything money could buy. Don't you care he's about to lose everything without my help?' His deeply carved frown added to the grave delivery of his words.

Allegra wished she didn't care. But the trouble was, she did. It was her Achilles' heel—her weak spot, the raw, vulnerable part of her personality—the need to feel loved and valued by her only living parent. She had sought it all her life to no avail. In spite of her father's shortcomings, inside she was still that small child looking for his approval. Pathetic, but true. 'I fail to see what any of this has to do with me. I simply don't care what state my father's business is in.' She knew she sounded cold and unfeeling but why should she care what Draco thought of her?

He studied her for a long moment. 'I don't believe you. You do care. Which is why you'll agree to marry me to keep the business afloat.'

Shock hit her in the chest like a punch. *Marry him?* Allegra widened her eyes. Not saucer-wide. Not dinner-dish-wide. Platter-dish-wide. Surely he hadn't just said that? The M word? Him and her? Married? To each other? She blinked and then laughed but even to her ears it sounded on the verge of hysterical. 'If you think for one second I would marry anyone, let alone you, then you are even more of an egomaniac than I thought.'

Draco's gaze continued to hold hers in an intractable

lock that was a tantalising tickle to her girly bits. 'You will do it, Allegra, or see your father's business die a slow and painful death. It's on life support as it is. I've been drip-feeding your father money for the last year. He hasn't got the funds to repay me even if I waive the interest. No one will lend him anything now, not after the way things have panned out in our economy. I came up with this solution instead. This way everyone wins…in particular, you.'

Allegra couldn't believe his arrogance. Did he really think she would agree to such a preposterous deal? She hated him with a passion. She couldn't think of a single person she would *less* like to marry. Well, she could, given her line of work, but that wasn't the point. He was a playboy. A fast-living Lothario who churned through women like a speed-reader churned through cheap paperbacks. Marriage to Draco would be emotional suicide, even if she didn't hate him. 'You're unbelievable. What planet are you on that you would think I would see this as a win for me? Marriage isn't a win for any woman. It's a one-way ticket to serfdom, that's what it is, and I won't have a bar of it.'

'You've been hanging around divorce courts way too long,' he said. 'Plenty of marriages work well for both parties. It could work for us. We have a lot in common.'

'The only thing we have in common is we both breathe oxygen,' Allegra said. 'I dislike everything about you. Even if I were on the hunt for a husband, I would never consider someone like you. You're the sort of man who would expect his pipe and slippers brought to him when he gets home. You don't want a wife, you want a servant.'

His half-smile was back, making his impossibly black eyes twinkle. 'I love you too, *glykia mou*.'

Allegra thinned her gaze to hairpin slits. 'Read my lips. I am not marrying you. Not to save my father's business. Not for any reason. No. No. No. No.'

Draco took a leisurely sip of his champagne and put the glass down on the coffee table with exacting precision. 'Of course, you'll have to commute between London and my home for work, but you can use my private jet—that is, if I'm not using it myself.'

Allegra clenched her hands into fists. 'Are you listening to me? I said I am *not* marrying you.'

He sat on the sofa and leaned back with his hands behind his head, one ankle crossed over the other with indolent grace. 'You haven't got a choice. If you don't marry me then your father will blame you for the collapse of his company. It's a good company but it's been badly run of late. That business manager your father appointed a couple of years ago when he had that health scare didn't do him any favours. I can undo that damage and turn the business around so it's profitable again. Your father will stay on the board and have a share of the profits I guarantee will be more than he has received in decades.'

Allegra bit down on her lip. It had been a worrying time when her father had had a cancer scare. She had flown back and forth as much as she could to help him through his bout of chemo and radiation. Not that he'd shown any great appreciation, of course. But to marry Draco to save her father from financial ruin? It was as if she had suddenly stepped into the pages of a Regency novel.

But her father needed her. *Really* needed her. There

could have been worse men than Draco to offer for her, she had to admit. The sort of men she faced down in court. Mean men. Dangerous men. Men who had no respect for women and who used their children as weapons and pay-backs. Men who stalked, bullied, threatened and even killed to get their own way.

Draco might be arrogant but he wasn't mean. Dangerous? Well, maybe to her senses, yes. Her senses went into a dazzled and dizzying frenzy when he came close. Which was a very good reason why she couldn't marry him.

Wouldn't marry him.

'Why me?' Allegra said. 'Why would you possibly want me for a wife when you can have any woman you want?'

His eyes did a lazy sweep of her from head to foot and back again, sending a frisson through every cell in her body. 'I want you.'

Those sexily drawled words should not have made her feminine core do a happy dance. She wasn't vain but knew she was considered attractive in a classical sort of way. She had her mother's English peaches-and-cream complexion, her dark blue eyes and slim build, but she had her father's jet-black hair and drive to achieve.

But Draco dated super-models, starlets and nubile nymphets. Why would he want to shackle himself to a hard-nosed career woman like her, especially when they fought at every chance they got?

Over the years she had done her level best to hide her attraction to him. The Embarrassing Incident when she'd been sixteen was filed away in her mind in the drawer marked 'Do Not Open'. These days she sneered instead of simpered. She derided instead of drooled. She flayed instead of flirted.

Falling in love with Draco Papandreou would be asking for the sort of trouble she helped other women extricate themselves from on a daily basis. Love did weird things to women. They got blindsided, hoodwinked, charmed into looking at their men through rosy love-tinted glasses that failed to show up their faults until it was too late.

Allegra wasn't going to be one of those women—a victim of some man's power game, leaving her as vulnerable as a rain-soaked kitten. 'Listen, I appreciate the compliment, such as it is, but I'm not in the marriage market. Now, if you'll excuse me, I'm going to—'

'The offer is for today and today only. After that I start asking for my money back. With interest.'

She sent her tongue over her lips but they felt as dry as the cardboard cover on one of her expert reports. The economic crisis in Greece was serious. So serious that many well-established companies had hit the wall like over-ripe peaches. She might have some issues with her father but not to the point where she wanted to see him ruined and publicly humiliated. Not now he had a wife and young baby to provide for. Allegra liked Elena. She hadn't expected to, with Elena only being two years older than her, but she did. It some ways Elena reminded her of herself—trying too hard to please everyone in an effort to be loved and accepted.

But if she married Draco to save her father from financial destruction she would be exposing herself to the sort of sensual danger she could well do without. For years she'd kept her distance from him. After that mortifying encounter when she was sixteen, it was her only way of protecting herself. But how would she keep her distance if she were married to him? 'This marriage you're…erm…proposing…' It was lowering to find her voice sounding so scratchy. 'What do you get out of it?'

His eyes shone with a devilish gleam that made her inner thighs tingle as if he had stroked her intimately. No one else could do that to her. Turn her on with a look. Make her so hungry for him she had trouble keeping her hands off him. She would like nothing more than to run her hands all over that strong male body to see if it was as deliciously hard and virile as it looked. When had she not burned with lust for him? Ever since she'd been a teenager with newly awakened hormones he'd been her go-to fantasy guy. No one else came close. He had all but ruined her for anyone else and he hadn't so much as touched her, other than incidentally, since that kiss. 'I get a wife who's hot for me. What more could a man want?'

Allegra kept her expression under tight control. 'If you want a trophy wife then why not select one from your crowd of sexy little sycophants?'

'I want a wife with a brain between her ears.'

'Any woman with half a brain would steer clear of a man like you.'

Her insult only made his smile tilt further, as if he was enjoying himself at her expense. 'And if you were to provide me with an heir…'

'A…what?' Allegra's voice came out like a mouse's squeak. 'You're expecting me to have…?'

'Now that I think about it…' He rose from the sofa with leonine agility. 'An heir and a spare might be a good thing, *ne*?'

Was he teasing or was he serious? It was so hard to

tell behind the sardonic screen of his gaze. 'Aren't you forgetting something? I don't want children. I have a career I'm not prepared to sacrifice for a family.'

'Lots of women say that but in most cases it's not true. They say it as an insurance policy in case no one asks them to marry them.'

Allegra's mouth dropped open so far, she thought her toenails would be bruised. 'Are you for real? What jungle vine did you just swing down from? Women are not breeding machines. Nor are we waiting around with bated breath for some man to stick a ring on our finger and carry us off to be their domestic slave. We have just as much ambition and drive as men, sometimes even more so.'

'I'm all for your drive.' His eyes did that glinting thing again. 'That's another thing we have in common, *ne*?'

The less she thought about his sex drive, the better. No one oozed it more potently than him. He was the poster boy for pick-up sex. He moved from relationship to relationship faster than a driver late for an important appointment changed lanes. What had brought about this sudden desire to play family man? He was only thirty-four—three years older than her. Or was it his way of twisting her arm? The arm that was attached to her hormone-charged body that strangely—since that night six months ago in London—kept reminding her every time she had a period she was over thirty and childless. 'I don't know where you got the idea I would agree to this farcical plan. Did my father suggest it?'

'No, it was entirely my idea.'

His idea? Allegra frowned. 'But you don't even like me.'

He came and stood in front of her, his superior height making her feel like a child's rocking horse standing up to a Clydesdale stallion. He didn't touch her but she could feel the magnetic pull of his body making every cell in hers gravitate towards him. She raised her eyes to his, momentarily losing herself in those bottomless pools of black with their fringe of thick lashes.

Why did he have to be so wickedly attractive? Why did her hormones jump up and down in ecstatic glee when he was close? Her gaze went to his mouth, drinking in the way his lips were both firm yet sensually supple, the lower one generous, the top one slimmer, but not enough to be considered cruel. It was a mouth always on the verge of a smile, as if he found life amusing rather than sad. Had she ever seen a more kissable male mouth?

'We could be good together, *agape mou*. Very good.'

Allegra suppressed the shiver his provocative words evoked. His voice was deep and mellifluous and his Greek accent—so much stronger than the faint trace of it in her voice—never failed to make her skin prickle in delight.

He always spoke English to her because she had let her Greek slip after living so long in England. She understood it more than she could speak it but she could hardly describe herself as fluent. She had always spoken English to her Yorkshire-born mother and she suspected her neglect of her father's language was a subconscious way to punish him for not being the father she longed for. 'Look, Draco, this has to stop. All this talk of a marriage between us is pointless. I'm not—'

He took one of her hands and enfolded it in the cage of his. His fingers were warm and dry, the tensile strength in them making something in her stomach drop like a book falling from a shelf. Make that a dozen legal textbooks. Who knew her hand was so sensitive? It was as if every nerve was on the outside of her skin, tingling, making her aware of every pore of his. 'Why are you so frightened of getting close to me?'

Allegra had to swallow a couple of times to find her voice. 'I—I'm not frightened of you.' *I'm frightened of me. Of how you make me feel.*

His thumb began a slow stroke of the fleshy base of hers. It was as light as a sable brush on a priceless canvas but it triggered an explosion of sensations that ricocheted through her body. Her heart picked up its pace as though she'd been given a shot of adrenalin with a crack chaser. Her brain was scrambled by his closeness, her resolve to keep her distance gone missing without leave.

His eyes searched hers for a long, pulsing moment. It was as if he was committing every one of her features to memory: the shape of her eyes, her nose, her cheeks, her mouth and the tiny beauty spot just above the right side of her top lip.

Allegra licked her lips, then realised what a blatant giveaway that was—the primary signal of attraction. It was as if her body was acting of its own accord. Her will, her determination to resist him, was overridden by a primal need to touch him, to have him touch her. To have him kiss her until she forgot about everything but how those firm, male lips felt on hers.

What are you doing?

The alarm bell of her conscience shattered the moment and she pushed against his chest and stepped back to create some distance between them. 'Don't even think about it, buddy.'

His mouth tilted in a knowing smile. 'I'm a patient man. The longer I wait, the better the satisfaction.'

Allegra had a feeling there would be a heck of a lot of satisfaction going on if she were to submit to his passion. The sort of satisfaction that had mostly eluded her in her previous encounters. She wasn't good at sex, or at least not with a partner. She could get things working fairly well on her own, but with a partner she found it too distracting to orgasm. Dead embarrassing, but at least she had been able to fudge her way through it. So far.

But she suspected Draco wouldn't be fooled.

Not for a minute.

Allegra refilled her glass for something to do with her hands. She was conscious of him watching her every move, his dark gaze resting on her like a caress. Her skin tingled, her pulse raced, her insides coiled tight with need. A need awakened by him. 'I think it's best if we forget we had this conversation. I don't want anything to spoil Nico's christening tomorrow.'

'What will spoil it will be you refusing to marry me to save your father's skin,' Draco said. 'You haven't got a choice, Allegra. He needs you like he's never needed you before.'

It was far more tempting than she wanted to admit. Not just because of how it would make her father finally appreciate her, but because she couldn't stop thinking about what it would be like to be Draco's wife. Sharing his life with him, sharing his luxury villa on his own private island. Sharing his body. Being pleasured by him, experiencing the full gamut of human passion. It was a dream come true for the gauche teenager she had once been.

However, she wasn't that girl any more.

But then a thought dropped into her head. Had her father and Elena only asked her to be godmother to Nico because of Draco and his offer? Would they have asked her without the merger and the marriage condition? Wasn't she good enough on her own to be Nico's godmother? Why did she have to partner with her enemy? A man she loathed with the same passion she desired him.

Allegra twirled her glass and placed it back down on the tray next to the champagne bottle. 'Here's a hypothetical question for you. If I were to marry you then how long would you expect the marriage to last?'

'For as long as I want it to.'

And how long would that be? Allegra turned to look at the view from the window to give herself more time to think. The sunlight was so bright it was almost violent. The intense blue of the Aegean Sea, and the equally vivid blue domes in contrast to the stark white of the houses, never failed to snatch her breath. It was picture-postcard perfect, especially from her father's luxury villa in Oia, where the best sunsets in the world were occurred.

It was home and yet it wasn't.

She'd always felt like she had a foot in both countries and it added to her sense of not really belonging anywhere.

If she married Draco to save her father from financial disgrace, where would that leave her when it was time to call an end to their marriage? Few marriages ended with a mutual agreement to part. There was nearly always one party who wasn't happy about the break-up. Would that be her? And—if he wasn't joking about the heir he said he wanted—there was no way she would have a child under such circumstances, with the knowledge that the marriage had no guarantee, no promise of full and lasting commitment.

Allegra turned back to look at Draco. 'Still speaking hypothetically here. What about my career? Or do you expect me to give that up?'

'No, of course not,' he said. 'But there will have to be compromises occasionally. I have business interests in London, as you know, but most of my time is spent in Greece. I think the fact you have your own career will enhance our marriage rather than complicate it.'

'And you would expect me to be with you most of the time?' Allegra said it as though it was the most unreasonable request in the world. As though she'd be committing to daily root-canal treatment.

His expression flickered with amusement. 'Isn't that what husbands and wives do?'

Allegra sent him a speaking look. 'Ones that are in love with each other, maybe. But that hardly applies in our case.'

One side of his smile went a little higher. 'You've been in love with me since you were a teenager. Go on—admit it. That's why you haven't got married yet or dated with any regularity. You can't find anyone that does it for you like I do it for you.'

Allegra affected a laugh. '*Seriously?* That's what you think?' What signals had she been giving off to make him think she was still that clumsy teenage girl?

She wasn't that infatuated fool any more. She was all grown up and she hated him. Hated. Hated. Hated him.

His eyes gleamed like wet paint. 'When was the last time you slept with a man?'

She folded her arms across her body and pursed her lips like she was a schoolmistress staring down an impertinent child. 'I'm not going to give you details of my sex life. It's none of your damn business who I sleep with.'

'It will be my business once we're married. I expect you to be faithful.'

Allegra unfolded her arms and planted her hands on her hips instead. 'And what about you? Will you be faithful or will I have to turn a blind eye to your little dalliances like my mother did for my father?'

Something hardened around his mouth, making it appear flatter, less mobile. 'I am not your father, Allegra. I take the institution of marriage very seriously.'

'So seriously you're prepared to marry a woman you don't love, for a short period of time, just so you can acquire a flagging business?' She made a scoffing noise. 'Don't make me laugh. I know why you want to marry me, Draco. You want a trophy wife. A wife who knows which knife and fork to use. A wife you can take anywhere without worrying she might embarrass you. Then, when you've got me to pop out an heir, you'll get bored, send me on my way and keep the kid. I'm not doing it. No way. Find some other puppet.'

She pushed past him to leave the room but he snagged her wrist on her way past, bringing her around to face him. Her skin burned where his fingers gripped her, but not a painful burn, more of a sizzling, tingling burn that sent heat rushing through her body and pooling in her core. He had rarely touched her since that kiss other than by accident. The contact of his flesh on hers was like being zapped with a lightning bolt. It made every nerve beneath her skin pirouette. His thumb found her thrumming pulse and soothed it with slow, measured strokes while his eyes held hers prisoner.

'I was only teasing about the heir,' he told her. 'But think carefully, Allegra. Yes, I am in the market for a suitable wife, and you fit the bill. But this is also your chance to get your father to finally notice you. You won't just be helping him, but Elena and little Nico, by providing them with security. If the business goes under, it will take them down with it.'

He had found another weak spot. Elena and Nico. They were the innocents in this situation and their future would be compromised if she didn't do something. Allegra could offer her father a loan but the sort of money Draco was talking about was in the millions. Many millions. She was wealthy, but not wealthy enough to float a multi-million-euro corporation. She let out a rattling breath and looked down at their joined hands. How could she turn her back on her father's financial plight when she was the only person who could do something? If her father went down, Elena and darling little Nico would be collateral damage. She couldn't stand back and let that happen. Not when she could help it. She would have to marry Draco. *Gulp.* 'It seems I don't have any choice.'

Draco brought her chin up so her gaze meshed with his. 'You won't regret it. I can guarantee it.'

You think? Allegra brushed his hand away from her chin and took a step backwards. 'I'm not agreeing to this for any other reason than to save my family. Are you absolutely clear on that?'

His eyes shone with a triumphant gleam that made the backs of her knees tingle. 'But of course.'

She disguised a swallow, trying not to notice the way his eyes kept glancing at her mouth. 'When are you thinking of…doing it? I mean, getting married?'

'I have already taken the liberty to make all the arrangements. We'll be married next weekend. I would have done it this one but I didn't want to steal little Nico's limelight.'

Allegra's eyes bulged in alarm. 'So soon?'

'It is a little rushed, but it will be a relatively simple affair. Just a handful of close friends and family.'

'But what if I want the whole shebang?'

'Do you?'

She blew out another breath and averted her gaze. 'No…'

'You'd be surprised at what can be done in a short period of time when you have money. If you want a white wedding, then that's what you will have.'

Allegra had never been the sort of girl to hanker after the fairy-tale wedding. She had rarely even thought of getting married. Her career had always been her top priority. She normally avoided bridal shops and didn't drool at jewellers' windows. But ever since she'd been a bridesmaid at a friend's wedding a couple of months ago she had started to think about what it would be like to be a bride. To be loved by someone so much they would promise to spend the rest of their life with her. It was indeed a fairy tale, one she saw turn to ashes and heartache every day of her working life.

'We'll be married on my island retreat,' Draco said. 'It will be easier to keep the press away.'

Allegra had never been to Draco's private retreat but she had seen photos. He had a villa in Oia, an apartment in Athens and other homes on Kefalonia and Mykonos. But his secluded retreat on his private island had the most amazing gardens and an infinity pool that was perched on the edge of a vertiginous cliff. It would make a stunning wedding location.

And a perfect spot for a honeymoon.

Do not even think about the honeymoon.

'Aren't you worried what the press will make of us?' Allegra asked.

He gave a loose-shouldered shrug. 'Not particularly. I've grown accustomed to them speculating on my private life. Most of the time they make stuff up.'

Not everything was fiction. She had seen enough photos of him surrounded by beautiful women to know he wasn't living the life of a Tibetan monk. Far from it. He was considered one of Greece's most eligible bachelors. Women were elbowing each other out of the way to score a date with him. What would everyone say when they heard *she* was to be his wife? A single-minded career woman like her, marrying a fast-living playboy like him.

It was laughable.

'You'll have to take a week off work, of course,' he said. 'We'll take a short honeymoon on my yacht.'

Her heart flapped like a goldfish trapped in the neck of a funnel. 'Hang on a minute—why do we need to have a honeymoon?'

There was a spark of something at the back of his gaze. Something dark and sensual and spine-tinglingly wicked. 'If you need me to spell that out for you, *agape mou*, then you've been living an even more cloistered life than I thought.'

Allegra crossed her arms, holding them tightly against her stomach. *A honeymoon? On his yacht?* His yacht was no cheap little fishing dingy, but it could never be large enough for her to feel safe. Safe from her own wicked, traitorous desires. She would need a cruise liner or an aircraft carrier for that and even that would be no guarantee. 'Look, I'm prepared to marry you for the sake of my father, but I'm not going to sleep with you. It will be an on-paper marriage. A marriage in name only.'

Draco came back to where she was standing but she had moved back against the wall, which gave her nowhere to escape. And with her hands crossed over her body she didn't have room to unwind them to push him away. She breathed in the scent of him—lime and cedar with a hint of something that was unique to him. It unfurled around her nostrils, making them flare to take more of him in. She felt drunk on him. Dazzled by the pheromones that swirled and heated and mated with hers.

He slipped a hand to the side of her head, his fingers splaying through her hair until every root on her scalp shivered in delight. His eyes had that dark, twinkling spark of amusement that did so much damage to her resolve. Lethal damage. Irreparable damage. 'And how long do you think an on-paper marriage between us would last, hmm?' His voice was a deep burr that grazed the length of her spine like a caress from one of his work-callused hands. 'I want you and I intend to have you.'

Allegra couldn't stop staring at his mouth—the way his lips shaped around every word; the way his stubble made her want to press her mouth to his skin to feel the sexy rasp of his regrowth. *Kiss me. Kiss me. Kiss me.* The chant was pounding an echo in her blood. She didn't want to be the one to make the first move. Not like she had done all those years ago, when she'd thrown herself at him only to be brutally rejected. She wasn't that girl any more. Making the first move would give him too much power. She could resist him. She could. She could. She could.

As if he could read her mind, he brought a fingertip to her mouth and traced a slow outline of her lips, setting off a round of miniature fireworks under her skin. 'Such a beautiful mouth. But I'm not sure if you're going to kiss me back or bite me.'

She inched up her chin. 'Try it and see.'

His smile was lazy and lopsided and sent her belly into free fall. But then he tapped her lower lip with his index finger and stepped back. 'Maybe some other time.'

CHAPTER TWO

DRACO PICKED UP his champagne glass because, unless he gave his hands something to do, he knew they would be tempted to jump ahead a few spaces. He could wait. Sure he could. Allegra was all for keeping things on paper but he knew she would crack before the ink was dry on their marriage certificate.

He knew she was attracted to him. She'd had a teenage crush on him, which had amused and annoyed him in equal measure back in the day. He'd been a little ruthless in handling her back then, but he hadn't been interested in messing with a teenager, especially so soon after his break-up with the ex he'd thought he was going to marry. Back then, Allegra had been young and starry-eyed, fancying herself in love, and had needed to be put firmly in her place.

But she was a woman now—a beautiful woman in the prime of her life.

And he wanted her.

Ever since London, Draco had realised Allegra was exactly what he was looking for in a wife. And when her father, Cosimo Kallas, had come to him for help, he had seized his opportunity and made his financial support conditional on marrying her. Besides, there were other men who were circling like sharks for the money her father owed them, men who he knew wouldn't hesitate to go after Allegra next. He couldn't stand by and let one of them force her into their bed to settle the debts he could pay without flinching. Who knew what might happen to her? Her father had angered a lot of his business associates. Draco wasn't going to let anything happen to her because her father was a fool.

Allegra was classy. She was well-educated, she was well-spoken and she was half-Greek. And, with her untouchable air, she was jaw-droppingly gorgeous. She could have graced a catwalk or been found starring on an old-world Hollywood movie set. She walked like a dancer, her slim figure moving effortlessly across the floor. Her glossy black hair was straight and hung almost to her waist. When she moved, it moved with her in a silk curtain that held his gaze like a super-powerful magnet. He couldn't stop himself from imagining that silky black skein draped over his chest, her long, slender legs entwined with his.

Draco suppressed a shudder of anticipation. He was hot for her. Seriously hot. So hot he only had to look at her and his blood would thunder. He couldn't seem to keep his eyes off her. When she'd spilled her champagne, the silk of her blouse clinging wetly to the perfect globe of her breast had made his blood shoot south in a torrent. He had rarely touched her in the past. Since that kiss when she was a teenager, he had respectfully kept his distance because he hadn't wanted any boundaries to be crossed. He had made it clear he wasn't interested back then and he hadn't wanted to give her mixed messages.

Now was different.

Their marriage wouldn't be for ever, just long enough to secure the business and get Allegra out of his system. Draco had nothing against long-term marriage, but he couldn't see himself doing the time.

He had teased Allegra with that talk of an heir to suss out her feelings on the issue of children. It wouldn't be fair to lock her into marriage—even a short-term one—if she was desperate to have kids. Thankfully, she wasn't, and it was the last thing he wanted from this marriage. Given his childhood, he wasn't sure he could ever see himself having a family.

When his mother had died from a gangrenous appendix when Draco was six, he and his father had been a team intent on survival in a world that didn't notice, let alone help, the desperately poor. Draco had a clear memory of walking with his fisherman father past the Kallas corporation headquarters one day only a month before his father's death. His dad had looked up at the building with its shining brass sign and expressed how he wanted Draco to aim high, to dream big and bountiful, to make something of himself so he wouldn't have to struggle the way he had done. When his father had been killed in a boating accident four weeks later, Draco had been left to fend for himself.

But his father's words had stayed with him, motivating him, fuelling his drive and determination. He'd clawed his way out of poverty, working several menial jobs while trying to get an education. At nineteen, he'd part-owned a business, and had gone on to own it fully when the partner had retired. He had gone from strength to strength after that, building and expanding each company he acquired. He was a self-made man and he was proud of it.

No one could say he wasn't a prize catch.

Not now.

And who could be a better wife for him than Allegra Kallas—the daughter of the businessman who owned the corporation his father had singled out that day with such aspiration? Acquiring the company would be a symbol of Draco's success. A token of the dreams and hopes his father had had for him and that he had now fulfilled in his father's honour.

Draco watched her sipping her champagne, sitting there on one of the plush leather sofas. Her long legs were crossed, one racehorse-slim ankle moving up and down in a kicking motion—the only clue she was feeling agitated. Her expression had gone back to her signature cool mask of indifference, which was another thing that secretly turned him on. He was amused how she took that schoolmistress tone with him. When she tried to stare him down with those flashing, unusually dark blue eyes, it made him hard as stone. Harder. He could feel the throb of it even now.

He'd wanted to kiss her. Of course he had. What man with even a trace of testosterone wouldn't want to feel that lusciously soft mouth? He'd tasted those sweet, hot lips once and couldn't wait to do it again. But he knew if he moved too soon it could shift the balance of power. He wanted his ring on her finger. He wanted her hungry. He wanted her begging. He wanted her to be honest about her lust for him. For lust after him she did. He should know the signs because he was experiencing them himself. He couldn't take his eyes off her generous and supple mouth. Couldn't stop thinking about that mouth opening over him, drawing on him, sucking him till he blew like the volcano Santorini was famous for.

Draco met her eyes across the space that separated them. She raised a perfectly groomed eyebrow at him, that starchy, English aristocratic, 'I'm too good for the likes of you' spark in her eyes making him want to carry her off fireman-style and show her just how good he could be for her. 'Another drink to celebrate our engagement, *agape mou*?' he said.

Her mouth was puckered like the drawstrings of an old-fashioned purse. 'Don't call me that. You know you don't mean it.'

He pushed away from the window where he had been leaning. 'Here's the thing—we have to act like a happy couple, even if in private you want to play pistols at dawn.'

Her chin came up to a defiant height. 'No one's going to believe it, you know. Not us. We're known to positively loathe each other.' Her cheeks went a shade darker. 'Especially after that night in London in December.'

He smiled at the memory. It wasn't the first time he'd felt that tingle of attraction. More than a tingle. A shockwave that had left him buzzing for hours afterwards. 'Ah, yes. It wasn't one of your best moments, was it? I was only trying to help and what did I get? A glass of red wine poured in my lap. Hardly the behaviour of a grown woman.'

Her jaw looked as though she were biting down on a metal rod. 'You provoked me. And it was either have that wine in your lap or splashed in your face, and your throat cut with the glass.'

He tut-tutted and shook his head at her as if she were a wilfully disobedient child who consistently disappointed him. 'It seems I may have to teach you how to behave. That will be fun: *Wife Behaviour for Beginners.*'

She sprang off the sofa as if something had bitten her on the behind, throwing him a look that would have stripped tarmac off a road. 'You think you're so smart, manipulating me into this farce of a marriage, but I've got news for you. I will not be a doormat. I will not be treated like a child. I will not sleep with you. Do? You? Understand?'

Draco loved it when she got angry with him. She was always so buttoned up, cool and controlled. But with him she showed the depth of passion in her personality others didn't see. She was feisty, a firebrand with a flaying tongue and a whip-quick wit. He enjoyed their verbal sparring. It was a big turn-on for him. Few women stood up to him or challenged him the way she did. He liked that she had spirit. That she wasn't afraid to lock horns with him.

He would much rather she locked those gorgeous lips on his, but all in good time.

'I understand you're a little apprehensive about sex, but I can assure you, I'm excellent at it.'

Twin pools of bright pink flared on her cheeks. 'I am not apprehensive about sex. I have sex—I have it all the time. I just don't care to have it with you.'

How he wanted to make her eat every one of those words and lick them away with that hot little tongue of hers. He wanted that tongue all over his body. *He wanted. He wanted. He wanted.* It pulsed through him like an ache. He'd been too long between relationships. It had been weeks—no, months—since he'd had sex. He'd been too busy, distracted by work and the dire financial situation Cosimo Kallas was in, to bother about hooking up with anyone.

But now he was ready.

He was so ready he could barely keep his hands off those slim hips, from pulling her against him so she could feel how ready. 'You will share my bed even if you don't share my body to begin with. I won't have my household staff snickering behind my back at my inability to consummate my marriage.'

She glared at him so hotly he thought the champagne in his glass was going to boil. 'If you so much as lay one finger on me, I'll scream loud enough for them to hear me in Albania.'

Draco gave an indolent smile. 'I can guarantee you'll scream, *glykia mou*. You certainly won't be the first. Most women in my bed do.'

Her mouth went into a flat line and her hands clenched into tight little white-knuckled balls. Her whole body seem to vibrate like a child's battery-operated toy. 'I'm surprised you want to wait until we're married. Why don't you throw me to the floor and have your way with me now?'

'Tempting, but alas, I'm a civilised man.' He swept a hand behind him where he'd entered the room earlier. 'See? No knuckle marks along the carpet.'

Her caustic look showed just how uncivilised she thought him. She swung away and put herself behind one of the sofas, as if she needed to barricade herself. 'I suppose you're only making me wait to ramp up the torture quotient.'

'The sort of torture I have in mind will be mutually pleasurable.'

She shook her hair back behind her shoulders in a

haughty manner. The silky swing of it always fascinated him. It was like the swish of a curtain. 'I find it hard to understand how you could want to bed a woman who hates you. It seems a little kinky to me.'

'You don't hate me, Allegra. What you hate is how you can't get your way with me. You need a strong man. Someone who will allow you to express that passionate nature you keep under wraps all the time. I'm that man.'

She gave one of her derisory laughs. 'Hello? We've actually had a women's movement during the last century. Didn't you hear about that or were you too busy clubbing mammoths and dragging them back to your cave?'

Draco's groin tightened at her witty come-back. She always gave as good as she got, which was another reason he thought her perfect wife material. He didn't want a doormat. He didn't want someone who didn't have the spirit to spar with him.

He wanted her.

It was as simple as that. Since he'd seen her in London he had lost interest in other women. He had found the dating scene increasingly boring and predictable. But every encounter, every conversation, with Allegra was full of surprises. She stimulated him physically and intellectually.

He reached into his top pocket and handed her the ring box he'd brought with him. 'That reminds me—I have something for you. If it doesn't fit, I'll have it adjusted.'

She took the box and cautiously opened it, as if whatever was in there might leap out and bite. But then she let out a breath and picked up the diamond solitaire with almost worshipful fingers. 'It's beautiful.' She looked up at him, her blue eyes showing a hint of uncertainty he found strangely touching. 'It looks frightfully expensive…'

Draco shrugged. 'It's just a ring. I threw a dart at the counter. This was the one it hit.'

She slipped the ring over her knuckle. 'It fits.'

'Must be an omen.'

Her gaze flicked to his. 'I'll give it back when we divorce.'

Draco didn't want her thinking there was any hint of romance in his choice of a ring. He'd done that once and it had been the worst mistake of his life. 'Keep it. I'm not sure any future bride of mine would want to wear a second-hand ring.'

She opened and closed her mouth, as if she couldn't find what to say. Then she looked down at the ring winking on her hand. It was a moment before she looked up at him again. 'How can I be sure you won't play around while we're married? You've played around all your adult life. Men like you get bored with one lover.'

Right now, Draco couldn't imagine ever being bored by her, but it didn't mean he would propose anything long-term. Long-term was for the in love, and that hardly described him in this case. He wasn't going to go down that path ever again. In lust? Yes. Big time. 'When I get bored, I'll let you know. We can end the marriage before anyone gets hurt.'

'Perhaps I'll get bored first,' Allegra said. 'Women have the right to choose their own husband, not have one thrust upon them. If I wanted to choose one, then you'd be the last man I'd consider. The very last.'

Draco smiled at the insult and moved across to

the door. 'We'd better let your father know the happy news. But, let me remind you, apart from your father no one—and I mean no one—must know this isn't a love match. I'm not interested in the press attention it would receive otherwise.'

Later, Allegra didn't know how she got through the rest of the evening, with Draco and her father chatting away over dinner like two good mates who'd just nailed a successful business deal. Damn it. *She* was the business deal. How could this be happening? Married to her worst enemy! And it was happening so quickly. Her phone hadn't stopped buzzing with incoming messages because Draco had taken the liberty of announcing their engagement on social media. Every platform of social media. *Grr.* It annoyed her because she'd been left looking like an idiot for not saying anything to her friends and colleagues about her 'secret relationship' with Greece's most eligible bachelor.

But when her secretary and best friend Emily Seymour texted, WTF? Is this a joke? Allegra couldn't quite bring herself to lie to her.

No joke but it's not what you think. Will explain later. Can't talk now.

Emily's text came back.

Can't wait! Knew you had a thing for him since that guy was a no-show. He's so HOT!!!'

She'd followed the word 'hot' with an emoticon of flames burning.

Allegra texted back.

MOC. No sex.

Emily sent an emoticon of a person laughing and holding their sides.
Allegra rolled her eyes and typed back.

I mean it!

She put away her phone before she was subjected to any more teasing. She wasn't sure how Emily had picked up on her attraction to Draco. But then, Emily was a bit of a romantic. What signals had Allegra given off? Or was she protesting *too* much?

'Well, I think I'll leave you two to chat while I head off to bed,' Allegra's father said, rising from the table. He paused by Allegra's chair and placed a hand on her shoulder. 'I know you'll be happy with Draco. He's exactly what you need.'

There were a hundred retorts she wanted to throw back but in the end she stayed silent. Her father gave her shoulder a quick pat, as if he were patting a dog he didn't quite trust, before he left the room and quietly closed the door behind him.

Draco twirled the amber contents of his brandy glass, his gaze steady on hers sparkling with amusement. 'Nice to know I've got the father-in-law's big tick of approval.'

Allegra picked up her wine glass and surveyed him over the top of the rim. 'What a pity you don't have mine. But that doesn't seem to matter to you—I wonder why? Maybe you've engineered this because you're secretly in love with me. Is that it?'

His expression became shuttered and he put down his own glass with a soft little thud. 'I'm not sure I'm capable of romantic love. I'm a little too practical for that. But I care about you, if that's any consolation.'

She gave a laugh. 'People *care* about their pot plants. How nice to know you'll offer me water and fertiliser occasionally.'

His crooked smile came back and sparked a sardonic glint in his gaze. 'Whenever you want fertilising, you just let me know.'

Allegra sent him a gimlet glare even though her ovaries were packing their bags and heading to the exits. And it was not just her ovaries that were getting excited. Her feminine core was contracting with a pulsation of lust that made it difficult to sit still in her chair. She had never really thought about having a baby before now. She was a career girl, not an earth mother. An image popped into her head of her belly swollen with his child. His DNA and hers getting it on and producing a baby with dark eyes and dark hair. She saw another image of him holding that baby, his strong arms cradling the tiny bundle while his eyes met hers in a tender look…

She gave herself a mental shake. 'So, you've never been in love? Apart from with yourself, I mean.'

He gave a soft chuckle and draped one arm along the back of the neighbouring chair. 'I'm not averse to a bit of self-love now and again. How about you?'

Allegra wasn't going to give him an account of her sex life even if these days it was mostly with herself. 'I thought I was in love with my first boyfriend but we both know how that ended.' And it had been Draco's fault. Damn him.

'Did you sleep with him?'

'Yes,' she answered in spite of herself.

'And?'

Allegra gave him a 'wouldn't you like to know?' look. 'You think I'm going to swap bedroom tales with you? It was your fault it was such a dis—' She clamped her mouth shut, furious she'd given away more than she'd intended.

'It was consensual...wasn't it?' There was a note of concern in his tone and he moved forward in his chair with a frown pulling at his brow.

'Yes.'

He was still frowning, his posture tense, on edge. 'What happened to make it such a disaster? Is that the word you were going to say?'

Allegra looked at the rim of her glass rather than meet his probing gaze. 'I wanted to get rid of my V card and he seemed the right one to do it with.' She twisted her mouth. 'Obviously these things are easier for you guys. You seem to have fun no matter what.'

'Biology isn't always fair,' Draco said. 'To women especially.'

There was a little silence.

'You were right about him, though,' Allegra said. 'He was such a loser in the end. He told all his mates what a disappointment I'd been in bed. Needless to say, I was completely and utterly mortified.' Why she was telling him that excruciating detail escaped her. Emily was the only other person she had told, because it was too painful to think about, let alone recount to someone else. And too skin-crawlingly embarrassing.

'Yes, well, I reckon he only said that to take the attention off his own inadequacies,' Draco said. 'He should've made your pleasure a priority. That's the golden rule of decent manhood.'

She was pretty certain none of Draco's lovers had ever complained about his lack of prowess in bed. Just the thought of him pleasuring her with that virile body of his was enough to make her get all excited downstairs. But why was she talking about this stuff with him? If she told him much more, he would realise she was practically a nun.

'Fancy an evening stroll out on the terrace?' he asked after a moment, as if he sensed she was uncomfortable with the subject.

'I miss all this when I'm in London,' Allegra said once they were outside and looking at the dark blue, wrinkled silk of the ocean below with its silver band of moonlight shimmering on the surface. 'But then, when I'm here I miss lots of things about London.'

His shoulder brushed against the skin of her bare arm, his left hand within a couple of millimetres of her right one where it was resting on the railing. 'It's a problem when you love two places. That's why I move between the two, so I get the best out of each of them by commuting between seasons. But, of course, not everyone has the financial flexibility to do that.'

The early summer evening air was scented with the salt spray of the sea and the faint but familiar fragrance of the vigorously blooming bougainvillea hanging in a swathe of crimson over the side of the terrace. The far off braying of a donkey and the clanging of the rigging of the yachts in the marina lower down carried in the light, warm breeze.

Allegra stole a covert glance at Draco. The moonlight put his impossibly handsome features into relief, making him look all the more like he had stepped off a marble plinth in an antiquities museum. The high, intelligent forehead with the prominent jet-black eyebrows, the strong nose and sculpted mouth were etched on her brain like a tattoo. What other man had ever compared to him?

It was a cliché, but tall, dark and handsome—and Greek—was her poison. She was lethally attracted to him. She knew it. He knew it. It swirled in the air when they were alone together like a potent but forbidden drug. One taste and Allegra knew she would be addicted. Which was why she had to keep her distance, even though every cell in her body was trembling with the need for contact. It didn't matter how much she fantasised about Draco in secret. No way could she afford to indulge in a physical relationship with him. He had rejected her once. She wasn't going to let him do it again.

But it would be kind of exciting to kiss him...

He turned and saw her looking at him, and before she could put any distance between them he lifted a finger to her face and tucked a breeze-teased tendril of her hair back behind her ear. His face was mostly in shadow, but she could see the moonlight reflected in his gaze like a glint of quartz in black marble.

Allegra knew she should step away, knew too she should brush his hand aside, frown at him and tell him to back off in her sharp, schoolmistress-y tone. But it seemed her mind and body had other ideas. Wicked ideas. Dangerous ideas. Ideas that made her picture her body crushed beneath his, his mouth clamped to hers, their bodies writhing in mutual, skin-shivering ecstasy. She drew closer to him as if someone had a hand in the small of her back, her hips brushing against his. The shock of the erotic contact made her insides twist and coil with lust, her breath hitch and her heart race. She saw her hands slide up to lie flat on his chest, the hard muscles flinching as if her touch electrified him.

Draco's hands went to her waist, his fingers gentle but as hot as a brand. His muscle-dense thighs were so close she could feel their heat and sense their latent strength. His head came down but his mouth hovered rather than landed, his warm, brandy-scented breath mingling with hers.

Allegra sent her tongue out over her lips to moisten them, her whole body poised in that infinitesimal moment before final touchdown.

Go on. Do it. Kiss me and prove that you want me as much as I want you. 'Are you going to kiss me?'

'Thinking about it.' His voice was two parts gravel, one part honey, making her insides quiver.

'What's to think about?' She moved even closer, her breasts bumping against his chest, making her flesh tingle. 'You know you want to.'

If she was wrong, this was going to be mortifying.

Draco's breath moved in a sexy waft along the side of her mouth, the rasp of his stubble grazing her cheek like fine-grade sandpaper. 'You've had way too much to drink,' he said.

'I'm not drunk—not even tipsy.' *Not on alcohol, that is.*

His tongue glided over her beauty spot, then circled it as if he were circling one of her nipples. A savage jab of lust assailed her, pooling in a liquid heat between her thighs. Then he moved his mouth to her jawbone, his lips working their way up in nibbles and nudge-like movements to the sensitive space below her ear. Her whole body shivered when Draco's teeth gently caught her earlobe, the tender tug sending a riot of sensations in a quick-silver streak down to the base of her spine. Her legs were without bones, without ligaments, trembling to stay upright and only doing so because his hands on her waist were keeping her there.

His mouth kept up its disarming of her senses, taking her on a journey of heady arousal unlike anything she had experienced before. Who knew her jawbone was an erogenous zone? Her jawbone! His lips nibbled their way down to the space between her lower lip and her chin. He was so close to her lips. *So* close... Close enough for them to buzz, tingle and ache for him to cover them with his mouth. But, still, he kept his lips away from hers as if he had made a private vow of kissing celibacy.

Draco's hands moved from her waist to cradle both sides of her head, his fingers splaying under the weight of her hair in a sensual glide that made something at the base of her spine heat, sizzle and melt. 'You are so damn beautiful,' he said in that same deep, gravelly burr.

'So kiss me, then.' Allegra slid her hands around his neck, which brought her lower body flush against his. She could feel the battle going on in his body where it was touching hers—the urge of the primal in combat with his iron will and steely self-control. Her own self-control was nowhere to be seen and she couldn't be bothered to send out a search party.

She wanted him to kiss her.

She needed him to kiss her.

She would *make* him kiss her.

She needed it like she needed her next breath. She would die if Draco didn't give in to the desire she could feel throbbing in his flesh where it was pressed against her. Mutual desire. Dark, wicked desire that refused to go back into its cage now it was released from its prison of denial. If he kissed her it would prove she wasn't the only one who was vulnerable. It would prove he had his weak spot—*her*. This time he wouldn't push her away with a cutting comment. This time she would kiss him as a woman kissed a man, not as a fumbling teenager. She would show him he wasn't as immune to her as he wanted her to think. 'Kiss me, Draco. What are you scared of?'

His hands came back down to settle against her hips, his fingers harder now—possessive, almost. His eyes were sexily hooded, his gaze honed in on her mouth. 'Are you sure you know what you're doing?'

Allegra moved like a sinuous cat against the hard frame of his body, her arms winding around Draco's neck, her fingers tugging, stretching and releasing his black curls. His erection was hot and heavy against her belly, the pounding of his blood echoing the deep, urgent thrumming of her own. She could feel her own moisture gathering, her body preparing itself for the pleasure it craved. Never had she felt desire like it. It was a raging fever, a torrent of need that refused to be ignored. Allegra wasn't going to sleep with him, but one kiss would be enough to take the edge off it, surely? What harm would one kiss do?

'You want me so bad,' she said.

His body pressed harder against her as if he hadn't

the strength of will power to do otherwise. His hands tightened their grip on her hips, his fingers digging into her flesh as if he never wanted to release her. 'Yes. I want you.'

Draco didn't say it out loud, but she could hear the word 'but' somewhere in that statement. Allegra brought her hand around to trace the outline of his mouth, her stomach pitching when the soft pad of her fingertip caught on his stubble. 'I bet you've kissed a lot of women in your time.'

'A few.'

She sent her fingertip down the shallow stubble-covered dip between his lower lip and his chin. Her eyes came back to his intensely dark gaze. 'Did you know you were my first kiss?'

'Not until you kissed me.'

Did he have to remind her how inexpert she had been?

'I've learnt since then. Don't you want to see how much I've improved?'

Allegra sensed he was wavering. He kept silent but his body spoke for him, his desire for her pulsing invisibly in the air like sound waves. His breath mingled with hers. His body was hot and urgent against hers, increasing her hunger for skin-on-skin contact. She slipped her arms back around his neck and rose on tiptoe, bringing her mouth to his in a soft touchdown. When she lifted off, his lips clung to hers like a rough surface to satin. Allegra touched down again, moving her lips against the warm, firm heat of his in an experimental fashion, discovering their texture, their shape. Their danger.

Draco drew in a breath and took control of the kiss,

crushing her lips beneath the fervent pressure of his. His hands went from bracketing her hips to cradling her head, angling it so he could deepen the kiss with a spine-wobbling glide of his tongue through her already parted lips. She welcomed him with a breathless sigh, his tongue tangling with hers in an erotic duel that had unmistakably sexual overtones. Her inner core recognised them, contracting in a fireball of lust that threatened to overwhelm her. Allegra kissed him back with feverish intensity, as if his mouth was her only succour and without it she would cease to exist.

He made a low, growling sound in the back of his throat and explored every inch of her mouth, his tongue sweeping, swirling, diving, darting until her senses were spinning like a top set off by a slingshot. Need ricocheted through her, clamouring to be assuaged. Begging, pleading, to be satisfied with every breath she snatched in while his mouth worked its fiery magic on hers.

One of Draco's hands went to her breast, cupping it in a possessive hold that sent another wave of sensation coursing through her body like sheet lightning. His thumb found her nipple, rolling over it through the fabric of her dress and bra, but she might as well have been naked. The thrill of his touch, even through two layers of fabric, was enough to make Allegra whimper for more. He moved to her other breast, cupping and caressing her through her clothes as if they were star-crossed teenage lovers on a clandestine date. His mouth left hers to blaze a blistering trail of fire down her neck and décolletage, his stubble ticking and tantalising her, his lips and tongue ramping up her desire until she felt like a pressure cooker about to blow.

But, while her self-control was shot to pieces, it seemed his was not.

Draco slowly drew back from her, still holding her in the circle of his arms but without chest-to-chest contact. She felt the loss keenly—her breasts were still tingling from his touch, from being crushed so tightly against his body. She searched his face for a moment but his expression was largely unreadable...all except for that glint of triumph lurking in the depths of his gaze.

Allegra slipped out of his hold and straightened the front of her dress. Time to rein things in. She couldn't allow him to think she was his for the asking. She had proved her point...sort of. But she had a disquieting feeling Draco had proved his own. 'Just to remind you. Kissing is fine, but that's as far as it goes.'

One side of his mouth came up in a slanted smile. 'You seriously think you can maintain that, even if by some remote possibility I agreed to it?'

Allegra raised her chin. 'Those are my rules.'

'Here's what I think of your rules.' He stepped back into her body space, standing close enough for her to feel the tug of attraction pulling at every one of her organs like invisible silken cords. His eyes moved back and forth between both of hers, searching, penetrating, challenging. She drew in a breath but it caught on something in her throat. Her thighs were less than a couple of centimetres from his, her breasts getting all excited about his chest being even closer.

Draco sent a fingertip idly down the slope of her cheek, then continued his tantalising pathway to the fullness of her bottom lip, his finger moving over its already sensitised surface like a mine sweeper. It took all her self-control and more not to take his finger into her mouth, to swirl her tongue around it and draw on it with her lips. The urge to do so was so primal and raw it made her insides quake with need. Allegra licked her lip instead, but her tongue came into contact with his finger on its return journey and an explosion of lust barrelled through her. She gripped the front of Draco's shirt, pressing her body against his, her mouth going to the exposed, tanned skin of his neck, sucking, nibbling, grazing him with her teeth and finally—*dear God, finally*—finding his mouth.

His lips moved with thrilling expertise on hers, his tongue delving deeply to call hers into sensual play. She made little breathless sounds of approval when his hands clasped her by the hips to hold her against his heat. She wanted more. Needed more. She sent her hands on a journey of discovery, sliding them over his hardened length, shaping him through his trousers, her own feminine muscles a frenzy of excitement.

After a moment, Draco placed a hand over hers to stop her from going any further. 'If we play by the rules, then those rules have to be fair.'

Allegra gave a shrug and stepped back, as if she didn't care either way, even though her body was crying out for release and her fingers were aching to feel the weight and heft of him. 'Can't take a little fooling around, Draco?'

His eyes glittered in the darkness. 'I would have you here and now but your father's household staff might be shocked. Don't look now, but his housekeeper Sophia's been watching from the window behind you.'

Allegra's cheeks grew so hot she was sure she was contributing to global warming. How had she let herself behave in such an abandoned way? She prided herself on always acting with poise and decorum around the staff. She wasn't the sort of person to behave recklessly or immodestly. But in Draco's arms she became a wanton woman with no thought for anything other than her body's needs. Needs that still thrummed and hummed inside her like a plucked violin string.

'Well, we are supposed to be acting like a couple in love,' she said. 'I might say you were doing a mighty fine job of it too.'

He gave a soft laugh. 'Don't confuse good old-fashioned lust with love.'

Allegra turned back to look at the ocean cast in its silver glow from the moonlight. She was conscious of Draco standing beside her, close enough for their arms to be touching. Even though his was covered in finely woven cotton, she could still feel the sensual energy of him. The potent vibrancy of him. Couldn't stop imagining how it would feel to have those strong, tanned arms wrapped around her in the grip of passion. 'What if you fall in love with me?' The question was out before she could block it. Had she sounded as if she *wanted* him to fall in love with her?

He turned and leaned his back against the balustrade, his hands resting on the railing either side of his hips. 'We've covered this, Allegra. I'm not sure I'm capable of loving you.'

Allegra flashed him a look. 'How charming of you to say.'

He gave a shrug, as if he recognised the veiled insult but was not going to apologise for it. 'Just saying.'

Of course, Draco falling in love was only a remote possibility. His heart was untouchable. He wasn't the type of man to allow himself to be vulnerable. He was the one who controlled his relationships to a set timetable. Few relationships of his had ever lasted more than a few weeks—one or two, perhaps, a couple of months.

Allegra looked down at her right hand resting next to his on the railing. His skin was so dark and hair-roughened compared to her pale, smoother hand. It was an erotic reminder of all the essential male and female differences between them. If she moved her pinkie a couple of millimetres she would touch him. The temptation to do so was a force inside her body over which she seemed to have little or no control. It was as though he were an industrial-strength magnet and she was a tiny iron filing. He had beautiful hands—broad and dusted with black hair that also lightly touched the backs of his long, strong fingers.

She couldn't stop thinking about those clever hands on her body. Not through her clothes, but on her naked skin. Draco wasn't averse to physical labour. He didn't sit behind a desk all day. He was the sort of man who didn't mind getting his hands dirty at the coalface of the businesses he ran. What would it feel like to have those hands gliding over her flesh? Touching her in places that hadn't been touched in so long she had almost forgotten what it felt like to be a woman?

She sent him a sideways glance. 'Why haven't you been in a long-term relationship before?'

'I have.'

'A month or two is not considered long-term.'

A beat or two of silence passed.

'I had a partner for close to a year once.'

He had? 'Really? I never knew. Gosh, you kept that awfully quiet. The press always—' Allegra thought it best to stop speaking before she revealed how closely she had been following his love-life in the media. It had been a bit of an obsession over the years One she wasn't too proud of, but she'd always had an unhealthy fascination with whomever he was squiring around town and for how long.

There was another long moment of silence.

'I was thinking about asking her to marry me.'

Allegra turned so she was facing him. Draco's face was backlit by the moonlight, so it was hard to make out his expression, but she could see his mouth had a rueful twist to it. 'You were?'

'I even bought the ring.'

She'd never heard even a whisper of an engagement. Why hadn't it been made public? Who wouldn't be interested in a self-made playboy like him settling down? Draco had dragged himself up from abject poverty to become one of Greece's most eligible bachelors. Who was the woman? Who had captured his attention to the degree he would offer to marry her? And, more to the point, why hadn't he gone ahead with the marriage? 'What happened?'

He pushed away from the railing and turned back to look at the moonlit view. She could only see one side of his face but it was enough to make her suspect he didn't like talking about the memory. His features had a boxed-up look about them, the line of his jaw tense, his gaze looking into the far-off distance. 'It turned out she wasn't the one after all.'

'She said no?'

He glanced at his watch and frowned. 'I'd better be on the move. I have some work to do back at my villa before I call it a day.'

Allegra placed her hand on his forearm when he turned from the railing. His muscular arm was warm and the dark, masculine hair faintly prickly under the softer skin of her hand. 'Wait. Tell me what happened.'

Draco went to brush her hand away as if it were a fly but she dug her fingers in. 'Leave it, Allegra.'

No darn way was she going to leave it. Not while she had a chance to find out who he was behind the persona of suave and ruthless businessman. 'I told you about my first time. It wasn't easy talking to you about that, let me tell you. I've only ever told my best friend, Emily. Surely you owe me this one confession?'

It was a moment before he spoke. He stood there looking down at her with her hand on his arm without seeming to move a muscle. But then his arm flexed under her touch and he let out a stream of air that sounded resigned. 'She had someone else lined up. Someone far richer than me. I ended up buying the guy's company a couple of years ago when it got into trouble. Sold it for a profit too. A handsome profit.'

As you do when you're filthy rich and want revenge.

It was a timely reminder to Allegra that the field they were playing on was tipped in his favour. He could be calculating and ruthless when he needed to be. Hadn't Draco already proved that with his non-existent marriage proposal? 'What did your ex think about that?'

He gave a breath of a laugh, a glint of cynicism entering his gaze, making it harder, darker. 'She asked to meet in private and offered herself to me.'

Allegra couldn't explain why she felt such a sharp dart of jealousy. What did she care who he slept with and why? She might care once they were married, but

his past was his past, and it had nothing to do with her.
'What did you do?'
'What do you think I did?'
'Told her to get lost?'
'Wrong.' His eyes contained a gleam of malice. 'I slept with her first and *then* I told her to get lost.'

CHAPTER THREE

ALL THROUGH THE christening service the following day, Allegra couldn't stop thinking about the ex who had spurned Draco's proposal. She'd tried searching for information on the net, but there was nothing about him having been in a long-term relationship. How many years ago had it been? Had it been long before he'd risen to the top, while he'd been still making his mark on the world?

Was that why he had never fallen in love and insisted he never would? Was that why he only ever hooked up with women for short periods of time—because developing an attachment would make him too vulnerable? If he had truly loved the woman, then Allegra could understand how hurt he must have felt—especially when his ex had supposedly chosen someone because they were richer than him. It would have been a cruel slap to the ego for someone as proud as Draco Papandreou.

There were few men richer than him in Greece now. His empire was vast, not just the luxury yacht building, which was growing exponentially across the globe, but also property. He owned numerous villas, not just for his own private use, but also for lease to super-wealthy customers. He had a sharp eye for business and had rescued many from collapse, building them up over time and selling them for a massive profit. He rarely spoke in public about his humble background as the only child of a fisherman, but she guessed it was a powerful motivator to keep expanding his business empire.

But Draco was also an enigmatic man. He only allowed people so close and he never allowed anyone to manipulate or hoodwink him. He was a good judge of character, a fact she had witnessed first-hand when he'd warned her about her first boyfriend. He'd been familiar with the boy's family—this being Greece and all—and had told her she was wasting her time with someone who only wanted to date her because she came from money. *That* had stung. No sixteen-year-old girl with confidence issues and a body she hadn't quite grown into wanted to hear something like that.

But, unfortunately, Draco had been right.

The boy had crowed about how he'd bedded her and then joked about what a disappointment she'd been as a partner. The vernacular he'd used had made the insult all the more hurtful and shaming. It had taken her years to sleep with another partner. Years. And even the last time she'd had sex—which was so long ago she could barely recall what he'd looked like—she had worried he was judging her on her performance, filing away notes to laugh about with his friends in the bar later. Allegra had blamed Draco for it all because she had only gone after the boy after Draco's rejection. The boy's cruel taunts had seemed to echo Draco's ego-crushing dismissal, further shattering her self-esteem.

Allegra looked across the formal room overlooking the terrace where everyone had gathered for drinks to wet the baby's head. Her father was doing more than wetting his son's head. She had lost count of the number of glasses of champagne he had put away. Was he worried about this merger or relieved it was now all sorted? He looked happy—the happiest she had seen him in years. But then, why wouldn't he? He had his perfect little family now, and his left-on-the-shelf daughter of thirty-one was being married off to solve his business woes.

Elena caught Allegra's eye and came over, carrying Nico in her arms. 'I haven't had a moment to speak to you in private, Allegra,' she said, smiling broadly. 'I can't tell you how happy your father and I are about you and Draco. Your dad's been so stressed lately but since he heard you and Draco are getting married it's like a weight's been lifted off him. You *are* happy about it, aren't you? It's just, you've been a little quiet and...'

Allegra forced a smile. Acting had never been her thing but there was no time like the present to learn. 'Of course I'm happy. I'm just feeling a little overwhelmed. It's all been such a whirlwind.'

'Yes, but Draco never waits around for paint to dry, does he?' Elena said with a light laugh. 'I think it's so romantic he wants to marry you as soon as possible.' She glanced at Allegra's abdomen. 'I don't suppose it's because you're...?'

Allegra avoided her gaze and looked at the baby instead, stroking a gentle finger down his tiny petal-soft cheek. 'No. It's just...we both have work commitments booked in months and months ahead and there's only this small window of time available.'

Who knew she could be so good at lying?

'But you do want children, don't you?' Elena asked, handing Nico over for her to cuddle. 'I mean, when you're ready? It would be awful to miss out. I thought I was going to until I met your dad and accidentally fell pregnant. I still pinch myself, you know.' Her gaze went to Allegra's father across the room and she sighed. 'I still can't believe he married me. I didn't think I'd ever find someone to love me.'

But did Allegra's father love Elena? The question seemed to hang suspended in the air like a cobweb. Whether her father felt the same love towards his young wife as she did towards him was questionable. He'd wanted a male heir, and he'd wanted a malleable Greek woman who wouldn't question his authority and who would be content to stay at home and rear the children.

'I've not really thought much about having kids. My career has always been my baby,' Allegra said. She had never been the sort of girl to peer into prams or go gaga at the mention of a baby. Her career had been her entire focus. She had put everything before it. But holding little Nico made a cordoned-off corner of her brain wonder what it would be like to have a child of her own. Nico's tiny rosebud mouth opened on a yawn and he stretched his little body, one tiny arm with its starfish hand flailing in the air. She captured his hand and pressed a kiss to each miniscule finger, marvelling at the perfect little fingernails.

Elena leaned in to straighten the hand-embroidered christening gown that had been in the Kallas family for over a hundred years. Allegra hadn't worn it as an infant because the privilege was exclusive to sons, a tradition that had been another reason to make her feel an outsider. Draco had mentioned the possibility of a child but he'd been teasing. It made sense that he wouldn't want any permanent legacies from their short-term union. And why was she thinking about having babies with him, anyway? She was supposed to be keeping their marriage in name only.

Good luck with that.

'Will you be all right with him for a moment?' Elena asked. 'I just want to pop to the bathroom and change my breast pads.'

'Of course.' Little Nico wriggled again then opened his eyes, looked at her and smiled a gummy smile. Allegra felt a wave of love so powerful it was like an invisible fist grabbing her heart. This was her half-brother and she was melting like honey on a hotplate. What would she have felt if it had been her own flesh and blood? She tickled the baby's button-sized chin. 'Hey, little guy, who's been a beautiful boy while all this fuss is going on?'

Draco came alongside Allegra and, slipping his arm around her waist, offered the baby a finger, which little Nico grabbed with his tiny hand. 'It's hard to believe how small babies are—he's like a doll.'

'Yes,' Allegra said. 'I keep worrying I'm going to drop him. I suppose you get used to it when it's your own.'

'You're a natural. You look like you've been holding babies all your life.'

She gave a wry movement of her lips. 'Yes, well, I like the ones you can hand back. Do you want a hold?'

'No way.' He took a step back and held his hands up like stop signs, as if she were handing him a ticking bomb. 'I'm no good with babies.'

'Go on.' Allegra kept coming at him with the baby. 'You're a big macho man. You're surely not scared of a tiny, defenceless baby?'

Draco looked as though he was going to resist, but then his expression took on a resigned set. 'If I drop him, then it will be your fault.'

'You won't drop him.' Allegra came near so she could transfer the baby into his arms. The closeness of him stirred her senses into a swarm of longing. The fresh lime scent of his aftershave with its woody notes was intoxicating and alluring.

He took the infant, holding him slightly aloft, as if not wanting to get too close. But then Nico smiled and gurgled up at him, and Draco brought him against his chest and gently rocked him in his arms, looking down at the baby with a small smile. Allegra hadn't expected the sight of him with a baby in his arms to stir her so much.

'I've never been a godfather before,' he said after a moment.

'Nor me a godmother,' Allegra said. 'I'm not sure what sort of spiritual adviser I'll make. Sometimes I feel I could do with some spiritual guidance myself.'

'Don't we all?'

She angled her gaze at him. 'What? The invincible Draco Papandreou in need of advice? Wonders will never cease.'

He gave her a self-deprecating smile. 'You'd be surprised. It took me a long time to get control of my life. I almost lost my way a few times.' He looked down at the baby again, his smile dimming slightly. 'Especially after my father was killed. I suddenly found myself all alone in the world.'

'How old were you when your mother died?'

'Six.'

Allegra had been twice that age when her mother

had died and she still missed her terribly. How hard must it have been for Draco as a small child to lose his mother, only to lose his father a few years later? 'It must have been awful for you when your father died so suddenly. Who looked after you?'

'I looked after myself.'

She frowned at the cynical edge to his tone. 'But how did you survive? Didn't some relatives take you in?'

His expression reminded her of a suit of armour. She could see the outline of his face but only through a mask of steel. 'What few relatives I had were not interested in a fifteen-year-old boy with an attitude problem.'

'So what did you do?'

'I fended for myself.'

'How?'

His eyes took on a sardonic glint. 'You really want to hear some of the wicked things I got up to? I might shock you.'

'Try me and see.'

He glanced down at the baby and then gave Allegra an inscrutable smile. 'Not in front of little Nico.'

Allegra was frustrated he didn't trust her enough to tell her what his childhood and adolescence had been like. Was his tragic past one of the reasons he wanted to settle down now? It was all very well, her harbouring secret little fantasies about having a baby of her own but, even if Draco had wanted one, having a baby together would cause a whole lot of complications she could well do without.

She had acted for a number of women divorcing husbands from a different country, which made the care arrangements for children particularly complex, especially if the split was acrimonious—and of course many, if not most, were. It was a legal and personal minefield and one Allegra wanted to avoid at all costs. She knew enough about Greek men, and Draco in particular, to know he would not want to live apart from his child or children. He would want control. And he would do whatever it took to maintain it. Luckily, a baby wasn't part of the deal.

Nico began to get restless and, as if tuned in to her baby's needs by radar, Elena came back and took him from Draco. 'Time for a feed, I think,' she said. 'You two make great babysitters, by the way.'

Once Elena left, Draco led Allegra out to a shaded part of the garden near a fountain where the tinkle and splash of water cooled the warm atmosphere. 'There are some legal aspects of our marriage to deal with. Can you free up some time mid-week? I'll be in London tying up some other business. I'll set up an appointment with my London-based lawyer so we can sort everything out.'

Allegra had no problem with signing a pre-nuptial agreement. She had investments, property and other assets of her own she didn't want to jeopardise when it came time to divorce. But it was a stinging little reminder of the cynical mind-set he had about their relationship. 'Sure. Just give my secretary, Emily, a call and get her to put it in my diary.'

'I know what you're thinking. But I have shareholders to protect, and I'm sure you too have assets you don't want to see compromised. It makes things less complicated when we wrap things up.' He waited a beat before adding, 'It's not meant to be an insult to you, Allegra.'

'I didn't take it as one.'

He lifted a fingertip to the space between her eyes and smoothed away a puckered frown. 'Then why are you frowning at me like that?'

Allegra forced her facial muscles to relax. 'I always frown when I'm thinking.' She moved closer to the fountain and trailed her fingers in the cool water. 'It feels weird to think this time next week we'll be married.'

His hands came to rest on the top of her shoulders, his tall, strong frame standing just behind her. The intimacy of his proximity sent a rush of fizzing heat through her flesh. She had to fight the urge to lean back into his embrace, to feel the stirring of his body.

'Having second thoughts?' he said.

And third and fourth and every number this side of a thousand.

'It wouldn't matter what thoughts I had, though, would it? I haven't got any choice. I have to do this or watch Elena and Nico suffer.'

He turned her around and meshed his gaze with hers, his hands going to rest lightly about her waist. His gaze searched hers for a long moment, his expression containing a hint of a frown. 'I know this has been difficult for you. Your father's situation has made things far more time pressured than they could have been. Creditors are impatient people these days. But, in time, I hope you'll come to see this as a good solution all round. For you especially.'

Why for her especially?

Marriage was such an enormous step for anyone, even when the two parties loved one another. But when neither of them were in love, then how did that bode for them? Sure, some arranged marriages seemed to work well, but surely that was good luck, or maybe one or both parties became so resigned to their situation they decided it was more tolerable to love rather than hate.

Allegra had felt such intense antagonism towards Draco for so long, she didn't understand why she felt so attracted to him. Was it her frustrated female hormones playing perverse tricks on her? The more time she spent with him, the more she realised she had fashioned him in her mind as an archenemy.

Funny, but he didn't feel like an enemy when he touched her. When he looked at her with those black-as-tar eyes with their unknowable depths. He didn't feel like her opponent when he kissed her, when his tongue played with hers in an erotic mimicry of sex that made her blood sing full-throated arias through her veins. Nor when his hands cradled her breasts or held her lightly by the waist, as he was doing now.

His fingers tightened a fraction and he stepped closer—close enough for her to feel the need rising in him that mirrored the ache rising in her. His eyes went to her mouth in a sexily hooded way that never failed to get her pulse on the run. He lowered his head as if in slow motion, leaving her plenty of time to block the kiss if she wanted to.

She didn't.

His lips were dry and warm on hers, just a brush stroke at first—a light touchdown of surface rediscovery. But then he touched down again, once, twice, and on the third time something restrained in him escaped and his kiss became one of passionate heat and urgency.

The same hot-blooded urgency coursed through her

from her mouth to the very centre of her womanhood. The sexy glide of his tongue into her mouth made her whimper in approval, her arms going around his neck to bring her body even closer to the glorious hardness of his. Draco's hands came up to cradle her face, his head angled to one side so he could deepen the kiss, taking her on a journey of thrilling, pulse-thudding excitement as her need for him built to a level she would not have thought possible even a few days ago. She tangled her fingers into the thick pelt of his hair, her mouth feeding off his. His teeth nipped her lower lip and then his tongue swept over it like a salve. He did the same to her top lip, his nip and tugs so gentle, but they caused a tumult of sensations to rocket through her body and pool in a liquid, sizzling fire deep in her core.

'Hey, break it up you two,' one of Allegra's father's friends called out from some distance behind her. 'Save it for the honeymoon.'

Draco set her from him with a smile at her father's friend Spiro while keeping her by his side with an arm around her waist. 'How's it going, Spiro?'

'Not as good as things are going for you, I'll wager,' Spiro said with a wide grin. 'So, you two finally got together. He's a good catch, eh, Allegra? You must be feeling pretty pleased with yourself, landing a man like him.'

Why's that? Because I was rabid-dog ugly and left on the shelf and no one in their right mind would ever have offered for me in a thousand, million years?

Allegra ground her teeth so hard behind her smile she thought she would have to be tube fed for the rest of her life. 'Actually, Draco is the one who got the prize catch, aren't you, darling?'

Draco's smile set off a smouldering glint in his eyes. 'But of course, *kardia mou*. I'm the hands down winner in this union.'

Allegra's back teeth went down another centimetre. But thankfully Spiro moved on to chat to other guests who had come out to the garden to enjoy the shade and light breeze coming in from the ocean. 'You're really enjoying this, aren't you?' she said out of the side of her mouth.

'You know what Spiro is like,' Draco said, leading her back towards the house with a firm, warm hand in the small of her back.

'Yes, he's a man who thinks all a woman wants is a man with a big bank balance. I find it *so* insulting. A man isn't a financial plan. I know there are probably some women out there who are gold-diggers, but personally I would never marry someone because of his wealth. It's no measure of who he is as a person.'

He gave her lower back a circular stroke, making her legs feel as though someone had snipped her ligaments. 'I agree with you. But, on the other hand, the fact that someone has had the discipline and drive to work and accumulate wealth must demonstrate some admirable qualities, surely?'

Allegra gave a snort. 'I had a client a couple of years ago. She married a man who'd inherited a veritable fortune from his parents. He was the laziest, most obnoxious man I've ever met. He was abusive to his wife, both during and after their marriage, and he was so darn mean about supporting his own kids once it ended. Money does something to some people. It brings out the worst in them, and then people get hurt. I see it all the time in my job.'

Draco tucked her arm through his. 'At least we come to this marriage as equals, or close enough to being equals.'

'I would hardly call my wealth equal to yours.'

'Perhaps not, but we've both worked hard for what we've got, and neither of us would like to lose it.'

There were worse things to lose...

Like my heart, if I'm not careful.

Emily was at Allegra's office door before she'd even had time to put her tote bag away when she arrived back at work on Monday morning. She closed the door behind her and pulled out the chair opposite Allegra's desk. 'Okay, so give it to me. What the hell is going on? Do you have any idea how gobsmacked I was to hear you're getting married?'

'I told you—it's a marriage of convenience,' Allegra said. 'My father's got himself into a financial pickle and Draco is bailing him out with a merger.'

Emily's brow puckered. 'But how come he wants to marry you?'

Allegra dropped her shoulders with a 'thanks for the compliment' look. 'Apparently he wants a wife and I tick all his boxes.'

Emily made an apologetic movement of her lips. 'Sorry, didn't mean to suggest you weren't marriageable or anything. You're gorgeous, and any man with a skerrick of testosterone would be thrilled to have you as his wife. But you've always been so against marriage—which to be frank is a bit of an occupational hazard around here. You broke out in hives before Julie's wedding, remember?'

Allegra remembered all too well. It wouldn't have

been a good look to be in the bridal party photos with red splotches all over her face and neck—but apparently it hadn't been hives but a reaction to the facial she'd had the day before as part of the hen's party spa day. Just as well the make-up artist had done an excellent job of disguising it with cover-up. 'That was an allergic reaction—'

'I rest my case.'

Allegra rolled her eyes. 'Anyway, I've agreed because...well... I've agreed, that's all. I've known him since I was a teenager. I used to run into him at corporate functions and stuff with my father.'

And proceed to embarrass myself with humiliating frequency.

'But six months ago you were spitting chips about how arrogant and up himself he was,' Emily said. 'Now you're wearing his ring. Show me, by the way.' She leaned across the desk to grasp Allegra's hand. 'Oh. My. God. Isn't it gorgeous?'

'Yes, I couldn't have chosen better myself.' Which made Allegra wonder if Draco knew her better than she'd thought, despite his claim he'd selected the ring at random. What else did he know about her?

Emily sat back down with a sigh. 'Gosh, I wish some handsome billionaire would force me into a marriage of convenience. *Is* he a billionaire?'

'Pretty close to it, I think.'

Emily leaned forward again, her toffee-brown eyes suddenly full of concern. 'You sure you're doing the right thing? I mean, you don't have to go through with it, you know. You can always say no even as the priest is asking you if you'll take this man and so on.'

Allegra couldn't say no, but explaining why to her

friend might make her look even more pathetic than she felt. She was ashamed about wanting to please her father at her age but there was no escaping it. 'I know what I'm doing, Em.'

'You said no sex, but surely you were joking?' Emily said. 'I mean, look at the guy. What's not to want?'

Allegra could feel her cheeks giving her away. 'I've told him it's a hands-off affair.'

Emily snorted. 'Like that's going to work. Did he actually agree to that?'

'Not in so many words, but he has to respect my wishes or—'

'Wishes, schmishes,' Emily said, eyes twinkling. 'You want him. That's why you were so cross about him that night in December. It was him you wanted, not that loser who didn't have the balls to show up when he'd been the one to ask you out in the first place.'

'I was cross with Draco because he seemed to be amused by the fact I was stood up by my date,' Allegra said. 'I didn't find it amusing. I found it humiliating.'

'What you found humiliating was Draco witnessing you being left high and dry,' Emily said. 'No girl wants a guy she fancies to see her rejected by someone else. It's not good for the ego. Speaking of egos—am I going to be your bridesmaid, or aren't you having one, since your wedding's so rushed and all?'

'Sorry, Em.' Allegra gave her friend a grimace. 'It's a really quiet affair with only a handful of guests on his private island.'

'His private island.' Emily grinned. *'No problemo.'* She slipped off the desk and straightened her skirt. 'But I expect a full report with photos when you get back from your honeymoon, okay?'

'Will do.'
'Where are you having your honeymoon?'
'On his yacht.'
Emily's eyes sparkled. 'You're toast.'

CHAPTER FOUR

ONCE THE LEGAL work had been seen to during the week, Allegra didn't see Draco again until the day before the wedding, when she arrived at his private retreat via a helicopter he had chartered to meet her at Athens airport. Her week had been a nightmare of juggling work, arranging a wedding dress and packing for their 'honeymoon'. Every time she even thought the word, much less said it, it made her pulse gallop. She knew he wasn't the sort of man to force himself on her. It was her own uncontrollable desires she was worried about.

Emily was right. How on earth was she going to resist him? Spending a week on a yacht with Draco was going to test her resolve like a chocolate addict standing in the middle of a chocolate fountain with her mouth open. She had no self-control around him. He only had to look at her with that black-as-sin gaze and her heart would skip as if it were jumping rope for England *and* Greece.

She had work commitments back home once the honeymoon was over, but apparently Draco had business meetings that week in London, so they would be travelling back together.

Just like a normal couple...

When Allegra arrived at the island it was like stepping into paradise. The eye-popping blue of the ocean with its fringe of sand on the villa side as white as powdered sugar was nothing short of stunning. The island was part of the Cyclades group and the andesite rocks, lava domes and prismatic columns of its cliffs and hills were geologists' eye candy. They were relics of the intense hydrothermal activity of millions of years ago and gave the islands, and this one in particular, a sense of timeless beauty.

But it was the villa itself that made her breath come to a slamming halt. It was eye-squinting white, built on four levels with an infinity pool that overlooked the pristine beach below. Gardens that looked like something out of a fairy tale surrounded the villa, and there were cypress pines everywhere, including a thick forest of them on the hills at the back of the island.

Allegra had expected Draco to meet her, as he'd arranged the day before. But only that morning he'd sent a brief text to say he couldn't make it. *Couldn't* or didn't want to? When she'd pressed the pilot for more information, he'd informed her Draco was tied up with something on the island which, considering a wedding was taking place the following day, wasn't such an unreasonable excuse. There was certainly a lot of activity going on for all that it was to be a small ceremony.

But when a woman in her late fifties came bustling out of the front door of the villa, welcoming Allegra in broken English, to her surprise she found herself feeling disappointed Draco hadn't welcomed her himself. What about his insistence they act like a normal couple in front of his staff?

'Kyria Kallas,' the housekeeper said. 'Kyrios Papandreou will be here soon. He is...how I say?...too busy?'

Allegra hoped it wasn't a foreshadowing of their future. She had never been important to her father. Work had always come first. Was she to suffer the same treatment by Draco? She might not want this marriage, but the idea of being so overlooked sent a shudder down her spine.

Allegra smiled at the housekeeper and assured her she was fine without him being there when he had so much to do. She found out the woman's name was Iona, that she had been working for Draco for five years and he was the best employer in the world. Allegra had trouble getting the woman to stop gushing about him. No doubt Draco's charm had worked its magic on the widow who, from what Iona said, he had rescued off the streets of Mykonos where she'd been left to fend for herself after her husband had divorced her, leaving her with virtually nothing out of a thirty-year marriage other than the clothes on her back. Allegra knew Draco was a financially generous man, but she hadn't seen him as the type to take in a homeless person and train them up to be his housekeeper.

Iona led her inside and showed her the wing of the villa she would be staying in prior to the wedding. It was a beautifully decorated suite of rooms with a marble bathroom complete with a freestanding bath with elegant gold taps and fittings. The furnishings in both the bedroom and sitting room were a lush combination of velvet, silk and brocade, and crystal chandeliers hung overhead. Allegra was no art expert, but the works on the walls were a mix of old and new, with a few pieces that looked like they were worth millions. The views from the windows were so breath-taking, she couldn't stop staring and wondering how anyone could ever get used to being surrounded by such beauty and the grandeur of nature at its finest.

One of the staff brought in her luggage and once he had gone Iona asked if she could press the wedding dress and any other clothes that needed attending to.

'That would be lovely, thank you.'

Allegra wandered over to the window overlooking the ocean and the gorgeous stretch of sand that sloped to the sparkling water below. Even though inside the villa was beautifully air-conditioned, the thought of a swim at the beach was so tempting she was rustling through her bag to retrieve her bathing costume before Iona could get it unpacked. She decided on her one-piece because she didn't feel like parading around in a bikini that was smaller than most of her underwear—a last-minute present from Emily.

There was a pathway with steps down to the beach that went past the infinity pool. Allegra decided against using the pool because it was so exposed to the villa. She didn't fancy the household staff watching her while she swam—or her version of swimming, anyway.

The sand was hot between her toes when she took off her sandals, and the sun beat down on her back and shoulders when she slipped off her light cotton beach poncho. The water was as warm as a bath and as clear as drinking water—so clear she could see fish darting away with every step she took. She went deeper and then did a shallow dive, her whole body sighing with pleasure when the water closed over her heated sticky flesh. It was like being baptised by nature, reborn and renewed by the elemental pulse of the water that had lapped this beach for aeons.

She swam back and forth, marvelling at the fish below her, and enjoying the sensation of the sun shining down on her back and legs after a miserable summer so far back in London. It was pure bliss to feel the water move over her body with every stroke she took, the sound of it splashing and the occasional cry of a seabird the only sounds she could hear.

Maybe she could get used to this sort of life—a week or two in London working her butt off and then coming back to this. To sun, sand and sea...and a sinfully handsome, sexy husband.

Draco came back to the villa, from seeing to an issue with one of his junior staff members at the staff quarters, to find Allegra had gone down to the beach. He could see her from the terrace, moving through the water like a mermaid, her long, black silky hair floating out behind her. His hormones shuddered at the sight of her. Her navy-blue and white one-piece highlighted her neat figure in all the right places—places he couldn't wait to get his hands on again.

He had only touched her breasts through her clothes and that had been enough to make him crazy with lust. She insisted their relationship would remain unconsummated, but every time he kissed her the message from her response was the opposite. He wasn't the sort of man to push a woman into doing things she didn't want to do, but everything so far told him Allegra *did* want him. Wanted him as badly as he wanted her.

He walked down to the beach and stood with one

hand over his brow, shielding his eyes from the sun, watching her slice through the water. But, as if she sensed his gaze on her, she stopped, stood upright in the waist-deep water and swung the wet curtain of her hair behind her back. She looked like a goddess arising from the depths of the ocean. The water droplets sparkled off her like a spray of carelessly flung diamonds, her creamy skin almost as white and pure as the sand.

Draco shucked off his jeans, T-shirt and shoes and walked into the water towards her. He would have slipped off his undershorts as well, but he decided to keep things in his pants, so to speak. Making love to Allegra with his staff watching from above was something he was keen to avoid. Once they were on his yacht and away from prying eyes, well, who knew what might happen?

He came closer to her and ran his eyes over her body. His flesh tingled, wondering if her hands and mouth would be as thorough as his searching gaze in the not-too-distant future.

Her eyes met his in a flinty lock. 'Is all your terribly important business sorted now?'

Draco placed his hands on her waist but, while she didn't resist, she stood statue-firm with her eyes spearing him like dark blue darts. 'Sorry, *agape mou*. I had an issue with one of my young staff. A homeless kid I took in a few months ago. He's having some problems with the rules I've set down.'

She blinked a couple of times and her whole body sagged as it lost its rigid stance. 'Oh...'

He moved his hands to her arms, stroking her wet skin cooled by the water. It was like caressing silk. Every cell in his body pulsed and strained to get closer to her. The blood pounded to his groin, his brain filling with images of him pinning her to the sand and getting all hot and primal with her. 'You can't be seen scowling at me the day before the wedding, *ne*?'

Allegra let out a breathy little sigh and stepped closer, placing her hands flat on his chest, making his blood roar all the harder. 'I'm sorry... I was just feeling a bit overwhelmed with it all. Is he OK, this employee of yours?'

Draco held her by the hips, his need for her closing the distance between their bodies like a bridge of lust. 'I found Yanni under the influence of something back at the staff quarters. I wasn't sure if it was alcohol or something else. I had to make sure, because he's got a history of substance abuse.'

She bit into her lower lip with her teeth. 'Oh, how terribly worrying for you. Is he all right?'

'Yes, but he's going to have one hell of a hangover in a few hours,' Draco said. 'I've got someone watching him and keeping him hydrated.'

'How old is he?'

'Sixteen going on thirty.' Draco grimaced and added, 'He's seen things you and I wouldn't dream of even in a nightmare. He's been living on the streets since he was ten years old.'

Her brow was as creased as the lines the wind had made in the sand. 'How did you come by him?'

'He tried to pick-pocket me. I caught him, and he fought like a demon, but then I realised he was sick with withdrawals from something. He was shaking and sweating and not in his right mind at all. He was barely coherent. I took him to a rehab centre and got him some help, but of course he relapsed as soon as he was released. You can't be on the streets and on God knows what substances for six years without having a struggle to get clean.'

Her brow was still slightly furrowed. 'So you took him in yourself? To live with you here on your island?'

'Yes, because he's safe here—relatively,' Draco said. 'This being an island, I can keep him away from the nightclubs and bars and seedy types who want to exploit him to do their dirty work for them. He's a good kid underneath all the bluster, he's just had some bad stuff happen to him.'

Her expression was thoughtful for a beat or two of silence. 'Did you spend time on the streets?'

Draco didn't like talking about the time after his father had died and he'd been left alone in the world. He had no money other than the pittance his father had saved which hadn't even covered the funeral expenses. It was a time he would rather forget because his life could have turned out so different—or ended altogether—if he had made some of the bad choices Yanni had made. Taking care of the teenager was a way of reaching back in time to be the sort of mentor he had found in his first boss, Josef.

'A few months. It was tough. I could have gone either way. But I managed to get out of there and make something of myself to honour my father.'

'How did you go from there to where you are now?'

'Guts and determination,' Draco said. 'And some luck. I got work down at the boat yard and the owner of one of the yacht-tour fleets took me on. I went to night school to finish my education and juggled a couple of other jobs to get some money behind me. I bought my way into the business and then bought it outright from Josef when he retired. I built it up and expanded it after that. I figured Yanni needs someone like Josef was to me. Tough but fair.'

Allegra gave him a lopsided smile and her hands slid up to link around his neck, bringing her body even closer to his until he could feel the cool, wet press of her breasts and the hot swell of her mound. 'I didn't realise you were such a nice guy underneath all that arrogance.'

Draco smiled and settled his hands on the sweet curve of her bottom, his gaze briefly dipping to the shadow of her cleavage. 'If you knew what I was thinking right now, there's no way you would ever call me nice.'

Her eyes shone with the same excitement he could feel throbbing through his body. Her fingers laced through his hair, her lips parting, and the tip of her tongue snaking out to leave a glistening sheen of moisture over them. 'Are you going to kiss me for the sake of any staff who might be watching?' Allegra's voice was husky, her warm breath wafting across the surface of his lips. She smelt of sun and salt and sunscreen, and something else that made his self-control throw its hands up in defeat.

Draco gave a mock 'let's get it over with' sigh. 'All right—if you insist.' He brought his mouth to hers in a kiss that spoke of the longing in his body. He explored the interior of her mouth, his blood rushing like a torrent at her response. Her tongue tangled with his, playing cat-and-mouse and hide-and-seek and I-want-you-right-now. He brought her as hard up against him as he could, his hands cupping her bottom until he could feel the intimate seam of her body. Never had he wanted someone so desperately. It was like a fire in his system, roaring through the network of his veins, making him zing from head to foot with sexual energy and demonic drive.

Her soft little whimpers drove him wild, so too the way her hands played with his hair, pulling and tugging until every hair root on his scalp tingled. Her mouth was wet and salty and he fed off it like an addict on a drug he couldn't resist.

He brought his hands up to stroke her breasts through the wet fabric of her bathers but that wasn't good enough for him. He wanted to feel those gorgeous globes of sexy female flesh, skin on skin.

He *needed* to.

He *ached* to.

Draco turned them around so his back was to the villa, somewhat shielding her from view. He slipped the straps off her shoulders as if he were unwrapping a gift. Allegra's breasts were neither small nor large but somewhere perfectly in between—creamy white with dark pink nipples erect as he was. He palmed them first, allowing her to get used to the slight roughness of his hands from working in his boat yard. She made a mewling sound when his thumbs rolled over her nipples, her mouth giving his sexy little nips and nudges that made his spine shiver as if sand were trickling down between his vertebrae. She caught his lower lip between her teeth in a little kittenish bite that made him wonder if he was going to jump the start like a teenager on his first sexual encounter.

He pushed her breasts upwards to meet his descending mouth, stroking his tongue around and over her nipple on her right breast, and then the left one, leaving them wet and peaking. Draco moved his mouth to explore the curve of her breast—the top side, the underside and the delectable space between. Allegra tilted her head back, her long hair trailing like black seaweed in the water behind her. She offered her breasts to him like a worshipper offers something to a god. He made the most of it. Beyond caring if his staff was watching from the villa. He subjected each of her breasts to an intimate exploration with his lips and tongue and with gentle nibbles of his teeth, evoking a panting response from her that thrilled every drop of testosterone in his body.

He was so hard, it was painful. But, as if she knew the agony he was going through, one of her hands slipped down between their jammed-together bodies and freed him from his undershorts. Her fingers were cool and firm around his length, stroking and squeezing him under the cover of the water. Not such a great cover, given the water was as clear as bottled water, but he was well beyond worrying about that.

He pulled her bathers down past her hips, slipping his hand down to cup her mound, letting her body feel the subtle pressure of his touch. She moved urgently against his hand, gasping against Draco's mouth. 'Please...' The cry sounded as desperate as he felt. 'Please. Please. Please...'

He traced his finger over her, teasing her with his strokes, finally slipping a finger into her hot, moist body, stroking the swollen heart of her until she came with a rush against his hand. He felt every contraction and ripple of her inner muscles, the sexy panting of Allegra's breathing delighting him more than he could have imagined. She was so responsive to him. What full-blooded man wouldn't be pleased about that? Nothing satisfied him more than giving a partner pleasure, but somehow Allegra's pleasure meant something to him.

Something he couldn't quite explain.

Draco withdrew his finger and held her while she recovered. Her cheeks were lightly flushed and it travelled all the way down to her décolletage in a rosy tide. She sent her tongue out over her lips again, her gaze a little dazed. 'That was…'

'Good?'

She pulled at her lip with her teeth, her gaze slipping out of reach of his. 'Unexpected.'

'In what way?'

'I don't normally… I mean I've never done that with a partner…'

He inched up her chin so her gaze reconnected with his. Allegra's blue eyes swam with uncertainty…or was it shyness, or a combination of both? 'The first time you've had sex in the water?' he asked.

She took a tiny barely audible swallow. 'The first time I've come with a partner present.'

Draco frowned. 'Really?'

She gave a self-deprecating grimace, her half-mast lashes screening her eyes. 'Yes, well, I can do it by myself, but as soon as a guy is there, pressuring me to get on with it, I just…freeze.'

To say he was stunned was an understatement. How had she put up with such an imbalance in her love life for so long? Or was it because of her first sexual encounter? The shame from being humiliated by some jerk who probably hadn't known how to make love to her anyway? Draco's guts roiled with anger at how she had been treated. She was responsive to him. Incredibly responsive, which meant she trusted him. Trust was an enormous part of sex, particularly for women, whose bodies could be so easily exploited by too rough a handling. He was all for a bit of athletic sex, but there was no way he would ever hurt or humiliate a partner during it, nor would he settle for anything less than mutual pleasure.

But, right now, his pleasure could wait.

He slid his hand along the side of her face, an unexpected wave of protectiveness sweeping through him. 'Listen to me, Allegra. You can trust me to always put your pleasure first. You can take as long as you need. Women are wired differently from men. A good lover will understand that and allow his partner plenty of time.'

Her smile was shaky around the edges and her cheeks still tinged with flags of pink. 'So much for the hands-off arrangement. We're not even married yet and look how I'm behaving.'

He brushed her wet hair back from her face, looking into her dark blue eyes almost the same colour as the ocean. 'This chemistry between us isn't something to be ashamed of, *glykia mou*. It's to be celebrated. It bodes well for a healthy marriage between us.'

She moistened her lips and her gaze flicked briefly to his groin. 'But what about you? Aren't you going to…?'

Draco shook his head. 'Not that I don't want to, but

the next time we make love it's going to be to consummate our marriage. And preferably we'll be alone on my yacht without half my staff watching from the wings.'

She sank her teeth into her lower lip. 'That hardly seems fair to you... I mean, things were getting pretty heavy there, just then.'

He took her hands in both of his and held them against his chest in case Allegra went in search of him. He could only take so much, especially from those silky little hands that seemed instinctively to know how to handle him. 'It's a man's responsibility to control his desires, at all times and in all circumstances. I want you. Make no mistake about it. I can't think of a time I wanted someone more. But tomorrow will be all the better if we wait.'

Her mouth formed a twist of a smile. 'Careful, Draco, you're starting to sound like our marriage is going to be a normal one.'

He held her gaze for a beat. 'In bed, it will be.'

Allegra walked back along the sand to the pathway leading to the villa with Draco's hand holding hers. Her body was still vibrating with aftershocks from the pleasure he had evoked. It made her aware of every inch of her flesh, as if all the nerves had been given steroids and were twice their size and three times as active.

How had it happened?

Why had she allowed Draco to touch her like that? He hadn't followed through to claim his own pleasure, so didn't that make her seem a little pathetic? Like that teenage girl she used to be? Her wanton response to him demonstrated her vulnerability. She was a fool to give him more ammunition. She was supposed to be resisting him. Rejecting his advances, not encouraging such intimate contact. Not only encouraging it but responding to it like she had never responded to anyone before. Her breasts felt fuller, more sensitive, her inner core tingling with the memory of his inserted finger. If she was going to shatter into a thousand pieces with the glide of his finger then what was going to happen when he made love to her fully?

What do you mean 'when'?

Allegra ignored her conscience. Her conscience could take a running jump off the nearest cliff and drown in the Aegean Sea. Her conscience didn't realise what it was like to be thirty-one years old and so feverishly in lust with a man she couldn't sleep at night without her body writhing in frustration.

What was wrong with having a 'married' affair with Draco? It was one of the perks of the deal. The *only* perk as far as she could see. Well, there might be a few more, but she didn't want to think about them just now. Perhaps sex could be fine as long as she kept her emotions out of it, which shouldn't be too much of a problem, because her emotions had never been involved before.

No. She was ready for this. More than ready. Her body deserved some excitement after the miserable drought it had been subjected to. It would make the prospect of getting married more palatable, knowing that as soon as they were alone they would be making love… No. *Having sex.*

Better get the terminology right from the outset. She wasn't a romantic. That was Emily's territory.

Emily was the one who dreamed of being swept off her feet and carried off into the golden sunset by a handsome prince. A fantasy that had so far done Emily zero favours.

Allegra was far too practical for all that nonsense, which was part of the reason why she had got to this age without falling in love. She had ruled it out. Put a line through the notion. She had always kept herself from getting too attached to the men she occasionally dated. She was a career woman through and through, but career women needed sex too, didn't they? They couldn't be expected to do nothing but work. It wasn't healthy. Balance was what she needed. A balance of work and pleasure, and how better to get it than to be married to heart-stalling, sexy-as-sin Draco Papandreou who would allow her to come and go for work and play?

Thing was… Allegra had a feeling she might want to play a lot more than work. And to come more than go—no pun intended. The thought of flying back to London, to dismal weather, traffic-clogged streets and difficult clients when she could have all this sunshine, white sand and water as blue as lapis lazuli didn't hold any of the appeal it used to, when she'd been desperate to get away from Greece after visiting her father and get back to her normal routine.

All the paperwork, the phone calls, the emails, the lengthy court appearances and the constant tension from dealing with difficult partners of distraught, angry or bitter clients…. Here all she had to listen to was the sound of seabirds, the ocean lapping the shore and the whisper of the wind in the pines.

When they got to the top of the path, Allegra pushed

back some wisps of salt-encrusted hair out of her eyes. 'I so need a shower.'

Draco's smile had a hint of devilment. 'I'd join you but that would be asking way too much of my self-control.'

A tiny doubt peeped out from behind the curtain in her mind... What if his self-control was only that strong because she hadn't done it for him? Down in the water, she'd been sure he would lose control and be swept away on a tide of passion just as she'd been.

But he hadn't.

He had stepped away from her as if they had innocently embraced and not been in the throes of making... Strike that. *Having sex*. Did it mean she would always be the one in the relationship with less power? The one who needed most, lost most. She saw it every day at work. Women who cared too much, loved or desired too much, lost out in the end.

Was she going to end up one of those women she privately pitied?

Draco's gaze went to the frown pulling at her brow before she could iron it out. He placed his hands on her shoulders and gave them a gentle squeeze. 'I know what you're thinking.'

Allegra screened her features. 'I'm hot and sticky and have sand in places I didn't even know I had places.'

He gave a soft laugh and stroked the back of his bent knuckles down her right cheek. 'Don't doubt yourself so much, *agape mou*. You have no reason to feel insecure with me.'

Like that's going to reassure me.

Allegra had never felt more insecure, more worried she was stepping over a vertiginous cliff into the unknown…or maybe not so much the unknown as the dreaded. Within less than twenty-four hours, she would be married to Draco Papandreou. She would wear his ring and share his bed and all his gloriously luxurious villas. But there was one truth she couldn't escape from no matter how much she tried to ignore it.

She would never have his heart.

CHAPTER FIVE

ALLEGRA PREPARED FOR her wedding day like any other bride, the only difference being that a knot of panic had settled in her stomach and, as each second climbed towards the time of the ceremony, the knot tightened, drawing all her intestines into a clotted ball.

Elena had flown in from from Santorini by helicopter first thing with Allegra's father and baby Nico, and was on hand to help her get dressed. Iona, Draco's housekeeper, was in her element, fussing over Allegra as if she were her own daughter. In spite of Allegra's reservations and nerves, she couldn't help feeling reassured by their cheery presence. They believed this was a romantic wedding day for the bride and groom and she didn't want to be the one to prick their bubble with the hatpin of honesty.

Along with Elena and Iona were a hairdresser and a make-up artist flown in specially, apparently at Draco's command. Allegra knew he was keen to keep up appearances, but it still touched her that he had gone to the trouble of organising their attendance. It might not be her choice to be married under such circumstances, but there was no way she was going to look like a fright show on her wedding day.

But that wasn't the only surprise.

The sound of the helicopter blades overhead announced yet another wedding guest arrival.

Not long after, Allegra was about to slip on her dress when there was a knock at the suite's door.

'That will be your bridesmaid,' Elena said, beaming.

'But I'm not having a—'

'Surprise!' The door burst open and in came Emily, carrying a garment bag folded over one arm. 'One bridesmaid arriving for active duty.'

Allegra blinked back a sudden rush of tears. 'Em, what are you doing here? I—'

'Don't cry! Your make-up will run,' the make-up girl said, dashing back over with a cotton pad, eye shadow and eyeliner brushes like an artist touching up her precious canvas.

Emily handed her garment bag to Iona, who bustled off to press the dress ready for her to put on. 'Draco called me at work a couple of days ago and asked me to come. He told me not to tell you as he wanted it to be a surprise.'

It was more than a surprise. Allegra couldn't understand why he'd gone to so much trouble, contacting her friend and workmate without telling her. But then he didn't know Emily knew their marriage was one of convenience. Had her friend blown it? Had Emily let slip she'd been let in on the secret against his express wishes?

Once the make-up artist had tidied up her face, Allegra clasped Emily by the hands. 'I'm *so* glad you're here.'

Emily grinned like a child let loose in a sweet shop with a platinum credit card. 'You should've warned me about Draco's wealth. I didn't realise you could have silver service on a helicopter. And he flew me first class from London to Athens last night and put me up in the most amazing hotel. I lost count of how many champagnes I was served on that flight. I felt like a movie star. That man has serious class.'

'Em...?' Allegra gave her a 'did you or didn't you?' look.

Emily's smile never faltered and she gave a covert wink. 'You should see the dress I've got. Actually, I've got three, so you could choose the colour you like best.' She went over to Iona who had hung the three dresses on silk-padded clothes hangers. 'Shell-pink, baby-blue or café latte?'

'The shell-pink,' Allegra said, turning to Elena, who was hovering nearby. 'What do you think, Elena? It would go best, don't you think?'

Elena nodded. 'Absolutely. It's perfect with the oyster silk white of your dress. Speaking of your dress—we'd better get you into it. We've only got a few minutes until the ceremony starts.'

Allegra felt like a royal princess when the girls and Iona helped her into her dress and veil. She had never had so much attention showered on her and she was surprised to find she was enjoying it. Having Emily there meant so much to her. Why had Draco gone to so much trouble? It made her feel that he cared for her. *Really* cared for her. Or did he just *really* care what people made of their somewhat hasty wedding?

Elena and Iona went ahead to take their positions on the velvet-covered and ribbon-festooned seats set either side of the strip of red carpet laid down in the formal garden.

Emily stayed to adjust Allegra's veil before they made their way out. 'You look amazing, sweetie. You could model for one of those bridal magazines.'

Allegra grasped her friend's hands again. 'You didn't let on that you know, did you?'

'No, but even if I took my contacts out I could see you're halfway to being in love with him, if you're not fully there already,' Emily said. 'Truly, he's something else to look at, isn't he? And that smile. Gosh, I'm halfway in love with him myself.' She winked. 'Only kidding.'

Allegra drew in a steadying breath and smoothed her palms over the satin of her figure-hugging gown. 'Are you sure I look okay? I don't look fat, do I? I bought this in my lunch hour and now I'm wondering if I should've—'

'You look a-maz-ing,' Emily said. 'That dress is perfect for you. It highlights everything I hate about you: your breasts, your hips, your bum—which is so tiny I wouldn't even classify it as a bum. Seriously, hon, you're going to pop Draco's eyeballs.'

Allegra adjusted the cleavage of her dress and grimaced. 'As long as I don't pop out of this dress.'

She stood at the top of the strip of red carpet with her father a short time later, trying to settle the hive of nerves in her stomach. While it was nice to have Emily here, and for Elena and Iona to be so kind and helpful, it didn't take away from the fact this wedding was not her choice. Not even marriage to Draco, the most attractive and sexy man she knew.

Especially because it was Draco.

He had too much power over her. Too much sensual power, which he had already demonstrated with stunning expertise. Seeing him in that sharply tailored suit and neatly aligned bow tie was enough to get her pulses racing. His dark-as-night gaze met hers and the edges of his mouth came up in a smile that spoke of triumph, rather than the emotion she hadn't realised till now she wanted to see.

But she didn't even like Draco. Of course she didn't... And marrying a guy who only wanted you to secure a much-prized business deal was a little lowering, to say the least.

'Ready to go?' her father asked.

'I could have done this on my own, you know,' Allegra said in a low tone so no one nearby could overhear. 'I don't believe in fathers giving away their daughters. It's positively feudal.'

Her father gave her arm a squeeze that was almost painful. 'Don't spoil it for me, Allegra. I've waited years for this day. I wasn't sure it was ever going to happen.'

She drew in a tight breath, stung by the partially veiled criticism in his voice. 'I'm only doing this for Elena and Nico. You do know that, don't you?'

'You should be grateful he was the one who won you,' her father said with a clipped edge to his voice. 'There were one or two other less savoury types who were interested but he outbid them with his offer of marriage. Hugely.'

A cold hand pressed on Allegra's spine. What did her father mean, Draco was the one who'd won her? '*What?*'

'Now is not the time to talk about it,' her father said. 'Ask him later.'

And then he led her inexorably towards Draco.

* * *

Draco had been prepared for Allegra looking beautiful. He had always known she would make a spectacularly gorgeous bride. And she didn't disappoint. She was a vision in an oyster silk slip of a dress that clung to all her assets like an elegant evening glove. Her simple white veil hung over her face and down her back in a floating cloud. Her hair was swept up in a coronet do that gave her the look of a princess that was nothing less than breath-snatching. He covered his reaction to seeing her with a smile that could have been termed gloating, but there was no way he was going to let her see he considered this ceremony as anything but a means to an end.

The deal was balanced firmly in his favour and he was fine with that. It was the way he did business and this was, after all, about business. He stood to gain the most out of getting her hand in marriage. Allegra didn't need his wealth or status because she had her own. He had played on her need to please her father who, in his opinion, didn't deserve it. Cosimo Kallas was a narcissist who was only happy when the attention was squarely on him. His wife Elena had been chosen because she was young and beautiful and attracted to him.

Just like you chose Allegra.

Draco shook off the jarring thought like he was shaking something off the back of his suit jacket. His marriage to Allegra was much more than that. He hadn't picked her from a line-up. He'd known her since she was a girl of sixteen. He admired her. He respected her. He *wanted* her.

And her father's business—and, more importantly,

her welfare—was a pressing issue that needed a solution, so here Draco was offering it. If he hadn't offered for her, another man would have done so with far more nefarious purposes. The business world was cutthroat and conscienceless. He knew enough about some of the rich and powerful creditors to know they wouldn't have thought twice about using her father's debts to force Allegra into their bed. If she thought being married to him was bad, he didn't like to guess what she would think about some of the alternatives.

This was his way of keeping them out of the equation.

It wasn't as if they would be living in each other's pockets. Draco liked that Allegra was independent, that she had her own career and commitments, because it would leave him free to see to his. He was prepared to be faithful because he didn't see any reason not to be during a short-term marriage. His father had instilled in him the trust needed to have a satisfying relationship. He had always admired his father for the commitment he had made to his mother that had continued long after her death.

And Draco knew the chemistry between Allegra and him was the best he'd ever experienced. He could only expect it to improve the more they explored each other. He couldn't wait for all this fuss to be over so he could get her alone and turn their marriage into a real one in every sense of the word. Allegra wanted him. Hadn't he proved that down at the beach? Their relationship would be one based on mutual lust.

The string quartet began playing 'The Bridal March'. Emily came up the red carpet first, but Draco couldn't take his eyes off Allegra, waiting at the end of the archway with her father, to begin the walk towards him. Had he ever seen a more stunningly beautiful woman? She looked like a bride from an old black-and-white movie. Her skin was luminous, her make-up emphasising the intense blue of her eyes, the aristocratic height and slope of her cheekbones and the pink perfection of her kissable mouth with that gorgeous beauty spot just above it. The silk dress moved with her body, making his hands itch and twitch to unpeel her from it and explore those delectable curves.

He drew in a breath but was more than a little shocked to find it caught on something in his throat. He'd always made a point not to be moved by weddings. They reminded him too much of his ex. Of all the hopes he had invested in that doomed relationship. Of his own calf-love foolishness. He'd been to a few over the years—friends' and colleagues' and business associates'—and he had never had his breath lock in his throat. It felt almost as if his whole life had somehow been slowly but surely heading towards this moment. That every road so far had led to this time, this place, this person walking towards him.

Allegra came to stand beside him and through the gossamer of her veil met his gaze. She gave him a trembling smile that plucked on a tight string deep in his chest. 'Hi…'

Draco had to clear his throat to speak. The uncertainty in her gaze, the slight wobble in her voice, made him wonder if she was experiencing the same unexpected groundswell of emotion. 'You look beautiful.'

The priest stepped forward with a broad smile. 'Dearly beloved, we are gathered here…'

Finally it was time to kiss his bride. Draco drew

Allegra closer and pressed his mouth to hers in a kiss that felt unlike any other kiss he had ever experienced. It wasn't because of the witnesses gathered or the solemnity of the occasion. It was a kiss that had a sacred element to it. A promise had been made and this kiss sealed it. Her lips clung to his, her hands resting against his chest, her right one over the thud of his heart.

Allegra smelt of summer flowers and her lips tasted of strawberries. He held her against him, praying his erection would cool it in time to turn to walk back through the gathered guests. He'd always considered it tacky when a wedding kiss went on too long. But now he wished he could freeze time. Stay right there and sup at her mouth until this burning ache in his flesh subsided—if it ever would.

He eased back to cradle her face in his hands. Her blue eyes shimmered as if she wasn't far off crying. '*Yia sou*, Kyria Papandreou,' he said.

She blinked a couple of times, as if to stop from tearing up any further. 'Thanks for bringing Emily here. It means such a lot to me. And for all the other… stuff.'

Was that why she was feeling emotional? The little jab of disappointment hit him under the ribs. Of course it wasn't about him. It was about her friend. He'd wanted to bring her friend here because Allegra no longer had a mother to support her and, besides, what bride didn't need a bridesmaid? He had asked his best friend to be his best man so it only seemed fair for Allegra to have someone she trusted and valued by her side. 'My pleasure,' he said. 'I thought she might hit it off with one of my friends from university, my best man—Loukas Kyprianos. He has a thing for English girls.'

'Even so, it was nice of you to go to all that trouble.'

He looped her arm through his and turned with her so they were facing the guests. 'Shall we let everyone get on with the party?'

It was a great party, Allegra had to admit, even though she spent most of it wondering about Draco's true motives in marrying her. She hadn't been able to get him alone to ask him to clarify what her father had told her. But it resonated with the sort of man he was. He might be ruthless when it suited him, but she knew him well enough to know he wouldn't stand for any sort of criminal behaviour. Who were the faceless men who might have blackmailed her into their bed if he hadn't intervened? The thought was too distressing to hold in her mind—like finding a cockroach in her glass of milk. It was revolting to picture herself with another of her father's business associates. Surely her father wouldn't have expected her to do it if Draco hadn't put his hand up and proposed marriage?

Why *had* he put his hand up? Could there be any other reason?

No. Why else had he said the marriage was temporary? Because he wanted to have her, but he needed an escape route, that was why. He'd been prepared to do the honourable thing by her, but promising to love, protect and provide for her for the rest of her life was a step too far.

Allegra looked around the party of revelling guests, her mind still in a whirling turmoil. It didn't take much for a gathering of Greeks to have fun when there was family, food and alcohol involved. Not that Draco had any family there. It struck her how alone in the world he was. He had friends and associates but no blood relatives. Weddings were times when families came together and celebrated with the couple.

She suddenly missed her mother with a pang that sat under her ribcage like a stitch pulled too tight. Not that her mother had really been there for her in the truest sense, but she ached for the mother she might have been if things had been different. But, strangely, she had a sense her mother would have approved of Draco. He was strong and disciplined, unlike her father, who had a tendency to live for himself rather than others. Draco didn't talk himself up, either. He did things in the background that one would ever hear of if he had any say in it. Would he have told her about the other men? He hadn't even told her about his commitment to Iona. His housekeeper had revealed it, not him. Iona had even told Allegra while she was helping her get dressed for the ceremony that Draco had set up a superannuation account for her with generous donations that set her up for a luxurious retirement.

Allegra stood with her arm looped through Draco's as various guests came over to chat. As if Iona could sense Allegra had been thinking about her, she came bustling over, cheeks pink from drinking champagne, and her eyes bright with happiness for her employer and his new bride. She grasped each of their hands as though she was making a pledge, her eyes going misty as they had during the service. 'Be happy. Be forgiving. Be friends.'

Draco leaned down to kiss his housekeeper on both cheeks. 'We will. I promise.'

Allegra waited until Iona had wandered off to talk to some other guests before she looked up at Draco. 'She's so lucky to have you. She told me she would've still been on the streets begging if it hadn't been for you.'

His arm went from around her waist to hold her hand, his thumb stroking the back of it in gentle movements. 'What she needed when her husband ditched her for someone younger was a lawyer like you. She had no one to stand up for her. She reminds me of my mother. She's a good woman, loyal and hard working.' He waited a beat. 'You rarely speak of your mother. Were you not close?'

Allegra grimaced. 'My mother never got over my brother's death. Losing him destroyed her. She gave up on life after that. My father would never admit it was suicide. He maintains the accidental overdose verdict the doctor put on the death certificate but I know she had given up. She simply couldn't go on.'

His hand cupped hers as if he was holding something fragile and precious. 'That must have been extremely tough on you, losing her under such awful circumstances. It's not as if your father is the nurturing type.'

'Yes, well, he wanted a son and heir, and when that son got sick he wanted another one to fix him, or—in a worst-case scenario—take his place,' she said. 'I turned up instead—female and an abject failure because I didn't have the right genetic make-up to save Dion or replace him.'

Draco's forehead creased into furrowed lines. 'But surely your father never said—?'

'He didn't have to,' Allegra said. 'I got the message loud and clear. Even my mother on a bad day would make it pretty obvious what a disappointment I was. That's why I was sent to boarding school in England so young. She didn't like being reminded of her failure to produce a healthy son and heir. I ruined her chances of falling pregnant again. She had to have a hysterectomy after my birth because I ruptured her uterus. I only found all this out when I was older but it explained a lot about my childhood. She wasn't the cuddling type, although there were plenty of photos with her cuddling my brother. She lost interest once he died and the only cuddles I got were from my nannies.'

Had she told him too much? Overloaded him with her Dickensian childhood drama? She rarely spoke of her childhood to anyone. Even Emily had only heard the cut-down version. She didn't like painting herself as a victim, but growing up without the security and comfort of parental love was something she carried like a scar. Mostly she could ignore it, but when she saw people interact with their parents, and in particular their mothers, the wound opened all over again. But she and Draco were alike in that they had both lost their mothers while young. If anyone could understand, it would be him.

Draco let out a long sigh and stroked the back of her hands with his thumbs, holding her gaze in a concerned manner. 'I've always been amazed at how well you turned out, given the tragic circumstances you were born into. But I had no idea you felt so unloved.'

And now I've signed up for a loveless marriage. Lucky me.

'To be fair, I think my father loves me in his way. Or at least, he does now that I've saved his precious business.' She met his gaze with a 'no secrets now' directness. 'He told me there were other men who had their eye on me. Why didn't you tell me that yourself?'

Draco's frown lowered as if he was thinking deeply and was troubled by those thoughts. 'I didn't want you to worry about it. I'd solved the issue as far as I was concerned.'

'It was an honourable thing to do...'

He shrugged as if they were talking about whose turn it was to take out the trash. 'I figured, better the devil you know.'

Allegra studied his unreadable expression for a beat. 'I'm starting to wonder if I know you at all. You're full of little surprises.'

'Don't read too much into my actions,' he said, expression still inscrutable. 'Your father isn't my favourite person in the world. I've always made excuses for him because the loss of a child is such a big thing. It's not the sort of grief you can easily move on from on. Although, he seems to have done so now.'

'Yes, his little affairs were his way of handling things,' Allegra said. 'My mother didn't seem to care what he did—she accepted it as normal. Even as young as I was, that used to really bug me. I often wondered if he'd stayed faithful to her would it have helped her heal a little better?'

'Maybe, maybe not.' He gave her hands a squeeze. 'Such sad talk for a wedding day, *ne*?'

Allegra gave a rueful smile. 'It's not like it's a normal wedding day, though, is it? I felt a little guilty acting in front of Iona. I hope she doesn't end up hating me for not being madly in love with you like every other woman on the planet.'

Draco's thumbs stilled on her hands as if they'd

been set on pause. His eyes held hers in a searching lock that made her feel that he was seeing more than she wanted him to see. Allegra's heart stammered. Had she given herself away? Shown how vulnerable she was to him? Not just in terms of physical attraction, but in terms of feelings she didn't want to feel but couldn't seem to control.

She couldn't fall in love with him. Couldn't. Couldn't. Couldn't. It would be unrequited if she did. He had locked his heart away and she had better not forget it. His reasons for marrying her were not just physical, but it didn't mean he loved her. He'd wanted to protect her. Any decent man would have done the same. The best she could hope for was the desire he had for her would last. But it was a fragile hope. A hope on a ventilator and a timer.

But then he slipped her arm back through his and smiled. 'Don't you have a bouquet to toss?'

CHAPTER SIX

THE SUN WAS setting by the time Draco steered his luxury boat away from the jetty on his island. Allegra stood beside him, a light wrap around her shoulders, and waved back to the guests standing on the jetty and the beach, including Emily, who was in proud possession of the bouquet.

Emily was standing a short distance from Draco's best man, Loukas Kyprianos, and Allegra could see the goggle-eyed looks Em was casting his way, as if she couldn't believe what she was seeing. On the handsome scale, Loukas was like Draco—*off* the scale. But, while Draco had a tendency to smile rather than frown, Loukas had a more brooding demeanour, hinting at a man who preferred his own company and kept his own counsel. Emily wasn't the sort of girl to get her head turned by a good-looking man, but she was a sucker for a man with secrets, given she had one or two of her own.

Draco manoeuvred the boat into the direction of the setting sun, which was now a fireball of red suspended on the smoky-blue plane of the horizon. A swathe of stratocumulus clouds reflected the burnished gold of the sun below and the grey and indigo bruise-like streaks of colour above.

A light breeze moved over the surface of the water, sped up by the passage of the boat. It played with Allegra's hair, which was already in two minds whether to stay up in her coronet do or give up and swing about her back and shoulders. She pushed the straying strands away from her face and resisted the temptation to slip her hand into Draco's outstretched one as he stood at the wheel.

He smiled down at her. 'All right? Not seasick yet?'

She shook her head. 'No. I'm pretty good on boats normally. Although, I guess I shouldn't speak too soon.'

'You'll be fine. The weather forecast is good.' He glanced back at the jetty. 'How's Emily getting on with Loukas?'

Allegra cocked her head. 'Are you trying to set them up or something?'

He gave a shrug. 'If it happens, it happens.'

'He doesn't look the type who needs a hand in that department,' she said. 'Who is he? He's seems familiar, but I'm sure I haven't met him before today.'

'He keeps a low profile—or tries to,' Draco said. 'We met at university. I was doing a business degree and he was doing computer engineering and software development. He's designed some of the most sophisticated security systems in the world. So secure, most government agencies such as MI5 and the FBI use his software.'

Good luck, Em.

'So is he on the lookout for a wife?' Allegra asked.

He gave her one of his crooked smiles. 'Not Loukas. His parents divorced when he was a young child and apparently it was one of those acrimonious, "use the kid as a weapon" ones. He doesn't talk about it and I know better than to ask. Both his parents have remarried and subsequently divorced, his father several times over. One thing I do know, he will never get married himself. It was hard enough getting him to agree to come to our wedding. You'd think I'd asked him to have a lobotomy.'

'Did you tell him it was a marriage of—?'

'No.' The tone of his voice underlined the word. 'We're close but not that close. No one is that close to Loukas. No one.'

Allegra chewed at her lip, watching the sun swallowed by the blue lip of the horizon. Why hadn't he told his best friend? Was it really because Loukas was a bit of a closed book himself? Why not tell his friend the truth? Or had he done it to protect her from anyone pitying her? 'I told Emily.'

'I know.'

She glanced at him in surprise. 'You do?'

Draco's expression was amused rather than annoyed. 'I figured you would. She's a nice girl. Seems to have her head screwed on.'

'Did you let on you knew she knew?'

'No.'

'I'm sorry, but I couldn't lie to her,' Allegra said. 'Everyone else, yes, but not Em. She would've figured it out anyway. She knows I'm not the sort of person to fall in love on a whim. But don't worry, she won't tell a soul. She's fiercely loyal and completely and utterly trustworthy.'

'Good to know.'

There was a little silence broken only by the slap of the water hitting the sides and hull of the yacht.

'Do you want to take the wheel for a while?' Draco asked.

'I don't know... I might run into another boat or something.'

'There's no one else out here. Come on. Stand in front of me and I'll steer with you.'

Allegra moved to stand in front of the wheel and he came in behind her, his arms either side of her body, his hands resting on top of hers where she was gripping the steering wheel. Who knew steering a yacht could be such a turn-on? The warm, hard presence of his body behind her made every nerve in her core jump up ready for duty. His broad hands almost completely covered hers, his fingers long, strong and so very capable. Deliciously, dangerously capable.

She could feel him against her bottom cheeks, the rise of his flesh an erotic reminder of what was to come. She shivered when he moved closer, his stubbly jaw grazing her cheek when he leaned down to help her navigate a larger than normal wave. The rocking motion of the yacht pushed her further back against him, sending her senses into overdrive. 'I want you,' he said.

'I would never have guessed.'

He gave a soft laugh. 'Minx.' He tongued the cartilage of her ear, the sensations rippling through her like waves. 'But then, I've wanted you since that night in London.'

Allegra shuddered when his teeth tugged on her earlobe. 'Funny, but I didn't pick up that vibe.'

He moved his mouth to the sensitive spot on her neck just below her ear. 'What vibe are you picking up now?'

'I'm thinking the honeymoon is about to start.'

He turned her so she was facing him, his eyes gleaming like high-gloss black paint. 'I need to drop anchor.'

Allegra linked her arms around his neck and gave him a sultry smile. 'I can think of something more fun we can do instead.'

He smiled and pressed a brief, hard kiss to her mouth. 'Go below and I'll be with you once I've got things up here under control…'

Allegra descended to the main cabin where a bar, sofas and large-screen television were located. There was a kitchen off that with a separate dining area, which wouldn't have looked out of place in a top-end-of-town restaurant. The master bedroom—one of four bedrooms on board—was big enough to sleep a football team as well as their support staff and sponsors. Maybe even some fans.

She was no stranger to luxury accommodation, but Draco's yacht was beyond anything she had seen before. Butter-soft leather sofas and ottomans, Swarovski light fittings and lamps and knee-deep, cream-coloured carpet. Polished timber woodwork and Italian marble in the wet areas such as the bathrooms. There was even a hot tub on the upper deck and a spa bath in the main bathroom. A bottle of champagne was in a silver icebucket with two glasses beside it, left by Draco's staff, along with their luggage, which had been unpacked and stored in the hand-crafted built-in wardrobes in the master suite. There was a supply of gourmet food in the fridge and pantry, both cooked and fresh ingredients, as well as a wine fridge with enough wine and champagne to host a cocktail party for a hundred guests.

Allegra couldn't look at the king-sized bed without a shudder of excitement. The same shudder of excitement she'd felt when Draco had said he'd wanted her when he'd run into her in London six months ago. She'd thought he'd been mocking her for sitting there so long, trying to make her glass of wine last the hour, trying not to check her watch and chew her lip and nails until they bled. But behind that glinting black gaze he had been sizing her up for himself. What had stirred his interest? Was it that he'd seen her as a convenient bride, a single woman on the wrong side of thirty who he'd assumed would stumble over herself with gratefulness when he offered for her?

But his motives had been far more honourable than that. Why had he done that? He was effectively saving her father's business and her, too.

Allegra sat down on the cloud-soft mattress and sighed. Why was she fussing over the fact he wasn't in love with her? People had sex without being in love all the time. It wasn't a prerequisite these days, even for marriage. Lots of people enjoyed a workable marriage with companionship and mutual respect holding them together. Romantic love didn't always last, anyway. The limerence period in a new relationship at best lasted two years. After that the relationship settled into the bonding phase…if it was going to, that was. Draco surely wouldn't let theirs go on for half so long?

It wasn't as if she was in love with Draco. But what if she succumbed to that lethal charm? She had already told him more than she'd told anyone about herself. It was as if her carapace had melted away. She actually liked him. As in *really* liked him. Liked his company, his smile, his dancing eyes, his body.

Dear God, his body.

The sound of his footsteps coming down to join her was enough to set her pulses off like thoroughbreds at the starting gate. Why hadn't she thought to buy some sexy lingerie? She'd been so determined to resist him but how long had that lasted? One kiss and she'd all but begged him to take her. One kiss! What if she was hopeless in bed? What if she couldn't orgasm with him? What if she took ages and ages, and he got fed up, and she had to pretend. and then she would be embarrassed and feel under even more pressure next time and—

The door of the bedroom opened and Allegra jumped off the bed as though she'd been shot out of a cannon. 'Erm… I think I'll have a drink. Would you like champagne? I feel like some, don't you? This is a good one. Wow… I've been to the vineyard. It was amazing, so picturesque.' She fumbled with the foil around the top of the bottle, sudden nerves and shyness assailing her.

Draco came over, took the bottle from her and placed it back in the ice-bucket. He put his hands on her waist, his expression as tender as she had ever seen it. 'You're nervous.' He said it as a statement, not as a question.

Allegra pulled at one side of her lower lip with her teeth, her cheeks feeling as if someone had lit a fire under them. 'It was probably a fluke down at the beach. I might not be able to do it again.'

He lifted her chin with the tip of his finger, holding her gaze with his. 'No one's keeping time here, *agape mou*. You can take all the time you need. We don't have to even do this tonight if you don't feel up to it. It's been a long day.'

'Don't you want to…?'

Draco's thumb brushed back and forth over her cheek like a metronome. 'Of course I do, but not if you don't feel in the mood.'

I've been in the mood for you since I was sixteen.

Allegra lowered her gaze to his mouth. 'I don't have any nice lingerie…'

He smiled. 'Do you really think I'd even notice? What I want to see is you. All of you.'

She shivered at the smouldering look in his eyes. The look that said 'I want you'. The look that spoke to her female flesh like the sun does to an orchid. Ripening it, opening it. Making it bloom and swell and release its scent. She placed her arms around his neck, moving closer so her body touched his from hips to chest. 'Make love to me…please?'

His mouth came down to cover hers in a kiss that spoke of deep, primal male longings only just held in check. Draco's lips moved against hers in a soft exploration, his tongue parting her lips with a gentle glide that made her skin prickle in delight. He courted her tongue, driving her senses wild with escalating need. She whimpered her desire into the warm, minty cavern of his mouth, her hips pushing against his with the need for more stimulation. His hands went from her waist to settle on her hips, holding her against his pulsing length. The eroticism of it thrilled her, awakening every nerve in her body, every sense on high alert.

Draco deepened the kiss with a bolder thrust of his tongue, a movement that made Allegra's inner core respond with a burst of feminine moisture, that instinctive, involuntary response that signalled her readiness, her eagerness, her desperation. One of his hands peeled away her dress as though he were removing cling film. It pooled at her feet and she blindly stepped out of it, her mouth still clamped to his. Her hands moved to undo the buttons of his shirt, her fingers struggling with the task in her excitement. With every button she undid, she placed her mouth to his skin, breathing in the intoxicating scent of him with that hint of lime and leather and late-in-the-day man.

He unclipped her bra and gently cradled her breasts in both his hands, his mouth moving from hers to glide down with blistering heat to her décolletage and over the upper curves of her breasts. The graze of his stubble made her insides clench with need, the glide of his tongue over her flesh evoking a murmur of approval from her lips. Draco's mouth opened over her nipple, drawing on it with light suction, the nerve endings responding with a frenzied dance of excitement she could feel right down to her core. He kissed the outside of each breast, then the undersides, and then her cleavage, his bristly face on the soft slopes of her flesh sending shivers of reaction all through her body.

Had anyone ever paid this much attention to her breasts in the past? Had anyone touched them with such gentleness? Cradled them and worshipped them? Treated them with such respect?

Draco's mouth came back to hers, subjecting it to another pulse-tripping exploration, his tongue mating with hers in a dance that made her ache for him become unbearable. She moaned her 'rescue me' plea into his mouth, her hands fervent, desperate on his body. She set to work on his belt and trouser fastening, sliding her hands over his flat abdomen, her palms and finger pads tickled by the prickle of his masculine hair.

He took over for her, shrugged off his shirt, unzipped his trousers and stepped out of them, his shoes and socks. Allegra couldn't help feeling touched he had left her knickers on until he was completely naked first. It showed a sensitivity she hadn't experienced with other partners. Only when he was fully naked did his hands go to her hips, gently sliding her knickers down her thighs so she could step out of them.

His gaze moved over her body, the desire in them ramping up her own. She pressed herself against him, her senses thrilling at the hard jut of his erection against her belly.

Draco moved her backwards towards the bed, laying her down and coming down alongside her, one of his hands on her abdomen deliciously close to the throb of her need. 'I don't want to rush you,' he said.

Rush me! Rush me!

Allegra was beyond words; all that was coming out of her mouth were breathless gasps and moans when his hand moved lower. She sucked in a breath when he brought his mouth to her belly button, swirling his tongue into its shallow pool until her back was arching off the mattress.

He moved his mouth down to the heart of her, preparing her by kissing her folds, stroking his tongue over her labia before separating her gently with his fingers and anointing her with his tongue in tantalising strokes and flickers that triggered an explosion of sensations that shook her like a rag doll. She bucked and arched and whimpered and cried as her flesh burst into a song that reverberated throughout her body until it finally subsided, leaving her in a languid, limbless state.

Allegra reached for Draco, stroking her fingers along his length, silently urging him to enter her body. After a moment, he eased back from her touch. 'What do you want to do about condoms? Are you on the pill?'

'I take a low-dose one to regulate my cycle.'

'Maybe we should use protection for the time being.'

It touched her that he'd given her a choice, not just gone ahead without consulting her on protection. He reached for a condom in a drawer beside the bed and sheathed himself. He came back to her, angling his body over hers so she didn't have to take his full weight.

That was another thing that struck Allegra about Draco. How many times had partners climbed aboard, so to speak, with little or no consideration for her comfort?

He smoothed her hair back from her face, his eyes dark and eager but with that element of concern that spoke of a man who didn't take consent for granted at any stage of the encounter. 'It's not too late to stop if you'd rather not do this.'

Allegra fisted her hands in the thick pelt of his hair. 'If you stop now, I'll never forgive you. I want you. Want, want, *want* you.'

His slanted smile made something in her stomach swoop. His mouth came down and covered hers in a drugging kiss that escalated her desire to another level that had her panting, writhing, wriggling to get the friction she craved. Finally, Draco came to her entrance, gliding into her with a smooth, thick thrust that made her gasp in relief and excitement. Her body welcomed him, squeezing him as if it never wanted him to leave. He moved his body within hers, deeper and deeper, gradually increasing his pace but making sure she was with him all the way.

Allegra was more than with him. She was a part of him. Consumed by the sensations ricocheting through her from the top of her scalp to the tips of her toes. Each thrust created friction against her, but not quite enough. It was like being suspended on a precipice, dangling there with the abyss beckoning. She whimpered and arched her hips, trying to position herself so she could fly.

Draco slipped a hand between their bodies and caressed her intimately, stroking his clever fingers over the swollen heart of her femininity until she broke free and flew and flew and flew. Fireworks, flashes, fizzes and floods coursed through her flesh. Her mind emptied of everything. It was as if, in those frantic moments, she'd become only flesh and feelings. Feelings that swept through her, flinging her out the other side just in time to sense Draco's final plunge.

He tensed above her, his breathing ragged, his guttural groan when he spilled making the surface of her skin tinkle and tingle with goose bumps. She held him during the short but savage storm, gripping his taut buttocks, holding him to her until he finally sagged as the waves of pleasure faded away.

Allegra couldn't remember a time when she had felt so close to another person. The skin-on-skin contact wasn't new, nor was having sex. The tangled limbs, and the sweat-beaded bodies and the crinkled bed linen were not foreign to her, either.

But the sense that her body had spoken to his, responded to his as it had responded to no one else, made her realise this wasn't just sex. What they had done was make love. Draco had worshipped her body, not exploited it. He had caressed it, not coerced it. He had respected it, drawing from her a depth of passion she had never given to anyone else. She hadn't been capable of it with anyone else. Her body had never wanted anyone like it wanted him. It was as if she was programed to respond to his touch and his touch alone.

Draco leaned his weight on one elbow and used his other hand to stroke her cheek. His eyes held hers in a gentle tether that made her feel even closer to him. It was as if he had glimpsed who she really was and liked what he saw. 'You were wonderful.'

Allegra gave him a shy smile. Silly to be feeling so shy after what they'd just done, but still. 'I don't suppose you've had too many complaints from lovers.'

He idly curled a strand of her hair around one of his fingers, the slight tug on her scalp making her shiver in delight. 'It's nothing any man should take for granted. What pleases one woman might not please another. Communication is the key and, of course, respect.'

She traced her fingertip around the sculpted perfection of his mouth, her core giving a little aftershock at the thought of the ecstasy his sensual mouth and potent body had given her. Pleasure she could still feel in every cell of her flesh like the echo of a far-off bell.

A thought suddenly crept up on her. What if Draco ceased to be satisfied by her? What if he became bored and went in search of someone else? She had witnessed first-hand her mother's shame at being shunted aside for a new mistress. It had made her mother even more depressed and disengaged from life. Allegra had often wondered if her father had been partly to blame for her mother's suicide by his inability to comfort and support her emotionally. She wondered if he was capable of doing it for Elena.

Draco smoothed a fingertip over her forehead. 'You've got that frowning look again. What's troubling you?'

Allegra gusted out a sigh. 'Nothing.'

He pressed his thumb pad on her bottom lip, moving it in a slow back-and-forth stroking motion. 'Talk to me, *agape mou*. It is good to communicate verbally and physically, *ne*?'

She couldn't quite meet his coal-black gaze and aimed for his stubbly chin instead. 'I guess I'm wondering how long this will last.'

He brought her chin up so her gaze meshed with his. 'This?'

Allegra licked her lower lip, tasting the salt of his thumb pad. 'Us. Having…sex. Don't most married couples drift into a less passionate relationship over time? What will you do then? Find someone else?'

A frown formed a bridge between his eyes. 'Didn't you hear me promise to be faithful above all others earlier today? While we're officially married I will be faithful, as I expect you to be.'

While we're officially married… Allegra searched his gaze, wondering, hoping, praying he meant every word. But how could she be sure? Didn't most people mean those vows at the time they spoke them? She was surprised to find *she* had meant them. She might not love him, but she still meant to honour the commitment as far as it was possible to do so. 'But our situation is a little different… We're not starting our marriage at the same place as other couples. What if you fall in love with someone? Someone you meet at work or wherever?'

His finger captured another tendril of her hair and began toying with it. 'What if you fall in love with someone?'

Allegra had trouble holding his penetrating gaze. She pushed out of his hold, swung her legs off the bed and reached for something to cover her nakedness. His shirt was the only thing handy and she slipped it on and crossed it over her chest without doing up the buttons. How could she fall in love with someone else when Draco was all she could think about? 'I don't think that's likely to happen.'

'Then why do you think it will happen to me?'

'Because it happens,' she said. 'It happens and you can't always control it. I represent so many clients whose partner met someone's gaze across a room and that was it. End of marriage. Most never thought it would happen to them. They thought they had a good relationship and then are suddenly left with the heartache of being rejected for someone younger and more beautiful. It's still easier for men to stray, especially when kids come along. It's hard work, bringing up a family, and some men can't cope with the focus not being on them any more.

'My father is a classic example. He got tired of my mother's depression after Dion died and got someone else on the side. Lots of them over the years—both she and I lost count. She was barely cold in her grave before he parked a new mistress in the house.'

Draco got off the bed, pulled on his trousers and zipped them. 'Not all men are your father, Allegra. Your parents' situation was tragic. The loss of a child would test any solid relationship and your parents' relationship, from all accounts, wasn't solid. But don't paint me with the same brush. It's insulting, for one thing. And, for another, I'm not capable of the emotions you describe.'

Allegra frowned. 'But you're not incapable of feeling love. I saw the way you interacted with Iona. And I know you loved your father and grieved terribly when he was killed because you hate talking about it. Look at the way you put everything on hold yesterday to see to Yanni. You *care* about people, Draco. You care a lot. You might not call it love but many would.'

His tilted smile had a touch of cynicism. 'Yes, I care, and to some degree that could be called love. But as for romantic love? I did that once and it was the most foolish mistake I've ever made. I'm not going to repeat it.'

'What happened between you and your ex?'

He made a move to the door but she intercepted him and stalled him with a hand on his arm. 'Talk to me, Draco,' Allegra said. 'I've told you so much about my own stuff but you keep your stuff to yourself. I would like to know so I can understand you better.'

'There's nothing to understand,' he said, but she noted he didn't pull away. 'I was nineteen and full of the confident arrogance of youth. I thought she cared about me the way I cared about her. She didn't.'

A penny dropped inside Allegra's head. 'You were nineteen?'

Draco gave her a rueful look. 'Yes, right at the time you made that pass at me. I was still feeling a little raw. You got the rough end of it. Under other circumstances, your crush would have been a compliment, but instead it was a brutal reminder of the one who got away.'

Allegra bit her lip. 'I'm sorry. No wonder you were so…so angry.'

He brushed a finger over her lower lip as if to remove the sting of the bruising kiss he had pulled away from so long ago. 'It was wrong of me to take it out on you.' His hand drifted away. 'That was why I was so against you getting it on with that boy a couple of years later. I saw something in him that reminded me of my ex.'

And for all these years Allegra had hated him for it. 'But weren't you rather young to be thinking about marriage at nineteen?'

'For some people, yes, that would've been too young. But I'd been on my own since my father died,' he said. 'I felt ready to build a life with someone. Turned out I wasn't as ready as I thought.'

Allegra wondered if Draco would ever be ready to settle down for life after such a disappointment. His commitment to her was conditional. A two- or three-year marriage was hardly a lifetime commitment. No mention of love, just caring. How long was that going to be enough for her? 'I wish I'd listened to you about that boy. It would have saved me a lot of hurt and embarrassment.'

He gave her an on-off smile and turned away to shove his feet back into his shoes, before he reached for a T-shirt and hauled it over his head. 'I'm going up on the bridge to check on things. I'll leave you to rest or whatever. We'll have some supper once I secure us for the night in a sheltered cove not far away from here.'

Allegra's shoulders sagged when the door clicked shut on his exit. She was being silly. What did it matter if he didn't love her? Refused point blank ever to fall in love with her? They could still have a satisfying relationship. Far more satisfying than any relationship she'd had before. Sure, it wasn't the fairy-tale relationship she secretly yearned for, but how realistic were those yearnings anyway? She knew more than most about the sort of heartache that came from idealistic expectations in relationships.

This way was safer. They had a mutual desire for each other and were both intelligent and rational people with a lot more in common than most.

Besides, she wasn't in love with him.

And she would be perfectly safe as long as she stayed that way.

CHAPTER SEVEN

DRACO DROPPED ANCHOR and stood and breathed in the warm night air scented with the brine of the sea. He loved being out on the water, away from all his responsibilities, the burdens he had been carrying since he was a teenager, when life had seemed so hard and impossibly cruel. Out here he could breathe. He could reflect on the goals he had achieved instead of dwelling on the ones he hadn't.

He wasn't sure why he'd told Allegra about his ex, not in so much detail. But she had shared a lot about herself, deeply personal stuff that couldn't have been easy to share. He enjoyed being out here with her—maybe a little too much. The desire that roared between them wasn't something that was going to fade away any time soon. Not on his part, anyway. Draco didn't know what it was about her that made him so fired up. She was beautiful, but then, he had slept with many beautiful women.

No, it was more than that. She was captivating. She was smart and funny and she responded to him with such fervency it couldn't fail to delight him. Hadn't he always known that? Wasn't that why he'd been so hands-off with her for all these years?

But he wasn't hands-off with her now.

And that was something his body was thrilled about. More than thrilled. Excited, exhilarated, ecstatic. He'd had great sex before, too many times to count. But with Allegra something else happened apart from the physical act of sex. Something deeper. Her trust in him gave their intimacy a quality he hadn't experienced quite like that before. Her lack of experience was uncommon in a woman of her age and Draco couldn't help feeling pleased about it. It reeked of a big, fat Greek double standard but he was privately pleased she hadn't shared her body with lots of partners. It gave her relationship with him more significance, as if she had waited for him. What man didn't want a wife who was fiercely attracted to him? It would at least keep her from straying. If Allegra wanted him, then she would think twice about leaving the relationship before he was ready for it to end. Her desire for him was something he could rely on to keep her true to the commitment they'd made that morning.

But as for loving her...

Of course he cared for her, in his way. Care, concern, tenderness, love—weren't they much the same thing? But being *in love*, well, he wasn't going down that road again if he could help it. Draco wasn't such a cynic he couldn't see it worked for some people. People who were less guarded about their emotions. Less... disciplined. But he wasn't one of them.

Not now.

He had learned his lesson the hard way and had learned it well. Opening his heart to love had been foolish and immature and he had paid a high price for it. A price he refused to pay again. He could live a perfectly satisfying year or two with Allegra as his wife without the complication of emotions he didn't need or trust.

The word love was overused these days. People tacked it on to the end of just about every conversation like some sort of verbal talisman. But how often did they mean it? *Really* mean it? He only had to look as far as Allegra's father to see how little those words meant. Cosimo Kallas bandied those three little words around his new wife all the time, but how long before he found someone else to play with when Elena was too tired, or preoccupied with child-rearing?

At least Draco had the self-discipline to refrain from such peccadilloes. His father had set him a good example. Loyalty ran deep in Papandreou blood. Papandreou men stood by their promises even when it hurt. When they made a commitment, they saw it to completion, even if things got tough. He wouldn't have offered to marry Allegra if he hadn't thought he was capable of seeing the commitment through while they wanted each other.

It was a perfect arrangement for both of them. She was a career woman with no immediate plans to have children. He had his own work commitments that took him around the globe at a moment's notice. This way both of them could enjoy the benefits of an exclusive relationship until it was time to move on. What wasn't to like about her? She was beautiful and amusing and sexy and had a whip-quick intellect. He was tired of dating women who didn't have any conversation or little if no sense of humour. Tired of being feted like he was some sort of guru or celebrity.

Draco liked that Allegra saw him as her equal. Liked that she argued with him, debated with him, stood up to him. He had a strong personality but, rather than it intimidating her, it brought out the steely, uncompromising will in hers. He enjoyed sparring with her. Their verbal spats were as exciting as foreplay. He got hard thinking about her prim little mouth firing off another vituperative round at him. Telling him what she thought of him when he could read her body felt the exact opposite. He found it invigorating to interact with her verbally and, of course, physically.

Once he got the yacht settled for the night, Draco went back below deck to find Allegra in the kitchen sipping a glass of water. She had showered and was dressed in yoga pants and a lightweight, dove-grey boyfriend sweater that had slipped off one creamy shoulder. Her hair was still damp from her shower and was in a makeshift knot at the back of her head. She had looked traffic-stopping stunning that morning at their wedding, but his body leapt at the sight of her, even in such casual clothes and with no make-up on, her unfettered breasts outlined by the drape of her top, and his breath caught like a fish hook in his throat.

She put her glass down and raised her chin in that aristocratic manner of hers, as if they hadn't been writhing around naked and sweaty on his bed less than an hour ago. 'I hope you weren't expecting me to get supper ready?'

Draco smiled at the tiny spark of defiance in her gaze. After their little heart-to-heart she was pulling back from him, resetting the boundaries after their intimacy. Was she unsettled by the intensity of their love-making? If so, he knew the feeling. He could do with a little regrouping himself to re-establish the balance of power between them. Sex had a habit of tipping things in a relationship. Good sex, that was. And it didn't get much better than what they'd experienced together. 'Are you hungry?'

The tip of Allegra's tongue passed over her lips, her gaze slipping to his mouth for the briefest moment before her chin came back up. 'Depends what's on the menu.'

He closed the distance between them, allowing her enough room to step aside if she wanted to, but she stayed where she was, her dark blue eyes showing nothing of the tug of war her body was undergoing. But Draco could sense it. He could sense her arousal, the silent thrum of it moving back and forth like a radar signal between their locked gazes. The blood surged in his veins, his need growling and prowling through his body in response to the tempting proximity of hers. He glided a fingertip down the hinge of her jaw, stopping below her up-thrust chin, feeling the delicate quiver of her flesh at his idle touch. 'How about we start with a little appetiser?'

He brought his mouth down to the side of her mouth, the tip of his tongue circling her beauty spot, evoking a tiny whimper from her and a sway of her body towards his. He traced his tongue over her plump lower lip, following the delicate ridge of her vermillion border like an artist drawing a fine line. Allegra made another soft mewling sound, her hands going to his chest, the press of her palms inciting a rush of red-hot desire, making his legs tremble at the knees and his groin bulge and burn.

Draco moved his tongue to her top lip, sweeping it across the soft surface before taking it lightly between his teeth, a soft little 'come play with me' tug that made her press even closer, her hands fisting into his T-shirt. He cupped her bottom, drawing her hard against him, torturing himself with the feel of her soft curves against the pulsing hardness of his body. 'I want you.' Those were the only three little words he wanted to say. The only words he wanted to hear from her. The only words that mattered right now.

'I want you too.' Allegra linked her arms around his neck, opening her mouth against his, inviting him in with a flick of her tongue against his lower lip.

Heat roared through his body, his desire for her like a wildfire that had jumped containment lines. Every cell in his body throbbed with it. Vibrated with it. He kissed her deeply, exploring every corner of her mouth, breathing in the scent of her shampoo and body wash—the frangipani and freesia mix that so bewitched his senses. Her tongue tangled with his in a duel that made the base of his spine hum. Her hands tugged and released his hair at the back of his head, making him even wilder for her. The intoxicating mix of part pleasure, part pain ramped up his desire until it was a dark unknowable, uncontrollable force deep in his body.

Draco lifted her to prop her on the bench behind, stepping into the space between her parted thighs. Her legs wrapped around his hips, her mouth clamped to his in a kiss that was more combative than anything else. It was as though she resented her attraction to him, wanted to punish him for it. He took the kiss to a deeper level, thrusting his tongue into the warm, moist recesses of her mouth until she was clinging to him and making purring, breathless sounds of encouragement. Her hands clasped his head, her fingers digging deep into his scalp, but he enjoyed the roughness of it, the urgency of it. The thrill of having her turned on like a wild cat.

He pulled up her boyfriend sweater, accessing her breasts with his hands, holding them, cupping them, and running his thumbs over the peaked nipples. He sent his mouth on a tour of discovery, down the soft skin of her neck, the delicate framework of her collar bone and the scented valley between her breasts. He licked each one in turn, taking his time, drawing out the pleasure until Allegra was writhing, and pushing and grinding her hips against him in an unspoken plea for more.

He hauled her top over her head and tossed it to the floor, coming back to cradle her breasts in his hands, holding their silky weight, watching the waves of sensual delight pass over her features. He released them to pull off his shirt so she could access his chest, her mouth burning him, branding him with hot, damp little kisses that made the need in him tighten, tighten and tighten... He tugged at her yoga pants and she slipped down off the bench to free them from her body, leaving her in a tiny pair of black knickers with tiny hot-pink bows.

Draco picked Allegra up, carried her to the living area and laid her on one of the leather sofas. He removed the rest of his clothes and came down beside her, his mouth coming back to hers in a kiss that sent incendiary heat throughout his body. Her tongue wrestled and writhed with his, her lips soft, supple and playful. Her teeth got into the action with little kittenish bites that made the blood thunder through his veins.

It had been a long time since he'd worried about losing control but, with her mouth working its mesmerising magic on his, he seriously wondered whether he would go the distance. Need pulsed, powered and panted through him. Allegra's body beckoned to him, her legs opening, her arms around his neck as tight as a vine.

Draco put his hands to her wrists, encircling them like handcuffs, but she was so slender his fingers overlapped. 'I should get a condom.'

She pushed herself back against him, her breasts cool and soft against the wall of his chest, her eyelids lowered to half-mast like a sexy siren's. 'I'm on the pill. Make love to me. *Now.*'

That was another thing he hadn't done in a long time and then only the once: gone bareback. But in the context of their exclusive relationship he didn't have the usual list of reasons why he should halt proceedings to access protection. Allegra was taking contraception, in any case. He cradled her face in his hands, locking his gaze with hers. 'Are you sure?'

Her pupils were wide with desire, her mouth plump and pink from kissing him. 'We're married. And we're not going to sleep around, right? I'm clean, but if you need to get test—'

'Done,' Draco said. 'I was tested six months ago when I ended a fling. I haven't been with anyone since.'

Her eyes widened in surprise. 'No one? No one at all?'

He brushed an imaginary strand of hair away from her face. 'Seeing you that night reminded me of the chemistry we've always had. We have a passionate connection that's not just physical but intellectual. I decided that night I wanted you and, with your father's business worries taking centre stage, I soon came up with a plan to have you before someone else did. I had already been drip-feeding him money. What was a bit more to get what I wanted?'

Allegra rolled her lips together, her eyes shifting out of reach of his. 'It sounds a little…clinical…'

He brought up her chin with his fingertip. 'Does this feel clinical to you?' Draco kissed her softly, lingeringly, allowing her time to respond with the fervent passion he knew she couldn't contain. Her mouth flowered open, her arms going back around his neck, her soft little moan of acquiescence as sweet as any music he'd ever heard.

He moved from her mouth to kiss a pathway down between her breasts to her belly button, swirling his tongue around the tiny whorl of flesh before going lower. Allegra gave another whimper—part excitement, part nervousness.

He calmed her by placing a palm on her belly. 'Relax, *glykia mou*. I won't hurt you.'

She drew in a breath and he separated her tender folds, discovering her all over again. The secrets of her body, the scent and softness, the thrill of feeling her respond to his lips and tongue, was intoxicating to him. She arched up and shuddered as the orgasm powered through her in waves he could feel against his tongue.

She flopped back against the sofa cushions and he came over her, gliding into her with a long, deep thrust that made the hairs on his head shiver and shudder at the roots. Draco cut back a groan, but he couldn't slow down. Not now. Not now this urgent, desperate need was on the run. It broke free from his body, exploding out of him in a hot rush of relief that rained goose bumps all over his quivering flesh.

He was floating...floating...floating...all of his senses dazed into somnolence.

Draco stroked a lazy hand up and down the slim length of Allegra's thigh as if he were stroking a purring kitten. 'I hope I didn't rush you. Things got a little crazy just then.'

She shifted against him, her head tucking underneath his chin like a dormouse preparing for hibernation. 'No, it was...wonderful.' Her voice was as floaty as he felt. 'Truly wonderful.'

Draco looked down at her, pleased to see a curve of a smile on her mouth. He played with her hair, freeing it from its elastic tie, lifting it up and letting it tumble back through his fingers. 'We're good together, Allegra.'

She peeped up at him. 'The best?'

He gave her hair a teasing tug and then brought his mouth back down to hers. 'The best is yet to come.'

Allegra woke in the quietude a little while before dawn. The only sound she could hear was the gentle wash of the water against the sides of the yacht. Draco was sleeping spoon-like behind her, one of his arms over her waist, his legs entwined with hers. She had never spooned anyone before. It was such a cosy, intimate feeling to be curled up together, skin to skin. She listened to the sound of his breathing, feeling each rise and fall of his chest against the naked skin of her back. She glanced down at the band of his tanned, hair-roughened arm around her waist, the contrast of his darker toned skin against her creamy white making something tingle and shiver deep and low in her belly.

The curtains weren't drawn as they were so far away

from anyone in the private cove they'd anchored the yacht in the night before. The stars were like handfuls of diamonds flung over a dark velvet blanket, twinkling, winking, existing in a timeless and spectacular array. It struck her how long it had been since she had seen the stars in such magnificence. Her life had become so busy with work she rarely saw the night sky, other than in the city, where the light pollution all but wiped their brilliance out, apart from a stubborn handful. Allegra hadn't even taken holidays lately...not since her father had his cancer scare and she had used up all her leave, so the occasional star-gazing she did while taking a break had gone by the wayside.

Draco sighed and shifted behind her, his arm tightening around her body. 'Are you awake?'

Allegra felt the stirring of his erection against her bottom, sending a rush of physical memory through her body. 'I hope that's not your idea of foreplay.'

He chuckled and turned her so she was facing him. His dark eyes glittered as brightly as the stars outside. 'Here's the rule. You don't get to leave my bed until you've had a good time.'

Allegra traced the line of his smiling mouth with her fingertip. 'I'm having a very good time. Better than I thought possible.'

He captured her finger and kissed the tip, holding her gaze with the ink-dark steadiness of his. 'Not sore?'

She surreptitiously squeezed her legs together but wasn't quite able to disguise her wince when the overused muscles gave a faint protest. 'No...'

One black brow rose, demanding the truth. 'Not at all?'

Allegra caught her lower lip in her teeth. 'Well… maybe a little bit. That was quite a workout for me, given I'm a little out of practice and all.'

Draco stroked her forehead with such exquisite tenderness it made her chest feel strangely tight. 'I'm sorry. I should've thought and taken it more slowly.'

She lowered her gaze and went back to tracing his mouth, lingering over his lower lip and the rich coating of stubble below it. 'I guess I must seem a bit of a pariah, getting to this age without a healthy sex life.'

He inched up her chin again, his eyes lustrous and dark. 'I have enough female friends and colleagues to know how hard it is for a career woman to juggle work and relationships. Some men don't like not being the centre of a woman's world. Some careers are more demanding than others.'

'Yes, well, I had to fight hard to get where I've got,' she said. 'And, in spite of all the sacrifices I've made, I've still not made partner in the firm, nor will I be.'

'Is that what you want? To be made partner?'

For years, it was all Allegra had wanted. It had consumed her—the drive to achieve, to be recognised as competent and capable amongst her peers, especially the more senior ones. But lately her motivations had undergone a change. She still loved her job, but it didn't feel as satisfying as it once had. She found herself thinking of all the bad things about her work instead of all the positive things. 'I don't know…maybe it's time I shifted firms or something. I seem to have come to a bit of a career dead-end.'

'The glass ceiling?'

'That and other things…' Other things such as that niggling sense she was missing out on something.

Something far more important than a partnership in a law firm.

Draco threaded his fingers through hers and brought her hand to his chest. 'Ever thought of working over here in Greece? You could set up a consultancy of your own. You could help women like Iona.'

Allegra had always resisted the thought of working in her homeland. She had been so determined to be independent of her father. But she knew there were opportunities over here that would be career enhancing and personally satisfying. 'I'm still trying to figure out how I'm going to juggle my London job without taking on anything else.'

'I'm not expecting you to quit your job to cater to my needs,' Draco said. 'You have the right to work where you please. I have business commitments in England too. I'm just putting it out there in case you'd like to think about it.'

'What would be the point of setting up a legal practice I will then have to close once our marriage is over?'

His gaze suddenly seemed to be darker than normal. More intense. His brows were drawn slightly together in a small frown. 'Wouldn't you have had to leave when you wanted children, in any case?'

'Whoa there, buddy.' Allegra pulled her hand out of his and got off the bed to put some distance between them. 'How did we get from clever career moves to kids? You know my feelings on this.' Even as she was saying it she was feeling the opposite.

I want kids. I want them with you.

How had it taken her this long to recognise that niggling sense of dissatisfaction with her life was because she wanted a child? She had never seen herself as a mother, but since she'd been with Draco she couldn't get the thought out of her mind. But her pride wouldn't allow her to express it openly. How could she talk of her longing for a child when Draco had married her for all the wrong reasons? A child deserved to be born in love, not convenience. A baby was a blessing, not part of a business deal.

Draco left the bed and slipped on a bathrobe, the twin of the one Allegra had shoved her arms through and tied around her waist. 'What's the matter? I'm not insisting we have a child together. I'm just putting it out there for discussion. There's no harm in that, is there?'

'Why discuss it at all?' Allegra threw him a brittle glance. 'We're not staying married for ever. That was the deal, wasn't it? Why are you shifting the goal posts now?'

A muscle moved like a tic near his mouth. 'Let's drop the topic. It was a spur-of-the-moment thing. Forget I said it.'

'No. Let's talk about it,' Allegra said. 'It's obviously been playing on your mind. I thought you were only teasing when you first mentioned it. But you have no relatives to speak of. Most Greek men want an heir, especially men as wealthy as you. *Were* you teasing?'

He released a long, slow breath as if he were regulating his response. 'I was. But now I'm…wondering.'

Allegra wasn't sure she wanted to discuss it when she already knew what the outcome would be. They could have a child together but it didn't mean Draco would fall in love with her and stay married to her for ever. 'It's all right for you men,' she said. 'You don't have to interrupt your career to have a family. You don't have to give up your body for nine months, and longer still to breastfeed, and then spend years putting your aspirations on hold. You want the joy without the hard work.'

She was on a roll but she was spouting forth stuff she no longer believed the way she had even a few days ago. But she didn't want him to think her so willing to give up everything for him.

Not when he didn't love her.

But you don't love him, so why does it matter?

Allegra sidestepped the prod of her conscience. She didn't want to think about her feelings for him. It was dangerous to think about how he made her feel. She was confusing good sex with love, just like so many of her clients did. A couple of good orgasms and she fancied herself in love? Ridiculous. It was oxytocin— that was what it was. The bonding hormone tricking her into thinking she was falling in love with him. She was in lust with him. That was all. Lust. Lust. Lust.

'I'm aware of the commitment it is for a woman to have a child,' Draco said. 'But you're in a much better position than most women. With or without a husband, you could hire any necessary help, so your career wouldn't be compromised.'

'A nanny, you mean?' Allegra knew all about nannies. Nannies who came and went, who pretended they loved you and then moved on with barely a moment's notice after their affair with the husband of the house came to light. Nannies who made you feel wonderfully secure, only to rip that rug of security from under your feet so you were left in the inadequate care of a mentally unstable mother. 'No way would I allow a stranger to raise any child of mine.'

She turned away to straighten the bed for something to do with her hands, pulling up the sheets with a vicious tug as if she was putting the subject to sleep once and for all. She sensed him watching her and tried to relax her jerky movements, to control her body language.

But then she felt Draco come up behind her, his hands going to her shoulders and gently turning her to face him. His dark brown eyes were full of concern, not criticism, disarming her completely. 'This is a painful subject for you, *ne*? Then we will leave it alone. I don't want to upset you. I want to spend this week enjoying your company.'

Allegra was enjoying his company a little too much. How was she going to keep her heart out of this when he was so damnably attractive? She blew out a long breath. 'It is a painful subject. I hated being brought up by nannies. I would only just get used to one and then she would leave unexpectedly—mostly because her affair with my father had ended. He went through three or four that way. I'm sure that's why my mother didn't protest about me being sent to boarding school so young. She figured it would keep my father's affairs off site, so to speak.'

Draco squeezed her shoulders. 'Was boarding school tough on you?'

'It wasn't a picnic, that's for sure,' Allegra said. 'I didn't feel I belonged there. I was half-Greek with an accent that was nothing like all the upper-class English girls. I got rid of the accent as soon as I could and tried to fit in. But going home for holidays was just as hard. It was like culture shock. My mother couldn't cope with a child underfoot. I reminded her too much of Dion.'

His frown was so deep it drew his eyebrows into a single bar of black. 'Why do you think your parents didn't divorce?'

'I don't know... I guess because my father would have felt bad about leaving her after Dion died,' Allegra said, moving out of his hold to fold her arms across her middle. 'In the end she left him. I thought he'd bring home a love child well before this. But he didn't seem interested in marrying again until Elena got pregnant.'

'Elena seems happy with her situation.'

'Yes, well, she would be, wouldn't she?' Allegra said. 'She has a beautiful baby boy and she's married a man she loves. What's not to be happy about?'

His frown deepened. 'I thought you liked Elena.'

'I do—a lot,' Allegra said. 'She's sweet and caring, and has a lot of sensitivity, and heaps of integrity too. I just worry she might not be able to hold my father's interest in the long term.'

The same worries I have about you.

'Your father might finally settle down now he has his son and heir,' Draco said. 'But I see why you'd be concerned for Elena.'

Allegra rolled her lips together for a moment. 'You don't see the similarity?'

A flicker of puzzlement passed over his features. 'What similarity?'

'Between our situation and theirs.'

A muscle tightened in the lower quadrant of his jaw. 'No, quite frankly, I don't. It's a completely different situation. I've told you our marriage has a time limit. I promised to remain faithful during that time and, unlike your father, I am a man of my word. You have no reason to feel insecure with me. I might have a more colourful past than you but I have never cheated on a partner. Never.'

'But we're not in love with each other, so in a way we're worse off than Dad and Elena.'

Something shifted at the back of his gaze, as if he was reordering his thoughts. 'Perhaps we're not, in the romantic sense of the word, but in every other way that counts.' Draco held out his hand. 'Come here.'

Allegra came as if he had an invisible cord attached to her body, tugging her back into his orbit. He took her by the waist, holding her against the frame of his body, his eyes meshing with hers in a lock that made her inner core tighten in excitement. There was no way she could resist him. It didn't matter if he didn't love her. She wanted him anyway.

He cupped her cheek with one broad hand, his touch as gentle as if he were cradling priceless porcelain. He brought his mouth down in a feather-down kiss that stirred her senses into a stupor. Her lips clung to his. Need rose in her like a tide, leaving no part of her body immune. Her breasts tingled where they were pushed against the hard wall of his chest, her legs feeling as if they had seaweed for bones. Draco's mouth came back down to claim hers in a firmer kiss, his tongue entering her mouth in a sensual glide that made her insides twist and coil like kelp.

He eased back for a moment to look at her with eyes glittering with desire. 'Breakfast or back to bed?'

Allegra pulled his head back down. 'Read my lips.'

CHAPTER EIGHT

DRACO HADN'T HAD a holiday for months, so he kept telling himself that was why he was feeling so relaxed after a week sailing around the islands. He'd chosen a couple of private hideaways he was familiar with where he and Allegra had swum in quiet coves with the fish darting below them or had lain on pristine beaches.

But, if he were honest with himself, he knew it was because Allegra was proving to be the best thing that had happened to him in a long time. Maybe ever. He woke each morning with a tick of excitement in his blood. Not just because the sex they had was getting better and better, but because the companionship they'd developed had settled into friendship unlike he'd had before with anyone else. He looked forward to discussing things with her—current affairs or business things that came through on email. She had a good mind and sound common sense and he enjoyed listening to her take on current issues. They had cooked together, read together, walked, swam and snorkelled together.

And made love.

Draco couldn't quite bring himself to call it sex any more. Weird, because sex was supposed to be sex. It always had been in the past. But with Allegra it was something more. Something more cerebral...even—*dared he say it?*—emotional.

He shied away from the thought and where it was leading. It wasn't love but physical bonding. It happened when the sex was particularly good. His body craved hers. Hungered for her closeness. Got restless when she wasn't nearby.

It was his hormones going crazy.

Nothing else.

Speaking of hormones, he hadn't returned to the subject of children. He still wasn't entirely sure why he'd brought it up when he had. When proposing, he had brought it up as a test to see what her plans were on the issue. But lately, he'd started to wonder if Allegra was projecting a cover-up opinion. He'd wanted to make sure he wasn't doing the wrong thing by her by tying her to a childless marriage. But she remained adamant that having a family was not on her horizon. It hadn't been on his either, but for some strange reason he kept thinking about it. He had no living close relative. It hadn't used to bother him but now it kept niggling at him. He was getting a taste of fatherhood with Yanni and it wasn't always pretty.

Did he have what it took to be a good father? His father had been a great dad. Hard-working and committed to him no matter what life had thrown his way. But his father had been killed tragically and life had been tough without a father to guide him. Tougher than he wanted any kid of his to experience...

But if Draco suggested he and Allegra have a child it would change everything about their arrangement. Make it more permanent. The only trouble was...

He didn't do permanent.

* * *

When Allegra came up on deck the last morning of their trip, she slipped her arm around Draco's waist and smiled up at him before looking at the sun rising over the water in a golden wash of glittering light. 'So beautiful.'

He dropped a kiss to the top of her head. 'I think so.'

She looked up into his dark gaze and wondered how she had ever thought she'd hated him. The last few days had been some of the most relaxing and enjoyable of her life. She couldn't remember a time when she had felt more in tune with her body. Not just its sexual needs but in terms of general health and wellbeing. She had energy, she slept well and she woke up feeling refreshed and excited about the day and what delights Draco had planned.

But now Allegra was starting to dread the thought of going back to the real world. The world where work, long hours and difficult people sawed at her nerves, kept her awake at night and turned her stomach into a churning mess. 'Do we really have to go back today? Why can't we stay out here for ever?'

He drew her closer, his hands settling on her hips. 'That would indeed be a dream. But duty calls, I'm afraid. I've already had five calls from various staff members over urgent matters. I shouldn't have turned on my phone until after we berthed.'

Allegra toyed with the collar of his polo shirt, her hips resting in the cradle of his. Such intimacy seemed so natural now. Her body still leapt at his touch, her skin tingling and tightening when he gave her *that* look. The 'I want to make love to you and make you scream with pleasure' look that spoke to her womanhood and made it do cartwheels, handstands and backflips in excitement.

But, while the intimacy was fabulous, their communication could do with some work, especially over the last twenty-four hours. She had sensed a subtle withdrawing in him, as if he was only comfortable with being intimate sexually, but not emotionally. There was so much they hadn't discussed in any detail about their relationship going forward. Where would they live? Would he expect her to move in with him? He had bought a new townhouse in Hampstead a year ago. Her little house in Bloomsbury was her pride and joy. She couldn't imagine giving it up, as it was a symbol of her independence. The first place she had called home.

Her home.

She lifted her gaze back to his. 'We haven't talked about our living arrangements when we get back to London. Will you stay with me or at your place in London?'

'Most married couples live together. But I don't expect you to move out of your home.'

Allegra wasn't sure what to make of Draco's answer. Did it mean he wanted to keep separate accommodation? Why would that be? The doubts gathered like seagulls above a fishing vessel, circling her brain, looking for a place to land. Would he keep his house in London so he could keep his distance when it suited him? 'So you plan to keep your place as well?'

'It wouldn't be a sound business move to sell just at this moment,' he said. 'I've recently spent a fortune on renovating it. But it's not a decision I have to make right now. I'll revisit in a year or so.'

How could she know for sure if that was his true reasoning? A business decision not a personal one? Was it a get-out clause? A back-up plan in case things didn't go according to plan? Over the last few days Allegra had been lulled into thinking he was developing feelings for her. The way he talked to her, listened to her, laughed with her.

The way he made love to her.

Yes, made love.

It didn't feel like 'just sex' to her. Not the way he worshipped her body, made it feel things it had never felt before, made her senses swoon and her heart lower its drawbridge.

She had fallen in love with him.

Not at first sight. Not since she was a teenager, but by degrees. Each time they made love the feelings would intensify. There was no denying them now.

She had fooled herself into thinking he would fall in love with her. Sooner. Later. Eventually. But how long was too long to wait? What if it never happened? What if he wasn't capable of being open emotionally?

'So, where will we go once we get back to London?' Allegra asked. 'Your place or mine?'

Draco slid his hand up between her shoulder blades and then under the curtain of her hair, cupping her nape. 'I have to fly to Glasgow for a meeting later that day. I got an email a few minutes ago about it. I won't be back for a couple of days so you'd be best to go to your place. I'll catch up with you mid-week.'

Allegra thought they'd be flying back together but now he was shooting off to Scotland. But she refused to show her disappointment. It was unreasonable of her to expect his career to take a back seat when she had her own professional commitments that couldn't be cancelled at short notice. It had been a logistical nightmare taking this week off as it was. But it worried her this would be an on-going pattern of their future relationship. How long before his 'catch ups' with her became not weekly, but monthly, or even less frequent? How long before he went from looking at her with those glinting 'I want you' eyes to avoiding her gaze altogether, as her father had to her mother when he'd come back from a new mistress's arms? 'Okay,' she said. 'Fine.'

Draco inched up her chin, his gaze searching. 'I know it's not ideal. I wish you could come with me to Scotland but I know how hard it was for you to get this week off. It was the same for me. There will be constant compromises as we juggle two demanding careers. But we'll figure it out as we go.'

Allegra stretched her mouth into a 'I'm cool with that' smile. 'That's what you get for marrying a career girl. You have to share her with her ambition.'

His thumb pad stroked over her beauty spot, his eyes still holding hers in a penetrating tether. 'I have a feeling you're not as ambitious as you make out.'

She forced herself not to shift her gaze but to hold his without wavering. How could he know how conflicted she felt about her career? She had barely acknowledged it to herself. She hadn't even talked about it to Emily. She'd played the 'career girl' card for years. Work had always been her top priority. But if she interrupted her career path with a baby what would happen to her place on the ladder?

And did she even care?

Allegra slipped out of his hold and held on to the

side of the yacht. 'I haven't even got time for a pet. I really don't know how women do it—have a family and keep their career on track.'

He put his hands on her shoulders from behind, his body brushing hers with its warm, hard temptation. 'These things have a way of working themselves out, *glykia mou*. Your circumstances might be completely different in a year or two.'

Yes, she would be divorced and single again.

Allegra turned around, her arms automatically going around his waist as if she had no will of her own to resist him. But then, she didn't. Not one little bit of willpower. She leaned her head against Draco's chest, his hand stroking the back of her head in a soothing motion. What if her body decided for her? She was on the pill but it was a low-dose one and she was woefully lax at taking it. They had made love numerous times now without a condom.

What if she was already pregnant with a honeymoon baby?

But, even if she was, it didn't change the fact Draco didn't love her. Not the way she wanted to be loved. Totally. Unconditionally. Bringing a baby into a marriage that wasn't based on love would not be the best start in life for a child. Didn't she see that every working day? Children traumatised by their parents' arguing, or worse, marked for life with the memories of their care-givers at bitter war with each other, sometimes even after the divorce.

Didn't she bear similar scars herself? Her parents hadn't fought overtly with each other, but she had seen the stone-walling and cold-shoulder treatment from her mother and the pay-backs with affairs and long absences from her father. Was it any wonder she had issues with trust? Big issues?

Draco brought up her chin, his gaze meshing with hers. 'We need to set sail soon if we're going to get back in time for our flights out of Athens this evening.' He pressed a soft kiss to her mouth and drew back to smile lopsidedly at her. 'Back to the real world, *ne*?'

I can hardly wait.

Emily followed Allegra into her office first thing on Monday morning. 'So, how was the honeymoon? Good? Bad? Sensational?'

Allegra put her tote bag and briefcase on the desk and gave her friend a prim look. 'Since when have I told you intimate details about my sex life?'

Emily's eyes twinkled like fairy lights. 'You haven't had one for the last year or more, so how could you? Did you do it with him?'

Allegra slipped off her jacket and hung it on the hook behind her door, hoping her hot cheeks weren't giving her away. Every time she thought of Draco and the intense pleasure he'd evoked in her over the last week it made her blush from head to foot. 'Isn't that what couples on their honeymoon do?'

Emily plonked herself on the corner of Allegra's desk, swinging her legs like an excited schoolgirl. 'So what happened to the marriage of convenience?'

Allegra gave her a self-deprecating look. 'It seems I have zero willpower when it comes to that man.'

Emily picked up a pen and examined it as though it were crucial evidence. 'Yes, well, I'm inclined to agree with you, given his best friend is enough to make a ninety-year-old nun think twice about staying celibate.'

Allegra angled her head. 'Don't tell me you…?'

Emily dropped the pen and jumped down from the desk, her arms crossing over her body. 'I don't know what came over me—I swear I don't. I've never had a one-night stand with a guy. Never, ever.'

Allegra looked at her friend in surprise. 'You *slept* with Loukas Kyprianos?'

Emily winced. 'Guilty, your honour.'

'So, are you seeing him? Dating him?'

Emily bit her lip, the earlier brightness of her expression fading. 'He didn't even ask me for my number.'

'Ouch.'

'Yeah, big ouchy-ouch. I have terrible taste in men. Why do I always pick men way out of my league? No. Don't say it. I know why. It's because I have this ridiculous life script where the only man I want is the one I can't have. I think my mum is right—I need therapy.'

I could do with some myself.

'But it's only been a week,' Allegra said. 'He might still get in contact with you. He could get your number easily enough through Draco or me.'

'I'm not holding my breath,' Emily said. 'I may have sabotaged my chances with him anyway.'

'How?'

She screwed up her mouth and nose in a bunny-rabbit twitch. 'I talked too much. It was like that third champagne did something to my tongue. No wonder they call it truth serum. My mum would say it's because I was subconsciously inviting rejection. You know how New Age-y she is.'

'But what did you say to him?'

'I told Loukas I wanted to get married before I turn thirty in March and I wanted four kids and an Irish retriever.'

'What was his reaction?'

Emily rolled her eyes. 'You would've thought I'd asked him to propose to me then and there. I might as well have put a gun to his head and said, "Marry me or I'll shoot". Although it pains me to admit it, my mother is right. I sabotaged what could have been a perfectly good relationship.'

'I don't know about that,' Allegra said. 'Draco told me Loukas isn't the marrying type. His parents went through a bitter divorce when he was a kid. He said Loukas would never get married. He made quite a point of it, actually.'

Emily's shoulders sagged. 'I sure can pick them. I thought I'd learned my lesson after my disastrous relationship with Daniel.' She sat down with a thump on the chair opposite Allegra's desk. 'Sorry. I shouldn't be dumping all my negative stuff on you. Tell me more about the honeymoon. Are you in love with Draco?'

Allegra avoided her friend's gaze and sat down opposite, making a business of straightening her desk as though she had full-blown OCD. 'It's not that sort of marriage.'

'Like hell it isn't,' Emily said. 'You've been in love with him for years.'

'I had a crush on him, that's all—'

'Crush, schmush.' Emily's playful smile came back. 'You so do love him. Look at you. You're positively glowing with oxytocin.'

Allegra could feel her cheeks warming up like hot-plates on a cook-top. 'Yes, well, Draco certainly knows his way around a woman's body... Thing is, am I going to be enough for him? He doesn't love me. He *cares* about me.'

Emily did her cute little bunny twitch again. 'Oh...'

'Not exactly what a girl wants to hear on her honeymoon.'

'No, but words aren't everything,' Emily said. 'Actions are what counts and it looks like you two have had plenty of that over the last week.'

'He's keeping his own house in Hampstead.'

Emily blinked. 'So? Aren't you moving in with him?'

'Why should I?'

'Because that's what brides do. They move in with their husbands.'

'But I don't want to move out of my house,' Allegra said. 'It's my home and I don't see why I should give it up just because my husband wants to live somewhere else. Women are the ones who always make all the compromises. And in the end they lose out. Big time.'

'You've been working in this job way too long,' Emily said. 'Compromise is the key to a successful relationship. Not that I can talk, as I've not had one, personally. But I live in hope.'

Me too.

CHAPTER NINE

ALLEGRA GOT A phone call from Draco later that evening when she got home from work. She had been waiting on tenterhooks all day for his name to pop up on her screen, the little kick of excitement when it finally did making her realise how much she'd missed him in the last twenty-four hours. 'Hi. How was your day?'

'Don't ask.' His tone was flat and jaded. 'I've got to fly to Russia in an hour. I'm at the airport now. I probably won't be back until Friday. Sorry.'

'Oh...that's too bad. Is it something serious?'

'Just business stuff.'

'You can talk to me about it, you know,' Allegra said with more tartness than she would have liked. 'I'm not some nineteen-fifties housewife who has no idea of how the real world works.'

He gave a rough-edged sigh. 'My client is a Russian billionaire who wants some face-to-face time over a design we're working on for him.'

'Couldn't you have sent someone in your place? You do have other people working for you, don't you?' Now she was starting to sound like a nineteen-fifties housewife.

'He's a difficult client,' Draco said. 'But his business is too valuable to compromise. I won't be away long—three days, five at the max. But enough about my business. How was it back at work?'

'Oh, you know, the usual stuff.' Allegra paused and added, 'Have you spoken to Loukas lately?'

'Not since the wedding. Why?'

'Just asking.'

'Just asking...why?'

She chewed at her lip for a beat. 'He and Emily got it on after the wedding.'

Draco gave a deep chuckle. 'Yes, well, I did tell you he had a thing for English girls.'

'He didn't ask for her number.' Allegra said it as if it was a personality defect.

There was a small pause.

'Was that a problem for her?' he said.

'A bit, I think.'

'She liked him?'

'She slept with him, didn't she? She's not the sort of girl to put it out for just anyone. Although she did have a bit to drink.'

'Loukas wouldn't have taken advantage of her, if that's what you're suggesting.'

'I wasn't,' Allegra said. 'She was keen on him but over-played it out of nervousness or something.'

'Over-played it?'

'She mentioned the M word.'

'Bad move.'

'Yes, it was apparently quite a dampener. Poor Em. She's such a sweetheart but she always falls for the wrong men.'

'Do you want me to have a word with him?' Draco asked.

'God, no. I think it's best if we keep out of it. We have enough problems of our own to interfere in anyone else's.'

Another silence ticked past.

'I mean...we have to sort out stuff, you know?' Allegra said. 'The living situation, for instance.'

'I thought we discussed that.'

'But what are people going to say when they find out we're keeping two houses in London on the go?' Allegra said. 'It's hardly the behaviour of a normal couple.'

'Then move in with me. Problem solved.'

'Why don't you move in with me?'

'Mine is a much bigger house,' he said. 'It makes sense to move in with me. You can rent yours out if you're not keen to sell it.'

'Why do I have to be the one who compromises?'

'It isn't about compromising, Allegra. It's about doing what's sensible.' Draco sounded as if he were talking to a child who had failed to grasp the simplest information.

Allegra wished she were still wearing her heels so she could dig them into the carpet. 'So far, I've made all the sacrifices in this relationship. You simply get on with your life as if nothing's changed.'

'Look, I have to go,' he said. 'I'll call you tomorrow.'

Allegra put the phone down and sighed. It wasn't the most satisfying way to end a conversation. But so far the only satisfying thing about their relationship was the sex. And even that was out of the question now, with Draco travelling thousands of miles away for days on end. Maybe she was being silly about the house. It made sense to use the bigger of the two. It was a big step for her, but not as big as marrying him. How could she expect him to fall in love with her if she kept harping on about silly little issues that weren't worth worrying about?

You expect him to fall in love with you?

Allegra chewed her lip until the skin felt raw. Was it too much of a dream to hope he would?

Draco leaned his head back on the headrest once he'd boarded his plane and closed his eyes, wishing he could close off his thoughts as well. Truth was, he could have sent someone else to Russia, but he needed some distance to sort out of few things in his head.

Why was everything suddenly so complicated? He had a filthy headache and a gut full of worry over Yanni back at home, who was giving his staff merry hell over being under house arrest. Now he'd upset Allegra over real estate. Her house was nice but it was practically a doll's house compared to his. Besides, he didn't want to live on her territory. He was the one calling the shots in their relationship. If he moved in with her, she would have the power to ask him to leave. He wasn't giving her that power, no matter how good they were together in bed and out of it. He could pack his house up and rent it out, but why should he? She was being stubborn.

Like you.

Of course he was being stubborn. Being stubborn was how you got things done. How you set goals and saw things through to completion. Being stubborn was how you built up a business into a global empire that was worth millions. Being stubborn was how you rescued a drug-addicted kid of the street and got him clean so he could have a life.

It meant Draco's life was a little more stressful than he'd like it, but that was the way things were. Allegra would come round. It was early days and she was still getting used to sharing her life with someone. As was he. This short separation would hopefully help him get some perspective. He had never been this close to another person. Not just physically, but emotionally. He looked forward to being with her, and he dreamt about her when he wasn't.

He had to rein it in. Draco didn't want to turn back into that callow youth of nineteen who'd fancied himself in love only to find it was a mirage. A fantasy. A dream built on air. He wasn't in love. His heart was in a straitjacket, where it belonged. He would miss Allegra while he was in Russia, badly. But it didn't mean he was in love with her. It meant he cared about her.

It was a mild word, yes, but the way he felt about her was anything but mild.

But when Draco got back to his hotel, from his third and final difficult meeting with his client, he sat in his suite and thought about how lonely it was eating yet another meal on his own. He could have gone out to a restaurant but the thought of dining out alone held zero appeal. No one to sit opposite him, challenging him, debating with him, smiling at his jokes and giving him those sparkly-eyed looks that signalled the same desire he could feel burning in his loins.

He missed Allegra. More than he'd thought he would. This time away was meant to give him some breathing room but instead it was stifling him. There was no trace of her perfume in the hotel room, not even on his skin. When he turned over in bed, the place beside him was cold and empty. That had never bothered him before. An empty space beside him meant he was free of emotional entanglements, but now it made Draco feel...well...empty. He'd tried calling her a few times but the time difference and the long meetings he or she had been in hadn't always worked in his favour. He'd been left feeling strangely out of touch with Allegra. Wanting her with an almost violent ache. Needing to see her like he needed his next breath.

He wondered if she was missing him. Did she stare into space and daydream about their honeymoon the way he did? Did she get a shuddery shiver all over her body when she thought about how they had made love on deck under the star-studded sky? Did she reach for him in the middle of the night and get a sinking feeling in her stomach when she realised he wasn't lying beside her?

Maybe it wouldn't be such a bad idea to move in to one house when he got back. A little bit of compromise wouldn't go astray, especially when it got him what he wanted—Allegra.

Allegra got back from court the following day to find a beautiful bouquet of flowers on her desk. She picked up the card and read the message.

Miss you. Draco.

Her heart gave a leap and she pressed the card against her chest just as Emily buzzed her on the intercom.

'Allegra, your stepmother is here. Have you got time to see her?'

Allegra put the card down on her desk. *Elena was in London?* Why hadn't she mentioned it at the wedding? Or was it a spontaneous trip? But that didn't seem like Elena at all. She was a homebody through and through. She didn't really enjoy travelling all that much and had said only recently how content she was to stay at home with little Nico. 'Sure. I haven't got anyone till four, have I?'

'No, you're all good. I'll send her in.'

Elena came in pushing Nico in his pram. Her eyes were red-rimmed and her face puffy, as if she had been crying. 'Sorry to barge in on you…'

Allegra came up to her and took her hands. 'What's happened?' She glanced in the pram to make sure Nico was all right but he was sleeping soundly. She looked back at Elena. 'What are you doing in London? Is Dad with you? Why didn't you tell me you were—?'

Elena shook her head. 'He's in Paris.'

An ice-cold tap began to drip down Allegra's spine. 'Paris? What for?'

Elena's bottom lip quivered. 'He's got a mistress there. I only just found out about her. He's been seeing her since I got p-pregnant.' The tears started in earnest then, accompanied by hiccoughing sobs.

Allegra hugged her close and stroked her back in soothing circular motions. What was her father thinking? He had what he wanted, didn't he? He had a son and heir and a loving and attentive wife. What more did he want? The selfishness of it appalled her. The cruelty of it made her stomach churn with anger.

Once Elena got some of her composure back, she

eased out of Allegra's embrace. Her watery gaze went to the bouquet of flowers on the desk. 'That's how I found out.' She pointed to the flowers. 'The florist must have got our names mixed up. I got this lovely bunch of red roses, and when I looked at the card it said "To Angelique, love always, Cosimo."'

'I'm so sorry.'

Elena turned a sharp eye on Allegra. 'Did you know? Have you known all along?'

'No, of course not,' Allegra said, shocked and more than a little hurt Elena would think it of her. 'Could it be a mistake? Another Cosimo?' Even as she said it, it sounded implausible.

'No, it's him,' Elena said. 'He didn't deny it when I called him. He ordered the flowers online for me and for her. He made some excuse about how he didn't want to pressure me for sex while I was pregnant. And here I was, thinking how kind and considerate he'd been when I was having all that wretched morning sickness. It makes me want to throw up all over again.'

Allegra wanted to throw up too. How could her father be so pathetic? 'What are you going to do?'

Elena's eyes streamed with tears and she brushed at them with the back of her hand. 'I want to leave him, but I've got little Nico to consider. If your father cuts my allowance, how will I afford a good lawyer to represent me?'

'I'll act for you,' Allegra said, handing her a bunch of tissues from the box on her desk. 'I know it's a little unusual, given he's my father, but I would never allow him to do you out of what's rightfully yours.'

'Oh, would you?' Elena asked, mopping at her eyes. 'Really?'

'Of course,' Allegra said, knowing it would be the end of her relationship with her father, but she no longer cared. Elena and Nico's welfare was a much higher priority.

Elena's situation was an unwelcome reminder of how much she herself had to lose. She was exactly like Elena—in love with a man who didn't love her back. He 'cared' for her. Like her father 'cared' for Elena. But at least Draco had had the decency to refrain from saying those three little words, unlike her father, who rattled them off all the time. And, unlike her father, he might be faithful to her for the duration of their marriage, but he planned to end it when it suited him.

He didn't love her.

That was the bottom line.

She would spend the next couple of years of her life—precious years she would never get back—waiting, hoping, praying he would fall in love with her. What if she had the baby she secretly longed for? She would be just like Elena, left holding it when he decided he wanted out. She didn't want to live like that. To be the sort of woman other women pitied. As she pitied Elena right now. If Draco couldn't say those words and mean them, then she had to make a choice.

'What are your immediate plans?' she asked Elena. 'Are you staying in London or flying home to Santorini?'

'I'm flying back to Athens to stay with my parents. I haven't told them yet. They'll be so disappointed but I have to leave him. I can't live with someone who doesn't love me enough to stay faithful. I just wanted to see you in person. I was worried you'd known about it.'

'I would never hide something like that,' Allegra

said. 'I'm appalled at Dad's behaviour. I'm shocked and sickened by it. I'm on your side in this. I'll get the paperwork drawn up and we'll take things from there.'

'I couldn't bear to lose Nico in a custody battle,' Elena said with a haunted look in her eyes. 'I'd rather die than face that.'

Allegra gave Elena another hug. 'I'm here for you every step of the way, okay? I can talk to Dad but I'm not sure it will do much.'

'No, please don't. This is my problem, not yours.' Elena took a calming breath and then gave a shaky smile that was a little off the mark. 'I'm sorry. I didn't even ask you how the honeymoon went. Did you have a good time?'

'It was lovely, thanks.'

'You're so lucky,' Elena said. 'Draco loves you. Anyone can see that.'

If only he did...

Allegra got home after a lengthy and arduous court hearing on Friday evening. She had only spoken to Draco a couple of times during the week, as he'd been in transit or busy with work commitments, or she had been in court and the time zones had made it even more difficult to connect. Besides, the conversation she intended to have with him was not one she wanted to have over the phone. She wanted to see him face to face. He'd arranged to meet her at her house. She had prepared a meal the night before and now she popped it in the oven to reheat before she showered and changed.

The doorbell rang as she was drying off her hair. The fact that he'd rung the doorbell was another reminder of how odd their relationship was. He didn't have a key to her house and she didn't have a key to his.

But then she didn't have the key to his heart, either.

Allegra's resolve took a punch when she opened the door to him. Draco looked as heart-stoppingly gorgeous as ever in an open-neck dark blue shirt and white chinos that showcased his olive complexion. 'Hi...'

He stepped over the threshold and took her in his arms, covering her mouth with his in a long, spine-melting kiss that made her resolve roll over and play dead. Her arms went around his waist, her hips flush against the potent heat gathering in his pelvis, her own body quaking with the need to get even closer. Draco pulled back to look down at her. 'That was a long week. Did you miss me?'

Allegra dropped her arms from his body and stepped back with a cool smile. 'I've been too busy to think about anything but work. How was your trip?'

His expression registered her response with a slight tightening around his mouth. 'Exhausting. I've crossed so many time zones in the last five days, I've got no idea what time to eat or sleep.'

'Come through.' She led the way to the sitting room where she had laid out drinks and some pre-dinner nibbles. 'Can I get you wine or beer or...?'

'What are you having?'

'White wine.'

'Half a glass will do.'

Allegra handed it to him with another impersonal smile. 'Here you go.'

He took the wine but put it straight back down on the coffee table. 'I have something for you.' He took out a package from his back pocket—a flattish square box wrapped in black tissue, tied with a gold ribbon.

She took it from him and carefully untied the ribbon and tissue to find a jeweller's box with a sapphire-and-diamond pendant inside. It was a delicate and elegant setting, almost simple in design, but the brilliant blue of the sapphire and the tiny sparkling diamonds that surrounded it made it one of the most beautiful pieces of jewellery she had ever seen. 'It's...gorgeous...' She glanced up at him. 'Thank you. It was very thoughtful of you.'

'Glad you like it,' Draco said with a smile. 'The sapphire reminded me of your eyes.' He took the box back from her. 'Here, let me put it on for you.'

Allegra turned around and lifted her hair out of the way while he looped the fine gold chain around her neck and fastened the clasp. The brush of his fingers against her skin made her whole body shiver in reaction. She turned back around to face him, her fingers absently playing with the sapphire. 'Thanks for the flowers, by the way.'

He placed his hands on her shoulders and meshed his gaze with hers. 'Why don't you tell me what's troubling you?'

Allegra pressed her lips together for a moment. 'I had a visit from Elena today.'

'Here? In London?'

She nodded. 'She flew over to talk to me face to face.'

'About...?'

'About my father's mistress in Paris.'

Draco's brows snapped together. 'He has a mistress? Already?'

Allegra slipped out of his hold and stood some distance from him with her arms crossed over her body, her hands cupping her elbows. 'Yes. Her name is Angelique. He sent flowers to her and Elena but the florist must have got the messages mixed up.'

He shook his head as if the situation was beyond belief. 'He's a fool. A damn fool. What's she going to do?'

'She's leaving him,' Allegra said, keeping her gaze steady on his. 'She says she can't live with a man who doesn't love her enough to stay faithful. I agree with her. You can't make someone love you—they either love you or they don't.'

There was a beat or two of pregnant silence.

'Allegra...' Her name came out on a heavy sigh that had 'don't do this' written all over it.

'I've been thinking this week while you've been away,' Allegra said, refusing to be daunted now she had made up her mind. 'This is how it's always going to be, isn't it? You don't love me. Not the way I want to be loved. The way most women want to be loved. The way Elena wants to be loved. I want love I can rely on, no matter what. Caring isn't enough for me, Draco. Flowers and expensive gifts and great sex aren't enough. I want you to love me. But, because you don't, our marriage has to end.'

He let out a harsh breath. 'Don't be ridiculous, *agape mou*. You're being—'

'You keep calling me your "love" but I'm not, am I?' she said. 'They're empty words. I want more than that. I deserve more than that.'

'Look, you're feeling let down about your father's behaviour and it's colouring your—'

'This has nothing to do with my father,' Allegra said. 'This is to do with us. But we're not an 'us', are we? Not in the true sense. We've married for all the wrong reasons and I can't be in a marriage like that. It will be like living my childhood all over again. Never feeling good enough. Never feeling enough, period.'

His brows came together over his eyes. 'You're not suggesting I'd carry on like your father? I told you I'd remain faithful. I promised you that.'

Allegra shook her head at him. 'Being faithful isn't enough. I can't be in a relationship that has a time limit. Every day that passes is a day closer to the one when you'll tell me you want out. That's not how a marriage should be. Even if you're not unfaithful, you could still fall in love with someone else, because without a solid commitment to me it leaves the door wide open for it.'

'I'm not going to fall in love with someone.'

'It's just as bad if you've ruled love out completely. I can't spend the next couple of years of my life hoping you will change. It's better to end it now. Before—'

'What about your father? The ink is barely dry on the deal.'

'You know something? Right now I don't give a fat fig if my father loses everything,' Allegra said. 'He deserves to lose everything, including his wife and son. I'm not going to be the sacrificial lamb for him. I've done it all my life. Papered over the cracks he made in my mother's and my life. I spent years compensating for his inadequacies but I'm sick of it. I'm reclaiming my life as of now, and it doesn't include you, because of the reasons I've stated.'

Draco showed no emotion. It was as if a curtain had

come down on the stage of his face. Allegra kept hoping he would say something...the words she so desperately wanted to hear...even though, if he did, she knew she would doubt their veracity. But why didn't he say them? What was so hard about saying 'I love you'?

'Is this about our living arrangements?' he said. 'If so, we can talk about a compromise. I was going to suggest it anyway, so...'

Allegra shook her head. 'Living together isn't going to solve this, Draco. Surely you can see that? We want completely different things out of life. Ultimately, you want your freedom and I want... I want a baby. A family.' There, she'd said it. Finally admitted the yearning that had been simmering inside her for the last few days. Maybe even longer...maybe since that night in London last December.

He flinched in shock. 'A baby? But you've always said you didn't want—'

'I know what I said but I've changed my mind.'

'Then let's have a baby,' he said, blowing out a breath as if everything was sorted. 'If that's the only issue, then it's easily solved. We'll have a baby and—'

'No,' Allegra said. 'I'm not having a baby to prop up a marriage that isn't working.'

'What do you mean it isn't working?' His gaze was forceful. Direct. 'Last time I looked, it was working just fine.'

'It's not working for me,' Allegra said. 'I'm not going to be second best, Draco. I want to come first. I deserve to be loved for who I am, not for what I can do. That was the script of my childhood; I don't want to follow it in adulthood.'

His expression returned to its inscrutable mask, all

except for a pulse at the base of his throat that seemed to be working a little overtime. 'Is this your final decision?'

Allegra set her chin at a determined height, even though everything in her was slumping, collapsing in despair. Why wasn't he saying it?

Tell me you love me. Tell me you don't want to lose me. Tell me. Tell me. Tell me.

'Yes.'

He gave a slow nod. 'We obviously can't get the marriage annulled.'

'No…'

'It will be embarrassing for both of us for a while,' he said. 'I won't speak to the press and I'd appreciate it if you didn't either.'

'Of course.' Why was he being so damn businesslike about it? So clinical and so composed, as if he wasn't ripping her heart out of her chest with his bare hands. Didn't that prove how little he cared? 'Erm…do you want this back?' Allegra touched the pendant around her neck. 'And the rings?'

'No. Keep them.' Draco's lips barely moved as he spoke, as if he resented the effort.

Allegra swallowed a puffer fish of sadness, but by some miracle she stopped herself from tearing up. Her eyes remained dry and focussed on his. 'I guess that's it, then.' She waved a hand towards the dining room. 'You could stay for dinner but I expect you'd—'

'No.'

'Right.'

There was another silence so acute Allegra was sure she could hear her heart beating. Boom. Boom. Boom.

'I'll see myself out.'

Allegra nodded, not sure she could take much more without showing the devastation she was feeling. Why wasn't he putting up more of a fight? Why wasn't he arguing his corner as he usually did? All he had to do was take her in his arms and show her what he found so difficult to say. Why was Draco walking away?

Because he doesn't love you.

CHAPTER TEN

DRACO WALKED OUT of Allegra's house as if he was on autopilot. His emotions were in lockdown. Emotions he hadn't known he had. He couldn't think past the thought of her pulling the plug on their marriage. He'd been blindsided. Again. What sort of fool was he to have fallen for it? He'd thought it was going so well. Why was she doing this? Why now, after that wonderful week away together?

All this talk of love... He hadn't said those words to anyone since he'd said them to his ex. He had sworn he would never say them in a subsequent relationship, and he had never needed to, much less wanted to. But Allegra hadn't said it, either. Somehow he had fooled himself into thinking she had, but then, he'd been wrong about that sort of thing before.

It was the same as all those years ago...

No. It was worse.

Much worse.

Back then, he'd been angry. Bitter. Furious.

Now all he felt was...*hurt*. Pain like he'd only ever experienced twice before, while staring at a coffin containing his mother and then later his father.

He had lost Allegra like he'd lost his parents. Without warning. Unexpectedly. They were there one minute and then they weren't.

Draco's chest was so tight it felt as if he was having a medical event. His throat was so raw it felt as though he'd drunk battery acid and swallowed the gear stick. Sideways. He walked to his car and got inside, gripping the steering wheel while he pulled himself together. But his thoughts keep running like a ticker tape in his pounding head.

Allegra wanted out.

She wanted him out of her life.

He was the one who was supposed to end things, not her. When he was good and ready. When it was time. She was supposed to be grateful he'd stepped in and saved her father's business and saved her from being blackmailed into bed by some sleazy creep.

Draco started the engine and backed out of the space. He had to get a handle on this. He couldn't allow someone to destroy him. Not like this. Not emotionally. He didn't do emotion. Or at least not emotion like this—the sort of emotion that pulled at every organ in his body until he couldn't draw a breath.

Fine.

He would get out of her life. What had he been thinking, trying to make a marriage between them work? Their relationship was doomed to fail and he was a fool for thinking he could pull it off.

All you had to do was say you loved her.

Draco braked on the thought. He didn't love Allegra. He hadn't fallen in love since he was nineteen and he wasn't going to do it now. He no longer had the 'falling in love' gene. Caring was his thing instead. He was damn good at it too. Look at the way Yanni was improving. Look at what he had done for Iona. Look at the way he provided for his staff all over the globe.

If Allegra couldn't settle for being cared about, then it was her problem, not his. So, he was alone again? He could deal with it. Would have to deal with it. He wasn't going to pay lip service to a concept he no longer believed in.

If he ever had.

Allegra wasn't sure how the press found out about her break-up with Draco but the newsfeeds were running hot by the end of the weekend. There was speculation on who was to blame for the split and she felt uncomfortable that most people assumed it was Draco. It seemed a little unfair although, given his 'playboy' track record and her quiet nun-like existence, it was an easy assumption to make. But it didn't sit well with her sense of justice.

Her father called and threatened to disinherit her for acting as lawyer to Elena but she'd simply hung up on him and blocked his number.

Emily called around to her house late on Sunday night with chocolates, wine and a shoulder to cry on. 'Are you sure you're doing the right thing, Allegra? I mean, it's only been a couple of weeks. Lots of marriages hit rough spots in the early days.'

'I had to leave him,' Allegra said. 'He doesn't love me. It's a deal breaker for me.'

'But some men are hopeless at admitting to loving someone,' Emily said. 'They literally can't say the words.'

Allegra sighed. 'I just can't bring myself to stay in a relationship that isn't equal. I love him. I think I probably always have. But he *cares* about me. That's not good enough. I want him to love me like I love him.'

Emily snapped off a big chunk of fruit and nut chocolate, ignoring the wine she had poured earlier. 'I don't know... I can't help feeling you're making a big mistake. But who am I to talk?'

'So, still no word from Loukas?'

Emily's shoulders drooped. 'Nope.' She eyed the chocolate in her hand for a moment then made a funny gurgling noise and dropped the chocolate to cover her mouth with her hand, her face draining of colour, as though someone had tapped the blood out of her body.

'Are you okay?'

Emily bolted out of the sitting room to the nearest bathroom. Allegra followed close behind and heard her being wretchedly sick. She pushed open the door and came over to where Emily was kneeling in front of the toilet. 'Oh, you poor darling.' She reached for a face cloth and rinsed it under the tap. 'You must have caught a bug or something.'

Emily buried her face in the cloth. 'Yeah, or something...' She came out from behind the face cloth and grimaced. 'You think you've got problems. Wait till you hear mine.'

Allegra frowned. 'You're not...?'

'I haven't done the test yet,' Emily said. 'I bought one—actually, I bought a couple—but I'm not game to do it. I keep hoping I'll get my period. I'm never late. I've never been even a day late. You could set Big Ben by me normally.' Her chin began to tremble. 'What if I'm pregnant? What am I going to do?'

'You'll have to tell Loukas. I assume he's the...?'

'Yes...'

'Are you going to keep—?'

'Yes.' Emily's expression had a look about it of a lioness protecting its cub. She even placed her hand over her flat abdomen. 'Of course I'm keeping it.'

'You'll have to tell Loukas.'

Emily scraped her hair back off her face. 'Yeah, really looking forward to that.' She gave a rueful twist of her mouth. 'You and I are a pair, aren't we?'

Tell me about it.

A few days later, Draco received a package in the post of Allegra's rings and the pendant he'd given her. There was a short handwritten note expressing her concern that he was getting the blame for their break-up.

But you are to blame.

He freeze-framed the thought. The last few days had been some of the most miserable of his existence. It was like reliving the grief of losing his mother and father. The unexpectedness of it. The blunt shock. The *how the hell do I cope with this*? The pointless 'what if?'s and '*what could I have done to prevent this from happening?*'.

Draco couldn't stay in his house with those gifts staring at him. They were the symbols of his failure. He walked out to the street but everywhere he looked he was reminded of what he had lost. Couples were walking hand in hand along the river. Families were picnicking on the lush grass, children playing and laughing in the summer sunshine. He saw a young father scoop a giggling toddler off the grass and hold her against him with a proud smile at her cuteness. His young pregnant wife came over and slipped her arm through her partner's, and beamed up at him with such affection it made Draco's chest tighten.

This was what Allegra wanted. Connection. Love. A family.

Didn't he want it too? Deep, deep inside was a locked compartment of his personality that secretly ached for what that young couple had. His parents had had it but it had been snatched away with his mother's early death. His father had done his best—more than his best—to provide a happy family life, but the threat of loss had hung over Draco and his father, until finally it delivered its felling blow.

Draco had shied away from loving people since because he always lost them. His mother, his father, his ex. Even his boss and mentor Josef had died soon after selling him the business. He had closed off his heart to protect himself from further loss, yet, by doing so, he had lost the person most important to him.

He had lost Allegra.

But, unlike with his mother and father, Draco could fix this.

He loved her.

Really loved her. Not just cared about her. But loved her with every cell of his being. Why else had he all but frogmarched her into marriage? He had married her before anyone else could because he loved her too much to see her suffer with a man who wouldn't respect and treasure her the way he would. His streak of protectiveness was a cover-up for love.

Everything he felt about her was real. Real love. Love that lived, breathed and blossomed for a lifetime. The sort of love he'd been too frightened to own because he didn't want to lose it. Like he had lost it when his gold-digger girlfriend had decided she wanted someone richer than him. But what he'd felt for that girl was nothing to what he felt for Allegra. He had blocked his feelings for so long, but they were seeping through the armour around his heart until it was all but bursting out of his chest.

It was time to fess up and win back the girl of his dreams. The love of his life.

Yes, that was exactly was what Allegra was—*his life*.

Allegra got home late after a mediation meeting ran over time and still the husband refused to settle. She thought longingly of that week, sailing around the Greek islands with Draco, when dirty divorces were the last thing on her mind. Not a minute went past without her thinking of him, wondering how soon he would find someone else once their marriage was formally over. She could have drawn up the papers herself, or got one of her colleagues to do it, but her heart wasn't in it. She would leave it to him to sort out. He was the one who'd wanted the marriage in the first place. It was his mess to undo.

She had only just got inside and slipped off her coat and heels when the doorbell rang. Something about how the bell rang made her pulse pick up its pace. Emily did a quick 'one-two' buzz. Her neighbour on the left held it down for three counts and the neighbour on the right used the brass door-knocker instead.

This sounded...urgent. Insistent. 'I'm not going away until you answer' insistent.

Allegra peered through the peephole and her heart did a backflip as good as any Olympic gymnast. She opened the door with a hand that felt more like an empty glove than a hand. 'Draco...'

'May I come in?'

She held open the door. 'Of course.' Allegra closed the door and turned to face him. 'Did you get the package with...? Oh, you've brought it with you.'

Draco placed the package on the hall table and turned to face her again. 'You didn't actually say you loved me the other day.'

Allegra licked her suddenly dry lips. 'I... No. I didn't see the point since—'

'Then let me be the first to say it.' He took her by the upper arms in a gentle grip, his dark, lustrous eyes meshing with hers. 'I love you.'

For a moment she just looked at him, completely stunned. She had longed to hear those words for so long and now she'd heard them she was too overcome with emotion to speak. She gazed into his eyes, her heart thumping so erratically, as if it was looking for an exit route out of her chest. 'You're not just saying it to get me to come back to you?'

His hands tightened as if he was worried she was going to slip out of his grasp. 'I'm saying it because it's true. I love you so much it, scared me to admit it. I've been a fool, Allegra. A stubborn, block-headed fool. Can you ever forgive me for putting you through the last few days? If you've felt even a quarter of the despair I've felt then I deserve to be horsewhipped.'

She touched his face, not sure if this was really happening.

He loved her. Draco loved her.

'I love you too. I think I may have done so since I was sixteen. But it's grown from a silly crush to love of such depth and intensity, I can hardly describe it. I just know I feel it and I can't imagine ever not feeling it.'

He smiled and hugged her close, rocking her against him as if he wanted them to be glued together. 'I'm sorry for the other night. I was blindsided by your decision to end things. I didn't see it coming because I was too proud to admit you had the raw end of the deal.' Draco eased back to look down at her. 'I've got a lot to learn about giving and taking in a relationship, but I hope you'll teach me. If you've got the patience, that is.'

Allegra pressed a kiss to his mouth, breathing in the familiar scent of him that thrilled her senses so much. 'Maybe you could teach me to be a little less insecure. I've been torturing myself with images of you taking up with someone else.'

'There is no one else for me, *agape mou*,' Draco said. 'I realised that during my epiphany earlier this evening. I made those promises when we got married because there could never be anyone else for me. My subconscious must have known it, even if I wasn't ready to admit it. I told myself I was marrying you to protect you, but what was motivating that protectiveness was love. You are my heart. My life. Can we start again? Stay married and live together for the rest of our lives, in a partnership others will envy and want to emulate?'

Allegra hugged him so tightly her arms ached. 'I can think of nothing I'd like better.'

'I wish I'd gone about this differently,' he said. 'It would have saved these last days of hell.'

'They were hell for me too,' she said. 'But that's all behind us now.'

A shadow passed through his gaze. 'I couldn't be in

my house after you sent back the gifts I'd given you. It was like coming back to the house after my parents' funerals. Even though they died years apart, the feelings were exactly the same. Seeing stuff sitting there but knowing they were never coming back to collect it. It's the worst feeling in the world. The sense of helplessness. Aloneness. Emptiness. That's when I realised I had blocked my feelings out of fear. I didn't want to lose you, like I'd lost everyone else I cared about, so I fooled myself into thinking I didn't love you. But then I realised why I was feeling so bad. Not out of pride or because of the business arrangement. But because my life is meaningless without you in it.'

Allegra stroked a fingertip around his mouth. 'I was so miserable after you left. I couldn't understand why you weren't fighting to keep our marriage. It sort of confirmed my doubts in a way. But now I realise how hard it must have been for you, with me springing it on you like that. I just couldn't go another day without knowing for sure how you felt.'

'I should have fought for you. But I guess I was feeling so raw I had to get away to process things. But it's not going to be how I solve conflict in the future.'

His eyes looked suspiciously watery. 'I saw a family today. A young family with a toddler, and the wife was expecting another baby. It made me realise what I was missing out on. I don't want to be surrounded by my wealth and possessions at the end of my life. I want to be surrounded by my family. *Our* family.'

She framed his face in her hands. 'You say you've been denying how you feel about me—well, I've been denying how I feel about having kids. I've suppressed my maternal longings for years as I worked to build my career. I don't want to get to the end of my life with a stack of legal documents for company. I want you. I want us to be family. And I want to live in Greece. It's my home. I want to set up a legal practice where I can help women like Iona and Elena. Iona might fancy a career change as a nanny. I'm going to ask her next time I see her. If ever there was a frustrated grandmother, she's one.'

His smile lit up his eyes, making them crinkle at the corners. 'That's been my mistake in the past—thinking "either, or" instead of both. We can both have what we want. It will take a bit of compromise on my part, but you're going to give me lessons, *ne*?'

Allegra gave him a teasing smile. 'When would you like me to start?'

He brought his mouth down to within a millimetre of hers. 'After I do this.' And he covered her mouth with his.

* * * * *

BOUND BY THE ITALIAN'S 'I DO'

MICHELLE SMART

This book is for the fabulous and
talented Pippa Roscoe.
Pippa, thank you for making our
collaboration such a joy. xxx

CHAPTER ONE

THE MESSAGE THAT pinged on Issy Seymore's phone was the notification that her taxi had been dispatched.

She met her sister's apprehensive dark eyes. This was it. Everything they'd worked towards this last decade about to come to fruition. All the late-night planning. All the scheming.

She'd imagined she'd reach this moment and be buzzing at this spring into action. She hadn't expected to feel such a weight in the belly she'd spent years working desperately hard to keep flat and toned. Gianni Rossi favoured a specific type of woman. Short brunettes that leaned towards plumpness were not in that favoured league.

'We are doing the right thing aren't we?' she whispered.

Amelia swallowed hard and nodded. 'But if you've got cold feet and want to back out then...'

'No,' she cut her off with a fortifying shake of her head. 'It's not cold feet. Just nerves, I guess.'

Amelia rubbed her arms and gave a rueful smile of understanding. If anyone understood about nerves, it was her sister. The faint bruising under her eyes was testament to the lack of sleep that had gripped them both since they'd realised five weeks ago that the stars had finally aligned and it was time to put the plan they'd spent so long finessing into action.

Amelia had taken all the risks to get them to this point, had spent two years in the enemy's camp, every minute of her working life spent with a cold knot of fear of being found out. As the Seymore sisters knew to their personal cost, the Rossi cousins were men without conscience. Without humanity. They'd ruined their lives and now it was the sisters' turn to repay the favour. Let them get a taste of what it felt to have your whole life destroyed. Because it could only be a taste. It was impossible to replicate the scale of the damage the Italian men had wrought on their family.

While Amelia had put herself on the line every working day for two years, Issy had worked safely behind the scenes, immersed in the online world. Now it was time for her to step up, step out, and play her part in the real world.

Straightening her spine, Issy stood as tall as her five-foot-one body would stretch.

Amelia's smile at this contained the first hint of humour either of them had been able to muster that day. 'Remember to keep your shoes on around him—you don't want him knowing you're short one end before you get him on the yacht.'

A splutter of laughter left Issy's lips, and she threw her arms around her big sister and hugged her tightly.

'You'll let me know as soon as you land?' Amelia asked into her hair, embracing her with equal intensity.

'I promise.'

'You've packed your charm repellent?'

She snorted and hugged her even tighter. 'You know I don't need it.'

Amelia disentangled her arms and cupped Issy's cheeks. 'Promise you'll be careful. Don't take any silly risks.'

'I won't. You be careful too.'

A shadow fell over her sister's face but she smiled. 'I'm always careful.'

Issy's phone pinged. Her driver had arrived.

One last embrace and a kiss to her sister's cheek and it was time to leave.

Time to fly to the Caribbean and put the plan they'd spent ten years strategizing into fruition.

Ten days earlier

Gianni Rossi knew when a woman was interested in him and the beautiful blonde with the fabulous legs at the bar of this ultra-exclusive, members-only club was definitely interested. She'd wafted through the swing doors with a feline grace and as she passed his table, her eyes had glanced at his. When she reached the bar, she'd turned her head to look back at him and this time the lock of her stare had not been fleeting. Now she sat sucking a cocktail through a straw with a gleam in her eye that suggested she would like to be sucking something else.

Never a man to turn down a beautiful woman blatantly showing her interest, Gianni excused himself from the company he was in. He indicated the stool beside her. 'May I?'

Wide, eminently kissable lips twitched. Dark blue eyes gleamed. 'Be my guest.'

He rested his backside on it and beckoned the barman over.

'Drink?' he asked her.

The gleam deepened. 'Sure.'

'A large bourbon for me and a...?' He raised a brow in question at her.

Dimples appeared on the beautiful face. 'Mojito. Please.'

'Mojito for the lady.'

While the barman fixed their drinks, Gianni ran his expert eye over her. Glossy shoulder length honey-blonde hair only several shades lighter than her perfectly plucked eyebrows. Beautiful elfin features. A short, silver sequinned dress with spaghetti straps that came from no high street store. A slim watch on her slim wrist from a brand also unavailable on the high street. The cut of her diamond earrings too showed that this was a woman with a discerning eye and access to an undiscerning bank account. He wondered how their paths had never crossed before.

He extended a hand. 'Gianni.'

Slim fingers wrapped around his. Her expensive, exotic perfume drifted into his space like a fragrant cloud. 'Issy.'

'I haven't seen you here before... Issy.' A name that rhymed with dizzy did not suit this sleek, confident woman with the melodious voice who pronounced her words with the same exactness as the English socialites who flocked to his parties whenever he was in London.

Gently extracting her hand from his, she flashed pretty white teeth. 'It's my first time.'

His lips curved. 'Is that a fact?'

She wiggled one of her perfect eyebrows knowingly and, enchanting blue eyes not leaving his face, closed her lips over the straw to suck the last of her original drink. The eroticism behind it sent a thrill racing through his bloodstream. Damn, this woman was *hot*.

Placing his elbow on the bar, he rested his chin on his closed hand. 'Waiting for someone?'

'My girlfriend. We're meeting here before we go to Amber's. She's running late.'

'Girlfriend?'

Amusement sparkled. 'A friend who's a girl. Why? What did you think I meant?'

He smiled slowly. 'I think you know very well what I meant.'

Another knowing, amused wiggle.

'Do you have a significant other?' he asked, cutting to the chase.

She shook her head slowly. 'Life's too short for significant others.'

A woman after his own heart. 'I couldn't agree more.'

'You're single too?'

'Always.'

'Now that is something I will gladly drink to.' Placing an elbow on the bar close to his, she mimicked him by resting her chin on her closed hand. 'So...' She tilted a little closer. 'Gianni... You're Italian?'

'Si.'

She grinned. 'An Italian stallion?'

How he loved a woman who knew how to use a good double entendre. 'So I've been told.'

She looked him up and down without an ounce of shame. 'I'll bet.'

Their drinks were placed before them. Gianni raised his. 'To being single.'

She clinked her cocktail to his glass, dark blue eyes bold on his. 'To having fun.' Then she pinched the straw between her thumb and forefinger and slowly inserted it between her lips. It could not be interpreted as anything but suggestive and the thrills racing through his veins ramped up.

Her phone buzzed.

'Excuse me,' she said, swiping to read the message. She replied quickly then fixed him with a rueful smile. 'That, I'm afraid, is my cue to leave.'

'Already?'

'I didn't expect to leave so soon but it's Camilla's birthday. She was going to meet me here but as she's running so late, she's got her driver to drop her at Amber's and sent him on to collect me. He'll be here in a few minutes.' She gave him an openly provocative stare, and added, 'I'm sure she won't mind if you join us.'

Gianni had been to Amber's, a tiny nightclub with a clientele comprised almost exclusively of British high society, a number of times. With regret, he waved a hand in the direction of the three men he'd not long ago abandoned. 'I'm on a poker night promise, but I can join you later…if you like?'

She finished her mojito and as she pulled the straw from her mouth, her bottom lip pulled down seductively with it. 'I do like,' she murmured, 'but I'm afraid it has to be an early night for me, midnight at the latest or I risk the danger of turning into a pumpkin.'

He rested his fingers on the hand with the immaculately manicured and painted nails that had incrementally moved closer to him and bored his gaze into hers. There was nothing he loved more than a sexy, confident woman who knew exactly what she wanted and wasn't afraid to show it, and this woman had all of that. She was sexy. Beautiful. Blonde. Long-legged. And she was unashamedly making it clear that she wanted him. The perfect temporary bedwarmer. 'I could do with an early night too.'

Her eyes gleamed and her pretty teeth grazed her bottom lip. 'As tempting as your unspoken offer is, regretfully I must decline. I'm flying to Barbados in the morning and need my beauty sleep.'

'Barbados?'

She nodded and got to her feet. 'I keep my yacht at a

marina in Bridgetown. I always spend a couple of months each summer sailing.'

'Now that is a coincidence... I'm flying to the Caribbean myself in a couple of weeks.'

Her eyes widened in surprise and delight. 'Really?'

He nodded. 'We can meet up... If you like?'

She didn't even pretend to think about it. She leaned closer to whisper into his ear, close enough that her silky hair brushed against his neck. 'I would like that *very* much.' Then, smiling widely, she stepped back and pressed her phone. 'What's your number?'

He recited it to her. She entered it into her phone, then held the phone up. 'My chariot is here.'

'Then it is best you go so you don't turn into a pumpkin.'

Eyes shining, she laughed softly. 'Great to meet you, Gianni.' Then she blew him a kiss and strolled away in her fabulously high stilettos with the same ramrod-straight sexy confidence she'd entered the bar, gently curved hips swaying.

Gianni watched her leave, shaking his head and trying to stifle a laugh at what had just occurred in a few short minutes.

Ordering himself another bourbon, he re-joined his friends debating whether to throw the evening's game so he could get himself to Amber's before Cinderella turned into a pumpkin.

A moment later a message pinged into his phone.

The ball's in your court. Hopefully meet you for some fun in the Caribbean soon. Issy x

He messaged her back.

Looking forward to it. I'll be in touch. G x

* * *

Issy hailed the first black cab that passed and jumped in the back. 'Nelson Street, Brockley,' she said to the driver.

Not until the club was a blur in the distance was she able to breathe with any semblance of normality.

She'd done it.

While she kicked off the awful shoes that made her feel like her feet were clamped in vices, she fired a quick message to her sister. Amelia, she knew, would be unable to breathe properly herself until she heard from her.

It worked! Hook, line and sinker. On way home. xx

That done, she rested her head back and closed her eyes.

She felt sick. And exhilarated. And unsettled. So many emotions, all sloshing in her mostly empty stomach.

The closer the time to acting out their plans had come, the more unsettled she'd become at going through with it. When Amelia had started work at Rossi Industries, she'd vowed to find concrete proof of corruption against the cousins. They'd both needed to know that what they were doing wasn't just revenge but a good thing, that they were saving other victims from the fate their family had suffered. When Amelia had told her five weeks ago that their time had come, all Issy had been able to think was they still needed that proof. Amelia had finally found it three days ago, exultantly messaging her with the news.

The mojitos Issy had drunk suddenly rose up her throat. Pressing her hand there, she squeezed her eyes even tighter and willed the nausea to pass.

She willed even harder to banish the image of Gianni Rossi looking at her like he would gladly eat her whole.

And willed even harder than that to forget the thrills that had run through her veins to see it.

Rob Weller, one of Gianni's favourite architects and a good friend though an infuriating timekeeper, arrived at the same time the barman brought Gianni's fresh bourbon to the table.

'Man, I have just seen the hottest woman leave this place,' he enthused as he slid his short frame onto the seat across from Gianni.

'Bet that's the woman Gianni just hooked up with,' Stefan said with a knowing grin.

'We didn't hook up,' Gianni felt obliged to point out.

'I saw you give her your number.'

Gianni smiled but kept his mouth shut. While he dated widely and enthusiastically, one thing he never did was kiss and tell. Not that there had been any kissing to tell about. Just one short, incredibly flirtatious conversation…and the potential for more than flirtatious conversation.

For fifty weeks of the year, he worked his backside off. For sure, he partied hard too, but work came first. It always had. It was the same for Alessandro, his cousin and business partner. Practically raised as brothers, the Rossi cousins had been twelve when they'd determined to carve their own path in life, paths that sped them away from their monstrous fathers, and they had worked their fingers to the bone and overcome huge setbacks to make their property development company the multi-billion-euro, internationally renowned enterprise it was today. Where Gianni and Alessandro differed was on the partying side of life. Andro lived and breathed Rossi Industries. He rarely took time off. He never dated. He liked his own company so much that Gianni had long ago taken to calling him The Monk. But for all his cousin's single-minded drive and monkish ways, he understood Gianni needed to occasionally blow off steam and recharge his batteries and so had never begrudged the two weeks Gianni spent in the Caribbean each summer. That fortnight was sacrosanct, highlighted in the diary of every one of the hundred thousand Rossi Industries employees. The company would have to be burning down before Andro bothered him during it or let anyone else do so.

'Leggy blonde, wearing a skimpy silver dress?' Rob asked.

'That's the one,' Stefan agreed.

'Man…' Rob shook his head. 'I almost threw myself into the cab she hailed so she could argue with me for it.'

'Bit creepy,' Gianni pointed out.

'How else can I get a woman like that to look at me without flashing my bank account at them?' Rob defended himself. 'It's all right for you. Women don't care about the size of your wallet. You only have to look at a woman for her to want to…'

'Did you say she hailed a cab?' Gianni interrupted before his friend could say anything that might prompt a passing woman to throw a drink over his head.

'Yes.'

'There wasn't a car waiting for her?'

'No. She definitely hailed a black cab. Why?'

He shrugged and raised his glass to his mouth. 'No reason.'

Intriguing. Issy had told him her friend's driver was collecting her, which did not imply the beauty hailing a black cab.

Why the lie?

He tipped the rest of his bourbon down his throat and

smiled. The only thing he loved more than a sexually confident woman was a sexually confident enigma begging to be solved.

His annual trip to the Caribbean couldn't come soon enough. If nothing else, it certainly promised to be fun.

Once Issy's stomach had settled a little, she took a deep breath and made the call.

'David?' she said when it was answered. 'It's Isabelle Seymore.'

'Issy!' he cried. She could hear music pounding in the background and guessed he was at a party somewhere. 'What can I do for you, my darling?'

'It's time.'

'Time? For what?'

'You know what. A yacht.'

There was a long pause. 'When do you need it for?'

'Next Friday.'

'That soon?'

'I did warn you that when the time came, I would need it to happen quickly.'

He sighed. 'You still need it for two weeks?'

'Yes.'

'With a full crew?'

She pinched the bridge of her nose. 'Yes. And a minimum of forty feet. As we agreed when I spent six months working for you for free.'

David liked to call himself a broker but really, he was a fixer to the rich. Want the use of a private jet for a weekend? Then David is your man. Need to throw a last-minute party on an obscure island with exquisite catering and hedonistic entertainment? Give David a call. In the mood for chartering a fully crewed superyacht? That's right—call David.

Issy had taken a six-month sabbatical from her job as an auxiliary nurse to work as David's girl Friday two years ago, when Amelia had first got the job at Rossi Industries. Six months of free labour at roughly one hundred hours a week, and all for this moment. If she hadn't once been best friends with David's little sister he'd have made her work a full year.

No one could accuse the Seymore sisters of slacking in their preparation. Or their research.

The cab pulled up outside the run-down block of flats she and Amelia called home.

Wedging her swollen feet back into the vices, she walked as gingerly as she could up the stairwell to her flat—the lift was, as always, broken—and Issy's mind drifted back to the day she'd learned monsters really did exist. She remembered it so clearly.

It had been a Sunday. Her mother had cooked a traditional English roast. Issy had been in charge of prepping the vegetables, Amelia in charge of making the batter for the Yorkshire puddings and the cheese sauce. During the meal, their parents had allowed thirteen-year-old Issy and fifteen-year-old Amelia to have a small glass of red wine each. Their parents had argued whether or not to take the girls out of school a week early so they could enjoy their Tuscan home a little longer than planned. None of them had known that in a matter of weeks the girls would be pulled out of their school permanently because the wealth that paid the fees would be gone.

When the doorbell rang, none of them had suspected what was about to happen.

Brenda, their housekeeper, was on her day off so the girls' mother, a vivid, beautiful woman with such *presence*, had answered the door. She'd returned shortly, anxiety on her face, and whispered to their father, who'd then excused himself.

Issy had just put a roast potato in her mouth when raised voices echoed from their father's study into the dining room. Without a word, the Seymore sisters and their mother slipped from the table and hovered outside it.

Male voices, heavily accented but with a precise pronunciation that meant the three of them heard every scornful, abusive word sounded through the crack in the study door.

'You're finished, old man. The sooner you accept that the better—for your sake.'

'What was yours is now ours, you washed-up, sorry excuse of a man. Accept it.'

'*Everything* is ours.'

'Everything. Say goodbye to your company...and hello to Lucifer. He's been waiting for you.'

Footsteps had neared the door. Issy and Amelia had held each other tightly as the door swung open and two tall, dark-haired men in impeccably tailored suits sauntered out of their father's study with all the swagger of a pair of gangsters in the films she was forbidden to watch. They failed to see the wife and daughters of the man they'd just ripped to shreds cowering behind the door. But the daughters had seen them.

Time had frozen. When their father finally appeared in the study doorway he'd aged two decades. The next morning, the frightened adolescent girls, who'd shared a bed that night, had woken from a fitful sleep to find his thinning dark hair had turned white overnight. A year later he was dead. A decade on, their mother was nothing but an empty shell of the vibrant woman she'd once been, distraught to wake each day, reliant on stimulants to get her out of bed.

Issy and Amelia had never been particularly close before that awful day. Close in age, yes, but nothing else. They'd have sooner scratched each other's eyes out than pay the other a compliment. That day, though, had pulled them together in a way the Rossi cousins could never have dreamed if they'd even bothered to consider the two innocent girls caught up in the collateral damage of their heinous actions. It had drawn them into a solid unit with only one purpose—revenge.

For the first time in a decade, Issy had the faint hint of what that revenge would taste like on her tongue.

CHAPTER TWO

THE *PALAZZO DELLE FESTE* gleamed under the dazzling Caribbean sun. It would have dazzled Issy even if it had been raining.

Blinking back her disbelief, she looked at David's deadpan face. 'How on earth did you manage to get this for me?'

He waved an airy hand. 'Just call me a magician.'

She turned her stare back to the humungous vessel docked before her. 'A magician? David, this is way beyond anything I asked for.' Their agreement had been six months free labour in exchange for the use of a sleek, modern yacht of at least forty feet, something a young, independently wealthy or trust-funded woman would reasonably own. This yacht had to be three times that size!

Heart sinking, she shook her head. 'It's amazing but it's too much.' It was too conspicuous. How could she blend in if things went wrong and she needed to escape? Plus something this size would give the impression she was in the league of billionaires. She knew how to pull off rich—after all, her family had once been rich—but this was a whole different league. This was Silicon Valley and oligarch territory. 'I need something much smaller.'

'Sorry, darling, but no can do. We're hitting the summer season. Everything's either booked or the owners are wanting them for themselves.'

'But this isn't what we agreed.'

'Darling, I've managed to acquire one of the finest superyachts in the whole of the Caribbean for your exclusive use, and you're complaining about it? Look at her! She's a masterpiece! She's got a helipad, two swimming pools, a library, an entertainment room, a games room, a movie room, a casino, a beauty parlour, a spa, *and* she has an inflatable slide that you can swish down straight into the sea. And if all that doesn't tempt you, she has her own speedboat, Jet Skis and a load of other water sports goodies tucked away for your personal use.'

No wonder it was named the Party Palace. This was a vessel equipped and dedicated to its owner having a good time.

'Does the owner know you're giving her away for a fortnight at no charge?' Chartering something of this size and opulence complete with full crew would generally set someone back around the hundred thousand mark. Per week. In English pounds. She would have had to work for David for free for ten years to pay for this.

'Ask me no questions and I will tell you no lies.'

She fixed him with a stare that, instead of making him quail, made him laugh and throw his arms around her. 'Oh, Isabelle, Isabelle. Why so serious? You're in the Caribbean. You have a superyacht with a crew of twenty at your disposal. *Enjoy it*, my darling. Everything is taken care of. Anything you could possibly want will be provided. If you're anchored at sea and want a Methuselah of Moët flown in or a hundred white roses, ask and it shall be delivered.'

'Have you really not got anything smaller I can use?'

'Do you know what the definition of stupid is? Asking the same question again and again hoping for a different answer.'

***

From the other side of the harbour, standing at the balustrade of his hotel room's balcony, Gianni watched the exchange between Issy and the broker through his binoculars. His beautiful hustler did not look pleased at the broker's offering. He didn't need to be a lip-reader to know she was arguing about it. He smiled when her shoulders sagged and she finally appeared to concede defeat. He was proved right a moment later when they climbed the steps onto the *Palazzo delle Feste*. The captain joined them. She shook his hand then followed the two men inside and out of Gianni's view.

Well played, David, he thought. There was nothing in the broker's demeanour to suggest anything was amiss. The promise of a further quarter million if the con woman accepted the yacht was too big a temptation for him to want to screw this up. That money was on top of the hundred thousand Gianni had already paid him. Information came with a price, and Gianni was happy to pay it.

He sent her a message.

Just landed. Can't wait to see you. G x

How did he know she was a hustler? His gut. It was never wrong. The one time he'd ignored it, the consequences had been disastrous. The evidence was pretty damn convincing too. Beautiful woman entering a club renowned as a haven for the rich and powerful, on the lookout for a man to reel in. She'd played her part beautifully. Those come-to-bed eyes. The seductive smile. The *pièce de résistance*—her enthusiasm for the single life. Unspoken had been the promise of a no-strings-attached fling that any man would salivate for while cleverly and subtly establishing that she *was* rich by mentioning her yacht. Putting herself on an equal financial footing to quell any doubts her victim might have. She'd been *magnificent*. If Rob hadn't seen her get into a cab and establish that she'd told at least one lie, Gianni wouldn't have doubted her at all. That's how good she'd been. And if he hadn't doubted her he wouldn't have got a close associate in Barbados to ask around at all the marinas in Bridgetown about a beautiful blonde called Issy who kept her yacht moored there. No one had heard of this woman... but all the digging around did reveal one delicious nugget. The slippery English broker David Reynolds was trying to pull in a favour and borrow—not charter—a modest yacht of no less than forty feet. What made this nugget so delicious was that the notoriously greedy David lived on his own yacht so was unlikely to need it for himself. Oh, and the date he needed it for was, coincidentally, the day Gianni flew out to the Caribbean.

On a hunch, Gianni got his associate to have a little chat with David Reynolds. After handing over considerable cold hard cash, he hit pay dirt. The yacht was needed for the exclusive use of a woman called Isabelle Clements.

It could have been a coincidence. Except Gianni didn't believe in coincidence. Only one way to find out, and that was to offer up his brand-new yacht, the *Palazzo delle Feste*, to the mysterious Isabelle Clements.

His gut and hunches had all been proved right. The beautiful Issy was indeed Isabelle Clements.

The beautiful Issy was indeed a hustler. A con woman.

His phone buzzed. The hustler had responded.

What a coincidence! Just docked! Still up for meeting at Freddo's later? x

They'd exchanged dozens of messages and numerous phone calls since their contrived meeting. It had been great fun stringing her along, asking her questions about what she was up to, wondering what outrageous lie she'd come up with next. 'Oh, I've spent the day snorkelling,' or, 'I spent the day with friends in St Lucia. Have you been? Oh, you must, it's to die for!' It was the phone calls he'd enjoyed the most, and not just because he could imagine her squirming over the lies he was forcing her to fabricate on the hoof. He kept capturing hints of genuine humour in her beautiful voice that only added to the anticipation. A hookup with a beautiful hustler with a sense of humour? What man could resist?

He fired a quick reply.

Wouldn't miss it for the world. 5 p.m.? G x

Her response flashed moments later.

Perfect. x

He read their most recent exchange a second time and grinned.

Let the games commence.

Issy was trying very hard not to panic. She needed to entice Gianni onto 'her' yacht by tomorrow at the latest. She knew that wouldn't be a problem, but what *would* be a problem was how she'd be able to act the role of superyacht owner when she didn't know her way around said superyacht.

She could have cheerfully kicked David in the ankle for screwing this up. She'd been specific about her requirements. Six months spent as his unpaid dogsbody meant she'd earned the right to be specific about them. Issy and Amelia had spent hours debating the best kind of yacht for Issy to have, and in all honesty, a battered old fishing boat would be better than this floating palace.

Still, David had assured her the crew would lie to any guest she brought on board and say she was the owner, and all that time spent as David's dogsbody meant she knew yacht crews were meticulously trained and would cater to her every need without her having to actually open her mouth and order them about. She'd never been any good at ordering people about, mainly because she hated being bossed about herself and so cringed to hear commands come out of her own mouth.

Knowing Amelia would be worrying, she took a picture of her opulent bedroom and sent it to her. She didn't dare tell her sister about David's cock-up, but a nice internal picture that didn't give anything away would do fine. Amelia needed to focus on her own task of pushing through her recommendation of a specific company for the Rossi Industries project she was managing. In reality, that specific company was nothing like Amelia had made it appear on paper. Going with that company would be an unmitigated disaster for Rossi Industries. The knock-on effects would destroy their entire enterprise. And destroy them. Perfect.

The sisters had known for a long time that the only way to topple the Rossi cousins would be by separating them. Together, they were as solid as rock, the cousins perfectly complementing each other so that nothing ever slipped past them. It would be impossible for Amelia to succeed if both cousins had to sign the project off and with it, sign off her recommendation. One cousin might miss or overlook something but the other would always pick it up.

Divide and conquer. It was the only way for the Seymore sisters to win, and it was with that thought at the forefront of her mind that Issy forced her feet into a pair of impossibly high wedged sandals—stilettos were forbidden on this yacht—and inspected her appearance one last time. Seeing as Gianni believed she'd been in the Caribbean for ten days already, fake tan had been a necessity, and she paid special attention to her exposed flesh to ensure her skin was streak-free. Satisfied she looked as good as she could for the money she'd paid, Issy made her way out of the floating palace to meet her handsome nemesis.

Here she came, striding gracefully towards the beachside restaurant, blonde hair blowing gently in the breeze, large designer shades covering much of her beautiful face, lithe body showcased to perfection in a pale green shirt dress that skimmed her deeply golden thighs and was complemented by a large, brightly coloured beaded necklace.

He rose from his chair to greet her.

Pretty white teeth flashing in delight, she strode straight to him and rested a hand on his shoulder so they could exchange kisses to each other's cheeks. A cloud of her exotic perfume enveloped him. He inhaled it as greedily as he relished the brush of her lips against his skin.

His memories hadn't played him false. She was every inch as stunning as he remembered.

'Well, here we are,' she said brightly once she'd settled herself in the seat across from him, lifting her shades to rest on top of her head.

He smiled slowly, noting the shirt dress was unbuttoned

enough to expose a glimpse of black lace bra, a deliberate tactic he was sure, and one he wholeheartedly approved of. If this was a taster of Isabelle Clements tactics for hustling money out of him then he was in for one hell of a ride. 'Here we are. I hope you don't mind but I've taken the liberty of ordering you a mojito.'

Those deep blue eyes he remembered so vividly sparkled. 'You have an impressive memory and no, I don't mind at all.'

For the longest time nothing was said as they gazed at each other, both feigning disbelief that they had actually made this happen, that they were sat across a table from each other in a restaurant located thousands of miles and numerous time zones from where they'd met.

Books had been written and films made about people like Issy Clements. Gianni cared not at all that he was the man her net had been thrown at. On the contrary. Anticipation as to how far she was prepared to go in her hustle thrummed heavily in him.

It had been a long, long time since he'd experienced excitement on a level like this. It wasn't that his life was boring—far from it—but Gianni and Alessandro had achieved such success with their business and after such torrid beginnings that there was no challenge left to it now. Nothing to strive for other than success on top of success. He would never be so immodest as to deny that Mother Nature hadn't blessed him with looks that most women found attractive but since his bank balance had sprung into the stratosphere, women had ceased to be a challenge too. Sometimes he would go to a party and have so many feminine eyes openly seduce him that he felt like a kid in a sweetshop who'd already gorged on all the chocolate. He could take his pick. And he did.

Like the cars he drove, Gianni liked his women fast, sleek and glossy; preferably tall and blonde. He also preferred them to have money, not from any form of snobbery—after all, he and his cousin came from nothing—but because he'd tired of reading about his 'sexploits' in the press. As he didn't date any woman long enough to learn if she was trustworthy or not, it made sense to shrink his dating pool to those he knew from the off didn't need to sell stories about him.

'So...' he said, breaking the silence with a seductive gleam. 'Do you come here often?'

Was it possible for the man to have a cheesier chat-up line? Issy wondered, mentally rolling her eyes. He was just so sure of himself, so keenly aware of the power of his sexuality and the effect it had on women that she supposed he didn't feel the need to bother using his wit. And he had wit. A great deal of it. She knew. She'd researched the man for years, night after night spent searching his name, learning the minutest detail about him. Of course, Amelia had got to know him quite well in a professional capacity and she'd grudgingly admitted he was as good-humoured in real life as he came across in interviews and the snippets of conversation attributed to him. Most of the time, in any case. It never boded well on anyone who dared cross him...but the Seymore sisters already knew that. They'd lived it.

His rampant sexuality had no effect on her. Gianni's handsome face, with its square jaw and the firm lips considered by many, many women to be *kissable* repulsed her. How many hours had she sat at her laptop staring into those light blue eyes with her stomach churning violently? Too many. There was not a millimetre of his face she was unfamiliar with, from the slight cleft in the tip of his broken nose—she would one day learn who broke it and shake their hand—to the way his left eyebrow sat a fraction higher than the right. She knew the dark hair currently exposed at the top of his unbuttoned black shirt whirled over defined pectoral muscles and down over a flat washboard stomach. She knew he was exactly six foot three. She knew he had his thick dark hair trimmed every fortnight. She knew that by the end of his two weeks in the Caribbean the currently stubbled square jaw would be covered in a thick black beard that would then be shaved before he returned to the world of business. She knew that if it was possible to think of Gianni dispassionately, she'd agree he was a walking shot of testosterone and that his muscular frame contained a potent sexuality that would make any other woman weak at the knees.

But not her. Issy was immune to any sexuality he exuded. The burn that had ignited in her veins in the London bar was the deep anticipation of impending revenge. The haunting of his gorgeous face in her thoughts was nothing new. He'd haunted her for years. What made the haunting bearable was imagining it crumpling the day he realised she'd taken everything he held dear from him.

Still, she'd thought better of him than cheesy chat-up lines.

Returning the gleam, she answered, 'Barbados is great, but I prefer to be out on the open sea. You?'

'Depends on my mood. When I'm on land all I require is great food, great beer and an excellent view.'

She let her gaze bore into his. 'The view from where I'm currently sitting is pretty something.'

He returned the heated stare. 'Really?'

She smiled suggestively and took great pleasure in watching his light blue eyes darken. Two years spent starving herself to create the feminine stick insect look he desired was paying off.

Her mojito and a fresh lager for Gianni was brought to their table. He held his bottle aloft. 'To the start of a beautiful new friendship.'

Smiling, Issy clinked her glass to it and took a flirtatious sip of her cocktail through the straw.

'I have to say, your command of the English language is seriously impressive,' she said, stroking his ego. 'If it wasn't for the hint of an accent, you could believe it was your first language.' A decade ago, his accent had been strong. 'Were you raised bilingual?'

'I'm self-taught.'

'Even more impressive. What spurred you on?'

'My business is based in England. I run it with my cousin.'

'What kind of business?'

'Property. What business are you in?'

'I'm not—I'm a trust fund baby.'

'Rich mummy and daddy?'

Ignoring the faint mocking tone of his voice, she nodded and had another drink.

'And what do Mummy and Daddy do?'

She told him the first real truth of their acquaintance. 'Daddy died quite a few years ago and Mummy's in rehab.'

Gianni made a suitably sympathetic face. So *this* was how the hustle was going to work. Personally, he would have put his money on her letting slip about a seriously ill close family member—a small niece or nephew would be ideal—whose life was hanging in the balance but who could be saved if only they could afford the excruciating amount of money needed for a proven but experimental treatment that poor Issy would love to pay herself if not for a temporary cash-flow problem. Mummy being in rehab was less heart-rending but, on reflection, a safer bet. No medical jargon to remember.

He mentally applauded her for sowing the seed so early, and made another private bet to himself that by the end of the evening she would have mentioned the excruciating costs of the rehab facility.

'That must be tough for you.'

'What doesn't kill you makes you stronger,' the clever hustler dismissed airily.

He raised his beer. 'I will drink to that.'

Clinking bottle to glass again, they finished their drinks. While they waited for fresh ones to be brought over, Issy scoured the menu searching for the meal that contained the least amount of calories.

When this was all over, she was going to hit her favourite fast-food restaurant and bury her face in all the burgers and chips and ice cream she'd spent the last two years denying herself.

She ordered a low-fat Caesar salad and made sure not to sound like she was ordering her personal equivalent of dog food.

'What does a trust fund baby do all day?' he asked once their order had been taken.

She fluttered her eyelashes. 'Why, has fun of course.'

'And where do you like to have your fun?'

Smiling suggestively, she wrapped a lock of hair around her finger in the same way she'd noted a couple of his old lovers had done. 'That all depends.'

'On?'

'My mood... And the company.'

Eyes gleaming, he laughed. 'Has anyone told you you're beautiful?'

I should ruddy hope I look beautiful, Cheesy Chat-Up Man. It cost a ruddy fortune to achieve this look.

Until exactly two weeks ago, when Amelia found the proof they'd been seeking and they'd realised the stars had finally aligned for them, Issy had rarely worn make-up, never bothered with fake tan and her hair had been a lank dark chestnut normally shoved back in a ponytail or plait.

'Has anyone told you you're an incredibly sexy man?'

He leaned forwards, wafting his cologne with him. 'Not in the last ten days.'

Been slacking, have you? Or too busy with the Aurora project that's about to come to fruition for Rossi Industries and is worth billions to you? Or so you think.

'Have you been hiding in a cave?'

He grinned. 'Not quite. Work has been all consuming. Believe me, I've earned this break.'

You certainly have. Earned it off the grave of my father when you forced a hostile takeover of his company.

'A week to unwind and recharge your batteries?'

'Two weeks.'

'Two?' She raised one of the eyebrows she'd plucked into submission, as if she didn't know exactly when he was due to return to what would be left of his business. 'How much fun can one man have in two weeks?'

'That all depends.'

'On?'

'If there's someone for me to play with.'

She held his gaze and smiled. 'Oh, I imagine a man like you would have no shortage of playmates.'

'It's never been a problem for me before.'

Such modesty. It was so becoming. Not.

'You know, my yacht has many toys on board.'

The sexy gleam shimmered. 'Really?'

'Uh-huh.' Emulating his gleam, she mimicked him further by leaning forwards, deliberately allowing him a good peek of her cleavage. 'I even have a slide.'

'Who doesn't love a good slide on a yacht?'

She grazed her teeth over her bottom lips and dropped her voice to a seductive purr. 'My thoughts exactly. If you haven't got anything planned, how would you like to join me on it tomorrow? We can take it to sea…try the slide out.'

'I can think of nothing I'd rather do.'

She raised her glass and flashed her first genuine smile. 'It's a date.'

He practically stripped her naked with his eyes. 'I'm already looking forward to it.'

CHAPTER THREE

ISSY EXAMINED EVERY inch of her bikini-clad body. The last time she'd worn a swimsuit she'd been twelve and forbidden from wearing anything but a full-piece swimsuit by her protective parents. She had a feeling if either of them could see the teeny-weeny white bikini she was wearing now, they would spontaneously combust.

She was scared she might spontaneously combust too, in embarrassment.

But this was the kind of bikini Gianni Rossi's lovers wore. She couldn't afford to disappoint him until they were far out at sea and she'd managed to throw his phone overboard.

But, heavens, it was revealing. Luckily it covered her bottom half quite well apart from where it tied together at the side of her hips, but about the only thing it covered up top was her nipples.

Feeling the panic that often tried to grab her throat rise, Issy breathed deeply and wrapped a sheer blue sarong around her to give herself the illusion of modesty. It was too late to back out now.

She only had to lead him on until she got rid of his phone, and then she could dress herself in a sack if she so pleased.

The problem was she could taste danger. It had been there on her tongue since she woke that morning. She had no idea where it was coming from, but her Spidey senses were warning her of *something*.

Warning her of Gianni? And if so, why?

Was she playing with fire?

Gianni was a playboy, but he was not a man to force a woman. None of his legion of lovers had a bad word to say about him and there was no way Amelia would have gone along with this if she'd thought Issy would be putting herself in any kind of physical danger with him. As she'd grudgingly put it, he was gentleman playboy.

Issy's gut had aligned with Amelia's description of him during their first meet in London. Her gut told her he posed no physical danger to her. So why did she feel so threatened? Was it even threatened that she was feeling?

Too late now. Today was the day Amelia made her bogus recommendation to Alessandro Rossi and the rest of the team. Issy needed to get Gianni out to sea and keep him there, without communication, until she had word that the contracts were signed and the deal that would destroy the Rossi cousins was done. That should take around three days but could be longer. She would have to flirt. Lead him on. Maybe allow him a kiss or two…and trust her sister and her own gut that he wouldn't force those simple kisses or two into anything more.

Heaven help her, she'd never led a man on before.

Truth was, she'd barely been kissed either. Her one barely kiss had occurred when she'd been David's dogsbody, by one of his caterers. Unfortunately said caterer had been handling fish and the smell oozing from him had put her off so much that she'd spent the rest of her dogsbody career avoiding him. There had been no one else. Between her real day job in the children's ward and her night job of learning everything there was to know about Gianni, there had been no time for anyone else. Besides, it was a bit hard to look at men in a romantic way when your thoughts were consumed by someone else, even if that was someone you despised with a passion, and she hated that she'd relaxed into his company over their meal and that the hours had passed so quickly. He'd regaled her with tales of his friends' exploits that had genuinely amused her. If she didn't know who he was, she would be in danger of actually liking him.

But that was the power of the man. Beneath the handsome, easygoing exterior, Gianni was the devil in disguise.

Straightening her spine, she left her bedroom and made her way to the deck Gianni would enter 'her' yacht from. After their meal, she'd spent a couple of intense hours familiarising herself with the main areas of the yacht and felt a lot more confident about passing it off as her own than she had when David had shocked her with it.

Two crew members were already on deck, ready to greet her guest.

Issy was about to take a seat in the shaded section when a tall figure emerged dockside in the distance.

Her heart and belly did a simultaneous flip.

The closer he strolled, the harder her heart pumped.

Even though he wore shades as large as her own, he still turned heads from both sexes. Maybe it was the black polo shirt he wore, which fit snugly across his broad chest and showcased his spectacular physique. Or maybe it was the canvas khaki shorts that she knew without having to check showcased his tight butt cheeks.

He stopped a few feet from the yacht, looking as if he were reading its name to make sure he'd reached the right one, then caught sight of her. A devastating smile stretched across his face and he bounded up the right-hand steps to board.

Her heart pumped even harder and faster.

'*Bella*, your yacht is as dazzling as you are,' he said as he closed in on her and laid a hand on her hip. He kissed both her cheeks before taking her hand and bringing it to his mouth. He grazed his lips over her knuckles. 'A stunning vessel for a stunning lady.'

To her absolute horror, Issy felt a burn crawl over her cheeks and knew she was blushing. Or was that flushing? Because she didn't know if it was the heat of his breath on her skin causing it or the seductive appreciation in his stare.

'I enjoy my time on it,' she murmured, hoping her own huge shades covered enough of her face to disguise the flush.

'I can imagine. Her name tells me you're a lady who lives to party.'

She bestowed him with a knowing smile and slowly extracted her manically tingling fingers from his hold. 'Today, the party is just you and me. Drink?'

He checked his thick watch and raised a neat black eyebrow. 'Too early for champagne?'

'It's never too early for champagne.' She nodded at one of the hovering crew, who bowed his head in answer and disappeared to sort the drinks for them, then turned to the other one. 'Tell the captain we're ready to set sail.'

Subtly bracing herself first, Issy tucked her hand into the crook of Gianni's muscular arm. 'That's if you're happy for us to set sail?'

Removing his shades, he practically stripped her naked with his hungry stare. 'I am at the mercy of your every whim.'

The sensation of being under threat hit her so hard that she had to grind her toes into her impossibly high wedged sandals to stop her feet running and throwing herself overboard. The flesh of Gianni's arm was warm beneath her hand. Smooth. A texture completely different to her own. The tingling in her fingers seeped through her skin and into her bloodstream, making her already frantic beating heart increase in tempo. There was nothing fake about the breathlessness of her voice when she managed to tease, 'Oh, I do love it when a man's at my mercy.'

Eyes alight with sensuality, he wolfishly, playfully, snapped his teeth together. The tingles in her blood seeped even lower. Deeper. Her legs had become distinctly wobbly.

They'd barely stepped inside when Danny, who'd worked for Gianni for six years, carried their champagne over, holding the tray out and not betraying by so much as a flicker that he knew him.

'Thank you,' the con woman said. 'Please tell Chef we will want lunch on the pool deck in an hour.'

Gianni didn't try to stop the swelling laughter. His head chef, whose name she'd clearly not learned, was called Christophe and had worked for him for even longer than Danny. This was all just too delicious.

Seeing Issy's curious stare, he merely held his glass out so they could make yet another clink, tipped half the champagne he himself had paid for down his throat, then took hold of her free hand and leaned his face close to her ear. She was wearing that wonderful perfume again and, having twisted her blonde hair into a chic knot, he could smell the underlying sweetness of her skin layered in it. For perhaps the hundredth time, he allowed his imagination to run riot as to how far Isabelle Clements was prepared to go in her hustle. He could only hope she would go far enough that he got to inhale more of her scent than the delicate arch of her neck. 'Show me around your party palace.'

The quiver of her skin was so subtle he could easily have missed it. But he didn't miss it. He saw it. He felt it.

He smiled.

This just got better and better. His hustler genuinely desired him. Since realising she was a con woman, he'd wondered if she'd targeted him deliberately—Gianni was well-known in the media and the club she'd turned up at was one he was known to frequent—or if any man there that night who'd caught her eye would have done. He didn't suppose it mattered. But it did make the game a lot more fun to suspect a genuine desire on her part.

As Gianni had yet to spend any real time in his new yacht, it was quite surreal to be given a tour of it by the great pretender. Everything had been designed with his input. The fact all the entertainment, from the casino to the movie room, was confined to the main deck was deliberate, and when they reached the games room with the full-size snooker table he couldn't resist raising a querying eyebrow. He suspected that when those heels were removed, Issy would reveal herself to be much shorter than she carried herself. Snooker was by no means a man's game but it helped to be able to see over the table. 'You're a snooker player?'

'Some of my guests like to play,' she neatly deflected. 'I'm not known as the hostess with the mostest for nothing.'

He grinned. She might be a con woman but beneath the high-society persona she was playing for all its worth he thought might lurk a woman who was genuinely fun. 'Want to play?'

'And miss out on the sunshine? We can play when the sun goes down.'

'You're not going to return me to shore before you turn into a pumpkin?'

Her dimples appeared—a sign he was starting to recognise meant she was genuinely amused. 'Want to swim?'

'Does that mean I get to go on your slide?'

Stepping closer to him, she picked a speck of flint off his polo shirt and huskily said, 'That all depends.'

He rested a hand on her hip. The gap between them was so small he could feel the heat of her hot body. 'Depends on what?'

Her teeth grazed her bottom lip and her eyes gleamed. 'On where we anchor, of course.' A smile lit her face and she tugged at his hand. 'Come on, I want to swim before we eat.'

Issy discreetly checked her watch as she removed it. The meeting in London would be well under way. Casually, she placed the watch with her phone on the table and made sure not to react when Gianni placed his own watch and phone next to them, then added his wallet to the pile.

She just needed to keep him off that phone until the moment to get rid of it presented itself...

Pondering on how to dispose of it dissolved when Gianni pulled off his polo shirt.

Suddenly she was overcome with the need to fan herself. Dear God in heaven, that body...

That thought dissolved too when his hands went to the button of his canvas shorts.

Her mouth ran dry.

It hadn't occurred to her until that precise moment that Gianni hadn't brought anything with him other than what was laid on the table.

The zip went down. Eyes locked on her face, his hands went to his hips and he tugged the shorts down.

Issy caught a glimpse of thickened hair at the base of his abdomen...at his groin...before the shorts fell to the floor and, with the hint of a wink, he casually pulled up the swim shorts he was wearing beneath them to a more modest level.

'Do you have sun cream?' he asked.

'Sorry?' she croaked.

'Sun cream. You know, the stuff you cover your skin with to stop you burning and hopefully prevent you from getting a melanoma?'

Pull yourself together! she shouted at herself. *You've seen his body before, many, many times.*

But, dear God in heaven, it was one thing to see that body on a laptop screen and quite another to see it in the flesh.

No picture, however talented the photographer, could do that body justice. Or that face.

'Yes.' That was better. More normal. She pulled a smile to her face and took out the expensive sun cream from the bag that had cost her two weeks' wages, and handed it to him. She was struck, not for the first time, by the size and strength of his hands, and fresh tingles zipped through her skin and veins to imagine those hands...

To imagine those hands *what*? Touching her?

Had she already had too much sun? Because she was fast starting to think her brain had become addled. There was no reason on earth for her to imagine that, just like there'd been no reason on earth for the heat that had pulsed through her when she'd picked at the imaginary fleck on his polo shirt a while ago, or for that heat to deepen in her most intimate part when his hand had rested on her hip and only the sheerness of her sarong had been a barrier between their flesh. No reason for that moment when anticipation had thrummed through her at the thought of his firm lips closing on hers.

Issy had a job to do. This man was her enemy. If her body was developing signs that could be mistaken for attraction then she had to rise above them. No way it was attraction. No way Jose.

'Would you do my back for me?' he asked once he'd finished slathering every inch of his limbs and torso.

Absolutely not!

'My pleasure,' she purred, taking the bottle from him and resisting squirting it in his eyes.

Standing behind him, she controlled the urge to squirt it cold straight onto his naked skin and dolloped a load into her hand.

Holding her breath, she put her hands to his back.

The muscles bunched.

Her heart clenched with her lungs.

She rubbed the lotion into the smooth skin. Her heart unclenched and began to pound.

Up to his neck her hands worked, over the shoulder blades, down the spine, around the sides. By the time she reached the waistband of his swim shorts her lack of breath was no longer deliberate and her lips were tingling as she fought their yearning to press a kiss right into the centre of this sculpted masterpiece.

She had to physically force herself to step back, and when he turned and caught her eye, every organ in her body made a double flip.

'My turn,' he said, a slow, sensual smile forming.

'I…' The urge to lie and say she'd already screened her back was almost stronger than any future potential melanoma threat.

The sense of danger was stronger than ever.

She turned around.

Saying a prayer for luck, she forced air into her lungs and untied her sarong. It floated to her feet.

She heard him take a sharp intake of breath.

Her refilled lungs expelled in a whoosh the moment his fingers made contact with her skin.

Sensation shivered through her, deepening as his fingers slowly caressed the lotion over her back. When they dipped under the thin string holding her excuse of a bikini together, a wild fantasy sprang into her mind of him untying the knot and cupping her aching breasts...

She didn't even know breasts *could* ache. She didn't have to look down to know her nipples had puckered. She couldn't look down even if she wanted. It was taking everything she had to keep her gaze fixed ahead and to stop her legs from collapsing beneath her.

His fingers skimmed the top of her bikini bottoms. This time she could do nothing to stop the betraying quiver of her body.

Too much sun.

But this was okay! The thought punched through. This was okay. Better than okay. Wasn't she supposed to be leading Gianni on? Holding his interest in the only way a woman could because all he cared about when it came to women was the superficiality of their appearance and what he could get out of them in the bedroom.

She just had to keep hold of herself and not let her sun-addled brain trick her needy virgin body into believing it could possibly be attracted to one of the men directly responsible for the loss of everything she'd ever held dear. Her body was so starved it would likely react in the same way to any man!

His hands clasped her biceps. He was going to press himself against her.

Without warning to either him or herself, Issy stepped out of his hold, kicked her sandals off and, only just remembering to throw a cheeky grin over her shoulder, ran to the pool and jumped into the cool water.

Gianni didn't hesitate to follow her.

Dio, there was something about Issy's skin he reacted to, from her touch on him to his touch on her, infecting the whole of him, soaking him in erotic awareness.

By the time he dived into the pool, she'd swum to the far end, treading water as she faced him.

Half a dozen long strokes and he reached her.

Although she met his stare with that fantastic insouciance, she was trembling.

He closed the gap, gripping the walls of the pool on either side of her slender body, trapping her, and drank in her beauty.

She was ravishing. The most beautiful con woman to roam the earth. And the sexiest.

Thrums of desire beat heavily in him.

From the darkness in her pulsing eyes and the unsteadiness of her breaths, Issy was feeling it too.

It was time to up the ante.

Let the pleasure commence.

He sank his mouth into the softness of her lips in a full-bodied charged kiss of attrition. *Dio*, she tasted of champagne with added heat, a taste that roused his already electrified body, and he wrapped his arms around her and pulled her tight against him.

Her surrender was immediate. Her lips parted and in an instant her hands clasped the back of his head, fingers scratching through his hair and into his skull, and she was devouring him with the same hunger infusing him. With her small, high breasts crushed against his chest and her legs wrapped around his waist, her tongue duelling with his, Gianni's arousal was as thick and heavy as he had ever known it, jutting hard against her inner thigh.

Kissing Issy was like tasting honey from heaven and his excitement somehow managed to thicken and tighten even more to wonder if the rest of her tasted as if she'd been giftwrapped by the king of the gods, Jupiter himself.

He would have to discover that another time because the moment he broke the kiss to drag his mouth over her cheek and to her neck, her fingers gripped his hair tightly and pulled his head back.

Her eyes were drugged with desire. He knew his eyes reflected the same.

She swallowed, then sucked in a breath. And then she released her grip on his hair, placed her hands to his chest and, with a giggle, pushed him back. 'Not so fast, big boy.'

He snapped his teeth at her. 'I can do slow.' Then he licked the lobe of her delicate ear and huskily added, 'I can do whatever you like.'

Hands laid lightly on his shoulders, she stretched her neck and, with a smile, gazed up at the clear azure sky. 'We have all the time in the world.'

Cupping her chin, he pressed a feather-kiss to her lips. 'All the time we need,' he whispered.

The drugged daze came back into her eyes but she blinked it away, then looked over his shoulder at something that had caught her eye and brightly said. 'Looks like lunch is ready. Come on, let's eat.'

Gianni stepped aside to release her. 'Give me a minute and I'll join you.'

Her pretty eyebrows drew in.

He grinned ruefully and dropped his stare to below the waterline. 'I need to cool off for a minute. I don't want to frighten the crew.'

She followed his gaze. A bright stain of colour crawled over her cheeks as understanding sank in, and it took her longer than normal to compose herself. 'Okay, probably best you stay here a while. Cold beer?'

'That would be great.'

She hauled herself out of the pool.

He didn't think he was imagining the slight stagger in her walk back to the lounging area.

Dio, her body...

No more focusing on that hot body, he scolded himself even as he internally sighed with disappointment when she wrapped a towel around it. Not while arousal still had its tentacles in him.

Maybe he should get Issy to bring the cold beer over and pour it down his swim shorts.

The staff were busy setting out plates and glasses on the deck's dining table. Issy had just finished retying her hair when she suddenly snatched her phone up and read whatever had just pinged into it. She was still reading when one of the crew approached her. She put her phone back on the table, nodded at whatever the crewman said, then indicated she would be two minutes to Gianni, and disappeared inside.

Gianni had never swum so fast in his life. He streaked through the water, hauled himself out and strode quickly to the table their stuff was on. Pressing his hand onto a towel a crew member had left for him, he grabbed Issy's phone.

'Tell me when she's on her way back,' he ordered the nearest crew member as he removed his own phone and top-of-the-range cloning device from the back pocket of the canvas shorts he'd left slung over a chair. In moments, he'd copied all the data from her phone onto his.

Carefully placing Issy's phone back where he'd found it, he dried himself off, removed his swim shorts, wrapped a dry towel around his waist, took a seat at the dining table and drank thirstily from the bottle of cold beer placed before him. Then, with a huge grin of satisfaction that came from knowing he'd upped the stakes in this game of chance in his favour, he swiped the screen of his phone for the first look at his bounty. Issy's screen saver appeared.

The grin died as his heart thumped then nose-dived in recognition.

He blinked, then blinked again, certain he must be seeing things.

The image of two young women, faces pressed together, smiling for the camera, remained.

The pulse at the side of his jaw throbbing, head pounding as he tried to make sense of something that absolutely did not make sense, he went into her messages.

The last of his euphoria died at the exact same moment his screen faded into nothing. Cloning Issy's phone had drained his battery.

But he'd seen enough.

This was no hustle.

This was a deliberate, targeted attack.

CHAPTER FOUR

Issy touched up her lip gloss with a shaking hand. She needed to touch up her eyeliner but was too scared of stabbing herself in the eye to dare.

The lip gloss dropped from her hand and clattered in the sink. She clutched her flushed cheeks and gazed at her reflection. Her eyes had a fevered brightness to them. It was nothing to what was going on inside her.

Her heart was a pulsating mess, her limbs weak, her stomach as tight a knot as she'd ever known it. Between her legs…

She squeezed her eyes shut and tried to fill her lungs.

Okay, so she wasn't immune to Gianni's animal magnetism. No point in denying it. The main thing to remember was that she'd come to her senses before the situation had got even close to getting out of hand.

The situation that entailed Gianni turning her into flames.

What did flames do? They burned the object into ashes.

She'd kept control of the situation. She'd dealt with it.

But, heaven help her, her body still felt scorched in all the places they'd bound themselves so tightly together.

She could still feel his mouth devouring hers.

As part of all her preparation for this, she should have found some men to practice kissing with. Maybe then she'd have developed some immunity to the act and wouldn't have turned into a molten flame for him.

A careful swipe of bronzer against her cheeks and a fresh sarong around her, and she was ready to face him again. As ready as she'd ever be.

She found Gianni at the dining table, leaned back in his seat, casually drinking lager from a bottle so cold rivulets of condensation dripped down it. Not until he rose to his feet did she realise he had a towel wrapped around his waist. A quick dart of her eyes to where they'd been sitting found his swim shorts drying on the back of a chair. His canvas shorts were where he'd left them earlier.

A pulse throbbed between her legs. Beneath that towel, Gianni was naked.

'Everything okay?' he asked.

She nodded and smiled brightly. 'Just needed to freshen up. I hope you're hungry—Chef's made us a feast.'

His gaze held hers then drifted slowly down her bikini-clad body. 'I'm ravenous.'

Their first course was a fire roasted tomato soup Issy had loved since she was a little girl but had never been able to re-create for herself. The French chef must have sought an authentic Italian recipe for it because it was even better than she'd tasted as a child.

'Don't you eat bread?' Gianni asked, nodding at the freshly made bread roll she'd left on her side plate.

She shook her head and offered it to him, then tried not to salivate when he ripped it in two and slathered each piece with butter.

Not long, she consoled herself. Not long until she could bury her face in an ocean of carbs and not care that they all landed straight on her hips. She could heap a spoonful of sugar into her coffee *and* a dollop of cream if she wanted. She could buy herself a huge bar of hazelnut chocolate and eat it all in one sitting.

She'd been hungry for two whole years. She could wait a few days more. She would celebrate Gianni and his equally abhorrent cousin's destruction by indulging herself in all the delicious foods and treats she'd had to deny herself to maintain the stick insect look.

For their second course she'd selected fresh tuna, pan-fried in Japanese spices and served on a bed of couscous with roasted peppers. Fresh tuna was an expensive treat she could never normally afford under the strict budget Issy and Amelia imposed on themselves, and as it was healthy and her portion small, she ate the lot, then made sure to drink a whole glass of water to fill her up.

Dessert was freshly made strawberry ice cream on a chocolate crumb base but, as divine as it tasted, she allowed herself only a couple of small spoonsful before pushing the bowl to one side.

'Are there no foods you enjoy so much that you allow yourself to gorge?' Gianni asked, watching her closely. Issy's return to deck meant he'd had to compose himself quickly. Years of being able to adopt a poker face in stressful moments, dating back to a time when he didn't even know what a poker face was, just knew he didn't want to give his father the satisfaction of seeing fear in his eyes, meant his outward composure was no effort at all.

What was occurring beneath his skin was a whole different matter.

He felt like he'd been sucker-punched.

The lying, conniving temptress shook her head in answer. *Mio Dio*, even Issy's slender frame was a lie.

Her screen saver kept playing in his mind's eye. He'd recognised the other woman before he'd recognised Issy. Well, what person wouldn't struggle to recognise the slender blonde picking at her food before him with the plump dark-chestnut-haired woman in the photo? The chestnut-haired woman, her face pressed against the other woman's, had gripped tightly to a huge ice cream sundae, as if afraid someone would snatch it away from her if she let go of it even for a photograph. Only the dark blue eyes had revealed her to be the lying, conniving temptress before him.

The broker must have lied to him about her name because the woman nibbling on a piece of lettuce was not Isabelle Clements. She was Isabelle Seymore. Daughter of the bastard who'd ripped off the Rossi cousins by selling them land it was impossible to build on and bribing the very people whose due diligence should have picked up that fact. Their first business deal still left a bitter taste on Gianni's tongue that even the revenge they'd taken on the man once they'd rebuilt themselves and conducted a hostile takeover of his company hadn't lessened.

Like father like daughter. Or, as he should say, like daughters. Plural. Because there were two Seymore sisters. And the other sister, the woman he'd instantly recognised in Issy's screen saver, was in a far more dangerous position to inflict lasting harm on the Rossi cousins.

Amelia Seymore. *Dio*, how long had she worked for them? Had to be two years. She was a good, diligent worker, the type who always arrived early, got her head down and got on with the job. No fuss. The kind of worker Gianni often wished others would be more like.

It had never crossed his mind that she was the daughter of the corrupt bastard who'd taken advantage of them in their first business deal. Not even her surname had given him pause for thought. Seymore was a reasonably common surname, and besides, who would be so blatant as to set up camp in the enemy's quarters under her real name?

Amelia Seymore, that's who.

Damn his phone for dying on him. He needed to warn Alessandro. He'd managed to get one of the crew to take it inside and charge it for him before Issy came back on deck, and it was taking all his willpower to keep his backside rooted to his chair and not storm inside to use it. To not unleash the full force of his fury on the conniving hussy actively seeking to destroy him.

He needed to keep his head. Give nothing away. Keep playing the game.

He took another drink of his second beer and contemplated Issy some more. There were many things he needed to do to shore up his defences, and warning his cousin was only one of them. From what he'd gleaned skimming her messages, the sisters were conducting a two-pronged attack, Amelia targeting the company, Issy tasked with keeping Gianni distracted until her sister's mission was complete. That mission revolved around the Aurora project for which she was the project manager.

Rossi Industries were on the cusp of making a creative partnership deal that would shake the property development world and send the cousins' already incredible wealth into the stratosphere. Today's leadership team meeting would be the decider on which company they partnered with. Gianni had already vetted it. He'd gone through every document with a fine-tooth comb. Nothing had jumped out at him. No warning flags about either of the final two short-listed companies. Nothing. He'd flown to the Caribbean content to leave the final decision on this to Alessandro knowing he would nip any trouble in the bud if it came to it. Whichever company they went with, they would be onto a guaranteed winner. Or so he'd believed.

What had he missed? He must have missed something. *Dammit!*

He drained his bottle and reminded himself that whatever the outcome of the meeting, nothing would be signed today. He had time in that regard.

Issy didn't know he'd discovered her true identity. He would make sure to keep it that way until they reached St Lovells, which was two days' sailing away from Barbados. Once on St Lovells, Issy would be powerless. St Lovells would be her kryptonite.

He needed to get rid of her phone. If he'd known when he cloned it the power it held, he'd have thrown it overboard or accidentally dropped it in the pool. It was seeing the two messages between Issy and her sister that had stopped his brain functioning as it should. The realisation that this was no mere hustle.

It was the message Amelia had sent to her sister two weeks ago that really churned his stomach.

They're corrupt. I have proof.

Churned it far more than the one written minutes after their meeting in London.

It worked! Hook, line and sinker.

What proof of corruption? Gianni and Alessandro were united in their demand their business be run straight down the line. They did not bribe. They did not lie. They did not cut corners. Their bastard fathers were the role models they used to work against and ensure everything they did was the opposite of how they would do it. Thomas Seymore's corrupt actions had only reinforced that ethos. Never mind the destructive fall-out such an accusation would bring, they'd been on the receiving end of malpractice and would never put anyone else through the same.

Any interrogation had to wait until they docked at St Lovells. Until then, he would take a leaf out of Issy's book and unleash the full force of his magnetism on her. Because that was the one big advantage he had—he knew damn well that for all her heinous plotting, Isabelle Seymore wanted him. He would play on that desire without mercy.

She didn't deserve his mercy.

He cast his gaze on her melting bowl of ice cream. 'May I?'

She lifted the bowl to him. 'Be my guest.'

'Grazie.'

'Prego.'

'You speak my language?'

There was a slight hesitation. 'Some.'

'I should have guessed seeing as you've given this beautiful vessel an Italian name.' Dipping his spoon into the ice cream, he lifted it to his mouth and added in Italian, 'I always think the best place to serve ice cream is on the naked body…and the best way to eat it is with my tongue.'

The dark stain of colour that flushed over her told him she'd understood him perfectly. The way she adjusted herself in her seat told him the image he'd evoked in her mind had infused into her body.

Smiling, he popped the spoon into his mouth.

Issy had to cross her legs tightly to stop herself from overtly squirming. But the bastard knew. She could see it in his eyes. He knew she'd understood his seductively delivered words and the effect they were having on her.

His command of the English language was so good it was easy to forget when speaking to him that Gianni was

Italian. Hearing that deep, sensuous voice in his mother tongue though...

It landed like a caress that penetrated deep into her core. His words had only added to the effect, and scrambled her brain to stop any quip forming.

Quite honestly, she needed to throw herself back into the pool to cool down.

God, she hoped the meeting in London was going to plan. Hoped the signing of the contracts was sped up and that it would all be wrapped up in a matter of days as Amelia expected and didn't drag on, because sitting there with Gianni's divinely masculine torso and heaven-sent face in her eye-line, the aftermath of the crush of their bodies still zinging through her skin and the mark of his mouth still on her lips...

This was hell.

Somehow she had to find a way to keep him distracted without compromising herself any further because she couldn't do this. It was too dangerous. Her awareness of Gianni was going through the roof. It was torture to even look him in the eye.

But look him in the eye she must, and she put her elbow on the table and rested her chin on her hand to murmur, 'We seem to be in a quiet stretch of water. How about I get the captain to anchor and we can get the slide out or take the Jet Skis for a spin?'

His eyes gave the sensuous glitter that melted her pelvis. '*Bella*, I've been fantasising about your slide since you first mentioned it.'

Issy contemplated the slide the crew had just finished inflating. Attached to the top sun deck and sweeping straight into the sea, it reminded her of a taller, narrow version of an airplane's safety slide. It wasn't just the slide that had been inflated. Next to where it jutted into the sea bobbed a giant square inflatable that could easily fit ten people on it. That too had been attached to the yacht.

She contemplated it because she wasn't the strongest of swimmers. She'd spent her childhood summers in and out of their Italian holiday home's swimming pool, but that had been a long time ago and, until that day, she hadn't been in a pool since. Even back then she'd never been interested in swimming itself, more interested in splashing around and trying to get a rise out of her sister by hurling beach balls at her head. Also, that had been a pool, with a definable bottom. She didn't dare ask the captain how deep the passage of water they'd anchored in was.

'Ready?' Gianni asked with that devilish grin of his.

Reminding herself that she was supposed to be a fearless society party girl, Issy grinned back. 'Race you to the top.'

She was off before she'd finished making her challenge, already darting up the steps to the next deck before Gianni realised what she was doing.

One good thing about working so hard on sculpting her body in recent years was that it had made her fit. Hungry, yes, but definitely fit. Also, it had made her quick on her feet, and she'd skipped up the first set of steps before Gianni even reached them. Laughing over her shoulder, she raced up the second set to the next deck, easily maintaining her lead, maintaining it too as she whipped up the third and final set... But no sooner had she put her foot on the top deck than a strong arm wrapped around her waist and lifted her in the air.

Legs flailing, she screamed, half in laughter and half in fright. For such a big man, she hadn't heard him closing in on her. He must have been holding himself back.

Dear God, she'd known Gianni was strong but he carried her near the top of the slide as if she weighed nothing, and when he put her down and twisted her round to face him, the size difference between them, even more prominent as she was barefoot, hit her starkly for the first time.

This man could break her in two with no effort whatsoever.

The sense of danger crept its way back through her but even as she tried to decipher it, she knew it was nothing to do with his size, that he would never use his physicality to hurt her.

He gazed down at her, blinked and shook his head. 'You're tiny.'

Uh-oh, she could feel a burn spread across her face. Gianni liked his women tall and leggy. In all her research she'd never learned of a lover who stood under five foot seven.

He placed his fingers under her chin and bowed his head. 'You carry yourself so tall but you're *tiny*.'

Impulsively, she pressed a finger to his lips. 'Don't tell anyone,' she said in a mock whisper. 'It's a secret.'

He stared at her for another beat and then burst into a roar of laughter. Issy couldn't help it. The sound was so infectious that laughter escaped her own lips, and when he put his hands to her sides and lifted her into the air so her face rose above his and her hair, which she'd set free, hung down like a waterfall, the compulsion to kiss him was so strong that it took everything she had to resist.

But resist she must. Even if her body did feel like it was on fire. 'Can you put me down please?'

His shoulders rose slowly before he acquiesced. But there was no time for her to make a break for distance. No sooner did her feet touch the deck than he pressed a hand into the small of her back and wiped a strand of hair off her face. 'You're beautiful.'

'Even though I'm short one end?' she quipped, a quip she was thankful and proud of making because those two words made her feel all fuzzy...but not as fuzzy as the look in his eyes did.

Heaven help her, everything about this man made her feel fuzzy.

Did she fancy him?

His gleaming sensuality burned through her. 'Small but perfectly formed.'

A sharp pang sliced through her chest and she had to work doubly hard not to show it.

It shouldn't even bother her! After all, wasn't this proof that all the money she and Amelia had scrimped and saved for over the years so Issy could pull off Gianni's version of perfection had worked? She should be glad they hadn't needed to invest in a stretching machine for her, not have her heart twist at the knowledge that he wouldn't look twice at the real Issy and certainly wouldn't consider her perfect.

Who *cared* what he thought? Not her. Once the deal in London was signed, sealed and delivered, she would disappear from his life and never see him again.

For the first time, Gianni saw the brightness Issy had maintained all this time in her eyes dim. In seconds she'd blinked it back to brightness, but he'd seen it and he wondered what had caused it, and then wondered why the hell he cared for the cause.

Aware of arousal strengthening in him, he reluctantly slipped his arm away from her, took a step back and indicated the slide. 'Ladies first.'

She smiled sweetly. 'Age before beauty.'

He sniggered. She might be a lying, conniving temptress

set on his destruction but she amused him. It had been a long time since he'd enjoyed a woman's company—anyone's company, come to that—so much, and when he cupped her cheeks and planted a hard, passionate kiss to her mouth, it was sheer impulse driving him with nothing calculated behind it.

Dio, she tasted so good.

'Seeing as I am here at your whim, ready to comply with your every wish, I will do the honours.' And with that, he climbed the three steps to the top of the slide, sat himself down and then let himself fall.

Issy peered over the balustrade and watched the enormous splash made when he landed. A knot of anxiety formed when he didn't immediately surface but it barely had time to root when his dark head suddenly appeared and, after wiping water from his eyes, his grinning face tilted up to hers.

Okay. Now it was her turn.

She could do this. To back out would only make him suspicious, and she couldn't afford that.

She remembered a time when a day at a splash park had been the height of fun, and charging down water slides of all shapes and sizes the biggest thrill of her life.

But those slides all landed in pools of water with a definable bottom and a host of lifeguards overlooking.

Stop being a wimp!

Resolved not to think about what she was about to do, she skipped up the three steps, waved at Gianni treading water a safe distance from the landing zone, plonked her bottom down and let go.

It felt exactly like what she imagined it would feel to free-fall. It was also much quicker than she'd anticipated, the water pouring down the slide as a lubricant hurtling her to the upward curving base so quickly she had no time to prepare or brace herself for the landing. Into the air she flew before slamming into the sea with a scream. Salt water shot up her nose and into her open mouth as she submerged into the depths.

CHAPTER FIVE

GIANNI'S AMUSEMENT AT the spectacularly ungraceful way Issy flipped in the air before crashing into the water vanished when she resurfaced in a panic of flailing arms. He didn't hesitate to streak through the water to her.

The moment he hooked an arm around her waist to stabilise her, she flung her arms around his neck and clung like a limpet to him.

'Hey, take it easy,' he chided when there was a danger she would drag him under. 'I've got you. Relax.'

Blonde hair splattered all over her face, dark blue eyes fixed onto his. She loosened her hold the tiniest fraction.

'Okay?' he asked.

Her lips pulled in before she nodded.

'Good.' Treading water for them both, he kissed her lightly. 'Can you swim to the inflatable?'

Still holding tightly to him, she turned her head to gauge the distance. It was only ten metres or so from where they were but he guessed from the look in her eyes that it could be ten miles as far as she was concerned.

'Hold on to my back,' he said. 'I'll swim us to it.'

Without losing her touch on his body, she twisted around him until she was gripping on to his back like a baby orangutan clinging to its mother.

'As great as it feels to have your legs wrapped around me

like this, you need to loosen up a bit if I'm going to be able to swim,' he told her drily. 'Trust the water's buoyancy and trust me. I've got you.'

Issy's definition of loosening up differed greatly to Gianni's, but at least she relaxed her hold enough for him to move his arms semi-freely.

Life took the strangest of turns he thought as he made his way steadily to the inflatable. Issy Seymore was here to destroy him and now she was holding on to him as if he were her personal life raft. If this had occurred two hours ago when he'd first learned her real identity, he'd have been tempted to let her suffer and flail her own way there. He almost grunted aloud to know this thought was a lie. He planned to make Issy Seymore suffer for the hell she intended to unleash on him but that didn't extend to physical harm.

Once they reached the giant inflatable, he helped her crawl onto it then hauled himself up beside her.

She'd laid herself on her back, her gaze fixed to the sky, breathing heavily.

Stretching himself out on his side beside her, he traced a finger along a high cheekbone. 'Better now?'

Her eyes closed before she turned onto her side to face him and locked on to his stare. 'Thank you for rescuing me.'

'My pleasure,' he murmured.

'Your pleasure? I almost drowned you.'

'*Bella*, you're half my size. You couldn't have drowned me if you'd tried.' Except maybe with her eyes. Gazing into them was like gazing into a deep, hypnotising pool. *Dio*, even half drowned, and with most of her make-up washed away apart from where her mascara had smeared beneath her eyes, she was ravishing. Desire stirred within him and he inched his face closer to hers and splayed a hand on her hip. Her drying skin felt impossibly smooth and soft to his touch.

But he could have drowned her, Issy realised, shivering at the thought even as tendrils of awareness unfurled inside her at his touch and the closeness of their bodies. It would have taken no effort on Gianni's part at all. He could have simply watched her splash around until exhaustion got the better of her. If he knew who she really was he'd probably have helped her drown.

Oh, what a plonker she'd made of herself, and it made her cheeks burn to think of how she'd banged on about 'her' yacht's slide, and then how, at the first go on it, she'd panicked at the speed she'd hurtled down it and flailed like a madwoman when she landed.

The burn deepened to recall how her fear had left her the moment Gianni had taken hold of her. She hadn't clung so tightly to him out of fear of drowning but because her body had instinctively equated Gianni, the man who'd destroyed her life, with safety. The irony was enough to make her splutter a laugh even as an ache deep inside her grew at the wish to wind her arms around him again.

'What's so funny?' he asked, nudging close enough for the tips of their noses to touch.

She plucked a plausible answer out of her scrambling brain; scrambling because it wasn't just their noses touching. The tips of her breasts had brushed against his chest and in an instant, the tendrils of awareness had turned into flames. She cleared her throat. 'I'm just thinking how undignified I must have looked when I landed in the water.'

Amusement played on the lips that had given her so much heady pleasure. 'It was one of those moments where you wish for a video camera.'

Her splutter turned into a giggle. As much as she despised

him, there was a dry wit about Gianni that tickled her, and she hated him even more for it. She loathed everything about him. Most especially loathed that he was the sexiest man to roam the earth and that she was practically melting with anticipation for his hand to move from her hip and explore the contours of her body properly.

God help her, she was aching for his touch.

God help her, she *did* fancy him. There was no other explanation for it. She desired the devil.

'I can't believe I panicked like that,' she bluffed, scrambling even more valiantly for clarity in her thoughts. She couldn't let her body's treacherous responses get the better of her, not when so much was at stake. Having sold herself as a party girl and water sports lover, she couldn't have Gianni think she'd panicked because she hated being out of her depth in water. That would contradict everything she'd purported to be.

His smile was lazy and totally belied the heat pulsing from his eyes. 'These things happen. No harm done.'

But she feared harm had been done. To her. Because the warmth of his breath brushing over her mouth and his thumb gently making circles on her hip was filling her with even more of those thrilling flames. An ache had formed deep inside her, the urge to press her pelvis forwards so that her groin locked with his almost unbearable in its intensity.

'Have you saved many hapless women's lives before?' she asked, striving for a form of nonchalant brightness in her tone but succeeding only in sounding breathless.

'You're the only one I've succeeded with,' Gianni replied, and as his fingers tightened their grip on Issy's delectable hip, his thoughts strayed to his mother. He'd wanted to save her and his aunt from their bastard husbands. Alessandro had too. When their fathers' mother, the matriarch of their family, died, the buffer to their cruelty had gone. Neither Gianni nor his cousin had appreciated how much their *nonna*'s presence at their farmhouse had kept a curb on her sons' malice. Her death unleashed it to a terrifying degree. How he'd longed to have superhero powers—he'd believed back then, when he was eight, that it needed a superhero to stop his father using his fists against himself and his mother— and the money to whisk them off somewhere safe. Turned out his mama didn't need saving. She'd saved herself. When Gianni was nine years old, he'd woken one morning to find her gone. He'd never seen her again.

Naturally, it had been a distressing time for a young boy, but he'd got over it. By the time he was twelve, Gianni and Alessandro had dreamed up their plan to leave. A cast-iron dream left little room for the adolescent Gianni to think about his mother or deal with the churn of anguish as to how she could have left him.

Strangely, he hadn't allowed himself to remember that long-ago anguish for so long that to suddenly think about it now was disconcerting. Emotional pain was something he'd never allowed himself to feel again. In this whole world he loved and trusted Alessandro, and that was it. This beautiful conniving woman gazing at him with eyes ablaze with desire was poison. If she had her way, she could destroy him as effectively as his mother had once done. But not emotionally. When it came to his heart, she couldn't touch him. No one could.

Issy was poison…but she was a hot poison. Her poisonous intentions couldn't quell the attraction smouldering thickly between them. Her poisonous intentions only added piquancy to it. Gianni wanted to taste her venomous lips again and, when her fingers finally closed around his hips and the tips dug through the material of his shorts, his desire ran free to imagine losing himself in all her beautiful toxicity.

'We'll have to get you a pair of red lifeguard shorts and one of those banana board things,' she murmured, her mouth so close to his that the scent of her sweetly toxic breath filled his senses.

There was venom in her breath for sure, a potent drug designed to bewitch and enthral and thicken the desire already rampaging through him. What she didn't know was that her poison could only work on a base level with him. He didn't deny that on a base level it was stronger than any other desire he'd experienced, infecting him right through to his pores, coming close to making him tremble with its strength. Dragging his hand around her back, he clasped her bottom and pulled her flush against him, letting her feel the strength of his excitement. 'Banana board things?'

She hitched a breath before answering. Her eyes had become glazed and when she spoke, there was a breathless quality to her voice. 'You know, those things lifeguards carry under their arms when they're running to save someone from drowning.'

He brushed his mouth against her toxically sweet lips. 'Do you mean a float?'

Her beautiful face flush with colour, she made a noise through her nose he supposed was meant to be a laugh and pressed her breasts tighter against his chest. 'Probably. I'll send you one for your birthday.'

He squeezed her bottom and ground himself harder against her, loving the barely perceptible shock that quivered through her and the pressure of her fingers on his hips. 'What if I need to save your life again before my birthday?'

Her eyes were now so dark and drugged with desire he could see the fight she was waging to keep control of herself.

There was barely any coherence in her voice, but somehow she managed to keep the banter going. 'You'll just have to use your superhero powers again.'

'I'm no superhero, *bella*. Just a man.' A man with a deep hunger for another taste of Issy's poisonous lips. Finally fusing his mouth to hers, Gianni rolled on top of her and sank into the heady pleasure of her mouth.

Oh, God, didn't she know how much of a man he was? Issy thought wildly as red-hot lava pumped through her veins. The feelings Gianni elicited in her were so out of this world, a craven need that his touch and ravenous mouth only fed, that she gave no thought to resisting. With his weight on her, covering her, subsuming her, the essence of herself slipped out of her grasp and she stepped into the flames of desire.

His kisses were hard and demanding, a devouring of mouths and tongues, a sensory whirl that had her press her screaming, sensitised skin tightly against every inch of him that she could. Dragging her fingers over Gianni's smooth, muscular back, she revelled in the groans he made at her touch and kissed him even harder, only breaking her mouth from his to gasp at the shock that thrilled through her when the weight and length of his excitement jutted through his swim shorts and jabbed against the scrap of material covering her most intimate parts. It was a thrill that burned deep in the heart of her and instinctively, she wrapped her legs tight around his waist and raised her hips.

She didn't know if the rocking motion was all them or if the swell of the water beneath the inflatable they were locked in each other's arms on was the cause and she didn't care. A burning coil had wound itself tightly in her core and was throbbing with a desperate need for relief, and she clung even tighter, kissing him even harder as the length of his thick hardness thrust against her swollen nub and...

The coil sprang free without warning. One minute she was rocking against him, caught up in the most heavenly thrills she'd ever experienced in her life; the next she shattered, and even as the unexpected explosions of her very first climax throbbed and raged through her, still she clung to Gianni, burying her face in his neck, desperate to keep the connection between them and draw out this most incredible moment of her life.

It was only when the spasms subsided and Issy realised Gianni had stilled that she came back to earth with a sharp bump. In an instant, the crest of the most glorious experience she'd ever ridden was over and sanity crashed into her like a bucket of ice being tipped over her head.

Oh, God, what had just happened?

She squeezed her eyes shut and wished for a hole to open in the inflatable and to sink beneath the surface and never come back up again.

This was terrible. Horrendous.

She tried to breathe. Tried to think. Then she tried not to think because even as the last thrills limped through her, her head was swimming with the fact that she'd just come completely undone and behaved in the most shocking, wanton, shameful fashion. And for *him*.

And all in her bikini. He hadn't even needed to touch her there.

The weight crushing her slowly lifted, but only the physical weight. She could feel Gianni staring at her. What must he think of her? She shouldn't care what he thought of her. She *didn't* care. She didn't.

She needed to bluff her way out of this, and as she realised this, the path of least humiliation opened to her. She just had to get back into character. It was beyond belief that any of his previous lovers had cared two hoots about seeming wanton to him. Wanton was what Gianni wanted!

As humiliating as her responses to him were, she needed to think of them in a positive light. Most importantly though, she must take more care than ever not to let desire for him overtake her sanity again. Use this as a warning to keep her internal guard up.

Gianni, struggling to find his breath, studied Issy's flushed face intently. His head was reeling from what had just occurred between them. Their kiss in the pool had blown his mind. This had come close to blowing his head off his shoulders. And hardly anything had happened. He was still to taste anything but her mouth.

But never had he experienced such unbridled hunger before. *Dio*, the ache in his loins was like nothing he'd felt before. Her passion...

His loins were on fire. He ached so badly to smother her mouth again and continue what they'd started. The fusion of their mouths had sent an inferno raging through them, from simmer to scorching in an instant. When he'd sensed what was happening to her... It hadn't seemed possible.

But it had been real. Issy had climaxed. He guessed from the ragged sharpness of her breathing and the way her eyes were still screwed so tightly together that it had been as big a shock to her as it was to him.

Just as shocking was how close to the edge he'd come too.

What the hell was happening to him? He was thirty-two years old. He'd learned to control his bodily responses to beautiful women before the end of his adolescence. He took *pride* in his control so to know that a few beats longer with their groins locked together would have tipped him over the edge too was beyond his comprehension. Issy was beautiful and sexy but so were plenty of other women. He'd never come close to losing control like that before.

Finally, Issy's eyes opened. After a moment's hesitation, they locked on to his. Gianni's heart slammed hard against his ribs.

After another beat, a lazy smile formed on her beautiful face. 'I need a drink. Let's go back.'

Disbelief almost made him mute. 'That's all you have to say?'

'I'm thirsty.' Laughing, she pushed at his chest and rolled out from beneath him.

His mouth opened and he shook his head. This woman was unbelievable, and he shook his head again as he watched her grip one of the handles around the inflatable's edge and slip into the water.

'Are you coming?' she asked with a tilt of her head and a knowing smile.

He laughed through the pain in his loins. 'I wish.'

She gave the faintest of winks. 'I guess you'll just have to wish harder.'

Before he could think of an answer, she'd pushed herself away from the inflatable and swum the metre distance to the steps the crew had earlier lowered for them.

Warm though the sea was, Gianni's body was on such a high simmer that when he followed Issy's lead, it was like sinking into a cold bath. He welcomed it. God help him, he was as horny as a sex-mad teenager, and as he watched her step onto the deck, all he could think of was untying those scraps of material covering her most feminine parts and screwing her until neither of them could stand.

Issy had no idea how she kept her back straight and stopped her legs from collapsing, and when she looked over her shoulder as she padded over the deck and saw Gianni's head appear by the railing, the swelling in her heart was so painful and the weakness in her legs so strong that the truth that she was in over her head slapped her like a wet fish.

She needed to message Amelia and beg her to at least try and fast-track the signing of the contracts. Get them signed immediately. She couldn't play this game for much longer. She needed to get as far away from Gianni as she could. He was just too much. All the research in the world couldn't have prepared her for the reality of seducing a man into distraction when the man in question brought out feelings in her that had never existed before. *She* was the one being seduced here, by the devil himself.

Upping her pace, mentally composing the message she would send to her sister, she reached the table she'd left her stuff on and in seconds found herself close to tears. Her phone had gone.

CHAPTER SIX

'SOMETHING WRONG?' GIANNI asked casually as he reached for his towel. He could not fathom why Issy's obvious anxiety should make his heart twinge.

She shook her sarong out. 'I can't find my phone.'

Of course she couldn't. He'd instructed the crew to hide it in his cabin, the only space in the yacht kept locked and off-limits to Issy. She could have it back when this was all over.

'It can't have gone far,' he assured her. 'Where did you last have it?'

'Right here. I left it on this table.'

He looked at his watch. It was coming up to ten p.m. in London. The meeting on the Aurora project would have finished hours ago. He could not let what had happened between him and Issy distract him from what needed to be done. He'd got rid of her phone so she was unable to contact her sister. His priority now was to warn Alessandro.

'Ask your crew,' he said. 'Maybe one of them took it inside for you when they took mine in to charge or when they finished clearing lunch.'

She bit her lip and nodded. 'Good idea.'

'If they haven't got it, it might be worth checking your cabin in case one of the crew put it in there for you and forgot to tell you.'

She nodded again, and hurried inside, forgetting to sway

her hips seductively in her distraction. For some reason, this too made his heart twinge.

Pushing away the strange feelings threading through him—he needed to work fast and concentrate—he indicated to Mara, the head of his crew, to bring his phone to him.

He switched it on and immediately called his cousin.

Alessandro's voice sounded down the crackly line. 'Gianni, how—?'

'Andro, listen, I don't have much time.'

'Okay, but what's the—?'

'Amelia Seymore,' he interrupted. 'She's Thomas Seymore's daughter.'

'*What?* I can't hear you properly.'

'Listen to me, Amelia Seymore is a traitor. She's been a spy this whole time. She's working with her sister to destroy us.'

'Amelia Seymore?' Alessandro's incredulity was clear.

'Yes! Seymore! The Aurora project is compromised. And listen, she claims to have found some kind of proof of corruption against us.'

'Did you say corruption? What corruption?'

'I don't know, but according to the messages I read, Amelia Seymore has found evidence of corruption by us. I'm in the Caribbean with her sister. I'll keep her out of the way here and stop her communicating with anyone and causing any more damage. Can you deal with Amelia? This needs to be nipped in the bud and damage limitation undertaken immediately.'

'Consider it done,' Alessandro said, his voice now low and dangerous.

Despite the bad reception, the message had got through, and a fraction of the tightness in Gianni's chest loosened. 'I may be out of reach for a while,' he said, 'but I'll try and get a message to you when I know what's going on.'

'Likewise. Speak soon, cousin.'

Gianni disconnected the call and took a deep breath of relief. His cousin was like a human missile when it came to taking down targets. Amelia Seymore stood no chance now she was in his sights. Whatever she and her sister had planned against them would fail.

But that still left Issy to deal with. She was an unknown quantity. The messages he'd read suggested her only job was to distract him while Amelia did the dirty work, but who knew what plans they'd concocted in the privacy of their home that had left no digital trace.

By the time she came back out on deck, now wearing a black vest with spaghetti straps over a black bikini and a pair of tiny denim shorts, her large shades once again covering much of her face, he knew the only safe thing to do was proceed with his own plan and get her to St Lovells. On the open sea at this time of year, there were too many other yachts about, too many ways for her to escape the *Palazzo delle Feste* and reach safety and communication with another vessel. There would be no escape for her from St Lovells. Not without his explicit agreement.

'Did you find your phone?' he asked as she approached him.

She shook her head. 'I have no idea what's happened to it.'

'It will turn up,' he assured her.

Flopping onto the sofa across from his, she tucked her legs under her bottom. 'I hope so.'

Unable to resist, he held his phone out. 'You can always use mine if you need it. It's fully charged.'

'Thank you but I don't know any of my contacts' numbers.' Her shoulders rose. 'I suppose it's the curse of the age we live in that we don't need to commit people's phone numbers to memory.'

'You mean you want to use your phone to make an actual phone call?' he asked in pretend horror, and was rewarded with a definite loosening of her taut frame and a snuffle of laughter.

'I know. Who'd have thought it, 'eh? Using a phone to call people on. Whatever next?'

'People using televisions to watch TV?'

'Now you're going too far.' The amusement on her face dimmed a little. She raised her face to the sky and sighed. 'When I was a little girl, my mum had one of those old-fashioned address books, you know the ones where you could write someone's name in it along with their address and phone number?'

'I am familiar with old-fashioned address books,' he said drily. His *nonna* had had one that had been crammed full of names, and random pieces of paper with scribbled numbers that used to fly onto the floor whenever the book was opened. 'Some people still use them.'

'Do you reckon? I used to laugh at Mum for keeping one and thought it hilarious that she could still recite her childhood phone number from memory. It just seemed so old-fashioned and unnecessary to me when everything could be stored on your phone. I know my phone will turn up and if it doesn't, I'll be able to buy another one and retrieve all my data, but I can just imagine my mum—as she was back then—laughing at me now for relying on technology when the old-fashioned way would have made it more likely I had it stored in my brain.'

'You say as she was back then… You mentioned before something about her being in rehab. If you don't mind me asking, what is she in rehab for?' He leaned back, managing to resist the temptation to fold his arms across his chest and stare at her like a headmaster waiting for a rule-breaking student to come up with a wild non-convincing lie to get them off the hook.

Slowly, Issy lowered her face and met Gianni's stare through the darkness of their respective shades. While she'd made her fruitless search for her phone and showered the sea salt off her skin, the space away from Gianni had been the space she needed to talk sense back into herself. She and Amelia had spent ten years working towards this point. She could not throw it away just because of a major case of hormone problems for the bastard she was so desperate to bring down. And one of those reasons she so desperately wanted to bring him down was because of her mother. Because one of the many consequences of Gianni destroying her life had been the loss of the mother who'd once cherished and adored her two daughters. Jane Seymore was alive only in the sense that her heart still pumped blood through her body. 'She has many issues. Drugs is the biggest one.'

'Your mother is a drug addict?'

Yes, you bastard. Because of you.

'She's not a junkie in the traditional sense that people think of drug addicts. She doesn't inject herself thank God but that's only because she has a needle phobia. It's mostly strong prescription stuff delivered to the comfort of her home—dealers nowadays have diversified into home delivery. Basically, she takes whatever she can get her hands on that stops her having to think or feel.' Anything that stopped her remembering all that she'd lost.

There was a flicker in his eyes and she suddenly had the sense that he was weighing up whether or not to believe her. 'How long has she been like this?'

'If you don't mind, I'd rather not spoil this beautiful day by talking about it.' Not with him, the cause of it all. Not when she was unlikely to be able to get through a conversation about it without breaking character and screaming and hurling anything she could get her hands on at him. It was hard enough maintaining the high-society character as things stood, what with all the awful, awful, *wonderful* feelings he'd let loose in her body. She'd deliberately seated herself on a separate sofa to him but the tempest happening inside her was as acute as if she'd curled herself on his lap. God help her, he didn't need to actually touch her for her to want him. All he had to do was look at her, and for the first time, she felt a pang of sympathy for all the women who'd fallen under his spell before her. She'd assumed for years that all they wanted of him was his money and the glamour of his lifestyle but as she was learning, there was far more to him than that. What chance had those women had? No wonder Gianni had a litany of broken hearts strewn in his wake.

After a long beat, he said, 'I respect that, but if you're worried about her not being able to contact you then we can get in touch with the rehab facility and give them my number to reach you on.'

Issy hated the pang that ripped through her chest and belly at this sincerely delivered offer. Her mother was in rehab because of him! She shook her head. 'It's fine. They can call my sister if there's a problem. It's Amelia I'm more concerned about not being able to reach me—I can't remember her phone number or email address off the top of my head.'

'Amelia is your sister?'

'Yes.' Mentally kicking herself for mentioning Amelia by name, Issy shifted in her seat and quickly changed the subject, moving the conversation along to the next phase of keeping Gianni distracted and preferably uncommunicable while Amelia made the final moves in the Seymore sisters' destruction of the Rossi cousins, casually saying, 'As we're too far from the nearest island to dock before night falls, I thought we could anchor at sea tonight.'

His eyes flickered at the change of subject before a slow smile spread across his far too gorgeous face. 'Is that an invitation for me to spend the night with you?'

'It's an invitation for you to spend the night on the yacht. Not necessarily with me.' Never, never, never. No matter how badly she burned for him.

A gleam formed. 'Playing hard to get?'

'Nothing good ever comes easy,' she riposted sweetly, thinking she didn't need to just play hard to get but needed to build a fortress of concrete to make herself immune to him.

He raised the short crystal glass filled with an amber liquid that she hadn't noticed him holding, probably because she was too mesmerised by his face. 'That's a truth I will gladly drink to.'

'So what do you say?' Issy asked after he'd taken a sip. She wished she had a drink. It was easier to play seductress with a prop in her hand.

'About me staying the night here?'

She nodded. If he said no then she'd move to plan B and order the captain to fake engine problems. 'All the cabins are made up.'

'As you just said we're too far from anywhere to dock tonight, that suggests I don't actually have a choice about staying on board,' he pointed out.

'You can always swim.'

His strong throat extended as he laughed. How she hated the way the sound of it rang like balm in her ears and hated the way it enlivened his face, amplifying his heartbreaking handsomeness. 'I'm a strong swimmer but as we've already determined, I'm no superhero.'

'You could steal one of the Jet Skis.' That would work. If she was lucky, he might fall off. But even as she thought that a nibble of panic chewed at her heart at the prospect of him falling into open waters without even a life jacket for safety, and she quickly scrubbed it from her mind.

He pretended to mull this over. 'Hmm... Escaping on a Jet Ski or spending the night with the most beautiful woman in the Caribbean... That's a hard choice.'

'Spending the night on board a *yacht* with, not necessarily in *bed* with,' she reiterated.

He sighed mockingly. 'It's the hope that always kills, but even so, that's hope enough for me.'

'You'll stay?'

The gleam in his eyes turned up a notch and lasered straight into her pelvis. 'Trust me, *bella*. I'm not going anywhere.'

'Nice cabin,' Gianni commented as he stepped through the door Issy had opened for him on the sleeping deck. He'd wondered which cabin she would put him in. He'd bet she'd been tempted to put him in the smallest. Not that any of the cabins were small by any reasonable judgement. Gianni loved to party and took his duties as host seriously. The last thing he wanted was for any of his guests to feel slighted by being given inferior accommodation. The irony that his first night on his new yacht would be spent in the third-best cabin—the master suite was locked and Issy had claimed the second-best for her own—did not escape him. Still, it was spacious and had a perfectly respectable king-size bed. Gianni usually slept in an emperor bed, but this would do for one night. He turned his gaze from the cabin to the woman hovering at the foot of the doorway.

'The en suite is filled with toiletries and there's robes in the wardrobe you can use,' she said. For once, she seemed to be avoiding his eye. She'd dodged the elevator that would have taken them to the deck, skipping up the stairs ahead of him and then heading straight to the cabin. He knew perfectly well Issy was doing her best to stay out of arm's reach of him and knew perfectly well why. When she'd set off on her mission to destroy him she hadn't factored that she would actually want him, that she wouldn't have to fake desire for him. It must be killing her. Great. Let her suffer, trapped in the web of her own making.

He had to give her kudos though for the slick way she'd engineered for him to spend the night and admire how she'd made promises that weren't promises at all. The promise of what could come…but only maybe.

Did she really think she could hold out against the scorching chemistry between them for the duration of however long she intended to entrap him for?

'I'm going to get ready for dinner,' she added. 'I'll see you in an hour.'

Before she could run away, he pulled his polo shirt off and dropped it on the floor. She hesitated, her gaze fluttering over his chest before rising to meet his stare.

Poor Issy. She had no idea how expressive her eyes were, how her desire rang out from them. If she knew, she'd wear her shades permanently.

He stepped over to her. Linking his fingers through hers, he gently pulled her hands above her head and trapped her against the wall. Her breathing shortened. That delicious colour he was coming to get such a thrill at provoking stained her cheeks.

'Want to take a shower with me before you go?' he murmured.

Her throat moved and her chest rose before she managed

to make her lips curve and huskily say, 'A generous offer but judging by the size of you, you'll hog all the water.'

'Oh, I can be generous, *bella*.' Dipping his mouth down to her neck, he traced his tongue over the delicate, toxically sweet skin, revelling at the quiver of her body in response. 'Before our time here is done, I'll prove just how generous a man I can be.'

'Your self-confidence is staggering,' she said, only the hitches in her voice betraying her nonchalance as a facade.

Dropping her hands, he dragged his fingers through her hair and down her neck until, for the very first time, he palmed a small, pert breast. A shock of electricity zinged through them both, so tangible he could swear he heard it crackle.

'*Dio*, you're sexy,' he muttered into her mouth before kissing her. His arousal, a semi-permanent state since their first kiss in the swimming pool, sprung back to full length at the first flicker of her tongue against his and when she cupped his head and her fingers dug through his hair to scrape against his skull, his intention of merely teasing her was completely forgotten as the heat she evoked in him unleashed in all its power, a surge of energy that burned from his loins to every crevice in his body.

The way Issy Seymore made him feel was more than a mere game. He'd never wanted anyone like he wanted her.

This time, though, Issy was the one to keep her head, suddenly pulling her mouth from his and pushing him away from her.

'I can't do this,' she croaked, breathing heavily.

'Do what?'

'This. Gianni…' Clearly flustered, she pressed a hand tightly against her heaving chest. 'I…'

'You what?' he encouraged. Would this be the moment

Isabelle Seymore confessed? Or did the little minx have something else up her sleeve?

Her dark blue eyes gazed into his with something akin to desperation. 'I'm saving myself for marriage.'

As soon as the words left her mouth, Issy wished she could take them back. She had no idea where they had come from. Of course she wasn't saving herself for marriage—she wasn't a Victorian!

But she *was* frightened. Terrified. Terrified at how easily her body overrode her sanity when it came to Gianni. Terrified at how deeply she was coming to crave him. So while her words of marriage had dredged themselves from nowhere, there was a slight calming in the wild thumps of her heart to know they were the words to make the commitment-phobic Gianni Rossi back off.

Gazing into his shocked eyes, she determined that when this was all over, she was going to find herself a boyfriend. She'd make Amelia get out there and find a boyfriend too. The Rossi cousins had stopped them living for long enough.

This craving for Gianni was all his fault. If Gianni and his hateful cousin hadn't ruined their lives then they would have continued developing like other teenage girls, getting boyfriends and partying, not trying desperately to save their father from himself and then trying to save their mother, and all the while working and working to reach this point where they could bring down the men who'd turned their lives into rubble. Gianni's actions all those years ago had stopped her forming the emotional and sexual attachments other twenty-three-year-old women took for granted. Something else to hate and blame him for.

Her loathing ratcheted up when his shock slowly dissipated and that hateful gleam flashed in his devil eyes. 'You're saving yourself for marriage, *bella*?'

Grinding her toes into her sandals, she jutted her chin. 'Yes. I'm sorry if that disappoints you.'

He shrugged with the nonchalance she kept aiming for, and, leaning his face closer to hers, folded his arms across his naked chest. How her fingers itched to swirl through the dark hair covering it. The bastard had probably taken his polo shirt off deliberately. She wished he'd put it back on.

'Why would I be disappointed? There are other ways to share pleasure.'

Oh, God, did he have to say *pleasure* so ruddy seductively? 'I just thought you might have expectations…expectations that I've admittedly fed…' There was no getting around that. She'd practically promised herself to him. Feeling more confident, she continued. 'I am very much attracted to you, Gianni…' She managed to flash a grin. '…as you've probably noticed.'

'I'm pretty damned hot for you too.'

'And I know I've led you on but it's only because I fancied you from the moment I met you and I thought you could be the one I dropped my morals for, but they're too strong. I can't give myself to you without a ring on my finger. I'm sorry.'

His mouth curved and his forehead creased in understanding. 'No need to apologise. If you have morals then you must stick by then.'

'I'm so glad you understand.'

'I understand perfectly. You'll only have sex with me if I marry you?'

'Yes.'

'Then I accept.'

'Accept what?'

'Your proposal.'

'I beg your pardon?'

'Your proposal of marriage.' He stepped forwards and pressed her back against the wall, bringing his face so close to hers that she could practically feel the glitter burning from his eyes in her retinas. 'I accept.'

CHAPTER SEVEN

THE MIXTURE OF emotions that flittered over Issy's beautiful face filled Gianni with amusement. He'd caught her out. Anticipation for what she would do now filled him.

'You cannot be serious,' she said incredulously. 'You want to marry me just so you can sleep with me?'

'Why not? We're having fun, just as you promised, aren't we? What could be more fun than getting married?' He cupped her breast. *Dio*, it felt so good against the palm of his hand. He'd be tempted to marry her for real just to feel it naked against him. 'Come on, Issy,' he goaded, moving his hand from her breast to thread his fingers through her hair and clasp the back of her head, 'what is life for but taking risks, and we're both risk takers. Let's get married and spend the rest of our time on the Caribbean having wild sex.'

He was playing her, Issy knew, even as a thrill of need pulsed low in her pelvis at the unbidden thought of locking herself away with Gianni and acting out every depraved need that had exploded for him. This was nothing but a Gianni tactic to get her into bed. Pretend to want to marry her so that she'd drop her bikini bottoms for him. The man must be a bigger sex-mad cad than she'd supposed.

Knowing this was all just a game made it easier to deal with. She didn't even have to fake her laughter at the absurdity of the swerve to their conversation. 'I'd be up for that but I'm afraid I'd need a ring on my finger before having the wild sex you promise, so unless you can think of a way for us to get hitched before our time here comes to an end...' She let her words trail off and raised a shoulder in pretend disappointment.

'The captain,' he said with a gleam.

'What about him?'

'Some ship captains have the power to conduct weddings. If yours has the requisite powers, he can marry us. Does he?'

'I don't know.'

'Let's ask him.' Unthreading his fingers from her hair, Gianni ran them down her slender, golden arms. 'I assume you have your passport on board?'

'It's right here in my cabin... What a shame you don't have yours,' Issy added with fresh pretend disappointment.

'Oh, but I do,' he said triumphantly, patting his back pocket. 'I always carry it with me.'

So he wanted to drag this absurd game out did he? 'Then let me get mine.'

Issy retrieved her passport from the handbag she kept it in, lifted the receiver of the cabin's phone, which connected to all the different parts of the yacht, and smiled beatifically at Gianni. 'Shall I call the captain then?'

Thoroughly enjoying himself, Gianni nodded. 'Tell him to meet us in the lounge.'

Gianni watched her press the captain's number, certain she'd slam the receiver down before the call connected and put a halt to this charade. It was ludicrous to think they could marry. Almost as ludicrous as Issy's declaration that she was waiting for marriage. Still, she'd upped the ante of their game superbly. He'd twisted and she'd matched. He couldn't wait to watch her fold.

But she didn't fold. Instead she politely asked the captain

to meet them in the lounge to discuss a personal issue. That was one thing he did like about her; that she spoke to the crew respectfully. Many yacht owners and charterers treated their crew like dirt; as if they were their personal slaves.

Call over, her lips curved. 'He'll meet us in the lounge now.'

He held his hand out to her. She laced her fingers through his and let him lead her down to the entertainment deck.

Captain James Caville entered the lounge at the same time as them. Not by word or gesture did he give away the fact he'd worked for Gianni for the last four years. Gianni was proud of his loyal crew. They'd transferred seamlessly to his new vessel and, when told that their boss—him—was being targeted by a hustler and to play along with the hustler's game, had risen to the challenge. It wouldn't even cross Issy's mind that Gianni and the good captain had spent more than a few evenings drinking their way through bottles of Scotch and playing Three Card Brag, or, on the occasions they were joined by other crew members, hunkered down at the poker table playing Texas Hold 'Em.

As a result of their friendship, Gianni thought he knew the captain pretty well and so was almost dumbstruck when, asked if he was allowed to officiate marriages, James nodded. 'The *Palazzo delle Feste* is registered in Bermuda and I have a Bermuda licence, so if you want me to marry you then I can. I'll just need to contact the ministry to go through the necessary requirements...' There was a beat of hesitation. 'Do you want me to do that?'

Gianni had to pull himself together quickly. He'd expected James to laugh at the request, had envisaged turning to Issy and teasing her about researching an island they could marry on and then winding her up into believing they would sail there. It had never crossed his mind that James would actually be allowed to marry them; he'd thought stories of ships captains marrying couples was an urban myth. He'd only chosen Bermuda to register the *Palazzo delle Feste* because that's where his last yacht had been registered.

Surely now was the time Issy would think this was getting out of hand and fold her cards. But instead of finding doubt or panic on her face, she simply gazed at him with challenge in her stare. She was waiting for Gianni to fold.

He'd never folded in his life.

Challenge accepted.

'Do it,' he said decisively.

James' only physical reaction to this was the slight raising of an eyebrow. 'And when will you want the ceremony?'

Gianni winked at Issy. 'Right now would be great but I appreciate that's unreasonable so as soon as possible. If anything can be fast-tracked then do it—money is no object if palms need to be greased.'

James pulled his phone out of his pocket. 'I'll get onto it now.'

'A drink while we wait?' Gianni suggested to Issy.

The beatific smile returned. 'Champagne would be fitting.'

The honours done, eyes locked together, they toasted each other and each drank half their glass.

Come on, Issy, fold, he mentally urged her. *You know neither of us will go through with this charade*.

How much longer until Gianni roared with laughter and admitted this was all just a wind-up, Issy wondered. She almost felt sorry for the captain working so hard to make a fallacy happen, but it was only when he covered the speaker on his phone and asked for their passports that the first twinge of doubt hit her.

She sipped on her second glass of champagne telling herself not to be silly. It didn't matter how much money Gianni had to grease palms, marriage was not something that could be fast-tracked. Any minute now and the captain would regretfully tell them it couldn't be done before Gianni flew back to the UK, and then they would both pretend to be disappointed and Gianni would have no choice but to back off from her physically for the rest of their time together. She would just have to think harder for ways to entertain him. The yacht was a veritable party palace—even its name denoted that—so in theory it would be easy.

Theory though, as she'd come to learn since arriving in the Caribbean, was no guarantee of success when put into practice.

A member of the crew came in with a sheaf of freshly printed-off papers in her hand, which she gave to the captain. Still talking on the phone, he riffled through them, then beckoned Gianni over. Their voices were too low for her to hear but when Gianni's gaze directed itself to her, there was a calculation in it that stiffened her resolve not to be the one to throw her hands in the air and say this had gone too far.

Stifling laughter, she drank more of her champagne and watched him do something on his phone that she suspected involved transferring money. Excellent.

A stronger pang of doubt hit a short while later though when the captain started laughing to whoever he was now talking to on the phone. The laugh and the tone his voice had now adopted reminded Issy of her father's the time she'd been playing on the floor of his study while he'd been conducting a business deal. He'd taken that same lighter tone and laughed in the same manner right before he'd ended the call. He'd been so happy with the deal he'd concluded that he'd scooped Issy up and spun her in the air.

She caught Gianni's eye. He'd topped them both up with

the last of the champagne then seated himself across from her, an ankle resting on a thigh, an arm strewn across the back of the sofa, the very epitome of nonchalance.

The devil raised his glass to her.

She raised hers right back.

'We're all set,' James said a minute later, rising from the table he'd set himself up on. 'We just need a couple of witnesses—I've sent a message to my officers—and we're good to go.'

The vaguely smug look that had been on Gianni's face while they'd waited, like that of a chess player waiting for their opponent to realise they were heading for a loss, flickered. He straightened. 'You can marry us now?'

The captain shrugged. 'It's cost you a lot of money, but I have the authorisation.'

Gianni somehow kept his features straight as he swore loudly to himself. This had gone too far. Issy *had* to fold now. He looked back at her. 'Ready to marry me?'

Eyes not leaving his face, she drained her champagne. 'Why not? Like you said, it'll be fun... Unless you have cold feet?'

'No cold feet from me.' He would *not* be the one to fold.

Two men in navy shorts and pale blue polo shirts with the same emblem as the crew had on their uniforms came into the lounge.

Gianni got to his feet. 'We need a ring.'

'Two rings.'

Issy got to her feet and realised she was a bit wobbly. Half a bottle of champagne on an empty stomach was probably not her best idea, but seeing as she was still sharp enough to recognise that, she wouldn't worry about it. This actually had become fun, and she giggled at the absurdity of it all, and giggled too, to think of Gianni wasting oodles of his money on a marriage that wouldn't take place. 'Any spare paper?' she asked the captain.

When he gave her a sheet, she knelt at a coffee cable and quickly ripped two strips off it. Each strip she rolled lengthways between her fingers until it resembled a long wriggly worm, then tied each one into a circle, which she held out to Gianni with a flourish. 'There,' she said, flashing a grin at him. 'Two makeshift wedding rings.'

'You're ready to do this?' he reiterated.

He wanted her to back out. He *expected* her to back out. She could see it in his eyes. And it was that expectation which filled her with serene defiance. Gianni had started this game of chess and it was up to him to put an end to it.

It was only when he clasped her hand and together they faced the captain that she realised neither of them was prepared to back down.

They'd reached stalemate.

Gianni had the strangest feeling of leaving his body and floating above and looking down on himself and Issy, hands clasped and reciting vows before the captain and growing number of crew come to see for themselves if the boss really was marrying the hustler. He watched himself sign the certificate where the captain told him to and watched Issy sign her name—her real name, Isabelle Christine Seymore—and the two witnesses sign theirs. Then he watched himself slide the paper ring over her finger and Issy slide the one she'd made for him over his finger, and continued watching with the same detachment while they kissed to seal their vows.

And then he re-inhabited his body as a flurry of handshakes and embraces were shared, the heavy beats of his heart rippling through him at the knowledge that the game of bluff he'd just played with Issy had backfired.

* * *

Issy popped two painkillers into her mouth with a shaking hand and washed them down with cold water. The after-effects of the champagne she'd drunk just a short while ago were making themselves known in the form of a headache. Or maybe the cause of it was the sudden loss of the adrenaline that had pumped through her in that mad hour that had ended with her married.

The amusement that had been carried with the adrenaline had gone too, reality as cold as the water she'd just drunk pouring over and through her.

She'd just married her nemesis. She hadn't merely exchanged fake vows but signed legal documents. Signed them in her real name. The only saving grace was Gianni had failed to notice anything about her surname.

But what on earth had possessed her? What had possessed *him*?

Amelia was going to kill her…

Oh, hell, she hadn't thought of her sister in hours, had completely forgotten about her lost phone and that her sister would be waiting anxiously with her own phone in hand for an update. She *had* to find her phone.

Closing her eyes, Issy took some deep breaths to force a modicum of calm into herself. It was the middle of the night in London. Amelia wouldn't be worrying; that was Issy projecting. Amelia would only worry if Issy went the whole of the next day without communicating. If her phone stayed missing, she would borrow one off the crew, search the main number for Rossi Industries and call Amelia through it. Her priority, she realised with a flash, was to tell the captain to destroy the marriage papers. If they weren't lodged, they wouldn't be properly registered, ergo, the 'marriage' would never be legalised.

These things decided in her mind, she expelled a more settled breath and called the captain. Told by one of his officers that he was currently unavailable but would call her back soon, she said, 'Don't worry, I'll speak to him first thing in the morning.' They were in the middle of the Caribbean Sea. Nothing would be done with the papers before morning and Gianni was due soon to escort her to dinner. She needed to work out how she was going to play things.

It was a thought that set her heart thumping again.

How was she supposed to brazen this out? Marriage.

Not marriage, she told herself stubbornly. Just a joke, a game, whatever, that had gone a step too far. So long as the papers weren't lodged, there would be no real marriage. She was safe.

Her head sorted and the painkillers kicking in, she decided the best thing to do was continue the joke and play up the marriage, so selected a slinky white fitted dress with spaghetti straps that came just below the knee and had a slit cut into its skirt that ran almost to the top of her thigh. For her feet she chose a pair of white spaghetti strap sandals to match. With her hair blow-dried into the illusion of thickness and her eyes painted a smoky grey, she finished the look off with a smear of red lipstick.

As prepared as she thought she was though, she still needed a moment to collect herself before answering the knock on her cabin door.

Gianni stood there, wearing the same polo shirt and canvas shorts that had been draped over his too magnificent body at various times throughout the day and with that devilish smile her brain hated but which her body adored on his too gorgeous face. 'Ready for dinner, Signora Rossi?'

The longing that ran through her came close to making

her legs collapse, and right in that moment Issy knew this had to end.

She couldn't handle Gianni or her feelings for him. She wasn't just in over her head, she was close to *losing* her head. She'd married him for heaven's sake! There was no way she could spend a whole week with him without losing her mind and probably the last of her self-respect. She had to trust that Amelia had done her part in the meeting that day and that their operation to destroy the Rossi cousins had reached the point of no return.

Because much more time spent with Gianni was going to push Issy to the point of no return.

She had to end this. She *would* end this.

A modicum of peace settled in her wildly fluctuating heart.

She would get their marriage papers destroyed and this horror story would end as soon as they docked on whichever the closest island was. She would insist they go off and explore and then she'd give Gianni the slip and escape without him, even if it meant abandoning the yacht.

All she needed to do was brazen things out and hold him off sexually for a few more hours.

'*Si, signor,*' she murmured, giving him a look of adoration that scarily needed no effort whatsoever.

He held his elbow out to her.

She didn't hesitate to slip her hand through it.

His eyes gleamed. 'I don't know about you but I'm already looking forward to dessert.'

The crew had transformed the dining room into a silver and gold extravaganza. It never ceased to amaze Gianni how ingeniously creative they could be in catering to his whims, and also the whims he hadn't even expressed. How they'd got hold of balloons, glitter and confetti and decorated the room accordingly would remain a mystery. He wouldn't ask. Sometimes the mystery was enough.

The dining table, which could comfortably seat twenty people, had been laid in an L at one end, with Gianni at the head and Issy to his right. Romantic candles had been lit, the reflection of their flames dancing off the crystal chandelier above. The huge windows lining the left of the dining room added to the romantic ambience, the setting sun on the horizon turning the sky a burnished orange that made it appear to be on fire. It perfectly matched the fire taking place inside him.

Gianni raised his glass of champagne to his bride and, for at least the dozenth time since he'd turned up at her cabin, marvelled at how ravishing she looked. He could hardly believe the beautiful creature beside him was the same woman in the screenshot he'd cloned. Alone in his cabin, he'd found himself staring intently at that picture with the strangest mixture of emotions playing through him. He strongly suspected the screenshot was Issy in her natural state and this blonde vision of perfection was a carefully curated image in which to ensnare him. What he couldn't understand was why the plainer, unpolished, plumper version on the screen made his chest tighten so much.

He'd shoved the strange emotions aside while showering for dinner, shaking off, too, the strange flux that had taken him out of himself during their 'wedding ceremony.' The papers they'd signed would never see the light of day. More than an annulment, their 'marriage' would never have happened. He was confident Issy shared the same thoughts on the matter but that, like him, she'd decided to play it out. How long did she think she could do that for?

Come the morning, they would dock at St Lovells and this charade would be over.

For tonight, he would enjoy his time with this dazzling woman and see what tricks she had planned to back out of consummating the marriage that would never be.

CHAPTER EIGHT

To Issy's surprise and relief, the dinner was actually fun. As course after course of the most exquisite food was brought out to them—the chef really had pulled out all the stops to create a feast for them—they slipped into light, impersonal conversation. Neither of them even bothered faking conversation about their future together. They both knew it wouldn't happen. It didn't need to be spelt out. The subjects they did touch on, though, gave her a greater insight into the man she'd believed she knew so well before meeting him, minor things no amount of research on Gianni could have dredged up.

'You don't read?' she asked in astonishment when they moved from music they liked onto books, and he couldn't name a single one he'd enjoyed.

'Not since I left school. The books they forced us to read were too boring and worthy for me to get any enjoyment from.'

'Didn't your parents encourage you?' She thought of how both her parents had helped and encouraged her to read, sparking a love of literature in her that she'd carried all her life.

His features tightened at this. 'My father is a homophobic and misogynistic bully. If he'd seen me reading a book for pleasure he'd have probably assumed I was gay and beat me.'

Shock at this brutal admission came close to making her choke on the raspberry she'd just popped in her mouth.

From the way he grimaced and the deep breath he took, she sensed this was an admission he hadn't intended to make. Swirling the wine in his glass, he tipped it down his throat. 'Sorry,' he said as he refilled both their glasses. 'I didn't mean to lower the mood.'

'That's okay... Did you mean it?'

His gaze was steady. 'I would never lie about something like that. My father is a monster.' The beginnings of a smile formed. 'But I don't want to talk about him on my wedding night so why don't you tell me about the books you enjoy.'

Issy had no idea why the thought of Gianni's father being a monster hurt her chest so much or why she felt something much like a yearning that he'd shut the subject down. It didn't make sense. She knew the bones of his childhood—the whole world did—so why the sudden craving to know more, to have flesh put onto those bones? She knew his mother had left his father when Gianni was a child and that she lived in Milan. She knew his father ran the same family vineyard in Umbria with his brother that the Rossi cousins had been raised in and that Gianni and his cousin were both estranged from their fathers, going so far as to change their surnames when they were eighteen. It was all part of their legend as self-made men who'd risen from nothing to the stratosphere. What more did she need to know?

It frightened her that she *wanted* to know more.

For the first time since they'd entered the dining room, she had to force a smile to her face. 'There's no point in me telling you if you haven't read any of them.'

Gianni stared at her for a beat. There had been a moment when he'd been certain she was going to press him for more information about his father. Instead, she'd chosen to respect his wish to end the subject. He never spoke about his father. He wasn't worth the wasted breath. He rarely thought about him either. He wasn't worth the headspace.

To find himself thinking about both his parents in one day and to actually mention his father, to confide a snippet of his life to Isabelle Seymore of all people, was perplexing, and he rubbed his hand over the thickening stubble of his jawline. What the hell was it about her that made the past feel so much closer than it had in over a decade?

'You've read a lot of books?'

She nodded.

'Don't tell me a party girl like you is a secret bookworm?' he teased.

She put a finger to her lips. 'Secret being the operative word.'

Unable to resist, he snatched at the finger and brought it to his own lips. 'Something tells me you're full of secrets, Signora Rossi.'

Her eyes glittered, and she stroked the finger pressed against his lips across his cheek, whispering, 'And something tells me it won't be long before you discover all of them.'

He captured her hand again and pressed a kiss into the palm. 'I look forward to it.'

The glitter darkened. 'So do I.'

An undercurrent had built, a tension laced with more than the sexual chemistry that kept drawing them so close together. Gianni could almost taste the deception swirling between them, nearing the surface, straining for the moment when their masks—already slipping—could be ripped away and nothing but the truth would be enough to satisfy them.

'What do you say to a game of snooker?' he asked.

'Only if you promise not to thrash me.'

He leaned his face close to hers. 'I never make promises I can't keep.'

Issy chalked her cue, watching as Gianni folded his huge frame to make the break. There was nothing gentle in his stroke. He hit the white ball with an accurate determination that rolled it forcefully along the table and smashed it into the red triangle of balls.

She smiled to herself. He'd played the shot like that for her benefit. Separating the red balls from their triangular cluster made it easier to pot them, not something a serious player—and she could tell from the way he played his shot that he was a serious player—would do if they didn't think their opponent would be easy pickings.

Deciding on and playing her shot quickly, she chided herself when the red ball she'd shot at missed the pocket.

Gianni didn't miss. He potted a red, then followed it by potting the pink, then potted another red. He missed the green by millimetres, switching the game back to Issy.

This time, she took her time, angled the cue carefully and made her shot. The white glanced the red, sending it into a pocket. She followed this with four successful shots, red, green, red, brown, but then, seeing there was no way she could pocket another red from where the white ball was placed, she hit the white softly, so it only brushed against the red, then gently rolled to slip behind the pink. She'd snookered him.

The look he gave her made her feel ten foot tall. Total confounded admiration.

'I thought you didn't play?' he accused, leaning over the table to reach the white.

'I don't remember saying that,' she refuted innocently.

His chin now lined against the cue, he raised an eyebrow at her. 'You implied it.'

Smirking, she shrugged. 'I haven't played for ten years.'

He took his shot. He managed to hit the red but didn't pot it. 'How old are you?'

'You should know that seeing as you're my husband,' she teased. 'I'm twenty-three. My dad had a snooker table. I always wanted to play but I couldn't reach the table so he bought me a child-size one for my seventh birthday and taught me. I upgraded to the full-size one when I was ten.'

'How were you able to see over the top of it?' he teased back.

'I used a stool. Being so small meant the distances looked longer to me but I think that improved my game.'

'Have you actually grown at all since then?'

'Very funny.' The red she was aiming for went straight into the pocket.

'Give me a chance,' he mock-pleaded. 'Go on, make it harder to see over the table. Take your shoes off.'

'They're sandals, you philistine.'

'A philistine?' His expression suddenly changed to serious and he lost the English accent he'd clearly worked so hard to make faultless. 'I do not think it means what you think it means.'

'Inconceivable.'

Their eyes met, identical amazed gazes at the recognition that they were with a fellow *Princess Bride* buff formed, and then they both started laughing. Issy laughed so hard she completely missed her next ball.

Grinning widely, Gianni took his shot and pocketed it, but missed his next one.

'Maybe I *should* take my sandals off if it gives you more of a chance,' she taunted.

His eyes drifted down her body. 'I don't know...' His voice dropped to a murmur as his gaze drifted back up to capture her eyes. 'Those sandals are very sexy.'

And just like that, the heat of awareness Issy had been vaguely dampening by sheer willpower flamed back to life, sending her heart into a pulsing mess at the strength of longing rampaging through her. If Gianni hadn't been standing on the other side of the snooker table her legs might just have propelled themselves to him.

She picked up her glass and took a long drink of her mojito, fully aware the skin on her face blazed with the same intensity as what was happening beneath it, fully aware too that Gianni knew exactly the effect those five little words had had on her.

But he didn't say anything, simply stood there waiting for her to take her turn, his cue in hand, that sensuous, knowing, *sexy* look...damn him...playing on his face.

Damn him!

Damn him too that, in order to stretch across the table and reach the white ball, she had to hitch the skirt of her tight dress up, something she'd done numerous times during their game already but which she'd done automatically, barely even thinking about it. This time, she was painfully aware of the suggestiveness that could be interpreted with the gathering of the silk, painfully aware too of how sensitive her thighs had become as the material rode up them.

Trying her hardest to control her breathing and concentrate, Issy draped herself over the table and aimed the cue.

'The rest of you is pretty damn sexy too,' he said at the exact moment she took her shot. 'Your backside is delectable.'

She misaimed the cue. The white ball scuttled off in the wrong direction, limping to a stop without hitting anything.

That pulled her together sharpish, and she glared at him. 'You said that on purpose to distract me.'

He raised a hefty shoulder. 'And?'

'And?'

He took his position at the table and winked at her. 'And what are you going to do about it?'

God how she hated how much she wanted him. Almost as much as she hated how greatly she was coming to enjoy their time together and how she could veer from amusement to full-blown desire from nothing but a tone in his voice or the raising of an eyebrow.

'I could sing to you,' she suggested, managing to sound reasonably normal in the process. 'People have offered money to stop me doing that before.'

He grinned. 'You can come up with something better than that.' He potted the last of the reds and fixed his stare straight back on her. 'I guarantee if you were to strip that dress off, I'd be unable to take another shot.'

She squeezed her eyes to counter the image that zinged straight into her mind of holding Gianni's gaze and peeling her dress off for his delectation. She had to force her eyes to open again and force her voice to sound blasé. 'I prefer the singing option.'

Chin on cue now lined up for the next shot, he smirked. 'I don't.' The yellow ball potted straight into the pocket.

Knowing she needed to steer them onto safer conversational territory, she asked, 'How come you're so good at this? At snooker,' she hurried to clarify before he could deliberately misinterpret her question and give a suggestive answer.

He took another shot. 'I have a snooker table in my London penthouse and my home in Tuscany. I like to play.'

'That fits in with your playboy image so well.' That's what she needed to remind herself of, she realised. When the force of Gianni's magnetism and personality was strong enough to blur the damage he'd wrought on her family; made it seem distant and faded, she needed to remember the chain of broken hearts he'd left littered around the world.

'I don't have a playboy image.'

'You do! I've looked you up.' About a gazillion times. 'You have your own hashtag. HotRossi.'

'Not started by me.'

'Started by your adoring groupies. You're a playboy who loves to party.'

'It's not a crime for a single man to party and date women.'

'I'm just saying your image doesn't fit a man who must have spent hours at a snooker table to get as good as you at it.'

'Snooker helps my brain relax. It's a good way to unwind in the evenings...' His lips curved in a lopsided smirk and he wiggled his eyebrows. 'When there's no hot woman available to help me relax, of course.'

This time she was able to maintain her composure, serenely saying, 'You're trying to needle me.'

'Am I succeeding?'

'No.'

His knowing grin showed he didn't believe her. 'It would be impossible for me to have such a successful business if I partied every night. I've reached the age where I get hangovers.'

'Oh, no. You poor thing.'

'Thank you for your sympathy.'

'You're welcome.'

'You do realise I've won?'

She looked at the snooker table. While they'd been bantering, Gianni had cleared the table so only the black ball remained. She couldn't beat his score with the value of it.

'Do I get my prize?'

'What prize? You cheated,' she accused.

'No, I didn't.' He placed his cue on the table and stalked to her. 'I was observing. Your bottom really is delectable.'

Heart thumping again, she sidestepped away from him and pulled the triangle for the red balls out of the slot. 'You distracted me. Play again without cheating.'

'You call that a distraction? *Bella*, that is *nothing* on what I could have done.'

Her pelvis practically contracted at the meaning, but she kept her focus. 'I call it cheating, and you're going to play fairly this time. I'll make the break.'

Completely blurring him from her vision, Issy ordered fresh drinks over the intercom then set the table. After chalking her cue, she folded herself to take the first shot but before she could hit the cue, she forgot to keep blurring Gianni and he appeared in her line of sight. He'd removed his polo shirt. His glorious chest was naked.

His eyes gleamed as he noticed that she'd noticed. Raising his drink to her, he said in an innocent tone, 'I was getting hot.'

'Then turn the air-conditioning up.'

'And waste power unnecessarily?' He tutted in disappointment. 'Feel free to remove your own clothes if you find it hot too.'

'Shut up.' Issy gritted her teeth to concentrate and hit the white ball with just enough force for it to reach the triangle of reds without breaking them up.

Gianni stepped to the table, hardly glanced at the balls as he took his shot and smashed them. Two reds dropped into the pockets.

Within ten minutes he'd cleared the table. Other than making the opening break, Issy didn't get a single shot. It was a masterclass in snooker, as good as anything she'd watched on TV as a child.

But she'd hardly paid attention to the shots. Throughout, Gianni kept his focus entirely on the table, not looking at her once. There had been nothing for her to fight against, no sensuous glances, no velvet-delivered innuendoes...

She'd fallen into a trance, mesmerised by the raw grace of the man and the beauty of his masculinity as he'd demolished the table.

By the time he potted the black ball for the last time and, finally, lifted his eyes to her, she couldn't have torn her gaze from him if she'd tried.

A smile slowly ghosted his face. Casually placing his cue on the table, he drained his Scotch and, with the gait and expression of a lion approaching its prey, stalked to her.

His eyes were intent, deadly, his words husky. 'I think that has earned me my prize.'

Her heart filled her chest with thick, heavy beats.

Fight or flight. That's what prey experienced when their senses registered the big cat emerging from the flora. Those semi-seconds of intuition and experience before adrenaline kicked in was the entire difference between life and death. Fight a lethal predator bigger than you and die. Take flight a moment too late and die.

There came a point when every captured prey gave up the fight and welcomed death to release them from the pain.

Gianni had captured her that night in London. She'd arrived at the club having badly underestimated the power of his sexuality and spent every waking moment since battling her own reactions to it.

She couldn't run any more. The will to fight had deserted her.

Submitting didn't mean death. Gianni wouldn't inflict pain on her, only pleasure, and for this one night, she wanted to explore where that pleasure could take them because she knew, with a marrow-deep certainty, that she could live a hundred lives and never feel what she felt for Gianni with anyone else.

Feeling a strange combination of shyness and boldness, Issy took a step towards him. 'What prize?' she whispered.

Gianni's chest swelled before he splayed a hand against her back to draw her flush to him. Her eyes were wide and filled with the desire he caught so often in them, but they were filled with something else too that he'd never seen before, an openness, as if she'd ripped an invisibility cloak away.

He dipped his face to hers. 'You.'

As their mouths fused together, Gianni had the strangest sensation that this was Issy kissing him. Issy, the young woman in the screenshot with the ice cream sundae, not Issy the polished seductress. Whichever Issy it was, he hungered for her with a power that was coming close to taking possession of him, and as her lips and tongue danced against his, the electricity that had flickered and crackled between them the entire day magnified and fired huge jolts through his veins and deep into his loins.

Dragging his fingers down her back, he clasped the bottom he'd spent most of the day fantasising about and gathered the silk of her dress until it was high enough for him to lift her onto the snooker table.

When she opened her eyes the strange sensation hit him

again, and with it the belief that he was looking into the eyes of the real Isabelle for the first time. There was nothing calculated in it. No guile. Just her. Just Issy and her desire for him.

He cupped her cheeks and kissed her so passionately she moaned into his mouth and scraped her fingers over his back. A zipper ran the length of her dress to her bottom and he pinched it and drew it down. Not breaking the lock of their mouths, she shrugged the spaghetti straps off her shoulders so they slipped down her arms and the dress fell to her waist, allowing her naked breasts to crush against his bare skin for the first time. *Dio*, he'd never known bare skin against bare skin could feel so incredible.

Breathing heavily, Gianni broke the kiss so he could gaze into her desire-drugged eyes again and drink in the heightened colour staining her cheeks.

He placed a hand to her chest and gently pressed her back. And then he brushed his hand over a breast that fitted into the palm as if it had been specially made for him. Pressing her back even further, he dipped his head and captured a dusky pink nipple in his mouth.

Issy jolted and gasped at the unexpected shock of pleasure that coursed through her. But it didn't end there, not with Gianni kissing and biting and sucking the overly sensitised skin, moving from breast to breast, flickering his tongue down lower still to nip at her navel, his hands roaming the contours of her body, fingers sliding over silk and flesh, leaving her skin flamed in their wake.

The flames deepened when his mouth found hers again and his hand slid beneath the bunched hem of her dress and grasped the band of her knickers. Thrilling at the hunger of his kisses, greedily devouring him with the same intensity, she gripped Gianni's shoulders and raised her bottom. He yanked the knickers down her thighs. A couple of flicks of her legs and they slipped down her calves to her feet, from where she kicked them off.

His desire when he pulled back to soak up her semi-nakedness, etched in every line of his hooded, heavy stare, overrode any of Issy's shyness at being displayed like this. There was a pained reverence in the look, as if she were the first woman he'd ever seen like this.

Could he see through her skin to the wildly beating heart? Could he see the flames licking her veins and bones?

One pop of a button and tug at a zip and his shorts fell down.

Issy roamed her gaze over him in the same way he'd soaked her up. She could hardly breathe. All her life, she'd thought the female body the more pleasing of the sexes. Gianni Rossi was the only man whose body had ever drawn her eye but for years she'd told herself it was because of her intensive research on him, that the reason she kept going back to pictures of him half-naked holidaying on his yacht was for whichever companion he happened to be with so she could study them in her pursuit of copying their look.

It had always been him. The devil disguised as Apollo. The sexiest man to roam the earth.

But she'd never seen a picture of him fully naked. Just as the pictures of him had never done him justice, seeing him naked was a revelation in itself. Magnificent was too lame a word to describe him. Every part of the devil was beautiful.

'Kiss me,' she whispered. There was something about his kisses that fed her hunger and made her greedy for more. Much more. Greedy for everything.

In a flash their mouths locked back together. Hands dragged heavily over skin, a need to discover and taste pulsing through them both, pulses that turned into throbs when Gianni cupped her sex and pressed his thumb against her swollen nub. Dear heavens, she'd thought it had felt good earlier... That was nothing...nothing.

She rubbed against him, moaning her pleasure into the deepening tangle of tongues.

Gianni could hardly believe how hot and wet Issy was for him. If the cells of the human body could make sound, hers would be crying out their need. He could feel it, taste it, smell it, and, keeping the pressure on the source of her pleasure, slipped a finger inside the sticky heat, his senses thrumming as her moans deepened and she clung even tighter to him.

Panting, she broke the fusion of their mouths and, still rocking into him, almost bit his cheek as she gasped, 'Condoms?'

He could hardly speak. 'In my pocket.'

'Get...' But her words died. Her eyes glazed, her pants shortened and suddenly her neck arched and her mouth opened. No sound came out. It didn't need to. Issy's silent climax shuddered through her, its ripples practically visible, and suddenly the need to take possession and lose himself inside her peaked to the point of desperation.

Only when he was certain that she'd passed her own peak did he gently remove his hand and kiss her. 'Let me get the condom.'

'Do it,' she whispered.

In a flash, he pulled a condom out of his back pocket, ripped the packet with his teeth and sheathed himself. Her hands were reaching for him, and when he stepped between her legs, she clasped the back of his neck.

He guided his erection to her damp opening.

Still breathing heavily, she swallowed and huskily said, 'Be gentle, okay?'

He jerked a nod, gripped a hip and, with anticipation almost too heavy to bear, was about to press himself inside her sticky heat when it flashed in his mind: the question *why* she would ask him to be gentle. 'Is this your first time?' He had to drag the words out.

Her grip tightened on his neck and she pushed back, encouraging him to take possession. His arousal throbbed so hard it burned through every part of him. 'Yes,' she breathed.

How desperately he wanted to thrust himself inside her. It was a desperation he'd never felt before. Not like this.

She was a virgin.

'It's okay,' she said raggedly, bringing her mouth to his and scraping the pads of her fingers over the bristles on the back of his neck. 'You won't hurt me.'

Her simple declaration landed like a punch to his solar plexus.

His confession came from nowhere. 'I know who you are.'

CHAPTER NINE

Issy was so consumed with the incredible feelings building on the tendrils of her climax and heightened anticipation for Gianni to take that final step and take possession of her that his words simply bounced like music through her head.

She wanted to experience everything, feel everything, lose herself in the hedonism of Gianni's touch...

But he was no longer moving. The fusion that would take her to heaven had stopped before it had properly started.

'Is something wrong?' she whispered, brushing her lips over his, trying to discern why his eyes were squeezed so tightly shut and his jaw clenched.

He breathed heavily through his nose before his eyes opened. His throat moved before he hoarsely repeated, 'I know who you are.'

Understanding seeped slowly into her dazed brain, and she had to blink a number of times to help clear it. 'You know...?'

'I know you're Thomas Seymore's daughter.'

But still her brain refused to fully comprehend. His words made no sense... Not until ice began to creep its way up her spine and through her chest, and the breaths she'd struggled to find in the throes of passion became lodged in her throat and lungs.

The dazedness in her head melted and swam, white lights

flickering, the ice in her body spreading until comprehension hit her fully and the breath exploded out of her. Slamming her fists against his chest, Issy pulled her thighs up and together, then twisted to one side and dropped off the table. Her feet slammed onto the floor, but she'd forgotten she was still wearing the stupidly high sandals and her ankle buckled at the impact, making her fall.

In an instant he was at her side, concern written all over his face.

Frantically trying to cover her modesty with the dress that until moments ago had been bunched around her waist, she huddled into herself. 'Get away from me.'

'Issy…'

She wanted to spit in his face. 'I said get away from me. Get out. Get out now.'

'Issy, please…'

'Get out!' she screamed, losing all control of herself. 'Get out, get out, get *out*!'

His broad shoulders rose and his chin lifted. Tension lined his face and made his body appear carved from stone.

She couldn't bear to look at him a moment longer and buried her face in her knees. She thought she might be sick.

As much as she tried to tune him out, she was acutely aware of movement around her and stiffened when a breeze feathered over her bowed head and the slightest pressure brushed against her hair.

She sensed rather than heard Gianni leave the games room. The emptiness he left in his wake confirmed he'd gone.

Gianni splashed cold water on his face and tried to regulate his breathing. Guilt pulsed strongly inside him.

Gripping tightly to the sink, he dragged air into his lungs

and tried to banish the image of Issy, humiliated and vulnerable, huddled on the floor.

The game they'd been playing had come to its conclusion but he'd been incapable of playing the final round.

He knew he'd done nothing wrong. *He* was the innocent party in all this. Issy had been playing him long before their first encounter, a meeting *she'd* engineered. Everything that had followed had been by her design. Everything. She'd played herself off as a socialite party girl and seduced him with her eyes and words. She'd even blagged his own yacht as a prop for her game. All he'd done was play along. Even when he'd learned her true identity and discovered she'd set all this up as part of a plan to destroy him and his cousin, the worst he'd done was hide her phone.

Yes. He was the innocent party in all this so why he should have had that awful paralysis of guilt when they were finally acting on the desire that had sparked at their very first meeting was inexplicable. And why he should still feel that guilt lying so heavily inside him was doubly so.

Issy peeked out of her cabin's curtains. The sun was rising, the last remaining stars twinkling before daylight extinguished them. The *Palazzo delle Feste* was already cutting its way through the Caribbean Sea.

She took a deep breath and put an internal call—the only calls her cabin phone could make—through to the captain.

By the time the call ended, despair had her in its grip.

The marriage papers were already lodged with the ministry.

Gianni showered and dressed. He'd spent the night in his own cabin. He'd been looking forward to spending his first night in it—sleeping in an opulent room with all the amenities a man could need, knowing how hard he'd worked for it and that no one could take it from him was a thrill that never grew old—but he'd been unable to settle. Sleep had been elusive. Every time he closed his eyes, it was Issy he saw, huddled on the floor, humiliated and vulnerable.

He'd put the order through to set sail for St Lovells before the sun had even risen and asked for the marriage papers to be destroyed. The captain had been able to comply with the first request. It was the second that was a problem. Believing the happy couple wanted the papers lodged as soon as possible, the captain had paid—well, Gianni had paid—for a member of the ministry to take a speedboat to the *Palazzo delle Feste* and collect the documents. Working back through the time line, Gianni estimated the official had arrived when he and Issy had been in the games room. All the crew had been under his strict instructions not to enter or disturb them unless specifically asked. Worse still, the bribed official had already lodged the papers. To disentangle them from their joke of marriage would now take an annulment.

That would teach him to give someone else power to spend his own money without limits, he thought wearily.

The marriage disentanglement was something that could wait. For now, it was Issy at the forefront of his mind. He knew he shouldn't care about her state of mind but that didn't stop his chest sharpening every time her image flashed in his head. Seeing as that was every other second, his chest felt like it had an ice pick jammed in it.

He found her on the sundeck, dressed in a long-sleeved sheer white kaftan eating her breakfast. She looked different, her hair tied in a loose ponytail, not a scrap of make-up on her face. She looked younger.

Breathing deeply to quell the tempest raging in his stomach, Gianni put his phone on the table and took the seat across from her. She didn't look at him, concentrating on the plate of eggs on toast with sides of bacon and mushrooms she was steadily making her way through, pausing only to pour herself more coffee from the cafetière. She added cream from the jug then a heaped spoonful of sugar, stirred vigorously, took a sip and then picked her cutlery back up and continued to eat.

Helping himself to coffee and a selection of the fruit, yogurt and pastries also laid out on the table but untouched by Issy, he had to force the food down his throat and into his stomach. He had no appetite.

'How long are you going to ignore me for?' he asked when her plate was empty and he could no longer tolerate the silence.

She responded by helping herself to a chocolate croissant and pretending not to hear him.

'I appreciate you are angry with me but you only have yourself to blame. You hustled me, Issy. You brought me here to distract me so your sister could set a bomb off in my company.'

That made her still. For a moment he thought she would speak but the moment passed when she took another bite of her croissant.

'I know this will disappoint you but your plans have been thwarted. I warned my cousin as soon as I discovered what the two of you were up to.'

There was the slightest flicker on the face that still refused to look at him.

'I knew in London that you were a hustler,' he continued conversationally. 'So I cloned your phone. Once I realised what you and your sister were up to, I had your phone locked away in my cabin. I will return it to you when this is all over and there is no longer danger in allowing you to communicate with Amelia.'

She pushed her chair back from the table and got to her feet. Still not even acknowledging his presence, she plucked an apple from the fruit platter and stepped away.

A flash of anger scalded him. 'I suppose I shouldn't be surprised at your silence. Your father had little to say for himself either when Alessandro and I confronted him with his corruption.'

For the beat of a moment her foot hovered in mid-air before she spun around and, ponytail swishing, stormed back to the table and grabbed hold of Gianni's phone. Moving too quickly for him to react, she raced to the railing and hurled it overboard.

Open-mouthed, hardly able to credit what she'd just done, Gianni watched Issy stroll back inside without once turning back to look at him.

Fury like she'd never known raged through Issy as she stormed over to the first member of the crew she came across. Realising her anger must make her look like a harpy, she took a deep breath before saying, 'Excuse me, but can I borrow your phone please? I still can't find mine.'

Leanne, probably even younger than Issy, bit her lip and dropped her stare.

Confused at her reaction, Issy put a hand to Leanne's arm. 'Are you okay? I'll pay for any roaming fees.'

Leanne shook her head. 'I can't. It's more than my job's worth.'

'What, lending me your phone? What do you mean?'

'We've all been ordered not to lend you our phones if you ask,' she mumbled.

'Ordered by who?' But she knew. Who else could it be?

'Mr Rossi.'

Issy gritted her teeth and filled her lungs to stop herself biting poor Leanne's head off. 'Look, Leanne, it doesn't matter what orders Gianni has given you. This is *my* charter. Please, let me use your phone, just for five minutes. Please.'

But the young woman only shook her head. 'This is your charter, but he's my boss.'

That swimming feeling in her head she'd experienced in the games room when she'd finally comprehended that Gianni knew exactly who she was started up again. She was almost afraid to say, 'Your boss? How?'

Eyes laden with sympathy met hers. 'Because this is his yacht.'

Issy's cabin phone rang. She glared at it. She'd spent the last hour locked away in here glaring at it, hating it for its refusal to dial out of the yacht. It was taking everything she had to maintain her fury because she knew the minute it started leaching out of her, terror for her sister was going to grab her.

Scrambling across the bed she'd been glaring at the phone from, she lifted the receiver and snapped, 'Yes?'

'Miss Seymore?'

Recognising the captain's voice, she closed her eyes and strove for a gentler tone. Much as she wanted to scream and shout at him, the captain had only been obeying orders from his real boss. 'Yes, Captain Caville. What can I do for you?'

'I thought you should know we'll be docking in twenty minutes.'

'Where?'

'St Lovells.'

'Is that an island?'

'Yes.'

'I've never heard of it...but thank you for letting me know.'

'You're welcome.' He hesitated before adding, 'My apologies again for the confusion about the wedding papers.'

But no apology for leading her on and letting her believe she'd chartered the *Palazzo delle Feste* for real when all the time he was working under Gianni's orders.

The entire crew worked for Gianni. The yacht belonged to Gianni. He'd played her like a puppet-master with sole control of the strings.

Oh, why hadn't she listened to her gut when David had shown her the *Palazzo delle Feste*? On some basic level that went beyond fear of not being able to pull off Silicon Valley or oligarch rich, she'd known the yacht was too much for what she needed. She'd known the charter was worth far too much for David to hand it over for free.

Desperation had made her ignore her gut. The window for her and Amelia to enact their revenge would only stay open for a strictly limited time and, once closed, the opportunity would likely never come again.

She'd ruined everything.

Putting the receiver back in its cradle, Issy covered her face. She mustn't cry. Not yet. Just as she wouldn't allow herself to think of how deeply wounded...broken... Gianni had left her last night. The tears would have to wait. The only thing she could allow herself to focus on was escaping Gianni. Once she'd accomplished that, she'd find a way to contact Amelia, not to warn her—she knew in her heart it was too late for that—but to make sure she was okay. That she was safe.

Both Rossi cousins were ruthless but it was Alessandro Issy found the most frightening. Unlike his cousin who the press adored, Alessandro stayed firmly out of the spotlight and so there were very few pictures of him online. Those there were showed a handsome but darkly menacing-looking man, the kind you crossed at your peril. His face perfectly matched the image Issy had conjured for him all those years ago when he and Gianni had walked out of their family home with all the swagger of a couple of gangsters who'd put a bullet in their mortal enemy. As far as Issy was concerned, they might as well have done. At least it would have spared her father a year of torment.

When she'd first seen a picture of Gianni, it had taken her a while to compute that the handsome man smiling so gregariously at the camera could be the same man who'd done and said such cruel things to her father. She'd had no such issue with Alessandro.

For all that, she'd thought Amelia was safe working for the Rossi cousins. Rossi Industries employed a hundred thousand people. Of course, only a fraction of them worked at The Ruby, the moniker given due to the pink tinge of the magnificent skyscraper the Rossi cousins had created in the heart of London as their head office, but there was safety in numbers.

Issy's negligence had put her sister in danger. She must have been negligent and overlooked something, or how could Gianni have got the measure of her so quickly?

Peering out of her cabin window, her spirits lifted the tiniest of fractions to see the small island they were sailing to. Very small. Too small for an airport but if it was big enough to dock a yacht of this size then that had to be a good thing. Her spirits lifted a fraction more to catch glimpses of pretty dwellings amongst the thick palms and verdant topography. Human life. Hopefully there would be an airfield with small charter planes. If not, there would be boats. She had emergency cash for this exact purpose. She'd known from the start that when her job was done, she'd need to make a quick escape.

It killed her to know the job would never be done. She'd blown it.

She waited until the yacht docked before slipping her feet into her rose-pink flips-flops—she would never wear heels again—and unlocked her cabin door. Satisfied the corridor was empty, she wheeled her suitcase down it. If she could make it to the metal stairs that would be unfolded for them onto the jetty without bumping into Gianni, there was a good chance she'd be able to reach safety without any further interaction with him.

The sun was high when she stepped out onto the deck, a warm breeze immediately blowing her hair around her face. She wished she'd kept her hair tied back in the ponytail, wished too that hadn't chucked her shades in her suitcase. She didn't want to waste time searching for them, not when escape was so close.

Members of the crew stood at the top of the stairs. Part of her wanted to snarl at them like a wounded cat, but she knew that impulse was unfair. Not only was Gianni their boss but his magnetism was such that even she'd come close to falling under his spell, so she fixed a smile to her face and thanked them for taking such good care of her.

About to take the first step on the stairs, a shift in the atmosphere made her hesitate. Despite the promise she'd made to herself to just leave and not look back, she turned her head before she could stop herself.

Gianni had appeared.

The punch to her heart was even stronger than the punch that had come close to flooring her when he'd joined her for breakfast.

In three long strides he was at her side and enveloping

her in a fresh cloud of his gorgeous cologne. 'Let me take that for you,' he said. Before she had time to react he'd lifted the suitcase from her hand and set off down the steps and onto the jetty.

Knowing that to open her mouth and speak would unleash the hellfire burning inside her, Issy had no choice but to follow him.

He walked purposefully, not looking back. The length and speed of his stride meant she had no chance of keeping up, so she set off at her own pace after him. If he refused to give the suitcase back then so be it. She had a bum-bag around her waist with her passport, bank cards and all her cash in it.

As she walked the long jetty, she tried to take in her surroundings. The harbour was small, only a handful of gleaming yachts moored. There were a few impossibly glamorous people in teeny bikinis and swim shorts milling around, all admiring the superyacht and no doubt trying to work out who the disembarking passengers were.

Issy tried so hard to take everything in but her eyes kept betraying her, seeking Gianni instead of seeking possible routes off this beautiful and clearly exclusive island.

He'd changed out of the familiar polo shirt and canvas shorts into a short-sleeved black shirt untucked over smart tan shorts that landed mid-thigh and a pair of brown deck shoes. He might have worn them at breakfast but she couldn't remember. She'd been too intent on comfort eating and keeping herself together to even dare look at him. Then, as now, she couldn't decipher the mountain of emotions thrashing through her. Too many. Too frightening to contemplate.

Seeing the fresh clothes he wore only heaped more humiliation on her. Gianni had embarked the *Palazzo delle Feste* with nothing but the clothes on his back and the items contained in his shorts' deep pockets. He must have had a stash of clothes locked away in the master cabin she'd been forbidden, by the owner, from entering. Forbidden by Gianni.

How she wished her heart didn't make such ripples to see the muscles of his calves tighten as he walked and the bunching of the muscles across his back.

And, when Gianni reached the end of the jetty and turned his gaze on her as he waited for her to join him, how she wished the burning ache he'd ignited inside her would douse itself to ash.

For the first time since she'd huddled on the floor of the games room, she was helpless to stop herself from meeting his eye. What she found in his glittering stare only compounded the ripples in her heart, a mirror of the tortured emotions racking her. For one mad moment, a longing ripped through her, for Gianni to cup her face in his hands and press his firm lips to hers and…

It all happened so quickly that there was no time for her to react. A man she hadn't noticed hovering beside Gianni grabbed hold of her suitcase at the exact same moment Gianni swept her into his arms and deposited her in the back of a black four-by-four car she'd also failed to notice. He quickly folded himself in beside her. The door closed.

'What are you doing?' Issy squealed, scurrying to the other door and immediately tugging on the handle. Panic gripped her harder when she found it locked. 'Let me out!'

'Soon.' He tapped on the dark window dividing them from the front of the car.

'Let me out, *now*!' The car started moving. Throwing herself forwards, Issy banged on the dividing window. 'Stop the car!'

'They won't stop.'

She banged again, harder. The glass must be reinforced otherwise her fist would probably have smashed through it.

'We're going to my complex. We'll be there in a few minutes.'

She glared at him and snarled, 'I'm not going anywhere with you.'

He sighed as if already weary of her anger and rubbed his hand over his ever-thickening stubble. 'The travel of this car says differently.'

'If you don't stop this car and let me out this minute I'll report you for kidnap.'

'Any report will have to wait until you leave St Lovells. I'm afraid you will stay here with me until I have word from my cousin that any damage you and your sister have caused our business has been contained and mitigated.'

'You can't do that!'

'I can and I will. It's not for ever, and I give you my word no harm will come to you.'

'As if I'd believe a single word that came out of your mouth,' she spat.

'That, I believe, is a classic example of a pot calling a kettle black.'

The look Issy gave him reminded Gianni of a wildcat that once made the mistake of hanging around his childhood farmhouse. This was before his mother left so he'd been nine at the most, but he remembered trying to befriend it and having a set of claws swipe his face in response. His bleeding face hadn't stopped him screaming and begging his father not to drown it. His father had proceeded to drop the cat in the well and then smack Gianni so hard around the back of his head that he'd actually seen the stars beloved of cartoon characters.

'You *can't* keep me here against my will. There are laws, you know.'

He almost felt sorry for her. '*Bella*, I *can* keep you here. I can keep you here because this island belongs to me and there is no way for you to leave without my permission.'

CHAPTER TEN

GIANNI HAD EXPOSED Issy for the conniving charlatan hellbent on his destruction that she was, so why the emotions that passed like a reel over her face made his stomach clench made no sense. The tenderness that kept slamming into him, the longing to gather her tightly and swear on all that was holy that he would never let harm come to her...it could only be caused by sleep deprivation. He should never have spent those insomniac hours looking through the data he'd cloned from her phone. So few contacts. So few photos. So few signs that this young woman had any form of a life that could be called sociable.

He'd read the messages between her and her sister hoping to learn more about their plans but there had been little more to be gleaned, and in any case it was the photos he kept coming back to. Every woman Gianni had dated catalogued every aspect of her life with selfies. He'd got so used to it that he barely even noticed their phones being permanently turned towards themselves. Issy had thirty-three photos stored on her phone. The ice cream sundae screenshot was the oldest. A handful of others were of her sister, who looked no different to the woman he'd last seen at The Ruby barely a week ago.

The first signs of Issy's weight loss began around the time Amelia started work at Rossi Industries, bookmarked in a series of photos of her smiling brightly with various equally smiley children. Her hair was that beautiful deep chestnut in every picture so he guessed she must have dyed it for their first meeting. So intent had he been on studying Issy and gauging from the timestamps that it had taken her four months to reach the size she still maintained that it was a while before he noticed all the photos were taken in a hospital and that many of the children captured had little or no hair.

'You own this island?' she whispered in horror, backing herself against the door on her side.

'Don't worry, your research skills didn't let you down.' Why he should want to reassure her on this aspect was anyone's guess. 'I brought St Lovells two years ago. I got all involved in the sale to sign a non-disclosure agreement to keep my name secret from the press—I know I can't keep it secret for ever, but I hope to enjoy it for a short while in peace. Your research skills didn't let you down with the *Palazzo delle Feste* either. The company I employed to build it also signed an NDA for the same reasons. It doesn't matter if they discover it's mine now—I've had anti-paparazzi technology embedded into it.'

'Since when has being in the press bothered you?'

He shrugged. 'The press are like the hangovers I've been getting since I turned thirty—wearisome.'

'Maybe you shouldn't court them then,' she suggested tartly.

'I don't court them, I engage with them, and always for business reasons. Believe me, I have never invited the paparazzi to send a drone over my yacht to take photos of me.'

'No, that would be your girlfriends.'

'My lovers,' he corrected. 'Girlfriend implies a form of permanence.'

Something spasmed across her face at his mention of the word lover. 'Don't worry, no woman would ever be stupid enough to date you thinking it could lead to for ever.'

But Issy knew more than a few of his lovers—hateful, hateful word—would have entered a relationship with him with their eyes wide open only to be dazzled and then blinded by the light he exuded. She'd had years to prepare and protect herself against his sexual magnetism but the reality of Gianni in the flesh had penetrated the thick stone wall she'd built.

'I should hope not,' he murmured, then looked outside the window. 'This island is the perfect sanctuary. There's tourist development on one side but it's limited. I've taken the south side for my personal use. There is no docking without permission. Any journalist stupid enough to send a drone over the island can expect to have it shot down.'

'And any kidnap victim can expect to receive zero help.'

'You will have half the island to explore and do as you wish in.'

'Great, does that mean I can swim to the nearest island?'

He pulled a face. 'If you like but I wouldn't rate your chances. Even the strongest long-distance swimmer would find it a challenge swimming forty kilometres without support.'

'You can't do this, Gianni. You know you can't.'

'How many times do I have to tell you that I can? And, please, stop with the outrage. What the hell did you think would happen if I found out what you were up to? You're a clever woman—you must have imagined the scenario.'

Feeling her temper rising, Issy closed her eyes and took a deep breath. 'Where's my sister?'

'In Italy with Alessandro.'

'Voluntarily?'

'I have no idea.'

'It can't be voluntary. She'd never go anywhere alone with that beast.'

His gaze swiftly darkened. 'Do not speak of my cousin in that way.'

'Or what? You'll hit me?'

He blinked as if surprised she would even suggest such a thing. 'Never.'

'Then what? Your cousin is a monster and you are too, and I want proof my sister is safe.'

'I would give you proof if you hadn't thrown my phone into the sea.'

'Give me my phone back then so I can call her.'

'No.'

'*Please*, Gianni. Please. Keep me locked in a dark basement with spiders if you must but please, let me call my sister. *Please.*'

It was the distress on her face that made Gianni come within a whisker of granting her request. When a solitary teardrop rolled down her cheek he had to clench his fist to stop from reaching into his back pocket for her phone.

'*Bella*, listen to me,' he said gently. 'Your sister is safe, I swear it. Alessandro is not the monster you believe him to be. He would never harm a hair on her head.'

Chin wobbling, her teeth grazed her bottom lip. 'You expect me to believe you?'

He brushed a finger across her cheek and gave a rueful smile. 'I expect nothing, but on this I want you to put your trust in me and believe me when I say Amelia is safe and no harm will come to her.'

He could not fathom why, after staring intently into his

eyes for so long it felt as if she'd delved into a lifetime of his memories, her soft nod and the loosening of her taut frame as she whispered, 'Okay,' should make his chest fill so strongly.

She must be mad. Issy knew that, gazing out of the window but with her thoughts too full to see. Trusting *him*? Trusting the devil? And it wasn't because she had no choice in the matter, it was a trust that came from her heart, a relief that spread through her and eased the tightness in her lungs. It was a trust she felt guilty for having, almost as guilty as she felt when she remembered how close she'd come to giving her virginity to the devil. If Gianni hadn't confessed to knowing who she was, she would have let him make love to her, and gladly. That he'd obviously had a fit of guilt himself to make such a confession at such a time should not mean anything. He'd led her on to that point. Every word he'd said had been a lie.

But every word you've said has been a lie too…

That's different, she argued with herself. Gianni was a corrupt…she almost called him a monster but for some stupid reason her brain recoiled from allowing her to think it. But he was definitely corrupt! He was the corrupt bastard who'd stolen her father's business and destroyed her life. He deserved everything she and Amelia had been planning for him.

Are you sure about that…?

Shut up! she shouted to her stupid brain. Of course she was sure! Amelia had discovered proof of their corruption and her sister wouldn't lie.

But why did you refuse to go ahead with the plan without proof?

Because I needed to be certain we were doing the right thing! They both had been! They had agreed from the off that they wouldn't go ahead without proof that it wasn't only their father the Rossi cousins had destroyed!

Why was she having this argument with herself again? Before meeting Gianni, as Amelia's side of the plan had been gaining speed, Issy had put her fresh insistence that Amelia find proof of corruption down to cold feet. Secret doubts had gathered, and she'd become increasingly needful of something concrete and physical to throw at the Rossi cousins if it ever came to it, a certainty that this wasn't just the vengeance of two adolescent girls who'd probably been blind to their father's faults.

It was working at the hospital, she was sure, that had put those doubts about her father in her head, and she hated herself for them, would never admit to Amelia that they even existed.

Working on the children's ward meant Issy spent a lot of time with parents whose precious children hovered between life and death. Those parents were fallible. Human. But the children never saw them like that. Their children trusted them implicitly. If Mummy or Daddy said they were going to get better then they unfailingly believed them, even if that assurance was a lie. Not one parent lied out of callousness but because they couldn't bear to deal with the consequences of the truth, both to their child and to themselves.

'We're here.'

Issy blinked herself out of her reverie and looked at her watch. Only ten minutes had passed since Gianni had kidnapped her into the back of his car and she hadn't paid any attention to her surroundings.

They'd stopped at an electric gate with a guarded security box built into a high stone wall that ran as far as the eye could see either side. The narrow road they'd taken continued on the other side of the of gate, surrounded by thick, tropical foliage. As they travelled it she tried not to marvel at the beauty surrounding them but when they emerged through it and the stunning vista revealed itself, she was unable to stop the gasp that escaped her lips.

A huge cove with the clearest turquoise water she'd ever seen lapped onto the cleanest, whitest sand she'd ever seen. The rays from the sun high above them made the water and sand sparkle like a billion tiny jewels had been scattered over it. Virtually hidden amongst the palm trees lining the beach was a handful of thatched roofed chalets. The central one, set back from the other four and easily the size of them all combined, rose like a Tibetan monastery.

It was the most stunning sight she'd seen in her life, beautiful enough to make her heart twist and then pump with a sigh.

The driver parked in a sheltered garage hidden from the naked eye.

'Let me show you around,' Gianni said quietly.

Issy closed her eyes before following him out of the car.

Close-up, the complex was even more stunning than it had been from a distance.

'This is the first time I've come here since the work was completed,' he told her as they neared the chalets, each larger and set further apart from the others than she'd originally thought. Reaching the first, she realised each chalet was set in its own private landscape.

'My original intention for this holiday was to spend a week sailing on the *Palazzo delle Feste* and the second week here,' he added when she made no response.

'You've spent an enormous amount of money on something you'll only use for two weeks of the year,' she observed as he guided her past a swimming pool that looked as if it were naturally created. Palms offered natural shade on one side of it, the other a sunbather's paradise.

'I'm planning for the future.'

'Oh?'

They'd reached the grounds of the second chalet. Leading her up the path to reach it, he explained, 'I work an average of eighty-hour weeks. I've worked those kind of hours since I was a kid. At some point in the future I will want to take my foot off the brake.'

'My heart's bleeding. Still, it's your money. You can spend it how you want.'

'You're too kind.'

'I know... Although I do wonder how you can be so free with it knowing everything you have came from stealing from my father.'

'We didn't steal from your father,' he bit back.

'Yes, you did.' She wanted to glare at him but her face wouldn't cooperate, the swell of emotions rising through her made her chin wobble and her voice tremble. 'I was there, Gianni. You invited yourself into our home and took everything we had from us. You ripped the business my father had spent his life building away from him and belittled and humiliated him. You didn't just steal his business—*you destroyed everything.*'

The darkness of his stare almost made her quail. When he finally spoke, there was an ice in his tone she'd never heard before. 'Your father stole from *us*. He sold us land unfit for development and bribed surveyors and officials to cover it up. It was our first business deal and we'd worked our backsides off from the age of twelve to pay for it *and* took a loan to make up the shortfall. Thanks to your father, we were left with crippling repayment charges for land that was worthless. It took us years of working every hour God sent to make those repayments and build a nest with which to start again, and the day we took control of your father's business and kicked him into the long grass remains the best day of my life. He deserved everything, had had it coming for years, not just for how he treated us but all the other businesses and individuals he'd ripped off over the years.' He threw the chalet door open. 'This is for your personal use. Do as you please.'

And with that, he strode back down the path, tension practically vibrating from his taut gait.

Gianni was too angry to appreciate anything about the sprawling lodge he one day intended to spend half of each year living in. He toured it fighting to stop himself from snarling at the housekeeper, who must have spent hours making everything shine so brightly and kept giving him anxious looks as if afraid he was about to explode.

It took a lot to make him lose his temper. His father was a squat bundle of aggression who used his fists as weapons and his tongue as a whip. Gianni had lived with him for eighteen years, but that aggression had neither been inherited nor rubbed off on him. If it had, he would have fought it with every fibre of his being. That didn't mean he disliked or avoided confrontation, just that the anger that could make a person's face go red and voice rise and words—often regretted after—splutter from his mouth rarely worked its way through him.

Issy's accusation that he'd stolen her father's business had slashed open a wound that had been sealed a decade ago when he and Alessandro had ousted him. It had taken every ounce of control to stop his voice from rising and to stop himself leaning right into Issy's face to shout his home truths and rip the blinkers from her eyes.

There had been no stealing. If Thomas Seymore had run his business legitimately they would never have been able to take it from him. They would never have needed to.

It had been the contempt in her stare while she'd thrown the accusation at him that had bit more than her words. Contempt laced with pain. Biting more than that had been the absolute certainty that she believed it. That Isabelle Seymore believed him a thief, that she believed him *capable* of being a thief. And corrupt. Mustn't forget that. He hoped like hell Alessandro had got to the bottom of the slanderous proof of corruption Amelia had messaged Issy about.

Alone in his master suite, he sat on the bed and rubbed his temples.

It shouldn't matter what Issy thought of him. It shouldn't matter that she hated him. He had no business feeling sick to the pit of his stomach that taking the business from Thomas Seymore had affected his youngest daughter so greatly. That was on Seymore. He was the father. It had been his duty to protect his children.

Gianni grunted a morose laugh and fell back. Spreading his arms out over the mattress, he gazed up at the ceiling. Fathers were supposed to protect their children. Mothers were too. The only person Gianni and his mother had needed protecting from was his father, and then his mother had run away and left him to take the blows and bullying alone.

Issy was refusing to leave her cabin. She'd asked the staff to provide her with food she could cook for herself and then locked the door. All this had been reported to Gianni, who was glad of it. In the short space of time that he'd known Isabelle Seymore she'd managed to get under his skin and dredge up memories of a past he preferred not to remember in any detail.

The tourist part of St Lovells was an exclusive resort he'd had built when he bought the island. Already it had gained a reputation as the ultimate luxury retreat for wealthy young things looking for a good time. Gianni was on his one full holiday of the year, the break he took annually to recharge his batteries and he was damned if he was going to let Issy's sulking prevent him from enjoying himself, not when it was her connivance that had stopped him making the usual plans in the Caribbean. On a normal holiday, he would hook up with a group of friends who spent their summers bumming around the Caribbean, invite along his latest lover to join them and generally have a great time doing nothing but enjoy himself for fourteen days.

He'd had a good night's sleep and now he was ready to enjoy himself and party. Issy could stay in her cabin and sulk for the duration of their stay here if she so wished but he was not going to let it stop him having fun.

The number of visitors was kept strictly limited, not as a means of keeping people out but as a means of preserving the island's natural beauty. One thing he'd learned in his career as a property developer was that there was always a trade-off when making a development between what humans needed and what the planet's other inhabitants needed. He much preferred developing on sites that had already been in use or on land that was ecologically worthless. The land they'd bought off Thomas Seymore was in the latter category, although just how worthless had been kept hidden from them until it was too late to do anything about it. The land Gianni's father and uncle owned containing the vineyards Gianni and his cousin had been forced to toil on throughout their childhood was heading the same way. Their fathers were ravaging the land, literally running their business into the ground.

When Gianni bought St Lovells he'd had a clear idea of how it would be developed: minimally. The work on both the tourist part and his private complex had been completed with ninety-five percent of the island left untouched. It was a tropical paradise alive with noisy, colourful wildlife, and as he took a golf buggy—his four-by-four was the only full-size motor vehicle allowed on the island—to the tourist part on his second day there, the darkness of his mood lifted.

One day, he would force his cousin to visit. Alessandro never took time off. The man was a machine. It still amazed him how two boys who were born only months apart, shared so much of the same DNA and had been raised like brothers could be so different and yet remain so close. Gianni would take a bullet for his cousin and he knew Alessandro would do the same for him.

He suspected Issy's relationship with her sister was similar. He didn't know Amelia well but knew she was a different kind of personality to her sister, more focused and analytical, more introverted. Issy had tried to hide her real self beneath the fake, polished exterior she'd projected to entrap him and portray herself as someone completely different to who she was, but he'd caught enough glimpses of the real Issy and studied enough of her photos and messages to know she was a smiley, kind, good person.

He stopped the buggy and rested his head back. Closing his eyes, he took a long breath. Issy had dedicated many years of her life to working against him, building a plan to ensnare him into a distraction so her sister could bring down his company. Good, kind people did not behave in that way. Just because she was a nurse who worked with sick children did not make her an angel.

Snapping his eyes back open, he continued his drive to the tourist resort.

The main resort pool was edged with beautiful people sunbathing and drinking cocktails. He rubbed his growing beard, fixed a grin to his face, and set off to join them.

The beach party went on until the early hours. Having had too much to drink to safely drive, Gianni got one of the resort staff to drive him back to his complex. Needing air to clear his head, he walked from the security gate and reflected on what a great day it had been. As he'd expected, he was already acquainted with a number of the vacationers: a supermodel whose best friend he'd once had a fling with and her latest beau, a genius app creator who frequented many of the same clubs and bars as him in London. They'd greeted him like an old friend and quickly introduced him to the rest of the party they were vacationing with, bright shiny, rich and beautiful twenty-somethings. One of them had been an American television actress he'd vaguely recognised, a tall, slender blonde with come-to-bed eyes she'd kept firmly fixed on him. She was exactly Gianni's type and he'd flirted with her for hours before realising his heart wasn't in it and that she didn't do anything for him. When she'd whispered in his ear on the beach about slipping away to her chalet, he'd graciously turned her down and called it a night.

He was still mulling over what it was about the actress he'd failed to respond to considering she ticked every box he wanted in a lover when he reached Issy's cabin. One of the lights was on. His heart turned over then rose up his throat, and he had to tread his feet firmly to stop them taking the path to her door.

CHAPTER ELEVEN

THE KITCHEN IN Issy's chalet was, in comparison with the rest of the place, tiny. Compared to the kitchen she shared with Amelia, it was humungous. Obviously installed with no expectation the occupier would ever use it—the staff had been astounded that she wanted to cook for herself, and had kept reiterating that there were world-class chefs on site who could whip up anything she desired—it nonetheless contained everything she needed.

Issy loved cooking. There were certain aromas, like freshly baked cakes and bread, that never failed to transport her back to a time when her family had been whole and happy. So far that day, she'd baked a lemon drizzle cake and made herself an Italian sausage pasta dish laden with parmesan. Comfort food. Instead of soothing her though, the aromas twisted her stomach to the extent that her plan to demolish the lot was foiled. It had been the same the day before, when she'd made profiteroles laden with whipped cream and chocolate and only managed to eat two of them.

If she was to believe Gianni's twisted accusation against her father then that meant the happy memories she relied on to lift her spirits and make her believe that good times could once again come for her and Amelia and maybe even their mother were built on a lie. She couldn't believe her father had been corrupt. She just couldn't. Until the day the Rossi cousins had barged into their home and destroyed their lives, her father had been a kind and loving man who'd lavished all the love and time he could spare on his family. Would a corrupt man cut short a business meeting so he could watch his six-year-old daughter perform the challenging role of a snowflake in a ballet recital? Would a corrupt man make every effort to be home by his daughters' bedtimes each night so he could read to them?

And would her mother, a once fun-loving, sweet, kind, joyful woman marry a corrupt man? Absolutely not.

Gianni was lying to her. He had to be. Probably because he didn't want to have to confront the damage *his* thievery and corruption had caused, and the more she thought this, the greater her outrage grew. How dare he twist things to make her father the bad guy?

There was a knock on her cabin's front door.

Crossing the airy living area adorned with the most exquisite furniture to the door, she guardedly asked, 'Who is it?'

'Me.'

She pressed a hand to her chest to stop her suddenly thrashing heart from bursting out. 'Are you here to set me free?'

'You are free, *bella*. You can go wherever you like in the complex.'

'Am I free to leave the complex?'

'No.'

'Then go away.'

'You can't spend all your time in here. It's not good for you.'

'If I was to leave this chalet I guarantee it wouldn't be good for you.'

His laughter rumbled through the door and made her

want to cover her ears. 'That's a risk I'm prepared to take. Come on, Issy, we could be here for a few more days. You can't spend it locked away. Come out and explore with me. We can talk.'

'In case you hadn't noticed, I don't want to talk to you, and I don't need to leave this cabin. You're a great host and there is plenty here to keep me occupied, so do me a favour and leave me alone. I'm not going anywhere until you let me go home.'

'You'll be free to go home as soon as I get word from Alessandro, but we will need to talk at some point.'

'We have nothing to say to each other.'

'We have a marriage to dissolve.'

'Then get dissolving it and leave me alone.'

Realising she was close to tears, Issy hurried back through the living area and out into her stunning private garden.

Gianni stared at Issy's chalet door. Still locked. Still no sighting of her. He regretted now making sure each chalet had all the privacy the occupants could wish for. These were the chalets for his close friends to use and for Alessandro, who he fully intended to one day drag here.

He knocked on the door. No answer came so he knocked again.

Her voice was even more guarded than it had been the day before. 'Yes?'

'It's me.'

She didn't respond at all.

'You can't avoid me for ever,' he said, and as he said it, he smiled ruefully to imagine her thinking, *Just you ruddy watch me.*

'Okay, you don't have to let me in,' he said after she'd ignored him for another twenty seconds, 'and I can't force you to talk to me. But I can sit here and talk to you and hope that you'll listen.'

Although the windows of the chalet were tinted to ensure complete privacy and her shutters closed so he couldn't see in, he sensed she was still at the door and hadn't rushed into the garden to escape his voice as she'd done the day before.

Lowering himself onto the front door step, he took a drink of the water he'd brought with him, made himself as comfortable as he could and rested his head back against the door.

'My father is a monster,' he said. 'A true monster. His brother—Alessandro's father—is the same. I don't know how they came to be that way, maybe their own father who I never met was the same, but their mother, our *nonna*, was a great lady. She lived with us and her presence tempered the worst of them. She died when I was eight.'

Gianni swallowed the acrid taste that had built in his mouth.

'Before she died, I was used to being hit. It was normal. Alessandro suffered the same. After she died the monsters came out. You know we were raised in Umbria?'

There was no answer but something told him she was listening.

He gave a morose laugh through his nose. 'I assume you know. I assume you know too that our fathers' business is wine. That's public knowledge for anyone who searches for it and I think you have searched my name and discovered everything the internet can tell you about me. If I were in your shoes and believed my father to be innocent then I would have done the same with the same intent, and I think that speaks of how different our childhoods were. If you were to tell me my father was innocent of something I would laugh in your face.'

Issy had tried to walk away from the door and out of the living area when Gianni had identified himself as her visitor but her feet had refused to obey. She'd tried to cover her ears when he'd started talking but her hands had refused to obey.

With a choked sigh of defeat, she slid her back down the door until her bottom reached the bamboo floor, then pulled her knees to her chest and hugged herself tightly.

'The wine they produce used to be great but when their mother died, they started cutting corners wherever they could. When Alessandro and I left, they cut even more corners. I give them two more years before the vineyard stops producing. At the most.' He laughed. Issy imagined his throat extending. 'Now, they're too lazy to even fertilise their land properly and since we left, too mean to pay anyone else to do it for them. Add all the other corners they cut and it's no surprise their Sangiovese tastes like battery acid.'

A long silence followed before he continued, still speaking in the same even tone as if relating a story he'd heard many times. But this wasn't *a* story. This was *his* story. All the things she'd longed to know even though it had had no relevance to her quest. Issy had wanted to know for her own sake because as much as Gianni had repelled her, deep down in the place she'd never dared acknowledge to herself lived an aching fascination for him.

'We were their little slaves,' he said. 'I remember crushing grapes with my feet until midnight and going to school the next day with purple feet and ankles. We were forced to work from sunrise until they said stop. If we complained, we were hit. Once Nonna died, we didn't have to complain to be hit. Her death unleashed them. They were our true slave masters and we their punching bags. Our mothers too. They never needed an excuse to beat them.'

Issy covered her mouth to stop a moan of distress escaping. She thought of the bump in Gianni's nose and how she'd wanted to shake the hand of the person who'd done it. That person must have been his own father.

'My mother ran away a year after Nonna died.' For the first time she heard an inflection of emotion in his voice. 'I haven't seen her since. She lives in Milan. I pay money into her account each month, but I never see her. She abandoned me to that bastard. It took months before I accepted that she wasn't coming back for me.' The tinge of sadness that laced his next laugh made her insides contract. 'My mother left me to my fate. Andro and I made a pact when we were twelve that as soon as we'd both turned eighteen we would leave and build new lives for ourselves. We worked even harder, taking jobs outside the vineyard wherever we could and saving every cent our fathers didn't demand we hand over to them. My father never knew, but I left school at sixteen and got a full-time job at a pizzeria—he'd have only taken my wages from me. The first thing we did when we finally left the vineyard was change our surnames.'

Vizzini, she remembered. That had been his original surname. It had taken her ages to dig that up. She remembered thinking Rossi suited him better and then had chided herself for thinking such a thing. Who cared whether his name suited him?

'We chose our *nonna*'s surname,' he said quietly, and though she had no way of knowing, Issy was certain he knew she was sat on the other side of the door to him. 'We sorted all the legal side out and then we made an offer on Tuscan land we'd huge plans for. We hadn't saved enough money to purchase it outright but we were able to borrow the shortfall.'

Dread crept its way up from the pit of her stomach.

'Only after the land was paid for and transferred into our

names did we learn it was unstable. There was no possibility of building a housing development on it. We'd been conned. The seller had seen two fresh-faced eighteen-year-olds and took advantage of our naivety. He bribed the surveyor and everyone else involved in the transaction and left us staring at bankruptcy.'

The seller. The man he claimed was her father.

'He underestimated us,' he said simply. 'We'd worked too hard and overcome too much to accept defeat. We started again. We worked like Trojans to repay the loan and build a new nest. As soon as we had the money we bought our first property and flipped it; gave it a makeover and sold it for a profit. We brought our second property and then our third and then we set our sights further taking on bigger and bigger projects with proportionate profits until we had the money to force the takeover of the business of the man who'd ripped us off. It took us four years. I don't think either of us slept more than four hours a night in those days. I do not regret what we did to that man. It didn't take much detective work to discover we weren't his only victims. I cannot abide corruption, Issy, and I hope that one day soon you will tell me of this proof of corruption Amelia spoke of because I swear on Alessandro's life that we are not corrupt. Everything we have we've built with our own toil using our own blood and sweat.'

Gianni's backside had become numb. Issy hadn't made a single sound but he was certain she'd heard every word. He rolled his neck and got to his feet. 'I'm going for a swim. Dinner will be served in the open dining room of my lodge at seven. All you need do is follow the path facing the beach and it will lead you to it. There is no pressure but know I would be glad to see you. I don't like to think of you alone with your thoughts...' He exhaled slowly before admitting,

'I want to get to know the real Isabelle Seymore because I already miss the Issy I spent that ride wild on the *Palazzo delle Feste* with. I know she's not the real you, but something tells me the things I like the most about her *are* real.'

Issy tried desperately hard to concentrate on the game of solitaire she was playing but her eyes kept being drawn to her watch. Gianni would be in his dining room, but he wouldn't be waiting for her. She'd left word for him declining his invitation when she'd requested dinner be brought to her cabin.

She couldn't face her stomach turning over at the aromas of her own cooking and she couldn't face him. It was too dangerous. She'd listened to Gianni relay the story of his life and wanted so much to open the door, crawl onto his lap and hold him tight. She'd long suspected his estrangement from his father was rooted in something bad—children rarely cut themselves off from their parents without good reason—but to imagine the suffering he must have gone through...

As hard as she tried to keep her emotions contained, the stone wall she'd built was breaking down, the contents of her heart bleeding out of it.

But there were three villains to his story. His father, his uncle and her father.

She couldn't accept it. Her bleeding heart wouldn't accept it. Her father would never treat two young men the way Gianni had described. He just wouldn't.

Are you sure...?

She slammed a card down then grabbed a chip. They were the most delicious chips she'd ever eaten in her life and she wished she wasn't feeling so down while eating them. She should be savouring their deliciousness.

Gianni must have been mistaken about her father. Because that was the crux of the problem—she believed him. Believed that he believed it.

And what about her sister? Because if Gianni was speaking the truth then it meant Amelia, the anchor that had kept Issy afloat all these years, had lied to her.

Mid-morning the next day, Gianni knocked on Issy's door again.

This time there was more hesitancy than guardedness in her voice. 'Yes?'

'It's me.'

Silence.

'I missed you last night.'

A long beat passed. 'Did you get my message?'

'I did.' He hadn't expected her to come. He'd hoped but his gut had told him not to hope too hard. He couldn't understand why her message, when it had come, had still landed like a blow.

There were many things about his reactions to Issy that Gianni didn't understand. Reactions and feelings he'd never felt before. They were growing stronger. The need to seek her out even if only to hear her voice gaining strength.

'Ready to come out yet?' he asked.

There was a slight hesitation before she said, 'No. Not yet.'

Not yet? That was a huge improvement and his chest lightened to hear it. 'That's a shame. It's a beautiful day.'

'I know. I've been in the garden.'

'Swimming?'

He swore he heard her laugh. 'No. I don't think it's safe for me to swim without a lifeguard close to hand.'

'That's one less thing for me to worry about,' he joked

back. He resisted offering to be her lifeguard. One step at a time. After days of silence and her cold shoulder, her voice sounded markedly warmer. Softer. 'Have you always been a lousy swimmer?'

'No... I... It's just been a long time. That's all. And I was never that strong a swimmer.'

He sat down in the same spot as he'd taken the day before. 'Tell me about it.'

'About what?'

'Swimming. Your life. Anything you want to tell me.'

'What do you want to know?' she asked doubtfully.

'Everything.'

When she next spoke her voice sounded so close to his ear that he knew she'd sat down too and that her back was likely pressed against the door the same as his, like two bookends. 'Be more specific.'

He wondered if her head touched the door too. She was so much shorter than him that it would rest lower than his. He wondered, too, why he'd always been inclined towards tall women before Issy. 'Tell me about your job. You're a nurse?'

'I'm an auxiliary nurse, not a medical nurse.'

'Is there a difference?'

'About four years of education.' Another quip? Things really were improving. He heard the smile in her voice as she explained, 'My job is basically to make sure the patients are comfortable and to help them with anything they can't do for themselves.'

'You work with children?'

'Yes. I'm on the children's ward.'

'You enjoy it?'

'I love it.'

'Is it not hard dealing with sick children?'

'It can be. You have to stay professional but it's hard not to build attachments. Especially with the really sick ones.'

'The ones you know will die?'

Her next, 'Yes,' was barely audible through the barrier of the door.

Her voice lifted a little. 'But they're incredible. All of them. Children are so brave, much braver than adults.'

'Do you really think that?'

'That's just from my observations over the last four years.'

'I know very little about children,' he mused. 'I've never been in a social setting with a child.'

'Never?'

'Never,' he confirmed. 'I've never held a baby either.'

'You've missed out.'

'How?'

He imagined the shrug she gave at this. 'Holding a baby is the most contenting thing in the world.'

'You want children of your own?'

'Definitely.' She paused before adding, 'You?'

'I've never thought about it until this minute, but I think I would like children. With the right woman.' The image of a small, plump, chestnut-haired Issy holding an ice cream sundae flashed in his mind. Immediately disconcerted, he blinked the image away and moved the subject away from children. 'Did you never want to be a real nurse?'

'Nursing was founded on caring for the sick and that's what I do, but originally I wanted to be a medical nurse.'

'What stopped you?'

There was another long beat before she softly answered, 'You.'

He closed his eyes and filled his lungs with air. 'Tell me, *bella*. Tell me everything.'

She took so long to speak he became convinced that she'd

slipped away. 'When our father lost the business it had a domino effect on the rest of our lives. Looking back, it feels like it happened overnight, but I must have been sleepwalking through it. One minute I was the luckiest girl alive, living in a big, beautiful house in London and spending my summers in our home in Italy. I went to a school I loved, I had great friends, a loving family... The next minute it was all gone. We lost our home. Amelia and I were forced to leave our school—our parents couldn't afford the fees—and start again at a new one where the other students hated us. Most of our friends abandoned us and our parents' friends abandoned them too. Dad always liked a drink, but I don't remember ever seeing him drunk before, but from that day I don't have a single memory of him sober. A year later he was dead. He literally drank himself to death.'

Gianni rubbed his temples. He remembered hearing on the grapevine about Thomas Seymore's death. The grapevine had whispered about alcohol. For once it seemed the grapevine had been correct.

'After his death, Mum was forced to file for bankruptcy and we were forced to move again—we'd become so poor the council had to provide us with accommodation. I think, though I don't know for certain, that that's when her drug dependency started. Amelia clocked on to it before I did—she's always been more observant than me—and protected me from it as much as she could but she couldn't protect me for ever. I just know that when I lost my dad, the last of the mother that lived in the woman that is Jane Seymore died with him.'

'She really is addicted to drugs?'

'Yes. We looked after her as best we could, but we were kids. As soon as Lia got the job with you, we could afford to send her to rehab in South America. Lia found it. Mum likes it there...as much as she likes being anywhere on this earth.'

A long passage of silence passed before she said, 'Everything we went through pulled me and Amelia together. Her strength was amazing and, in a way, inspired me to be strong too. She kept me sane. We took care of Mum and each other, and we vowed revenge on the men we believed killed our father and drove our mother into addiction. We wanted to hit you where it hurt and that meant your business. Every single thing we've done since Amelia went to university to get the qualifications that would make her the ideal candidate for your company has been with that end goal.'

'You've played the support act?'

'No. I was the backroom worker in the project but we've supported each other. Every decision we made together. All the money we earned went into the same pot.'

'But you wanted to be a medical nurse.'

'I needed to be earning money. Believe me, we both made sacrifices but neither of us saw it as that, and it worked out for the best. I love my job and being so hands on with the kids. It's the most rewarding job in the world and I wouldn't change it for anything.'

The ache that formed in Gianni's chest at this was so acute that he had to exhale slowly to relieve it. 'A few times just then when you were speaking of your revenge, you spoke in the past tense...' He was, absurdly, almost afraid to ask. 'Does that mean you believe me?'

CHAPTER TWELVE

Issy bowed her head and breathed deeply before leaning back against the door and dragging her hair off her face. 'I don't... Gianni, please...' She pinched the bridge of her nose and fought back the hot swell of tears. 'I've... I've had some doubts.'

'What kind of doubts?' he asked gently.

Bitter-tasting guilt rose up her throat at what she was about to admit. 'We took everything he said in blind faith.'

'I know it hurts, *bella*, but admitting that he was a bastard in business does not have to taint your memories of who he was as your father.'

'But I feel disloyal for even questioning it to myself,' she whispered.

'A child is programmed to trust their parents,' he said in that same gentle tone. 'When my mother ran away without me... It came close to breaking me. My own mother abandoned me and I've never been able to trust anyone but Alessandro since.'

Not wanting to inadvertently offend him, Issy hesitated before asking, 'Is that why you've never had a long-term relationship?'

He gave a low laugh. 'I never think about it but that's very likely. My social life is great fun and I have many friends, but no one I would consider close. That includes my past lovers. I've never had a conversation like this with anyone before or shared the confidences I did with you yesterday.'

'It's the same for me,' she admitted. 'I've always had Amelia to talk to and we confide absolutely everything in each other, but I think that's because we *had* to pull together. If she hadn't been there I think I would have grown to hate my parents for sinking into dependency, you know, for not being enough to keep them sober. I always make myself remember how it was before the business was taken and how happy we were as a family and how secure I felt—I *have* to hold on to that. When I FaceTime my mum, I sometimes catch glimpses of the mum I remember and I cherish those moments, and when I think of my dad I remember the man who read to me and led all the standing ovations at my ballet recitals, and it kills me to think that wasn't who he really was.'

'That *is* who he was, *cara*. The family man and the businessman were separate parts of him.'

'But if he sold you that land fraudulently and bribed officials to make it happen then his protestations of innocence after you forced the takeover were lies, and if you're right that there were other victims then that means my entire childhood is tainted.'

'Only if you let it be tainted.'

'But it means everything we had, all the privileges Amelia and I enjoyed, were built on fraud and lies.'

'But the father he was to you wasn't a lie. He loved you and Amelia and it seems to me that he destroyed himself in alcohol because he couldn't live with the repercussions of what his business decisions had done to his family.'

'I can't believe you're sticking up for him.' Not after everything. How could Gianni give her reassurance after what she'd tried to do to him?

'He must have had some good in him to produce a daughter like you.'

'What, a vengeful liar who was hell-bent on destroying you?'

'No, a fiercely loyal, kind-hearted, beautiful woman who couldn't go through with her vengeance without additional evidence. Don't forget, I have read the messages between you and your sister. When she messaged you that she'd found proof of corruption against us, your reply said, Thank God for that. That same day you took a photo of yourself with a patient and your hair was still chestnut. In the few days between that message and photo being taken to when we met in the club, you'd dyed your hair. You had doubts, *cara*, I know you did, and your sister knew it too and told you what you needed to hear to get you to actually act on your plans.'

The tears Issy had been holding back fell down her cheeks. How could a man she'd known for such a short time have the power to decipher her own thoughts and feelings better than she was able to?

'Bella?'

Breathing deeply, she wiped her eyes on her knees. 'I can't believe I'm admitting this but you're right, I've had doubts about his version of what happened between you and him.' Doubts that had grown the deeper she'd delved into Gianni's life and found nothing remotely untoward about his business conduct, doubts compounded with every gushing interview and profile published about him. No one had a bad word to say about him, not even his broken-hearted lovers. 'But, Gianni, I don't have any doubts about Amelia. None at all. She's my rock and guardian angel rolled into one. I can't bear to think of what would have happened to me without her. Why would she lie to me? *Why?*'

Now he was the one to take his time to answer, saying

slowly, 'I can't answer that but you need to think on this—why did she message such important news to you instead of calling you? Your whole plan hinged on Amelia finding proof that we were corrupt to push you into action. Consider if it is possible she messaged instead of calling because she was afraid you'd hear the lie in her voice.'

Issy sat on the edge of her private swimming pool with her legs submerged in the warm water up to mid-calf. Soon, the sun would make its descent and fill the sky with the orange haze that had captured her attention every night she'd stayed on this island. It had been her only respite from thinking of Gianni.

She was still thinking of him.

Gianni Rossi had occupied much of her thoughts in the years since she and Amelia had first hatched their plan. At the start of it all, it had been a tiny flightless fledgling plan but over the years it had grown in substance. Grown wings. As the plan had developed and she'd begun her research on him, slowly but surely Gianni had begun to occupy more headspace. By the time she'd started her job at the hospital he was the first thing she thought of when she woke and the last image she saw before she fell asleep.

She would never know the truth of what happened between Gianni, Alessandro and her father but she accepted that whatever Gianni had done, he truly believed her father had fleeced him. She did believe that. Gianni was not the monster she'd believed for so long; a belief she'd had to keep feeding to herself over the years to stop from faltering in her quest.

Amelia had sensed Issy's doubts. She was certain of it.

She closed her eyes and pressed her hand to her belly to ride the spasm of guilt that came from her own doubts. She couldn't think of Amelia right now, couldn't bear to let her mind take her where it so desperately didn't want to go.

Her eyes snapped back open. What she wanted was Gianni. To feel the light that always filled her when his gaze captured hers. To go to him as Isabelle Seymore, the auxiliary nurse who liked ballet, books and junk food more than was good for her, both of them stripped back to just their essences, all pretence and deception between them gone.

And she wanted to know the real Gianni, the man who'd opened up to her and without an ounce of self-pity told her his story.

She had a strong feeling that all the things she'd been helpless to stop herself from liking about him were the real Gianni.

No more thinking about the past.

Gianni sat at the end of the twenty-foot dining table laid for two, as it had been on board his yacht that night, and had a large drink of cold white wine.

Would she come?

He hadn't felt this nervous since his first date all those years ago.

He'd invited Issy to share dinner with him. Again. She hadn't given him an answer. Again. But her silence had been different this time. Allowed a sliver of hope to settle in him.

She hadn't left a polite message declining. Yet. He looked at his watch and popped a large green olive in his mouth. There was still time for her to back out…not that she'd actually said yes.

Hope was dangerous, he rued, now reaching for a breadstick and forcing his gaze on the spectacular sunset unfolding before him rather than keeping it fixed on the path she would join him from. If she came.

How had this happened? Going from a potential fling to a seductive game with a hustler, to learning the truth about her, to this? All along this was supposed to have been nothing but fun, the same as all his other flings but with added bite.

He'd never imagined he would feel like this, that he *could* feel like this. Like he was losing his head.

The hairs on the back of his neck rose. His heart thumped.

He whipped his head to the left before his brain caught up with what his senses were telling him.

Emerging from the darkening shadows of the foliage-lined path, her eyes locked on his face, was Issy.

The closer she moved towards him the harder his heart pumped. Dressed in a pretty pale yellow sundress with the spaghetti straps she favoured but which caressed her body with a swing around the knees rather than constricted it, barely a scrap of make-up graced her face. It had no need of it. Her silky blonde hair hung loose, sweeping over her shoulders, the first real hint of chestnut that had so captivated him in her photos emerging at the roots, the two colours blending together to create something uniquely beautiful.

Unable to tear her gaze from Gianni's face, Issy climbed the three steps onto the podium that served as his outside dining room. In the periphery of her vision silver fairy lights twinkled the perimeter of the wooden roof, a row of nightlights flickering on the table. With the sound of the sea lapping on the beach behind her, the whole scene was so dreamily romantic her whole being felt consumed by it.

But it was the man in the crisp white open-necked shirt and smart dark grey shorts who'd risen to his feet and taken slow steps towards her who consumed her the most. To see the way his chest was rising and falling as if it had a weight in it and the expression in the eyes as rooted to hers as hers were to his, an expression that was more, much more, than hunger...

Standing before him, she raised her arm and palmed his cheek. The thick stubble from four days ago had grown into a fully fledged beard. The pads of her fingers tingled madly in reaction to the sharp yet soft texture and her longing for him intensified.

His nostrils flared. His strong throat moved.

The tiny gap between them closed. His hands skimmed her waist then tightened around it.

Without a single word being uttered, he lifted her into air. Her face hovering above his, her hair brushing against his face, he continued to stare at her as if she were a miracle come to life before lowering her gently and then sweeping her into his arms so she was cradled against his chest.

Nestling her cheek against his beating heart, Issy breathed him in. The freshness of his cologne mingled with his clean skin enveloped her open senses. Open because she would no longer close any of herself off to him.

Gianni carried Issy up the stairs to his bedroom. She fit perfectly in his arms.

Gently, he sat her at the foot of the bed. Her eyes were open. Trusting. She reached a hand out to him. Capturing it, he kissed her pretty fingers, then stepped back to strip his clothes. First came the shirt which he shrugged over his head and let drop wherever it landed. Next came his shorts. He unbuttoned them and tugged the zip down, then, pinching his snug boxers with them, pulled them down his hips and thighs until gravity took care of the rest. Stepping out of them, he kicked his deck shoes off and had to force air into his lungs at the expression on Issy's face as she drank him in… Because that's how it felt. As if she were drinking in every part of him.

For the first time in his entire life, Gianni felt stripped to his marrow.

He took a step to close the small gap between them but she shook her head softly to stop him and got to her feet.

His heart had swollen so hard it came close to choking him. He watched as she pulled the dress up her beautiful body and over her head. Just as he'd done, she gave no care to where it landed.

Her hands went around her back. A moment later her pretty white silk bra fell the same way as her dress and all that was left were the matching panties. Clasping them with the tips of her fingers, she pinched the sides and pulled them down until she was able to step out of them. And then she straightened, cheeks flush, barely breathing, and it was his turn to drink *her* in.

During their time on the *Palazzo delle Feste*, Gianni had feasted his eyes on her for hours and hours. It felt like he was looking at her anew. Slowly, he soaked in every inch of her, from the tiny brown mole on the side of her neck to the small, pert breasts with their beautiful dusky pink nipples to the neat triangle of dark brown hair between her legs all the way down to her painted toes.

Head tilted back, eyes wide on his, she took the step to him. His arousal jutted into the base of her belly. Her lips parted, a small breath pulled in. Her eyes darkened and pulsed.

Slowly, he ran his hands down her bare arms. *'Tu sei bella...'* he whispered hoarsely.

Her chest rose, her voice barely audible as she whispered back, *'Anche tu.'*

So are you...

He lifted her back into his arms. Her arms locked around

his neck. Carrying her around the bed, he laid her down so her head rested on a pillow. Her hair spilled around her like a fan.

He didn't know what ached the most, his heart or his arousal.

He had never felt like this. Never felt such need for someone that his whole body trembled at the strength of it.

Issy felt like she'd been transported into the fairy lights that had barely penetrated her consciousness before Gianni swept her into his arms, a magical dreamlike reality filled entirely with him. When he laid himself on top of her, resting his weight on his elbows either side of her head so as not to crush her, the tips of her breasts pressed against the hardness of his chest, she would swear she felt the strength of his heartbeat as clearly as she felt her own.

The wonder in his stare as he lowered his face to hers made her heart beat even faster, and when his lips finally captured hers, flames ignited in it, pumping fire through her veins and melting the last of her thoughts.

Closing her eyes, she sank into the wonder that was Gianni and the tenderness underlying the passion of his kisses.

His mouth and hands explored her with a reverence that left her molten. Barely an inch of her flesh went untouched, unkissed, unloved. When he trailed his tongue up her inner thigh and pressed it against her swollen nub, every nerve ending in her body responded and she was helpless to do anything but cry his name and ride the thrills of the climax he slowly brought her to.

Dazed, drugged on bliss, she pulled herself up as Gianni raised his head. This time she was the one to kiss him. This time she was the one to lay him down and worship every inch of the body of the man who had captivated her for so long.

With the taste of Issy's climax still on his tongue, Gianni submitted to an assault of his senses that would have lost him his mind if it wasn't already gone. Every touch and mark of her mouth and tongue scorched him. Never had he been on the receiving end of such pleasure, but it was much more than that, more than a bodily experience, this transcended *everything*...

He groaned and had to grit his teeth when she took hold of his erection, then grit them even harder when she took him in her mouth.

Mio Dio...

He looked down and her gaze lifted to his. His heart punched through him to see the desire-laden wonder in her stare.

Closing his eyes, he gathered her hair lightly and let her take the lead, throwing his head back as her movements, tentative at first, became emboldened. The fist she'd made around the base tightened and she took him deeper into her mouth, moaning her own pleasure at the pleasure she was giving him.

If heaven existed he'd just found it.

Mio Dio, this was like nothing...*nothing*...

The tell-tale tug of his orgasm began to pull at him, and with an exhale of air, he gently pulled away from her.

Her gaze lifted to him again, a tiny knot of confusion on her brow.

Throat too constricted to speak, he cupped her cheeks and kissed her deeply, pushing her onto her back and sliding himself between her legs with the motion.

The tip of his erection brushed against her opening, the urge to just bury himself inside her with one long thrust so strong he had to clamp his jaw and squeeze his eyes shut to stop his basest instincts from taking him over.

Issy was a virgin. They needed protection.

The burning desire to say to hell with the consequence of no protection...

Keeping himself positioned between her legs, he stretched his arm out. No sooner had he tugged open the drawer of his bedside table than Issy lifted her head and began open-mouth kissing his neck while dragging a hand down his chest and abdomen to take hold of his erection.

Dear God in heaven...

He groped and fumbled for a condom; fumbled because she was masturbating him and deepening the French kisses on his neck.

The foil open, he removed the condom and took the hand Issy was giving him such glorious pleasure with. Her mouth moved up to his jaw until she found his lips, and, somehow, tongues fused and their hands clasped together, they rolled the condom on. Barely a second passed before she was flat on her back again, short, jagged breaths coming from her mouth, her eyes boring into his, his erection jutting and straining against her heat.

Issy felt possessed, that there was every chance she would go insane if Gianni didn't take possession of her. She had never wanted anything as badly as she wanted this. Every inch of her body was alight with the flames he'd ignited, her senses consumed with him. His beautiful face was all she could see, his ragged breaths all she could hear, his musky skin all she could smell and all she could taste, the smoothness of his skin all she could feel.

His lips grazed hers lightly and then he began to press his way inside her.

There was no pain, no discomfort, just a slow-building sensation of being deliciously filled and stretched until their groins locked together and they were as one.

Gianni thought he'd found heaven when Issy had taken

him into her mouth. If that was heaven then this was paradise, a miracle of the flesh and soul.

They could just stay like this, he thought dimly. Fused together. As one.

Never had the need for release burned so deeply but the urgency had gone. Now all he wanted was to savour this moment, savour Issy...

Issy had thought she'd already experienced all the sensual pleasure there was to feel but when Gianni began to move inside her, a whole new feeling grew, the burn in her core deepening and then uncoiling like tendrils through her very being.

Hooking a hand to his neck, she kissed him and closed her eyes.

Slowly, slowly, his thrusts lengthened and deepened. Slowly, slowly, the incredible pleasure increased until she was nothing but a mass of nerve endings and the burning pressure deep inside of her exploded.

With a long cry, she buried her mouth into his neck and held tight as rolling waves of bliss flooded her. Somewhere in the recess of her mind, she heard Gianni groan loudly, and then there was one last furious thrust that locked their groins together for one final time.

Buried as deep inside Issy as he'd ever dreamed it was possible to be, Gianni's climax roared through him. And still he tried to bury deeper, still she tried to pull him deeper, both of them desperately drawing out the pleasure for as long as they could until there was nothing left but stunned silence.

CHAPTER THIRTEEN

GIANNI STARED AT the sleeping face turned to his and smiled to see the light smattering of freckles highlighted on Issy's nose and cheeks by the early morning sunlight streaming in.

The temptation to wake her was strong but his conscience would not allow him. She must be exhausted. Three days and four nights of almost constant lovemaking had left her with faint bruises under her eyes. As for him... Despite the lack of sleep, Gianni felt the best he'd felt in so long that he couldn't remember when he'd ever felt this good. This alive.

Carefully rolling onto his back, he stretched an arm above his head.

'Morning.'

He turned his head. Issy's eyes had opened, a sleepy smile playing on her lips.

He leaned his face to hers and brushed a kiss to her lips. Her smile widened.

'It's early,' he said quietly. 'Go back to sleep.'

She nudged herself closer to him and placed a hand on his chest. 'I don't want to sleep.'

Taking her hand, he took a long breath knowing exactly what she meant. The four days they'd spent as lovers had passed almost like a dream. It had been just them. Gianni's room covered the whole second floor, a sprawling open-plan space with his hand-crafted emperor bed, a small dining table, a large corner sofa with accompanying entertainment centre, a bar, a walk-in wardrobe and en suite. They'd eaten in this room food brought to them by staff who left it at the door, drank from his bar which was topped up the few times they'd escaped to his private pool. It was as if they were the only two people in the whole world.

He raised his head at the sound of rustling and saw a note being pushed under the door.

Kissing Issy first, he climbed out of bed for it. As he opened it, he looked at her. She'd thrown the bedsheets off and struck such a provocative pose that he almost threw the note away unread. Almost.

The message was from Alessandro, four words: The business is safe.

That was it. No other information.

He read it again and waited to feel something lift in him. Something didn't come.

Why wasn't he ecstatic? For sure, he'd known Alessandro would fix things. He'd never doubted that. But he'd expected to at least feel relief, not an immediate plummet of dread in his stomach.

'What's wrong?' she asked softly.

He met her stare. For a long moment he debated whether or not to tell her. 'Alessandro has sorted everything.'

'With the business?'

'Yes.'

'Oh.'

He had to swallow to make his throat move but before he could speak, she said, 'I'm glad.'

'You are?'

To his horror, tears filled her eyes. She nodded. 'I'm sorry for what we tried to do to you. Really sorry.'

His lungs compressed. 'I know you are.'

'Please forgive me.'

Sitting on the bed, he brushed away the tear that rolled down her cheek. 'It's already forgiven.'

Issy tried desperately hard to stop any more tears from leaking. She didn't want to cry in front of him but reality had just inserted itself into the dream of their life. She'd refused to think of anything but Gianni since they'd become lovers. It had been the same for him too, she was certain. It had been the two of them in a private, dreamy bubble. When not making love they'd spoken about so many things, had long, laughter-filled discussions about their lives and interests, getting to know each other as who they really were, but by unspoken agreement there had been no mention of his cousin or business—other than generically—or her sister or parents. What they'd found together was too special, too *magical*, to allow the things that meant it had to come to an end spoil it for the time they had.

He wiped another tear. 'You are free to go home now.'

But that only made her want to cry harder. 'Do you want me to go?'

He shook his head with vehemence. 'No.'

'Good,' she said in a whisper. 'Because I don't want to go either.'

He closed his eyes as if in relief, his shoulders rising before he locked them back on hers. 'Your phone is in my dressing room.'

That made her smile. 'I'd forgotten all about it.'

'You can call your sister.'

But there was a reason Issy hadn't allowed herself to think of her sister let alone talk about her. 'You said she was safe.'

'She is.'

'Then I don't need to call her. Not yet.'

From the way Gianni's eyes were searching hers, she had the feeling he knew exactly how torn she was about Amelia.

Wrapping her arms around his neck, she pulled him down for a heady, passion-filled kiss.

The man who made her feel so, so much didn't have to return to his real life for another four of five days…oh, hell, she was losing track of time…and she would extract every ounce of the pleasure and joy being with him brought her until their time ran out.

Reality could wait a while longer.

The sea was much warmer than Issy anticipated, and she didn't even flinch when it reached the top of her legs. When it reached her bellybutton, she stopped. 'This is as far as I go,' she declared.

'Wimp,' Gianni teased with that smile that never failed to make her heart go all squidgy.

'I am not a wimp!'

He threw the beach ball at her. 'Yes, you are.'

She caught it and threw it back. 'No, I'm not.'

His grin widened. 'How am I supposed to pull you under if you won't go any further than your stomach?'

'You want me to drown?' she asked in mock outrage.

'No.' He lobbed the ball hard at her. 'I want to save you from drowning so I can give you the kiss of life.'

'You need one of those banana float things if you're going to act as lifeguard again,' she reminded him.

'I can't wait to unwrap it on my birthday.

'I'll need to use a whole tree's worth of wrapping paper,' she said, and used all her strength to chuck the ball at him and laughed with glee when her aim finally came good and the ball bounced off his head.

'You did that on purpose!' he accused, scooping the ball up and tucking it under his arm.

'I don't know what you're talking about.'

He strode through the water towards her. 'You have an evil streak in you.'

Giggling, she waded backwards, trying to escape him. 'Only when it comes to beach balls.'

He held the ball above his head, eyes gleaming as he loomed down on her. Having such long legs and only being thigh-high in the water meant he'd closed the gap far quicker than she'd been able to flee. But instead of dropping the ball on her head, he threw it aside and then, with a speed and grace that had no place on a man of his size, lifted her by the waist and threw her in the air.

She landed backside first with a squeal, kicking feet and flailing arms submerging at the same time as her face went under. Rising back to the surface, trying her hardest not to laugh, a task made harder by the throaty, uproarious sounds coming out of Gianni's mouth, she half crawled to him and grabbed his calves.

'You think you can knock me over?' he mocked, and in a flash he had her by the waist again and for the second time in less than two minutes, Issy was flying in the air and landing with a splash. When she resurfaced, the ball was in reach. Grabbing it, she threw it at him and got him on the forehead.

'Oh, that does it,' he said with a shake of his head, now wading towards her like a panther on the prowl.

By now breast height in the water, Issy, cackling with laughter, tried to swim away from him. She'd barely managed three strokes when he captured an ankle and pulled her under. She came up for air with a splutter, only to be bodily lifted from the sea by a single arm wrapped around her waist and carried to the beach.

Laughing too hard to scream or pretend any form of protest, the most she could do was slap feebly at his shoulders when he laid her down on the sand.

'I just saved your life!' he admonished sternly, which only made the absurdity of it all funnier. 'Now stop laughing so I can give you the kiss of life.'

Clamping her lips together so stop any more giggles coming out, Issy immediately played dead.

The expected kiss took much longer to press against her expectant lips than she'd anticipated. She peered through one eye to see what the hold-up was and found Gianni gazing down at her with an expression in his eyes that made her heart clench. Breaking character, she pressed a hand to his cheek and rubbed her palm against his beard. He captured the hand and kissed it reverently. 'You're beautiful, did you know that?'

Her chest filled with an emotion she didn't understand but which was thick enough to cramp her lungs. 'You make me feel beautiful,' she whispered.

'You are beautiful, Isabelle, and I want you to promise me you will never starve yourself again.'

She thought of the meals they'd shared these last six days, how happiness and wonderful sex had increased her appetite, how her bikinis—literally the only clothing she'd worn since they'd become lovers—were already feeling tight at the hips. The emotions filling her swelled even more. 'I starved myself to entrap you.'

He kissed her hand again. 'I'd already guessed that. And I can guess why you felt you needed to do that and to dye your beautiful hair.' He shook his head tightly. 'None of those women were real to me, Issy.'

'What do you mean?'

Gianni took a breath and tried to collate his thoughts. 'They were status symbols, like my penthouses, the watches I wear, the cars I drive or have driven for me. A way for me to flaunt the man I'd become to my father.'

She just stared at him.

'I've not seen him since we left Umbria,' he explained quietly. 'I never want to see him again.'

She threaded her fingers into his and squeezed.

'We knew, Alessandro and I, that changing our surname from theirs would hit them where it hurt the hardest.'

'Their egos?' she guessed.

He smiled at her astuteness. 'I know it must kill my father to see my success and know his place in my history has been severed. I wanted him to see me with the best of everything the world has to offer and not even be able to take credit for my name.'

'And the best of everything included women?'

'Yes,' he agreed unflinchingly. It was only now, speaking it aloud, that Gianni understood how shallow and, yes, misogynistic his attitude to the women in his personal life had been. 'If I had passed you as you were two years ago in a street I would never have looked twice at you. I wanted what I believed was the male dream; the killer supermodel on my arm and in my bed.'

He deserved the hurt and distaste curling Issy's mouth, and gently tightened his hold on her hand to stop her pulling it away.

'I need to be honest with you,' he said. 'I have to be. After the way we started and all the lies, I don't ever want deception of any kind to come between us.'

Her eyes flickered.

'I wouldn't have looked twice at you because I'd trained

myself only to see tall, blonde, obviously rich women,' he continued. 'I didn't need to see anything more than that because I wasn't looking for more. I had no interest in anything real.' He managed a smile and kissed her clasped hand. 'It's all this time with you, Issy, the way you make me feel... I didn't stand a chance. And being with you, the uniqueness of how we came to be; it has brought the past back to me in a way it hasn't been in a long, long time. I think of my mother now, alone in her Milanese flat and for the first time in over two decades, I don't hate her for not coming back to me.'

'Maybe she couldn't,' Issy suggested quietly. There was something about Gianni's tone and the way he was looking at her that made her heart thump. For the first time in what felt like for ever, there was dread in the beats.

He grimaced and shook his head. 'She could. The first place she fled to was a woman's shelter. I know this because my aunt told me. The people there would have helped her but she chose not to tell them about me.'

A whimper crawled out of her throat.

The grimace turned into a smile. 'Don't be sad for me, *cara*. It is thanks to you that I can now confront my past in a way I never let myself before—I *have* to confront it. I don't want it to have power over me any more. My mother left me because she didn't love me enough to take me with her. That is the crux of it.'

'I don't believe that,' she whispered vehemently. How could any woman on this earth fail to love Gianni, let alone the woman who'd given birth to him?

He brushed a finger against her cheek. 'I think my father beat the love out of her. She has never remarried or taken a lover. She doesn't even have friends. That used to make me happy but now...' His chest rose then fell with flump.

'*Bella*, your mother abandoned you too in her own way, but you don't hold any anger or bitterness towards her. Instead, you try to understand and help her. You forgive her. And that is what I must do. Forgive my mother for the hand life dealt her and trust that her abandonment was not my fault.' His eyes held hers. 'And trust that it doesn't have to affect the rest of my life.'

The dread that had been building in the thumps of Issy's heart were now so loud they almost deafened her. Instinct was screaming at her to change the subject now, right now, another, stronger part yearning to wrap her arms around him and hold him tight and swear that he could put his trust in her, that she would never let him down, that she would always be there for him. That she would never leave him.

But those words would be a lie. There was no future for them to place his trust in her, not in the way she sensed he'd been driving this conversation towards. In a few days they would go their separate ways. They would leave each other. That's how it had to be, and she stared at him, pleading with her eyes for him to understand, silently begging him not to say the words that would force her to hurt him, hurt them both.

Just two weeks ago Issy would never have believed she or any woman would have the power to hurt Gianni Rossi. But then, two weeks ago, she'd never believed he would have the power to hurt her. She'd thought herself immune to him. She'd been too stupid to see that she was already half in love with him.

His lips parted.

No! She wanted to scream. *Please, don't.*

'I love you, Issy,' he said quietly. Sincerely. Breaking her heart. 'I love you. I know our marriage was a game of bluff we both told ourselves we'd lost but…'

She scrambled up and onto her bottom and shook her head frantically. 'Please, Gio, don't.'

He blinked as if something had flown into his eye.

'Don't say it,' she begged. 'It can never be. You must know that.'

He stared at her for the longest time, fingers still tight around hers, a contortion of emotions flickering on his face. 'Tell me you don't love me.'

'Don't do this.'

'Tell me you don't love me.'

'Please.'

'Tell me you don't love me and I will end this conversation and seek an annulment as soon as we return to the mainland. All you have to do is say the words.'

'I don't l…' But her tongue refused to cooperate. Refused to tell the lie. Finally snatching her hand free from his she buried her face in her knees and cried, 'I *can't.*'

Gianni made himself breathe through the sharpness in his chest. Issy's inability to refute her love didn't ease the tension tightening throughout him. 'You do love me, *bella*,' he said steadily. 'What we have found together is something we had no choice over. I couldn't stop myself falling in love with you and you couldn't stop it either. That spark was there from the very first moment. Our wedding was a farce but our marriage doesn't have to be. I have no idea how we will make it work but I know we can because what we have is too special to throw away. I never in a million years expected to feel like this about anyone and yet here we are. Give us a chance. Please, don't turn your back on something we could both search for another million years and never find.'

When she lifted her face to him, tears were streaming down her face. That was the moment Gianni knew he'd lost.

Chin wobbling manically, she shook her head and choked, 'I *can't*. You must understand that.'

He had no idea how he was able to keep his voice even. 'I understand that we love each other.'

'Stop saying that, it only makes it harder. We can never be. I can't betray Amelia. You have to go back to your own life and let me go back to mine.'

'Amelia betrayed *you*.'

She shook her head violently. 'No. Never.'

'She lied to you. You know it in your heart.'

'No! She wouldn't! And even if she did, she would have had her reasons. Oh… You don't understand!'

'Then make me. Tell me. Tell why you are so ready to throw us away.'

'I don't want to throw us away! I want to be with you but it's impossible.'

'Explain it to me. You owe me that much.'

'Gianni… You said I don't hold bitterness and anger towards my mother, and that I learned to understand and forgive her and help her…none of that came easy. There were times I *hated* my mum for what she was doing to herself but I never let myself fall into despair because through it all, I had my sister. I have looked up to her my entire life, even when I was a brat to her in the days when I believed everything was perfect. Amelia's the one who held what was left of our family together and held me together. She's the one who helped Mum, not me; I only helped Amelia help her. She's the one who protected me from the bullies at the horrid school we were sent to after Dad…' She cut herself off and took a long breath before looking him squarely in the eye. 'I know dad ripped you off. I believe you. If you say he ripped off other companies and people too then I believe you. And if you say Amelia lied to me about finding proof of corruption against you then I believe that too.'

Oh, but it *hurt* to finally admit that, and Issy had to wipe away more tears before adding, 'I believe you, Gianni. She lied to me.'

God help her, she was taking Gianni's word over her own sister's. But she knew it. From the moment he'd denied it, she'd known in her heart, just as he'd said, that he was telling the truth. It was a truth she'd locked away from herself in the beautiful days they'd just shared, burying it because she'd fallen madly in love and had selfishly wanted to have this time with him, because he was right about that too—what she felt for him would never be replicated.

All along though, she'd known it would have to end. What she hadn't known was how much it would hurt.

'You believe me?' He grabbed the back of his neck and sucked air in.

'It doesn't change anything. She hates you and your cousin too much. Her lie must have been born out of desperation, there's no other explanation for it. You should have seen her in the days leading up to my leaving for the Caribbean; she was so tense at the thought our time was finally coming that I thought she would snap. That we've failed will be destroying her. I can't add to that. I just can't. I can't betray her.'

'You already have,' he stated flatly.

'I know.' God, she was going to cry again. 'But this… here…what we've shared…soon it will be just a memory. For me to leave her and make a life with you… It would devastate her. She would never forgive me.'

'Do you not think it is the same for me?'

Taken aback at the tightness in his voice, Issy met his stare. The coldness shining from his eyes made her quail.

'Do you not think Alessandro will think I have betrayed him? Me, the one person in this world he trusts, falling in love with one of the women who set out to destroy us?' The more he spoke, the more the ice-like fury that had been building in Gianni while Issy had been making all her excuses spread. 'Me, falling in love with Thomas Seymore's daughter and wanting to build a life with her? Do you not think that will land like a kick in the teeth to him? And do not forget, Alessandro is as much of a victim in this whole charade as I am. More so. While you and I have been having fun here in the Caribbean, he's been fighting for the very existence of our company. Don't you think I know what the consequences could be? Exactly the same as what you fear. The difference is I love you enough that I'm willing to lose everything to be with you. I would walk on hot coals for you, but you…' He laced his voice with all the contempt he could inject into it. 'You're a coward. You won't even try, and you're using your sister as an excuse.'

She looked like he'd slapped her. 'How can you say that? You know what we've been through and what we mean to each other.'

'That's my whole point,' he spat. 'If your sister loves you as much as you love her then she will want the best for you. She will want you to be happy. If you wanted it enough, you would convince her. I don't deny she will be angry and betrayed but in time she would come round. Maybe she would never accept me as a brother-in-law but she sure as hell wouldn't want to lose you, but we will never know, will we? And I will never know if Alessandro would forgive me because you're so scared that I'll end up abandoning you as your parents did through their addictions that you'd rather cling to your sister's skirt and use her as an excuse than take the leap of faith with me.'

'I'm not scared,' she whispered.

'Liar.' Rising to his feet, he dusted the sand from his hands. 'And so much for trusting me.'

Unable to bear looking at her stricken, cowardly face a moment longer, Gianni turned on his heel and walked away from her.

'Where are you going?' Issy scrambled to her feet, panic suddenly clawing at her.

'To call Captain Caville. The *Palazzo delle Feste*'s moored on an island fifty kilometres away. It will not take long to reach us. I suggest you start packing.'

She had to practically run to catch him. 'What, we're leaving?'

'I have no wish to stay here another minute longer than necessary.'

'But we're not expected back in London for a couple more days.'

'Our time here is over.'

'Please, Gianni, don't let it end like this.'

He came to an abrupt halt and spun around to face her. 'What the hell do you expect? A few more days of *fun* together? No, you have made your decision and I have made mine. We will sail to the nearest island with an airport that flies to the UK and I will buy you a ticket for the first flight home.'

'And what about you?' she asked, almost numb with shock at his implacable coldness.

'That, *bella*—' he virtually spat the endearment '—is none of your business. My lawyer will be in touch over the dissolution of our *marriage*...' There was even more venom in his voice. 'Do not expect anything from me. This marriage meant nothing. *We* meant nothing. Enjoy your life.'

When his long legs set stride again, Issy let him go.

CHAPTER FOURTEEN

Issy sat on the balcony of her cabin on the *Palazzo delle Feste* gazing up at the stars. There were so many of them twinkling down on her from the moonless sky. She wished they injected warmth as far as Earth. Despite the balminess of the night she was huddled under the wrap she'd packed for the unpredictable weather when she returned to London. She'd felt chilled to the bone since Gianni had so coldly and ruthlessly severed her from his life.

And it had been a severing. A member of staff had collected her suitcase from her chalet and walked her to the yacht. Since embarking, she hadn't caught a glimpse or heard a whisper from Gianni. She'd wandered aimlessly through the familiar rooms, half hoping and half dreading bumping into him. She'd even knocked on his cabin door and still didn't know if she'd been relieved or devastated that it went unanswered. She'd tried the handle but it had been locked. Probably for the best. She didn't know what she'd have said to him.

He must have had a change of heart and stayed behind on St Lovells.

Maybe it was better this way. A clean break. It would have happened in a few days anyway. It was just in the few times she'd envisaged it—only brief visions, because nausea had roiled strongly inside her at the images in her mind's eye—they had parted with tender words. She'd imagined a life spent weaning herself off her internet addiction to him.

She pulled the wrap tighter around her shoulders and wished she could call Amelia, tell her she knew what she'd done but that it didn't matter because whatever reason had propelled her sister to act so out of character and lie to her must have been important. The more she thought about it, the more it hurt her heart that Amelia hadn't felt able to confide that reason in her.

But she couldn't call her. In the days of bliss when she'd been blocking the world from her head, she'd left her phone in Gianni's dressing room. To take it back would have let the world intrude and she'd been desperate to avoid that. And then everything had crumbled between them and she'd hidden in her chalet until the call to leave had come. She'd been too numb to think about anything.

She wished she was still numb. Now, she felt sick to the pit of her stomach and it hurt even more to know that even if she had remembered her phone, she'd not be able to confide any of the pain she was feeling to her sister.

Or would she?

Gianni's cold voice kept echoing like a taunt in her ear. *Coward.*

How was she being a coward? And as for his ridiculous assertion that she had abandonment issues?

A spark of fury suddenly fired in her. If she did have abandonment issues—which she didn't—hadn't his behaviour proved her right to have them? And just like that, the coldness left her. Jumping to her feet, Issy paced her balcony, wishing Gianni was on board so she could confront him with the home truths she wished she'd thought of earlier. That it was grossly unfair to call her a coward just because she put her sister's feelings above her own. That if he thought she had abandonment issues, at least she didn't cut the abandoner from her life even if they did deserve it, which Gianni's mother undoubtedly did. That...that...that...

The stars began to blur. And then they began to spin.

Dazed, Issy staggered back to her seat and breathed deeply, waiting for the dizziness to pass.

But it didn't pass, just built up and up more and more as the truth rose in her stomach and chest and up her throat and she had to cover her mouth to stop the agony escaping.

She *was* a coward. Of *course* Amelia would forgive her. Maybe not overnight but in time she would, just as Issy would forgive her anything, even lying to her about something so dangerous as the Rossi cousins.

Gianni wasn't dangerous. Not in the way she'd once believed. He was dangerous in the way he could sever a relationship without batting an eyelid. Issy had obsessed over him and witnessed from afar his litter of broken hearts for so many years that taking that final leap—what had he called it? A leap of faith?—had been too terrifying to contemplate. Because her parents' addictions *had* felt like abandonment, like she wasn't enough to keep them sober and on this earth with her. Not even enough to keep her mother in the country with her. Yes, she'd long ago accepted it and forgiven them both for it but it had done something to her she hadn't even realised and so when the chance had come to give herself properly, heart, body and soul to Gianni, she'd cowered in fright because deep down she was so goddam scared he would leave her too. And so she had pushed him away before he could push her and now the truth was demanding she confront it, and she realised he never would have. Gianni would never have left her. It wasn't that she had tamed the lothario or anything clichéd like that, but a magical alchemy of chemistry and passionate desire sprinkled with a meeting of minds and humour had captured them and woven their hearts together. They belonged together.

And she'd thrown it away. Been too frightened to take what he was so gladly offering.

No wonder he'd been so cold and furious. For the first time since his mother had abandoned him, Gianni had handed his heart over on a plate and Issy had rejected it.

In the distance the dark shadow of approaching land appeared and it was the knowledge that on that island sat the airport from which she would take the flight that would fly her away from him that finally broke her.

Sliding off the chair, Issy fell onto her knees with a thump, opened her lungs and howled.

Gianni had been sat on his balcony for over two hours hardly daring to breathe in case Issy heard him. He'd cursed to hear her step out on her balcony, cursed himself too for not putting her in a cabin far from his.

He wanted nothing to do with her, not even a glimpse of her, and when she'd knocked on his door he'd taken great pleasure in ignoring her. What the hell did she even want with him?

And now he was trapped on his balcony waiting for her to do the decent thing and go back inside so he could wallow in the bottle of Jack he'd brought out here for company.

Movement came. Great! She must be going inside.

No, she was stomping around, which was unusual as she had such a light, graceful tread to her step.

Dammit, all he wanted was to wallow until he reached the bottom of the bottle and be drunk enough not to notice when the yacht docked and Issy disembarked for the final time from his life. He was going to sail on to Barbados and take his jet back to London from there. It was safer that way. No risk of accidentally bumping into her.

She stopped stomping. Excellent.

He folded his arms across his chest and waited impatiently for her to finally disappear inside. Except there was no obliging sound of a door being slid open or closed.

A loud thud made him jump to his feet.

What the hell...?

But the thought had barely formed when an animalistic howl of agony rent the air.

'Issy?' he shouted, rushing to the barrier separating their balconies. Dammit, why the hell had he insisted the barrier be high enough for complete privacy? He called her name again but the only sound from her balcony was heart-wrenching sobs. 'Stay where you are,' he ordered, trying not to let the panic that she'd seriously injured herself consume him. 'I'm coming.'

Racing through his cabin, he yanked his door open and ran straight to Issy's door, praying she hadn't locked it. God answered that one, and he pushed it open before racing to her balcony door and sliding that open too.

What he found stopped him in his tracks.

Issy was curled on the floor in the foetal position, great sobs racking her entire body.

In an instant he was beside her and hauling her into his arms so she was cradled on his lap.

'Where are you hurt?' he asked urgently. 'Please, *mia amore*, tell me where you're hurt.'

Slowly it dawned on Issy that she wasn't dreaming. Hallucinating Gianni's voice had been more than she could endure and she'd covered her ears like a child against the cruelty of it, crying so hard her ribs felt bruised.

She hadn't hallucinated it. She hadn't hallucinated him.

Tentatively, still afraid he would disappear in a blink, she touched his cheek. It was as warm and solid as it always was but still she whispered, 'Gianni?'

'Tell me where it hurts,' he repeated in the same urgent tone that had finally cut through her despair.

'Hurts?' she echoed.

'You have hurt yourself. You are in pain.' His Italian accent was stronger than she had ever heard it. 'Please, you must tell me where it hurts.'

More tears streamed down her face as her hand fluttered to her chest and pressed against her left breast. Against her heart. 'Here.'

'What have you done?'

'Pushed you away.'

He didn't understand.

'Oh, but I'm the biggest fool in the world.' Trembling, she cupped both his cheeks tightly. 'Please forgive me. Please give me another chance. Please don't give up on me and cut me from your life. I couldn't bear it. I *can't* bear it. I love you, Gianni, and I want to build a life with you.'

He hardly dared believe what her lips were saying and her eyes were pleading.

'It's not even been ten hours since you walked away from me and they've been the longest ten hours of my life. What we have found together…you're right. I could walk this earth for a million years and never find it again.'

'And your sister?'

'She loves me. She'll forgive me in her own time, but right now it's you I need forgiveness from.'

'Mia amore…' A bubble of hope was starting to build inside him. 'There is nothing for me to forgive. I didn't react as well as I should and lashed out at you and for that, I am sorry too.' He took a deep breath before admitting, 'I think I have a problem with rejection.'

Her chin wobbled but she managed a smile. 'A small one, maybe.'

He raised an eyebrow which made her smile widen and a small laugh escape her lips, and then before he even knew it was happening, her arms were wrapped around his neck, his hold around her had tightened and they were kissing with such passion and love that the bubble of hope exploded in a blaze of joy so strong that the last of Gianni's fears abandoned him.

'Your reaction was understandable,' she murmured when they came up for air. 'We both have abandonment issues.'

'Had,' he corrected, kissing her again. 'But not any more. You love me and you'll never let me go.'

'And you love me and will never let *me* go.'

'Never.'

'Never.'

And they never did.

Issy stretched luxuriously within the silk sheets of Gianni's bed...*her* bed...and yawned widely. She loved this room. This bed. This penthouse. She'd only spent two nights in it but already she felt at home. Gianni had made it feel like home for her.

The only thing that stopped Issy feeling like she could spring to the clouds in a single leap was dread about what was to come when Amelia finally arrived back home. Gianni had given her phone back to her and when she'd checked it, there hadn't been a single message or voice mail from her sister. Just a wall of silence. In a way, that had made it easier for her to maintain her own silence too, especially when Gianni's contacts had quickly confirmed she was still abroad with Alessandro.

When the bedroom door opened, she sat up, a smile already on her face at the joy that fizzed through her at the mere anticipation of seeing her husband—it was taking some getting used to, actually thinking of him as her husband—after being separated from him for fifteen whole minutes while he made them eggs for breakfast. One look at his face and empty hands wiped the smile away.

'What's happened?' she asked.

He shook his head and sat next to her to stroke her hair. 'Alessandro has sent me a message.'

Issy's heart thumped. Like her, Gianni had been waiting for his cousin's return to London before telling him about their marriage. 'He knows about us?'

'I'm not sure but that isn't why he messaged me. He's asked me to bring you to the airfield.'

'Why?'

Sympathy lined his face. 'Amelia's flying back to the UK. Alessandro says...he says she needs you.'

It was like ice had been injected into her veins. As sisters, they'd pulled together and always been there for one another emotionally, but Amelia had never *needed* her.

Gazing into the steadfast eyes of the man she still couldn't quite get her head around was her husband, bone-deep certainty grew that her sister was in great distress.

'You'll come with me?' she whispered.

Strong arms wrapped around her and held her close. '*Mia amore*, I would follow you to the ends of the earth.' He kissed her gently. 'I'll call our driver. We can leave in ten minutes.'

Our driver. *We*. Simple words but words infused with meaning.

It was the two of them. Together. For always.

EPILOGUE

Gianni closed his eyes contentedly as he swayed gently on the hammock under the rising early sun. Snuggled on him, his chubby cheek pressed against his chest, his youngest son, Matteo, slept. At only eighteen months, the little ratbag—an affectionate term Gianni's beautiful wife called him—had recently mastered the art of escaping his cot. That morning he had toddled into his parents' bedroom and woken Gianni by prodding his nose. With the rest of his family sleeping, Gianni had taken him outside to watch the sunrise.

He tried not to sigh to think that soon they would have to return to Europe. Mia, their eldest child, was a couple of weeks away from starting school. They'd debated whether to employ a tutor so they could continue spending six months of each year in their Caribbean hideaway but decided that would be selfish of them. As far as they were both concerned, children needed playmates. St Lovells would be there for all the school holidays and then, when their brood had all flown the nest, they would make it their permanent home. At least, that was the plan. How long it would take for that to happen was anyone's guess, a thought reinforced when a sound made him peer through one eye and spot his heavily pregnant wife sneaking towards him, carrying a huge, elaborately wrapped box, Mia bringing up the rear with carefully balanced, much smaller boxes in her own tiny hands.

His family. God, he loved them. Sometimes he would look at his children's happy faces and his heart would squeeze so tightly it left a bruise. Sometimes he would look at his wife and take in her flowing dark chestnut hair and curvy body and those beautiful blue eyes that always shone with such love, and thank every deity he could think of for bringing them together. Six years of marriage and their devotion to each other had only grown. She was his entire world. Their children were their universe.

'Happy birthday, Daddy!' Mia suddenly yelled.

He opened his eyes fully and feigned surprise.

Matteo lifted his head and grinned at him. ''Ap Birfday.'

Pressing his son's button nose, Gianni then held him tightly and swung himself off the hammock. Issy was beaming at him. The box was practically as tall as she was.

'Happy birthday, you gorgeous man. Bet you can't guess what your present is...*don't* tell him, Mia!'

Watching his daughter carefully place the other boxes on the table, he pretended to ponder. 'Hmm. Whatever can it be?'

Issy's beam grew.

Somehow they managed to exchange Matteo for the box, and then Gianni ripped the wrapping, already grinning, imagining what she'd come up with this time.

It was a banana float. At least, that's what Gianni and Issy called it. Every year she brought him the same thing for his birthday. He was growing quite the collection. But each was decorated in its own unique way and he burst out laughing when he pulled it out of the box and found it had been cleverly painted with caricatures of his wife and two children's faces squashed together.

Placing it against the tree the hammock was tied to, he wrapped his arms around her as much as Matteo in her arms would allow, and kissed her deeply. 'Thank you,' he murmured.

'My pleasure,' she murmured back, before dropping her voice to a whisper. 'You can have the rest of your present when the children go to bed.'

He snapped his teeth with a mock growl and squeezed her delectable bottom. 'I look forward to it.'

'Stop being soppy and open our presents!' Mia demanded, spoiling the moment in the best possible way.

Laughing even harder, he scooped his daughter up and planted an enormous kiss to her cheek.

Not a day went by when Gianni didn't consider himself the luckiest man alive.

* * * * *

COMING SOON!

We really hope you enjoyed reading this book. If you're looking for more romance be sure to head to the shops when new books are available on

Thursday 21st May

To see which titles are coming soon, please visit
millsandboon.co.uk/nextmonth

MILLS & BOON

FOUR BRAND NEW BOOKS FROM
MILLS & BOON MODERN

Indulge in desire, drama, and breathtaking romance – where passion knows no bounds!

OUT NOW

Eight Modern stories published every month, find them all at:

millsandboon.co.uk

LET'S TALK
Romance

For exclusive extracts, competitions and special offers, find us online:

- **f** MillsandBoon
- **X** @MillsandBoon
- **◎** @MillsandBoonUK
- **♪** @MillsandBoonUK

Get in touch on 01413 063 232

For all the latest titles coming soon, visit
millsandboon.co.uk/nextmonth